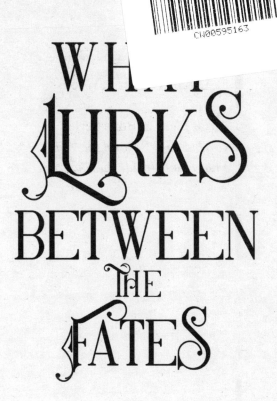

WHAT LURKS BETWEEN THE FATES

Also by Harper L. Woods

Of Flesh & Bone Series
What Lies Beyond the Veil
What Hunts Inside the Shadows

WHAT LURKS BETWEEN THE FATES

HARPER L. WOODS

HODDER

First published in Great Britain in 2023 by Hodderscape
An imprint of Hodder & Stoughton
An Hachette UK company

1

A CIP catalogue record for this title is available from the British Library

Paperback ISBN 978 1 399 71176 0
eBook ISBN 978 1 399 71843 1

Typeset in Times Ten LT Std by Manipal Technologies Limited

Printed and bound in Great Britain by Clays Ltd, Elcograf S.p.A.

Hodder & Stoughton policy is to use papers that are natural, renewable
and recyclable products and made from wood grown in sustainable forests.
The logging and manufacturing processes are expected to conform to the
environmental regulations of the country of origin.

Hodder & Stoughton Ltd
Carmelite House
50 Victoria Embankment
London EC4Y 0DZ

www.hodderscape.co.uk

For the survivors who rise like the stars.

About What Lurks Between the Fates

Once, I'd chosen my mate instead of freedom.

For weeks, we retraced our steps back to Mistfell and the lingering shadow of the Veil at the boundary between realms. Traveling through the kingdom, I denied the evidence in front of me, unable to fathom that I wasn't the lost princess of Faerie. Instead, it is Fallon who must fear the consequences of her heritage. Which leaves me with a single, unanswered question.

Then, I awoke, caged high above the throne of the Queen of Air and Darkness.

Mab is the Queen who keeps all of Alfheimr held squirming within her clawed grasp. She uses the children of Faerie to sustain the magic granted to her by the cursed gem atop her crown, which has carved her from the girl she once was into a dark vessel, obsessed with power. She thrives on cruelty, and wields our love as an instrument for pain.

Now, I'll play the games of the Fae.

I'm a curiosity, my presence an enigma that was never foreseen. I may not be Mab's daughter, yet she still keeps me close, as she forges me into a weapon against humans and Fae alike. Mab may not own me yet, but she controls the life of the man I love. There is nothing I wouldn't do to see him freed.

Even if I have to become the villain to do it.

Trigger & Content Warnings

The Of Flesh & Bone series is set in a medieval style world where human women are subservient to their male counterparts. The world is a dark dangerous place for women, particularly those who do not conform to societal standards and the purity culture that determines how they live.

The Fae realm of Alfheimr is even darker and the violence in this world gets darker and more graphic with each book. There is murder, torture, and elements of assault.

As such, some elements may be triggering to certain readers. Please proceed with caution.

- Religious purity culture
- Verbal & physical abuse (NOT the male lead)
- References to grooming behavior & assault of a minor by an authority figure (NOT the male lead)
- References to past physical and sexual abuse
- Ritualistic sacrifices
- Suicide
- Suicidal thoughts & ideation
- Graphic death, violence, & torture
- Attempted sexual assault (NOT by the male lead)
- Graphic sexual content
- Flesh-eating creatures

Prologue

Caldris

One of the twin moons flickered as my mate blinked rapidly. She swayed in place as stars shot through the darkness, cruising toward the earth as if the Primordials themselves wept upon all of Alfheimr. My nails dug into the flesh above my heart, feeling the snake that coiled around that beating flesh pull tighter. Mab's gaze sat heavy upon me, her command bearing down on my soul as I pushed myself to my feet.

I did not feel the pain of the wounds already inflicted upon me—only the pain of that flickering bond between Estrella and me. Her consciousness faded slowly as I watched. The pain blooming at the side of her head made my own throb in response.

Mab squeezed her fingers tighter, driving me back to my knees with a strangled roar. For centuries, I'd suffered beneath her hand, compelled to obey her whims and commands. I'd always thought them a burden, a torture unique to the Queen of Air and Darkness.

But *nothing* could compare to the pain of kneeling helplessly as Ophir lifted Estrella into his arms, then hoisted her over his shoulder like a sack. Her eyes connected with mine for a brief moment before they went hazy, and I knew the woman I loved could not see me any longer as the darkness pulled her under. Tears pooled in the shocking green of those unseeing eyes, the color all the more vivid for it, before they shuttered and she was lost to me completely.

The bond snapped shut between us, like the closing of windowpanes in the harsh winter breeze. I stared at her temple where Ophir had struck her; the bruise blooming darker as I watched. I pushed against that metaphysical window, hoping to throw open the shutters and feel through the chasm between us for any sign of life. It lingered there, her mind trapped in the total darkness that only unconsciousness could bring, but her heart still beat in tandem with mine.

She would sleep for a time but wake soon enough. I couldn't determine if that was a blessing or a curse, knowing what awaited her in the Court of Shadows with the queen who would use her to punish me for the secret I'd kept.

Mab summoned the shadow realm once again, allowing Davorin to step through with Fallon. She didn't make a move to fight as he walked into the shadows with her. Her gaze connected with mine for only a moment before she looked back at Estrella, her face twisting with regret.

We'd all been so fixated on Estrella being Mab's daughter, so convinced by the evidence of her powers, that we'd never stopped to consider the alternative. I couldn't imagine what was racing through Fallon's mind, what she must be feeling with the sudden realization that she was the very thing we'd *feared* for Estrella.

And she didn't have a bit of magic to show for it—that we'd seen, anyway.

Several of Mab's children chained my wolves, snapping muzzles around their mouths while she used her control over them through me to force them still. I growled low in my chest, feeling more wolf than man as the cwn annwn were pulled through the shadow realm.

Imelda looked at me, her eyes filled with regret. We'd both failed them. Both failed to prepare them for what was coming and failed to deliver them to safety, as we'd promised. She closed her eyes for a moment, forcing herself to step away from where Fallon had stood. She went to where Estrella's mother wept silently, holding the wound on her face with quiet resignation. Whatever her experience had been in Mistfell, she never moved to fight for her daughter.

She knew it would be pointless and would only lead to her death. A death that Estrella and I had only just managed to distract Mab from claiming.

Imelda took her, wheeling her chair through the snow to put some distance between the Queen of Air and Darkness and the only one of us who had any chance at freedom.

"Take her to my mother," I whispered as she passed me to stand with Holt and the Wild Hunt. Her nod of affirmation soothed the frayed part of me that hadn't been able to save my mate.

At least I could give her human mother a safe place to live out her life, even if Estrella never saw her again.

"Do try not to have too much fun without me, boys. I need him alive still," my stepmother said, her lips curving upward as her dark eyes shone with malice.

Mab stepped through the shadows next, disappearing into Tar Mesa as Malachi lingered at the edges of my vision. He didn't demand my attention in the final moments where I could see my mate before his brother led her through to the Court of Shadows, allowing me to fixate on the sight that would forever stain my memories.

"Ophir!" I roared, flinching back from a kick to my face from one of Mab's more enthusiastic children. Malachi scolded him for interrupting the moment, but the blow had never landed in truth anyway, only skimming my nose. "I will feed you your own intestines if you hurt her. Mab cannot always be there to protect you." I coughed, spitting blood from the previous beating on the snow. From the injuries that would blend into new ones shortly enough.

"Perhaps you should be more concerned with what I have planned for you. Mab won't hurt your mate just yet. She likes her victims aware when she plays with them," Malachi said, chuckling beneath his breath as he closed the remaining distance between us.

He and his twin brother, Ophir, had been the fascination of Alfheimr when they'd been born all those centuries ago. Twins were unheard of among the Fae with the witch's curse upon us. Naturally, Mab had felt compelled to add them to her collection, a rarity she needed to own for herself. Whereas many of her children were decent Fae—twisted by the bond forced upon them as children—the twins were demented, cruel things. They didn't require Mab's bond to behave in ways that should have horrified any living creature, because they enjoyed it.

Ophir stepped through the shadows, vanishing with the love of my life as the rest of Mab's guards ushered the Fae Marked and humans who had joined us on our journey to follow. They struggled as they were led by their chained hands, being treated as prisoners in ways we hadn't allowed.

They'd always thought of us as captors, and we were, to some extent, but not all villains were created equal. Some thrived off of suffering and lived to hear their victims' screams.

There was only one creature in this world who could force me to do harm, and one more who could motivate me to do *anything* if it meant keeping her safe.

Neither could make me enjoy the suffering of innocents.

Malachi stepped forward, closing the distance between us as he pulled his iron blade from its scabbard. He ran his thumb along the sharp edge as he stared at me. "What should I do with you? It is so rare that Mab allows me to be the one to remind you what happens when you disobey her."

"I think you've already made your point," Imelda said from behind me, ignoring Holt's attempts to quiet her.

It comforted something in me to know that my best friend would protect the witch, keeping her from interfering in things she could not change. I glanced back at her, watching as he grasped her around the waist and pulled her struggling frame against his side.

"Quiet, Witch," he warned, his voice dropping low as he leaned down to murmur the words against the side of her head.

Imelda shuddered, squirming in his grip to get free. "Unhand me, Huntsman."

"You don't know Caldris very well, do you?" Malachi asked, touching the edge of his iron blade to my neck. My skin heated beneath the touch, melting away until his blade touched the sinew of muscle. "No, I think something much more severe is in order for his treachery in keeping this secret from our queen."

I gritted my teeth, glancing toward Holt where he stood with Imelda and guarded Estrella's mother.

"Get them to Twyla," I said.

He was duty-bound to follow Mab's command as they related to his position as leader of the Wild Hunt, but that didn't infiltrate the rest of his life. He was free to do as he pleased as he went about his duty, and he'd clearly claimed the witch as his. Since she had no loyalty or affiliations within Alfheimr, he would care for her as long as she allowed him to do so.

Mab's ownership of me made Estrella Mab's property by extension, and I'd never hated the snake wrapped around my heart more than I did in that moment.

Holt held my gaze for a brief moment, then glanced toward Estrella's mother and finally nodded. He led the Wild Hunt to their horses, taking Imelda's hand and guiding her to follow him. He settled the witch upon his skeletal steed in front of him, ignoring the way she struggled against his hold even in the moments where her fear should have driven her to seek safety, in whatever form it came.

Aramis hoisted Estrella's mother up onto his horse in front of him, helping to support her when she swayed slightly.

"I should take your head for the way you ignore me even now," Malachi said, demanding my attention as the Wild Hunt departed for the Winter Court. For the capital in which I'd been born but had no memory of ever residing in.

Catancia.

"It will grow back," I said, forcing a smile to my face.

My blood coated my teeth from my beating, thick and viscous, making my smile grim and disturbing. The pain of being beheaded was but a shadow compared to the fact that it would take me time to heal that wound.

Time I didn't have to waste while my mate would be in Mab's clutches without me to protect her.

"You're right about that, and you would remain blissfully unaware of each hour that passes. I cannot allow you to return to Tar Mesa quickly and ruin our fun too soon, but I want you to be in *agony* for every hour she is with us. I want you to suffer, wondering what we'll do to her when she wakes," Malachi said, pulling the sword away from my neck. He tapped it on the ground twice, the edge sinking into the snow before he lifted his leg and pressed a boot against my chest. He kicked me backward, watching as his minions moved to pin me to the snow.

"One of these days, I will return this *kindness*," I said sarcastically, snarling up at him as he raised his sword above his head.

He brought it down across my elbow, severing my forearm from my body with a single swing. Pain clenched my teeth together, throwing my head back as he repeated the motion with the other arm. The wound sizzled from the iron upon my flesh, and I watched through dazed eyes as he wiped my blood off his sword on the leathers of my armor.

Then he slid it back into his scabbard, pulling a simple long dagger from his thigh. He placed a foot on either side of my body, lowering until he hovered just over me.

"Goodbye, Caldris. I very much look forward to getting to know your pretty mate while you sleep," he said, shoving the dagger into my upper arm. The burn of iron lit me aflame from the inside as he left the long dagger there, pinning me to the snow and the frozen ground beneath.

I lifted my other arm to touch it, trying to reach for it to pull it free even though there were no fingers to grasp it with. So long as the iron was in my body, it wouldn't heal. One of his minions grappled my arm back to the ground, stabbing through my bicep and pinning me there as well. He spat on me as he stood, turning toward Tar Mesa and calling to the shadows that would take them home.

Each one followed until the last of Mab's children stepped up, leaning over me with his iron dagger. He used it to nudge my chin higher, glaring down at me cruelly as he touched the tip to the front of my throat.

He held my eyes intently, slowly pressing the blade forward until the tip penetrated my throat. I gasped for breath, and the sound came out wet as my mouth filled with blood. He pushed forward slowly, spearing me alive until the hilt of his dagger touched my Adam's apple. Only then did he step away, following after the others and leaving me to bleed out, unable to heal myself.

They stepped through the shadowed walkway they created, leaving me alone at the entrance to Alfheimr with the golden gates gleaming behind me. Only snow existed in front of me, a yawning chasm of winter on all sides.

I lifted my right arm along the blade of the dagger, wincing through the pain as I fought to loosen it from the frozen ground beneath me. It pulled on my flesh, slicing through new tissue every time I moved. I'd do whatever it took to get free, because my mate needed me.

She needed me *now*.

1

Estrella

There was no time in the darkness inside my head. There was no pain or strife, only a strange sort of peace that seemed unnatural. It repelled me, telling me it was not my time to rest.

There were things to be done. There were Fae to be slaughtered.

Clink.

Clink.

Clink.

My shoulders throbbed with each sound of metal smacking together. An involuntary noise that seemed to come from above me, pulling me from the moment of peace that wasn't mine to have. I lingered in that strange place between sleeping and awake, where the sounds surrounding my body filtered through my mind without drawing me from my slumber.

"I don't want to wake up," I whispered, uncertain if the words ever reached my lips or if the protest was only inside the confines of my mind.

"And yet you must. It is not your time to die just yet, Estrella Barlowe," a male voice answered.

My eyes popped open, actively searching out the man who spoke the words. The man who had the voice that felt so familiar and somehow wasn't all. He was a stranger to me, a haunting from the deepest recesses of my mind that I couldn't seem to grasp. He slipped through my fingers like water in the river, drifting away before I could focus on him.

My stomach swayed as reality crashed down upon me. My vision lurched, and my head throbbed. My shoulders strained as I unsuccessfully tried to move them. I was strung up by my wrists, and the bite of pain spread through them and down my forearms as I hung over a pit in the stone floor.

Snakes coiled among themselves in that crater, their bodies twining and writhing as if they could climb upon themselves to reach me. I didn't fear snakes any longer, but I tried to curl my legs up for a moment, avoiding them. Would the serpents of Alfheimr obey my command just as those of Nothrek had?

Hands touched my feet, and I swung forward. My stare locked on the eyes of the male who had knocked me out and carried me. His stare was intent, a smirk gracing the lips on his ethereal face. His eyes glowed green in a way that put mine to shame, almost luminescent in the darkness of the room surrounding us.

"Ah, the pretty birdie is awake at last," he murmured, turning toward the dais and leaving me to sway like a pendulum.

Back and forth. Over and over. My joints groaned with every swing of the iron chain above my head. Rope had been wrapped and knotted around my wrists and was attached to the chain. It chafed my flesh where it restrained me, growing slick with the blood that leaked from the abrasions.

The male's steps were casual as he approached the stairs at the front of the room, relaxed as I squirmed through the pain in my shoulders.

Two enormous stone columns stood to either side of the staircase the Fae male ascended. A snake entwined each of them, etched in perfect detail and looking eerily similar to the ones below me that waited for their next meal. At least two dozen Fae waited at the foot of the dais, staring up at me with devious grins on their faces. They murmured softly, their voices echoing and carrying around the room. I couldn't isolate a single whisper or voice. They droned, buzzing like the bees in the gardens during summer.

Metal cages hung from the ceiling high above, filled with creatures. Human and Fae alike, they existed in various stages. Some still breathed, though the wounds upon their bodies implied they'd be better off dead.

A woman sat in the cage closest to me, what remained of her face pressed against the iron bars so that I could stare into the eyes of one of the first women to show me kindness in Nothrek. Half of her face was untouched, unblemished by the violence that had torn the other side to shreds. Her body lacked skin. One side was burnt, blackened by flame, while the other half had been peeled away in strips, hanging from the bars of her cage like ribbons.

Adelphia stared, blank and unseeing, at the wall of the throne room, her eyes clouded over in white. I squeezed my own closed, swallowing down the burn that tried to claw its way up my throat. The knowledge that her death had been so horrific clung to me, promising to taunt me in the dead of night. I would see those eyes for the rest of my life, the first injustice of what I suspected would be many to occur during my time in the Court of Shadows.

I forced my eyes open, following the path the male cut up the steps. At the top of the stairs was a stone dais, and Mab sat upon a throne crafted from skulls. Fallon stood beside the throne where Mab perched, wincing back from her so-called mother as Mab poked and prodded at her with a disgruntled look upon her face. My heart soared at the sight of seeing Fallon alive and unharmed—at least as far as I could tell.

Given the fate that had met Adelphia in the time I slept, I couldn't begin to guess how long I'd been unconscious.

Or the things Mab could do to my friend during that time.

"What do you mean you haven't got any magic? You're my *daughter*," Mab said, her voice ringing through the crowded throne room. I glanced at the select few Fae who had been chosen to stand with Mab on her dais, noting the way they watched Fallon with a mix of both trepidation and excitement.

None stepped forward to help Fallon when Mab reached out with thin hands, grasping Fallon by the chin and pressing a black nail into each of her cheeks.

"I've never used magic," Fallon said, and it was only through the bond between us that I heard the whisper of her words. Only through my knowledge of her that I read them upon her lips. I would have known her voice anywhere, been able to separate it from a crowd of hundreds.

Blood welled beneath Mab's thumb as her talon dug into Fallon's flesh. I pulled on my bond with Caldris at the sight of it as I looked around the room for him, not allowing myself to feel the panic and worry over where he was and what might have been done to him. I would have known if he'd been taken from me. It would have splintered my soul in two. There was no sign of him in the groups waiting; no sign of the male who would have never chosen to be far from me—especially not when I suffered. The bond between us was silent, the threads associated with his magic frayed and faint.

I grasped one of the golden threads that radiated off a skull from Mab's throne, twisting my numb, bloodless fingers around it and pulling it toward me. The edges were frayed and blackened, as if the thread itself was ready to fade into the shadows as it stretched out toward Mab herself, swaying to be closer to her.

The skull shifted, turning to face Mab. It drew her attention, and her face paled for just a moment before the thread fell out of my hold. I couldn't hold on to it, and worry struck me in the gut for my mate. For what must have been done to him to weaken him so much that I couldn't pull from his power at all.

I didn't dare to touch my own magic, having the distinct feeling that it would only draw attention to myself that I didn't want. I wanted Mab to release Fallon, wanted her to forget all about her fury over her daughter not possessing magic, but I didn't want to turn that anger on myself.

Mab narrowed her eyes on Fallon, glancing cautiously back toward the skull that had changed positions and shaking her head before she finally turned to look at me. Her dark eyes collided with mine from across the cavernous throne room, making my heart skip in my chest. There was something so empty in her gaze. It lacked all humanity and emotion until only a thirst for power remained.

She stood from her throne as the Fae male reached the top of the stairs, using graceful hands to lift the skirts of her gown as she descended the first steps. Her pointed shoes touched the red carpet that ran up the center of the stairs, the train of her dress gliding out behind her smoothly as she moved.

The stone of the steps was gray, but the dark speckles upon it reflected centuries of torment. There was only so much one could do to wash away the relentless flow of blood that must have lain upon those steps through time. The crown atop her head gleamed with silver, the bright color jarring against the darkness of her hair. Shadows bled from it the same way they did with Caldris's crown, but it was the shimmering black gem the size of my palm that drew my eye.

I knew it from the story Caldris had told me all those weeks ago in the sanctuary of our cave, huddled beside the fire.

The Cursed Gem. Delivered to the Seelie Court by the dwarves of Elesfast. Created by Edrus himself.

Mab said something to the male at her side as she walked, and he hurried down the steps until he stood on the edge of the floor before me. Grabbing hold of the rope where it was tied to a pole on the wall, he let out slack until I dropped by a margin. Then another and another, until I approached the mouth of the pit. He stopped lowering me then, not allowing me to drop into the pit itself but hanging at eye level with those standing on the edge.

I tried to keep my face blank, knowing most would be consumed by fear of the snakes in the pit below. While I wasn't certain what to think of them, it probably wasn't even close to the reaction Mab would expect. I had to wonder who the snakes would favor in the end. Would my affinity for them be enough to outweigh Mab herself?

I swallowed, wincing when another male stepped up and hooked me around the waist with a shepherd's crook, pulling me toward the ledge. He held me there as the other male untied me, and then they let me fall to the stone on the ledge.

My bare feet hit the ground suddenly, the cold of the stone radiating up my ankles and calves. Like a shock to my system, it overrode the torment and the warmth of numbness within me.

My knees gave out beneath me, and I collapsed. The side of my face smacked against the stone when I couldn't move my arms to catch myself. No matter how hard I tried, they wouldn't move.

How long had I been unconscious and hanging there?

I slowly managed to move my right arm, dragging it closer until I got it beneath my body. My other followed with painstaking slowness as I glared at Mab's feet and her blood-colored shoes where they peeked out from beneath the hem of her dress. She came closer, the sharp, pointed heel gleaming with a polish that made it look wet when it caught the light.

My shoulder cracked as I drew my arm down and got my hands beneath me. Pushing, straining, on those hands, I lifted my upper body from the floor as Mab came to a stop in front of me.

I turned my stare upward, dragging it over the gleaming black of her gown and to the pale skin of her chest. Up her slender neck, and to the harsh, beautiful features set as if encased in stone. Rigid and unmoving, she looked down at me as if I were a worm beneath her feet. Her eyes were angular, her nose pointed and dainty. Her raven hair fell to her waist, as straight and smooth as silk, with the tips of her ears protruding slightly through the sides. The angle of her eyes made a perfect line with the tips of her ears, her face somehow proportioned in ways I hadn't known possible.

She was a great beauty, despite the coldness that radiated off from her.

She took a step forward, pressing her toes onto my starry-night painted fingertips. Sinking her weight into that foot, she ground my finger bones into the stone beneath my hand. I gritted my teeth, grimacing through the pain as she smirked—cold and calculating—as she watched the hints of pain on my face.

"What are you, Little Mouse?"

"I don't know," I ground out, clenching my teeth as she crushed my fingers.

She chuckled, a deep throaty laugh that lacked any sort of humor. It was vicious, tinted with evil itself, as if the lack of answers only pleased her. She bent forward, putting more pressure on my crushed hand, then wrapped her bony fingers around my chin and gripped my face with black talons in the same way she had Fallon.

"Well then, we'll have fun trying to figure it out, won't we?" she asked, stepping back and turning away to dismiss me.

My fingers twitched with the sudden freedom of not being crushed. They'd only been a moment away from cracking beneath the pressure. I pushed to my feet slowly, stumbling as they fought to remember what it was to have the ground beneath them.

"I am no mouse," I said, forcing my back to straighten despite the pain in my shoulders.

Mab spun to face me slowly, quirking a brow in something that almost resembled surprise. "That's odd, because I am the snake, and you look like dinner to me," she said, dropping her gaze to my bare feet and sliding it up my body.

Whatever she saw, she found me wanting.

"Have you ever encountered a Matagot, Mab?" I asked, tilting my head to the side as a hush filled the cavernous throne room.

Mab's eyes hardened into a glare at my faux pas, at the lack of respect I showed her in using her given name when I had no right to.

"Be very careful, girl," she said, lifting a hand when one of her men took a step toward me.

"They're small. Like barn cats, and most villagers think of them as unassuming pests. But the farmers and harvesters know better than to chase them off," I explained, pausing as I glanced to the side as if she wasn't worth my time. I glanced toward the cages, to the people hanging within them who still breathed.

Yet I could not stop myself from pushing the Queen of Air and Darkness, from voicing the first thought in my brain.

"And why is that?" she asked, steepling her hands in front of her.

"Because they eat the snakes when they grow too large and crush the plants beneath them." My fingers twitched at my side to prove my point, and her eyes fell to the bruising skin in acknowledgement.

She laughed, showing her teeth in something that felt far more terrifying than her boredom. She took a step toward me, staring down at me from her much taller height. "I am very much going to enjoy breaking you, Little Mouse," she said, turning her attention to the male who had cut me down from the snake pit.

She pivoted to look toward her throne as a hand buried in my hair, gripping so tightly that my arms flailed, and my hands rose to try to get free. The male shuffled me toward one of the stone walls where black spikes protruded, threatening anyone who wandered too close with impalement. A set of iron shackles hung from the ceiling in front of one particularly vicious spike. I thrashed and dropped my weight to the floor suddenly.

"Damn it to Tartarus," the male cursed, hoisting me up.

I lifted my feet from the ground, forcing him to support all of my weight. It wasn't a difficult task for a Fae, but it did throw his balance just the slightest bit forward. I reached up, grasping him around the back of the neck and yanking him down. As his body bent toward the ground, I jerked and shifted his balance off until he flipped over my head and landed on his back on the stone in front of me. He vaulted to his feet quickly, spinning to face me as I hurled myself to my own feet and threw my weight forward. Knocking into him, pushing him back a few more steps, I retreated as quickly as I'd assaulted him to avoid the black spike that stabbed through his abdomen.

The Fae male glanced down at it, and the sharp point of it sticking out through his stomach, before he raised his eyes to mine once again. "That hurt."

"Do not touch me again," I warned, glancing to where Mab watched with her arms crossed and lips pursed, as if she couldn't decide if I was a curiosity, entertaining, or a pain in the ass. I'd do my best to be the latter if she didn't kill me first.

"You do realize that I'll only add a lashing to your punishment with every moment you spend wasting time, don't you? I do hate to be kept waiting," she said, tapping her black talons along her forearm for effect as the Fae male slowly peeled himself off the spike.

He stepped forward, ignoring the hole in his stomach in a way that I never could have dreamt of before I'd entered the realm of the Fae. The spike behind him glistened with blood.

"Stop it. Please," Fallon suddenly said, as the Fae male approached me. "Don't hurt her."

Mab looked at her daughter, considering her carefully. Fallon kept the emotions open on her features, her concern for me showing in every line of her face. But Mab was not the kind to care.

Not for me. Not for her daughter.

All the things Caldris had told me were true. She cared for nothing but herself. That much was clear from a single glance into the emptiness of her eyes.

"Chain her, Malachi," Mab instructed, not even bothering to look away from where Fallon's face twisted with remorse. "No child of mine will put herself on the line to protect someone else. You will learn very quickly that it is you or her in this place, Maeve."

Malachi used my distraction—my dawning horror for the callous way Mab treated her long-lost daughter—against me and grasped me by the front of the throat. He squeezed until my air was cut off, then lifted me from my feet, shifting me until my stomach touched the very tip of the spike.

I struggled as much as I could, pushing back into the wall of his body and trying to avoid the impalement that threatened if I shifted even a hair forward. Grasping one of my arms, he wrenched it above my head and shackled me.

The moment the metal touched my skin, it sizzled with the familiarity of iron. I sagged in Malachi's grip, all the strength leaving my body quickly, but he used his free arm to wrap around my waist and hold me up as he latched the other wrist into the shackles above my head. Once that was done, he grabbed the end of the chain where it met the wall, yanking it higher until the shackles pulled me up. Only my toes scraped the ground, grappling for purchase and stability.

"I hope you're good at holding still, Pet," Malachi murmured as he stepped up beside me.

He touched his thumb to the healing wound on his stomach, gathering blood and reaching up to spread it across my lip.

Revulsion slid through me. I only desired my mate's blood anywhere near my mouth.

He stepped around to my back once again. His fingers brushed against the skin at the top of my neck as he grasped the collar of my dress. There was only a moment of pause, distinctly for dramatic effect and to give me time to realize exactly how this punishment would go. Then the fabric pulled tight against my body, tearing as he ripped it down the back and shoved the scraps to the side to leave my spine open to view.

"How sweet," Mab cooed, forcing me to glance over my shoulder at her. "She matches her mate." The scars I'd come to be ashamed of were so publicly on display. Knowing that the woman who had given Caldris the scars—which were so much worse than mine—would be responsible for making us a true matching pair made rage simmer in my veins.

I met her glare, watching as one of her males handed her a black whip. It looked as if it had been crafted from the shadows themselves, but it couldn't have been. Not with the iron tips protruding from all sides.

I turned forward, hanging my head and trying to will my body to remain still. The pain would be unbearable, but so would allowing myself to be impaled by the spike a mere breath away from my stomach.

I drew in a deep breath and planted my toes against the stone floor, sinking into the darkness inside of me. Making a home there and hoping it could protect me against what was to come.

The whip cracked as Mab swung it, the distinct sound echoing through the throne room.

But the pain never came.

A body pressed into mine lightly, and an arm wrapped around my stomach, a large hand between my stomach and the spike threatening to torture me. I glanced over my shoulder, finding Caldris's burning blue eyes on mine as the whip cracked again.

"Caelum," I murmured, fighting back the choked sob that wanted to emerge at the sight of him.

He was alive, even if he was not well. The circles under his eyes were deeper than I thought possible, his skin lackluster, as if he were ill.

The hand at my stomach was covered in dried blood, and his tunic and armor were adorned with holes all the way up his arms.

"I'm here now, my star."

"What did they do to you?" I asked, wincing when the whip cracked again. Caldris's body jolted when it collided with his back, but he didn't allow the strike to push me forward or bring me harm.

He didn't answer, only taking his eyes off mine when the whipping stopped. He reached above my head, risking the burn of iron to unshackle me and helping me get my footing when my body sagged.

"You know I don't take kindly to anyone ruining my fun, Caldris," Mab's deep, empty voice said. The tone of her words echoed through the cavernous room as Caldris reached up to loose my second hand. I wavered in his grasp, struggling to find my footing after being hung over the pit for the countless hours I'd spent unconscious.

As soon as I was steady on my feet, Caldris reached up to the clasp at the top of his neck, shucking off his leather and armor without a word. The armor fell first, hanging off his body until it clacked dramatically against the stone of the floor.

"You would give me your own flesh to protect hers?" Mab asked as I spun in front of my mate. Putting the iron spike at my back and leaning into his body, I stilled his hand as it went to the buttons fastening the leather he wore atop his tunic. "It is always such a shame to ruin the skin that so many would appreciate if given the chance."

"No," I protested, shaking my head as he tried to shake off my grip.

"This is nothing compared to the misery I would endure if it meant you would never know pain again, *min asteren*," he murmured, guiding my hand away and slowly unfastening the buttons.

I glanced at where Mab stood, staring at her nails and toying with the shadows extending from her hands. Her eyes connected with mine, a tiny smirk gracing her blood-red lips as if she knew as well as I did that watching my mate endure my fate was worse than if I suffered it myself.

I closed my eyes, imagining that bedroom window held tight against the cold lurking outside. Reaching up with trembling fingers and preparing myself for the unique sense of wholeness that came with being connected to Caldris, I flipped the clasp open. A gust of wind blew them open, surging into my lungs and burning me from the inside out with the warmth of the hearth in winter.

Caldris's eyes glowed with a frosty blue, a surge of gold tinting the edges of his irises for a moment before the light faded from them and I wondered if I'd imagined the entire thing. So caught in the wave of feelings coursing through me, I brushed the unfastened leather off his shoulders until it fell to the floor and pulled his tunic free from his trousers, shimmying it up his body until I could pull it free from his head and drop it to the floor while I looked around his form and met Mab's dark stare.

I raised a tentative hand to grasp the iron shackles above our heads. Lifting one of his hands to them, I ignored the searing of both our flesh as I clanked it closed around his wrist. I repeated it with the other wrist, touching my ruined skin to his cheek gently as he bowed his forehead toward mine, his eyes fluttering closed as he let out a shuddering breath.

"Until chaos reigns," I whispered.

He flung his eyes open the moment he sensed my intention coursing down the bond, no longer hidden in the deepest recesses of my mind. "My star," he said, shaking his head as he struggled against the shackles holding him prisoner.

I sensed Mab's whip of shadows preparing, gathering at her side as she allowed one of her minions to sprinkle it with iron dust, as clearly as if it had been an extension of me. I smiled sadly for my mate, knowing he would have given anything to prevent me from taking his pain.

He'd suffered long enough. He'd been tortured for longer than I remembered existing, feeling me and never having me while *this* was his reality.

The whip cracked as I stepped around his tense form. His body shifted as he tried to prevent me from moving into the path of harm. Mab's court cheered as the whip cracked through the air, eagerly waiting for the agony that would follow when the shadows struck against Caldris's skin.

I turned my face to the side as I blocked it with one arm, thrusting the other up above my head to catch the blow. The whip wrapped around my forearm, searing into my skin and imbedding itself there as it sank through my flesh. I pulled my face away from the hand that had sheltered me, watching my flesh melt as the iron burned me. My bones throbbed, but I turned my glare to Mab and forced myself to wrap the shadows around my hand.

It burned its way through me, but I grabbed it with a firm grip, anyway. Melding it into my body, accepting it as part of me until we forced it out from the valley it created in my skin. Mab narrowed her eyes as I wrapped my fingers around her whip, then glanced at the court who had suddenly gone silent.

I screamed through the pain, raising my arm up even higher and then forcing it down toward the floor. The whip slammed against the floor, cracking the stone in a distinctive path toward Mab. It moved as if in slow motion, echoing the movement of the whip as Mab's weapon came back toward her.

The whip left her hand, pulled from her grasp with the force of my fury. The very tail end of it sliced her cheek in an upward swing before it dissolved into nothing. It vanished in a slow arc toward me; the very thing that seared my skin disappeared without a master to empower it. My skin hung in ruined tatters, gaping and open where the shadows had once filled it.

Mab's eyes dropped to my arm, studying the slight, pulsating golden glow that filled my flesh as my body worked to repair the damage. Cold filled the marks, soothing the burns as she and I watched my skin knit itself back together. The wounds healed slowly, the golden light spreading through them. Only I saw the golden threads wrapping themselves around my forearm.

Mab reached up a hand to touch her cut cheek, her crimson blood covering her fingers as her own wound sat unhealed.

None in her court dared to move. Part of me was convinced that they didn't dare to breathe while her jaw was clenched. I took a single step forward, pausing only when she raised a hand and Caldris groaned behind me.

I gnashed my teeth together, gritting out the words. "I do hope that doesn't scar."

"It seems having a mate is not the only secret you've been keeping, my darling Caldris," Mab said, ignoring me entirely as she stepped forward. "She'll make such a fun new pet for me to play with." She paused at my side, glaring down at me as I lifted my eyes to hers. Caldris's chains rattled as he struggled, while Mab's men let him loose from the chains.

"The last person who tried to own me now lies dead," I warned, forcing myself not to look away from her as she tipped her head to the side and smiled at me.

"Is that a threat?" she asked, a slight giggle slipping free from her lips. "It has been so many years since someone dared to threaten me, I'd almost forgotten what it feels like. I believe I've missed it."

"You could have all the threats you wanted if you released the children you've collected and allowed them to return to their families. Only a coward would use them to maintain power," I said.

Caldris sighed. "*Min asteren*—"

"Better a coward than dead," Mab said, shrugging her shoulders as she turned to look at Malachi, severing the eye contact I hadn't been willing to be the first to break. "Take them to the dungeon until I've decided what to do with my new curiosity."

She turned away, leaving us to the men who looked at me as if they weren't certain they wanted to risk touching me.

Caldris struggled in his chains, trying to get free from the shackles so that he could get to me.

His fury was tangible in the air, and because of the bond, I knew it was rage for me.

I'd revealed too much, played my hand too soon, but I would never regret getting between him and the pain coming for him. Not when I suspected it was the first time anyone had ever done something like that. Beneath his fury, I felt his confusion. Even a God wanted to be loved so thoroughly that someone would sacrifice themselves to protect him.

The hilt of a sword crashed against my temple, forcing me to stagger on my feet and stumble to the side. Malachi caught me, steadying me as he raised his sword once more.

Caldris roared. "There's no fucking need for—"

Another blow knocked me fully into his grip, and my body went lax.

Then everything faded to black.

2

The feeling of water sluicing over my skin drew me from the depths of slumber. I opened my eyes suddenly, staring out at the dark, reflective surface beneath me. All around me, faint lights twinkled in the darkness like the night sky, stretching on and on for what seemed like an eternity. There were no mountains, no trees, no signs of life—merely an endless void.

My arm lay against the water beneath me, supporting me above the surface as I stared down through the murky, flowing surface. I lifted a hand, studying my fingers before I pressed it against the water once more. It slid beneath the surface, and the water streamed over my hand, flowing as quickly as the waters of a rapid river. Shifting, changing, moving. I couldn't see the bottom of the strange river beneath my body. Shadows and specters twined together seamlessly, writhing and filling the water.

The macabre, weathered face of a man passed beneath my hand—his skin was pulled taut to his skull, his eyes closed and cheeks hollow. I pressed my face closer to the water to study the way my fingers moved within the fluid. A spectral woman passed by, her eyes closed as if she was in eternal slumber until the moment her torso passed by my hand.

Her eyes flung open. She grasped onto me, and her mouth opened into a scream, revealing razor-sharp teeth. I tugged on my hand, trying to pull it free, but she and the water held me captive.

"Let go!" I screamed, pulling as hard as I could.

Those teeth seemed to rotate in a circle within her mouth, spinning in a vortex that felt like it would suck me into an entirely different world. She slowly dragged herself toward my hand, while I desperately fought to pry her fingers off mine.

"Let it be a lesson for you," a male voice said as he pressed the paddle end of his oar against her torso.

He pushed her away, and her shriek and wail echoed through the cavernous empty space as she drifted off. I was finally able to yank my hand free. My lungs heaved as I cradled it to my chest, having nearly lost it to my own curiosity.

"Do not play with things you don't understand, girl."

"What was that?" I asked, rising to my feet.

The water supported me as I stood; whereas his skiff seemed to float within the liquid that somehow solidified for me. Skulls hung off the sides, the flesh melting from the bones in various stages of decay. The bones of a person's spine lined the seam of the boat itself, curving around the edge.

"Something that would have done anything for even just a taste of your blood," he answered vaguely. His face remained hidden by his hood that draped over the front of his head and torso. Whatever existed below it was lost to the darkness within, making me wonder if he was even a man at all or something else entirely.

"Why?" I whispered, and the sound bounced between us.

He chuckled, the sound deep and entirely otherworldly. "You might be oblivious to your true nature, but that doesn't mean there aren't creatures out there who see you for exactly what you are, girl," he said, slipping his oar into the water. He rowed away, turning his skiff away from me as I scrambled after him.

"Wait! Tell me what I am!" I called after him, watching as he moved impossibly fast. I seemed unable to follow. My feet moved, but it was as if I ran in place. "Please!"

"Be careful what you ask for, *Little Bird.*" He stopped rowing, turning back to me slowly until only the glow of golden eyes came from beneath his hood as his stare met mine. "Some secrets are better left in the dark."

My world spun, his face disappearing as he turned away, leaving me to collapse in the water. My lungs filled with air, as if they'd been deprived the entire time I was in this place. What absorbed me wasn't the river.

It was the hard stone floor beneath me in a cell.

I suddenly thrust myself into a sitting position.

Caldris stared at me, his expression as confused as mine.

***

"Estrella?" Caldris asked.

He sat on the opposite side of the iron bars of his cell. A stone passage separated us, hobbled and broken between the two free-standing prisons holding us separate. I *felt* the iron surrounding me, elevated slightly over the damp passage between us. Something scurried in the back corner of my cell, tempting my eyes away from the mate who stared at me as if he couldn't believe I existed.

"Thank fucking Gods. Do you have any idea how worried I've been?"

"Some secrets are better left in the dark..." I whispered, my voice trailing off as the words fell from my lips. A reiteration of something I knew well; the words slid off my tongue like a well-known, familiar mantra.

"What did you just say?" Caldris asked, maneuvering to his knees. He paused with his hands only a breath from the iron of the bars, his head cocking to the side as he studied me intently.

"Nothing," I said, shaking my head, determined that it had been only a figment of my imagination; a moment in a dream where I tried to grasp onto something even remotely familiar in a time when everything I'd ever known had been torn from my hands.

"Say. It. Again," Caldris ordered, his voice dropping lower with the tone of command I recognized. It was the same one he'd used on me that day in the tunnels, when something had compelled me to flee the cave beast and leave him behind.

My mouth dropped open, ready to confess all my secrets at the first word from him.

I clamped it shut in defiance. "You will *not* do that ever again," I snapped, forcing the same tone to my voice.

Caldris's eyes flashed in a moment of darkness, black bleeding through the bright blue of his stare. We didn't know what I was; we didn't know if whatever it was would ever stand as his equal or if I would remain lesser next to his status as a God.

His lips tipped into a smirk, confirming my suspicions that he would enjoy every second of the battle if I proved to be a worthy opponent in every way. Just as he enjoyed me when I threatened to bleed him, he would never desire a mate who *always* did as she was told.

"All right, my star. Then tell me what I want to know. I can feel it rattling around inside your head, but I want to hear you say the words," he said, dropping his hands to his side. They clenched into fists, his frustration pulsating down the bond. He wanted to touch me, wanted to reach me, but the hall that separated us and the iron bars prevented it.

I raised my chin, severing our eye contact to look around the cell that would probably be my new home. Water ran down the stone in the hallway just outside, and iron bars surrounded me on all sides of the small square I occupied. Chains dangled from the ceiling in the hallway outside, and torture instruments hung from the walls. I swallowed.

"Some secrets are better left in the dark," I whispered, raising my eyes to his dark stare once more.

"Show me," he murmured, the command less forceful than the last. Instead of feeling like it would tear submission from me, it tickled the edges of my consciousness, playing the threads of our bond like a violin.

I closed my eyes, drawing in a deep breath as I drew the memory of what I'd seen, of the teeth and golden eyes, to the forefront of my mind. My father's words struck me in the chest, haunting me from the form of someone who was not him. Someone who could not and would never be him.

No father of mine would have rowed away from me, leaving me lying on the top of the river. He'd have pulled me up and put me in the boat with him, finally reunited with me after death had separated us for years.

And my father did not possess the glowing golden eyes that sank into my soul and tormented me.

"The ferryman," Caldris murmured softly, his gaze snagging mine as the memory ended.

I jolted back to my body, pulled from the immersive experience of witnessing it with Caldris for the first time.

"Why would the ferryman use the same phrases as my father?" I asked, swallowing as my mate's stare turned confused.

"Your father said, 'some secrets are better left in the dark'?" he asked, pushing to his feet.

He lifted a hand to his face as he paced around the cell. He limped lightly, as if his body was still repairing itself from whatever harm had been done to him before he'd found his way to me.

His hand brushed against the front of his throat, drawing my attention to the remnants of a white scar. I swallowed, knowing his face and his body by heart. *That* scar had not been there before we'd arrived on the shores of Alfheimr.

Rage simmered in my blood, forcing me to my feet so that I could pace around my own cell. He would bear the scar of that iron for the rest of his days. I glanced down at my forearm, at the unblemished skin that had glowed with golden light. I'd somehow known for a fact that the shadow whip had been dipped in iron, that it was the very tool Mab had used to scar Caldris's back.

Yet my skin was free from scars.

I swallowed, looking back at my mate, who couldn't seem to take his eyes off the unblemished parts of me. It wasn't jealousy or bitterness that flowed to me through the bond, but curiosity and comfort.

Whatever I was didn't matter to him. All that mattered was that it seemed I would be even harder to *kill*.

"He did," I agreed finally. "It was a frequent saying of his when I grew too curious. When I'd wander toward the Veil as a girl or get into some kind of trouble meant only for boys." I rolled my eyes. The phrase was meant to warn me away from exploring things I shouldn't have any knowledge of, and somehow that mentality had carried through my life.

Even now, I felt guilt over my desire to know what blood flowed through my veins. Logically, I knew that the secret was better left untouched so that it couldn't be used against me.

"His nickname for me was Little Bird," I said, watching as Caldris froze, turning his head to face me suddenly.

"Interesting," he said, nodding. I knew that Caldris and the ferryman knew one another, that they'd often worked in tandem to deliver souls to the Void.

"Is my father the ferryman somehow? I don't understand how any of this is possible," I asked, running my hand over the unblemished arm. I couldn't shake the feeling that I didn't belong in this place, that its very nature was wrong for me.

I came alive in the darkness, but something about the Court of Shadows made my skin crawl.

"The ferryman isn't any one person. They are a collective entity composed of souls chosen by the Fates to be the keepers of the Void. The collective is meant to erase human experience and create an unbiased guardian with only the best interest of Fate in mind, creating something new. Their interference in not allowing you to be devoured by the lost spirit goes against everything they're meant to be," Caldris said.

"A lost spirit? Is that what that thing was?" I asked with a swallow. "With the teeth?"

"Yes. Every moment they spend lost in the River Styx without passing into the Void strips away more and more of what makes them human or Fae. They become hollow entities with no persona, desperate to devour the flesh that could make them whole again," he explained.

"And what does that have to do with my father? The Fates chose him to become part of the ferryman?"

"He must have already had that connection to the Fates prior to your childhood, otherwise he would not have known that phrase," Caldris said, his gaze falling to the flowing water spreading across the stone floor. It was just a trickle, a tiny stream at the center of the hall between us, but it was clear this was the part of a great and terrible court that lay forgotten and dismissed.

All who entered here were lost, much like those lost to Styx.

A snake slithered up the stream, navigating around the discarded torture instruments and stains from centuries of blood. He paused at the bars to my cell, rising onto his tail to look at me as he cocked his head to the side. Bending down, I squatted in front of him and held out a hand.

His delicate tongue snaked out, brushing against the skin of my fingers before he allowed himself to slither between the bars and curl up in my palm. I rose to stand, brushing the fingers of my free hand over the back of his head as his yellow eyes stared at me.

"It just had to be fucking snakes," Caldris said, his face twisted in disgust.

Pursing my lips, I furrowed my brow at him but kept my eye trained on the helpless snake in front of me. "They're just misunderstood, aren't you?" I asked, smiling as he leaned into the pressure from my finger scratching the back of his... neck?

Did snakes have necks?

What was my life? I shook my head, watching as he slithered his way up over the back of my hand and up my arm. He continued over my shoulder, curling around my neck and tickling my skin as he made his way to the top of my head, using my braid to put himself there. He curled up in a circle on top of it, seeming quite cozy as Caldris stared at me.

"Problem?" I asked.

"That's hardly sanitary. You never know what he's crawled through," Caldris said.

"Snakes don't crawl," I returned, pretending that I hadn't just wondered if they had necks. "Besides, I never know where you've been, and somehow I still like you."

"Ouch," Caldris said with a laugh that defied the circumstances surrounding us. "I haven't *been* anywhere in centuries."

I hummed, resisting the urge to pet the snake atop my head. I needed something to do with my hands, a way to keep busy, to distract me from the emptiness of my cell. I needed a fucking book to read, but I doubted Mab was going to give me access to her library. Caldris's face softened as I glanced around the cell before my gaze fell upon him again.

"I'm going to get you out of here, I promise."

"And what about you?" I asked, trying to tell him through the bond that I would never leave him behind. The only way to get me out was to get *him* out, and the snake wrapped around his heart would make that nearly impossible.

"We'll worry about that when you're safe," he said, hanging his head.

"No."

"Excuse me?" he asked.

I glared at him in response. The God of the Dead wasn't used to being told no—not when the only person who dared to defy him was the Queen of Air and Darkness herself.

"You dragged me here against my will. I will *not* be sent away like an incompetent child. I am the only one of the two of us who can act outside of Mab's will. You need me, and we both know it," I explained, stepping up to the iron bars that held me captive. The snake upon my head felt like a crown, like a twisted joke. Mab was the queen known for her power over snakes, and here one rested with me even still.

"She will *use* you in ways you cannot imagine. You cut her, *min asteren.* I could not tell you the last time someone was able to do that. You should have allowed her to scar me as she has countless times and stayed hidden. Now she *sees* you. What do you think she would do to possess a weapon like you?" he asked, making my lips twist into a grimace.

"I'm not a weapon," I argued.

"You are. We cannot even begin to understand what you're capable of yet, but you healed from iron. You used Mab's own shadows against her. You will strengthen her reign. If for no other reason than that, we have to get you away from her."

"I'm not going to leave you behind," I stated firmly, staring at my mate across the hall between our cells.

There was nothing but a determined stare on his face as his gaze held mine, his jaw clenched, immovable as solid ice. But enough force could break it, could shatter the ice around him like the Veil upon the grass of the gardens at Mistfell.

I wouldn't bow, wouldn't break. Not when the alternative meant that the past weeks I'd spent coming to terms with the mate who'd claimed me would be for nothing. Not when the bond we'd created and the love we now shared would haunt me.

I wouldn't allow Mab to be what drove us apart when I'd tried and failed to do so on my own.

"You aren't supposed to be here. I didn't believe it when you said that you felt like something within you revolted against these shores. You are far too dangerous to exist in the clutches of the one person who would use you to burn the world as we know it to the ground. With you at her side, she could be unstoppable," Caldris explained, his gaze softening for a single, delicate moment.

"She already is. If she wasn't, someone would have stopped her by now," I said, hanging my head as I considered that freeing my mate from Mab may be impossible in the end.

It seemed unfathomable that one person could have so much more power than what I'd observed in him. There'd been a time when the power my mate possessed seemed infinite, and in truth, it still did in so many ways.

What must Mab's power have looked like if it was too much for the male who'd decimated Calfalls to fight?

"Maybe we were just waiting for you. Even if we didn't realize it," Caldris said, his voice dropping to a whisper. "It has been suggested that my mate may be enough to increase my power so that I could stand a fighting chance, but we never considered what you may be. You are more than just a mate for me to love, and your power will feed our bond far more than a human's life force ever could. No matter what you are, there is something inside of you that will frighten Mab when she comes to realize how deep it runs in you. When you factor in our bond, the two of us would be unstoppable if we could only complete the ceremony and tie our lives together in truth."

I sank to my knees on the stone beneath me, touching a hand to the rough surface and wishing the iron around me didn't dull my senses so much. I'd never healed from it before stepping foot in Alfheimr, so something about this land strengthened me.

As much as I felt like I wasn't supposed to be here, this was where I'd been born in my first life.

This was the land that coursed through my soul, that powered my very existence. So why did it repulse me, as if the earth itself wanted to send me away?

I shuddered as I bent my fingers, digging my nails into the stone and pressing down with every bit of the aggravation I felt. The stone cracked beneath my touch. Jagged pieces jutted up from the surface to surround my hand. I picked them apart slowly, nudging them out of my way as I touched my fingers to the soil beneath.

It was rich, hearty, even in this place that seemed so devoid of life. The grains were perfect for growing plants, wet and healthy in ways the grainy sands of Nothrek could never be without the magic of the Faerie. I cupped a handful and lifted it from the ground, curling my arm toward my torso as I stared at the dirt that felt so different from the soil I'd spent an entire lifetime toiling away in.

"What are you doing?" Caldris asked, his voice muffled, as if I was drowning beneath the surface. As if the water that flowed through the hills of Faerie raged inside my head, making it so that I could barely see him.

"I don't know," I admitted, staring down at the hole in the earth where I'd taken the dirt from it. I returned the soil, placing it gently and touching my fingers to the earth once again. My fingers curled into it, the individual grains imbedding themselves under my nails and staining my fingers.

I ignored the pulsing whisper, the driving force to remove my hand from the thing that did not belong to me. It did not claim me, that quiet murmuring of the soil that echoed in my head.

Abomination, it seemed to say; and if dirt and soil and all those things had the ability to speak, I might have taken that insult to heart.

A trick of the mind, I reminded myself, finally pulling my hand away. I covered the hole with the stone once again, piecing the shards together like a puzzle until it wasn't readily apparent to any guards who might intrude on my personal cell.

"It doesn't want me here," I whispered, trying not to acknowledge the melancholy in my voice. It was foolish to care what something that did not live thought of me, but I couldn't shake the stinging feeling of rejection.

I'd never belonged anywhere, and it seemed I still wouldn't.

"What doesn't?" Caldris asked.

I could feel his gaze on me. I hadn't yet met his face, not wanting to see the concern in his eyes. I wondered if whatever had changed within me had also taken something from me. If it had changed me into something less stable, crafting me into something that would always struggle to separate the truth from fiction.

I raised my eyes, finally meeting his blue stare. The dirt seemed to cling to the Fae Marks on my palm and fingers, as if it could hide who and what I was.

"Faerie," I answered, not knowing what else to call it. The magic that coursed through the dirt was natural, derived from the Primordials who'd crafted the world themselves.

Was it the Primordials who did not want me here, if that was the case? Or was it purely the result of their magic?

"You say that like it spoke to you," he said, his brow furrowing.

I was sure he'd heard the whispers that danced in his head; and given that I, myself, questioned if they were real, I could just imagine how difficult it must be to hear them through the bond. Like a secret whispered through people, how much of what we sensed from one another was diluted or altered?

"It wasn't words so much as a feeling," I confirmed, because the word I'd put to it was my own. The only word to match the feeling it gave me. How could I possibly thrive in this place where I was a prisoner in a land that didn't want me?

"What's happening to me?" I asked instead, tears pooling in my eyes. My nose stung with the threat of them, as if they could burn a path up my throat and scorch the world. The realization of all that had happened, all that I'd lost, overcame me.

I'd known being with Caldris meant sacrificing my freedom, but I hadn't been expecting to be held within a literal cage.

There was sacrificing my freedom for love, and then there was having it stolen for no reason. This was the latter, and I wanted to do whatever it took to get back to the sacrifice.

"I don't know," my mate admitted. He didn't shrug his shoulders. The movement would have been far too casual for the seriousness of our conversation, but the lack of commitment was there, nonetheless. "We'll figure it out when we can. For now, we're better off not having the answers. Mab can't demand information we do not have."

I nodded, trying not to let my curiosity get the best of me. *Some secrets are better left in the dark.*

I could hear my father's voice as clear as if it had been yesterday, the mantra of the ferryman a gentle hum in my soul. I didn't understand why, and I'd have been lying if I wasn't curious to see him again, to demand the answers I was due. It was a stark contrast to the girl who had always been content to stay oblivious, who felt the truth in that statement.

Where had that gotten me? What good had my willful ignorance done for me in the end?

I was done being kept in the dark about the things that concerned me. My birth was one mystery I was determined to solve the riddle of. Why was I protected? What was I that I had to be smuggled out of Faerie as an infant with Mab's daughter?

Caldris smirked, rolling his eyes slightly as he stared at me across the void between us. Even if it was only a few paces, it felt like a chasm determined to keep us apart. To separate what Mab knew would be too powerful for her if we could only come together in the truest sense of the mate bond.

"You aren't going to leave this one alone, are you?" he asked, shaking his head as if I was impossible. It was done with genuine amusement alongside his frustration, as if this was just further evidence of all the reasons he loved me.

I smiled back at him, silently shaking my head.

"I thought as much," he said with a sigh.

Warmth pulsed down the bond, striking me straight in the chest. His feelings on the matter were clear, as if I couldn't read them on his face. We'd always been able to communicate somehow, even without words, prior to the bond linking our minds together as one.

I twiddled my thumbs, dropping my gaze from him as I debated whether I wanted the answers to the question I would ask. Part of his mind was protected, the memory of exactly what they'd done to him fuzzy, as if he'd hidden it behind a veil so that I couldn't access the fine details of his pain. Only the swift, unyielding agony he'd experienced came through, as if whatever wall he'd erected in his memory wasn't enough to block it out and keep it from me.

He shifted his neck, the thin line of white that he hadn't yet healed seeming to gleam in the dim light coming from the sconces on the wall.

"What did they do to you after they took me?"

He hesitated, his body freezing as he gave up on trying to roll the tense muscles that accompanied his injury. "You shouldn't ask that question," he said simply, his voice dropping deep with warning.

I pushed at the wall he'd created in his mind, probing along the edge of it with gentle fingers that couldn't seem to get through. I didn't dare to push too hard, not knowing what damage I might cause by being forceful.

"And yet I am anyway," I said with a subtle smile. "I need to know what they did to you so that I know how much to make them suffer when I'm given the opportunity."

He grinned in response, his love for my violence showing even in the darkness that surrounded us and the fate that seemed impossible for us to escape. "This hardly seems like an appropriate place for foreplay, my star," he murmured gently, the slight teasing lilt to his voice confirming that whatever they'd done, he would survive it.

"I think the atmosphere is perfect. Everyone wants to fuck surrounded by rats," I said, shaking my head from side to side. "No matter how hard you try, this is not a question I will let go. Tell me what they did."

"Leave it alone, Estrella," he snapped, his teeth clacking together with the force of his frustration.

"No," I answered simply, pushing against the wall firmly enough that he turned his head to the side with a snarl.

"Would you just let me protect you from how ugly this world is?" he asked.

"To what end? You think Mab doesn't intend to do the very same to me once she figures out what I am? She'll torture me; and hiding me from the pain that awaits isn't going to do either of us any good," I said, rolling my eyes to the stone ceiling that hovered too close.

It wasn't high, but it somehow felt even more claustrophobic than the tunnels the resistance favored had been. I supposed that was the point, and the closest comparison I could make was the kennels the Mist Guard kept their hounds in. It felt more like a prison than I'd ever experienced, and that said something when my entire life had been one.

"Stop it," he said, shrugging me off and pushing back through our link.

"Tell. Me," I ordered, my voice dropping low with the command. I felt it rumble in my chest before the words escaped, the bass of it seeming too deep to be natural.

Caldris froze. His eyes flew wide open as his lips parted, but he quickly clamped them shut. I tilted my head and watched his physical struggle play out, as if he'd been compelled to admit the truth to me.

"Tell me what they did," I said, allowing my voice to resonate in that deep place. It was the same home to the darkness that lurked within me, to the void of nothing just waiting to consume me.

"Little One," he said, his voice dropping into a deep groan as he reached up to his throat and wrapped a hand around it.

His eyes narrowed as he realized I was already aware of what I'd done.

I'd already figured it out, even if I didn't understand how it was possible.

"Tell. Me." My voice was barely a whisper, hardly even a breath.

"They cut off my hands," he said, the words torn from him as he sputtered. "And then as I bled, they stabbed me through each of my arms and my throat with iron so that I was pinned to the ground and had to tear myself free."

I swallowed hard. The haunting image of his memory surged free from his walls and struck me straight in the chest. The pain that hit me was beyond imagining, tearing me in two in a way I'd only ever experienced when I'd been remade when I touched Alfheimr.

The image of him pulling on his arm until the blades cut through him and his flesh hung off his body in ribbons would never be erased from my mind. I swallowed, holding my head in my hands as I watched him yank the knife from his throat, struggling to get to his feet. He couldn't do it, his body too weighed down by the iron weapons that had been used to immobilize him. He fought his way to his hands and knees, his bones protruding from his wounds as blood poured out of the hole in his throat that refused to heal.

He slipped in his own blood as he crawled across the snow, staining the ground red as he went.

"I would have dragged my broken body across the snow until I reached you," Caldris said, forcing me to remove the hands from my face and meet his stare. Both empathy and fury lurked in his eyes, somehow a mix of softness and rage coming through our bond. I couldn't even blame him.

What I'd done was a violation, and even after realizing what was happening, I'd continued on, anyway.

I clamped my mouth shut, swallowing the apology that tried to make its way up my throat. If the roles had been reversed, he wouldn't have apologized for doing it to me.

But neither of us had expected for me to have that kind of power over him, and I didn't know where that left us. What could I be that would be more powerful than a God?

The son of two Gods. The grandchild of the Primordials. He was one of the only second-generation Gods in existence, purely because he was so powerful that none could possibly compare.

"We need to set boundaries," he said, swallowing as he realized how unfair that was.

"Funny that when I use it against you, it is time for boundaries, but when you do it, it's for my own good," I said, raising an eyebrow and trying to highlight his ridiculous double standards.

"I do it to protect you. Not to make you confess your secrets," he said.

"Perhaps it is time for you to realize that I am not the one in need of protection," I murmured, letting the words linger between us.

Silence met me in response, because neither of us had been willing to consider the fact that I may be something *more*.

More powerful than my mate.

3

Estrella

I woke slowly, the feel of unyielding stone beneath me far from the most comfortable of surfaces I'd ever experienced.

I couldn't say it was the worst either, though.

My body ached as I stretched out my limbs, uncurling from where I'd twisted my body into the fetal position in an attempt to keep warm. I didn't know where exactly Mab's court was located, but the distinct chill in the air felt far too much like winter for my comfort.

Why did it always have to be fucking cold? I wanted a land of eternal summer and warm, balmy nights or, at the very least, a fire to read beside with a pile of blankets to keep me comfortable.

"Be warmer if pretty dress wasn't torn," a small voice said, the deep tone of it so at odds for how quiet it seemed. Even in the silence, it was barely murmur in the dungeon we now called home.

I sat up suddenly, glancing around the cell and heaving a sigh of relief when my eyes landed on the figures of two very different shades looming beside me. The one who had spoken was small enough to fit in my hand. His silver beard was pulled into two braids that went down to his feet. A purple hat rested above his head, slightly too large for him so that it appeared to be drooping down into his eyes. With his beard covering most of his mouth, all that I could truly see of his face was a bulbous nose.

The other shade was the spectral form of a woman. Her legs were bare, only small strips of cloth covering her breasts and intimate area. I glanced toward Caldris's sleeping form, relieved to find his eyes still closed. The jealousy that pulsed through me wasn't natural, but neither was it something that could be contained—even despite the fact that she was dead. Turning my attention back to her with guilt in my heart, I watched as her skin shimmered in the dim lighting. She shifted beneath my scrutiny, the lines of the scales of a fish covering her flesh.

"It's rude to watch people sleep," I mumbled, tearing my eyes from the unusual sight. I'd barely seen fish, what with them being inedible according to the laws of Nothrek because of the magic of Faerie coursing through the waters between realms.

"It's rude to make yourself at home in someone's favorite haunt, but you don't see us calling you out for your lack of manners," the small male figure said, the tone in his voice scolding.

He took a step toward me, bold and brave despite his size. I supposed a small stature hardly mattered after death, but there were those who lurked within the walls of the Court of Shadows that I suspected could make even the dead suffer.

"Trust me, you'd be welcome to your favorite haunt if I had my way," I said, shifting and continuing to stretch out my aching back.

The scale-covered woman lingered behind him; her features carefully blank as she studied me. I watched as her attention drifted to the other cell, pausing on my mate where he slept. The low growl in my throat shocked both of us, drawing her eyes back to me as I curled my legs beneath me and glared at her.

The little creature shrugged, oblivious to the moment passing between the women inhabiting the cell. Such was the way of men, existing with their heads buried in the sand so much that they didn't see the threats coming until it was too late.

"Human won't be here long, anyway. They never are," he said, shrugging his shoulders as if my life, and subsequent death, were inconsequential to him. Unsurprising, if he'd seen countless victims come and go in this very cell.

"Lozu!" the woman said, her eyes bulging wide. In spite of the moment that we'd shared before, her gaze softened as she refocused on me. Her pupils were unnaturally large, the color surrounding them a hazy white. "It is rude to discuss the impending death of a still living creature."

"If it doesn't have manners, why should I?" the male asked, his nose twitching with his irritation.

The part of me that had been tormented into having manners recoiled, immediately bowing forward as if I might apologize for my lack of decorum. I shook it off with a frustrated twist of my lips, wondering if those memories would ever fade—if the reaction they elicited within me would ever dampen.

"Ignore Lozu. He isn't usually so brutish. Welcome to our cell. You are free to share it; though I am sure you do not desire such things," she said, crossing her arms across her stomach. "My name is Monos."

I held on to my name, knowing the games the Fae so often played. There'd been rumors when I was a girl, even if the whispers of them had been faint and overshadowed by the teachings of the New Gods and the priests who worshiped them above all.

"You can call me E," I said.

Her brow rose, then she bowed her head, both a moment of respect and a challenge flashing between us. She turned to look toward Caldris in his cell, the shimmer of scales on the side of her head distracting me from the way she watched my mate.

"He is yours?" she asked, turning her attention back to me for a moment before she glided forward. Her legs moved as if she were walking, but her feet never seemed to touch the floor. She drifted through the bars holding me caged, fading into Caldris's cell and lingering over him as she stared down at him.

Everything in me tightened when he did not wake. He always woke when anything came too close, his instincts protecting him even in his sleep. Concern for his injuries and worry about the female I wasn't certain I could trust slithered inside me, but I shoved it away.

Caldris remained shirtless despite the bitter cold temperatures of the dungeon, but where I'd been curled up into a ball and unable to keep warm, it didn't seem to faze his sleeping form.

"Yes. He's mine," I said, making sure to put my claim to words when I recognized the way she looked at him.

"He's a good male," she said, and I wished it surprised me that she recognized him. "He was the only one who was kind to me when I was locked away down here, separated from the sea I called home. My mate was killed in the battle that led to our capture; I was barely alive. But Caldris sewed my scales back on so that I would not die," she said.

She knelt beside him, reaching forward as if she might touch a hand to his face. Her touch went through him, unable to make contact with the male she clearly respected. It didn't look like love that graced her face, but pity. As much as I knew my mate would hate to see that, it soothed the jealous parts of our bond that would drive me to do something irrational.

"He's a good mate to me," I said, recognizing that he would truly do anything to see me freed from the chains that bound him. I might not understand the reverence the Fae had for the mate bond just yet, but I knew I loved mine.

"He was sorry when I died down here alone, but it is him whom I feel sympathy for. At least I can no longer feel the pain," she said, rising from his side. She came back to my cell. Curling up against the wall, she looked at the smaller creature, who seemed to study me. I couldn't be certain without seeing his eyes, but his nose pointed in my direction.

"He would not want your pity," I said, drawing a sad sort of smile from Monos. She knew him well enough to agree, but she cast her gaze back over to where he slept.

"He would not," she agreed, sighing lightly as she lowered herself to the floor. She sat upon the stone, leaning into the iron bars of my cage and picking up a piece of rubble. She tossed it into the air, catching it when it fell back down to her hands. "I suspect he has the pity of many, anyway."

My face slackened, a bittersweet huff of laughter escaping me as I nodded in agreement. Aside from the monster capable of such atrocities, who would not pity a creature who had spent his entire life in servitude and suffering?

"Is it considered rude to ask what kind of Fae you are?" I said, raising a brow when she smiled slightly.

"Very," she said, her lips peeling back into a grin that revealed sharpened teeth at the corners of her mouth. There were two rows of them, twice as many teeth as any human I'd ever met. "I am a Selkie, a creature that prefers to live in the water. Lozu is a gnome, though he'll never admit it."

"What good does it do to deny what we are?" I asked, glancing down at where the smaller creature stepped up to my legs. He leaned forward, grasping my dress in his hands and rolling his fingers over the fabric.

He pushed it up slightly, moving it out of his way as he stepped in. I scrambled to press the fabric against my body, watching in confusion as he leaned forward and pressed his nose to my ankle. It twitched as he sniffed.

"What is it?" he asked. He pressed his nostrils against my skin, breathing in so deeply that I felt the suction. That nose pointed up in my direction, and I caught the briefest glimpse of red, slitted eyes beneath the hat as he shifted.

"I… what is what?" I asked, swallowing past the haunting feeling of even a moment with those eyes settled upon me. They were all red, with the narrowest diamond of black at the center like a pupil. There were no whites or iris, only the color of blood where it consumed the eye.

"You. He means to ask what you are," Monos answered. She didn't seem surprised by Lozu's fixation with my ankle, with the way he tried to shove more of my skirt out of the way so that he could get to more of my skin. "You look like a Sidhe, but you do not smell like one."

I glanced down at the smaller creature when he finally stepped out from beneath my dress. He tipped his head back, his nose continuing to twitch as looked at me. I considered looking away, wanting to avoid that unsettled feeling of his red eyes again, but if I could not withstand the first of the creatures of Faerie I encountered, how would I fare when I faced the monsters of legends?

"Can I taste? Just a small one?" he asked, his lips part-ing just enough to reveal the sharp row of teeth that filled his small mouth. He ran a sharpened claw over my ankle, a red line blooming on my skin as he scraped it. He didn't draw blood, only scratching the surface.

"No, there will be absolutely no tasting," I said with a swallow.

His lips turned down, his beard falling with the motion. It was the closest I'd ever seen to an actual frown on any face, his pout making him appear somewhat less menacing.

"We are most curious," he said, as if that curiosity enti-tled him to a taste of my flesh. His tongue ran along the seam of his lips, wetting the dry flesh as he waited, hoping that he would change my mind.

Over my dead fucking body.

"I truly do not know what I am. I'm sorry I cannot pro-vide the same answers you offered to me," I said, biting the inner corner of my mouth as the gnome moved away. He went to Monos, curling up in her outstretched hand and making himself comfortable.

"Mab knows you are not Sidhe. This is where she puts the creatures she thinks are beneath her. The ones who are not Faerie enough for her to see value in. Something about you does not pass her standards," Monos said, laying her head upon the stone. She curled up as if sleep was next on her agenda, forcing me to cast another concerned glance toward my mate.

"Is he all right? Surely, he should have heard us speaking by now," I said, using Monos's affection for my mate to try to gain some reassurance. She'd been close to him; she would have known if he no longer breathed.

If his heart no longer beat.

She tilted her head to the side with a disbelieving smile. "He has not heard us, because there is nothing for him to hear," she said, reaching out a hand. She leaned forward, crossing the distance between us until she grasped my bare ankle in her grip. I felt the hand that wrapped around my flesh, immediately thinking about how her touch had gone through Caldris when she tried.

"I don't understand," I said, staring at her hand and the talons upon it. She didn't hurt me, shifting my leg to the side. But I didn't feel like she'd moved me, didn't feel any sort of connection to the muscle and sinew that had changed positions.

"You have not yet awoken for the day, E," Monos said, dropping her stare to look at something behind me.

Turning, I took in the sight of my body lying curled on its side, my leg positioned awkwardly as I hadn't been the one to do it.

"The veil between life and death is the thinnest when we slumber, and the Winter Solstice approaches. You should take more care the next time you leave your body and enter the spirit realm, Wanderer. Not all the spirits you encounter will be so kind."

I reached out a hand, touching the side of my arm as my horror mounted. It drifted through, sliding straight to the floor of the dungeon as if my body were nothing but air.

"I don't know how to leave my body, let alone how to stay," I admitted, swallowing as I stared at my body and at where Caldris had begun to stir in his cell on the other side.

He mumbled my name, shooting to a sitting position quickly as he spun to look at me. His eyes went to my body immediately, his gaze fixated on it.

As if the three shades didn't exist, and I realized the truth in Monos's words. He couldn't see me, and I wondered if he could feel that my soul—the other half of his—had vacated my body.

"Is this how I'm to die? A soul separated from her body and left to wander for eternity?" I asked, tears burning my eyes as I studied Monos. "Is that how you died?"

"Silly creature," Lozu said with a yawn. "We died because the Queen of Air and Darkness locked us in here and left us to rot. She forgot we ever existed, and we simply wasted away."

"That's horrific," I said, my empathy growing as I considered what it must have been to die so slowly. Even as I watched Caldris panic, clutching his chest as if the pain in his heart—the pain in his soul—was something he felt physically.

Lozu shrugged. "Been here centuries. Dying here was a blessing compared to what Mab does with her playthings. Better to hope for starvation, then I can eats you when you're gone."

"Can a shade eat?" I asked, swallowing my fear.

It shouldn't have mattered, as I would already be dead and gone. I laid my soul on the top of my body, mimicking my position and hoping for the best. The warmth of my body sank into my chilled soul, welcoming me home as I fell back into the rhythm of my heartbeat.

It lulled me to sleep, a soft and steady drum as I tuned out Caldris's panic and fear. The only way to calm him was to return, to become one with my body once more.

Everything faded to gray as my eyes drifted closed, Lozu's last foreboding words reaching me in the final moments before sleep claimed me.

"Perhaps we'll find out."

4

Estrella

Time passed slowly.

I did not again venture into the spirit realm while I slept. Caldris's horror and relief when I'd returned was enough to keep me firmly planted within my body. I didn't know how to control it, only that I desperately wanted to. Monos and Lozu had followed me into the physical realm, haunting me and informing my mate of what I'd done.

Boredom made every single one of my bones hum with the need to do something, with the need to move. Caldris watched me from his own cell, tossing the body of a rat into the air and catching it for entertainment. I tried not to think of how disgusting that was, because we both knew he'd probably touched more disgusting things in his centuries of life. His comment about my snake friend was rich, considering he had no qualms about toying with a corpse.

Playing with the body of a rat was a new low, and it forced me to look over at where Lozu watched me like I was his next meal.

"You could eat him too, you know?" I said, nodding my head toward Caldris.

"Too tough. You just soft enough not to get stuck in my teeth," Lozu said, not even bothering to look over at Caldris as the words rolled off his tongue.

My mate, for his part, seemed unbothered by Lozu's half-assed threats. I was nearly certain that we both knew the gnome had grown fond of me during our time in that cell, that his affections would at least give him *some* pause before he consumed my flesh.

"We've had this conversation," Monos said, a sigh leaving her lungs. "You do not need to *tell* her you're planning to eat her. Just do it once she is already dead and gone." Her casualness made me rethink my assurance that my friendship with the shades had changed anything. Perhaps they, better than anyone, knew how to separate the flesh from the soul. My body was but a vessel, useless to me once I abandoned it in favor of the Void.

"That's very reassuring, Monos. Thank you for that wonderful endorsement," I said, rolling my eyes.

Caldris chuckled, the rat squelching as his body hit the ceiling of the cell. Caldris looked at his largely flattened toy in disappointment the next time he caught it, tossing it to the side and looking for another one.

"You aren't going to die in here," he said, rooting around in his cell.

In the time that had passed—which felt like an eternity but was impossible to know or measure without evidence of the sun rising and falling—his body had finally healed. Only the thinnest of scars remained on his throat. They were tiny blemishes in his Fae Mark that felt unforgivable to me.

I would skin the male who did it alive if I had it my way.

"Your wishful thinking does not make that true," I snapped, pacing back and forth in the too-small cell that I couldn't seem to escape. For once, my height worked to my advantage, allowing me to stand without having to bend forward. Caldris wasn't so lucky, having to bend at the waist in order to fit in the cage when he stood.

He didn't seem bothered, having spent his fair share of time in Mab's dungeon over the course of his life. "Mab is far too curious to know what you are to allow you to die before she gets her answers," he explained, a sad smile gracing his face. His words only served to confirm what I'd already learned from Monos, that what waited for me outside of the monotony of this cell was far worse than the threat of starvation.

"Lets me have a taste and I'll tell her. Then we can eats," Lozu said, his nose twitching happily as he stepped closer to me.

"If you bite me, I will tear the nose off your face, gnome," I snarled.

His beard shifted as his lips pulled into the semblance of a smile. "Does you not want to know what you're made of?" he asked, stomping his foot in frustration. "Lozu can tell you."

"I am not even the slightest bit tempted to sacrifice part of my flesh to you so that you can chew on it long enough to tell me what I am," I said, rolling my eyes to the ceiling. Even dealing with the conflicted feelings of wanting to know the truth of my heritage and not wanting the answer to be available to Mab, there had to be slightly less painful ways to uncover the truth than being eaten.

The gates of the dungeon clanged in the distance, signaling a guard coming to deliver the meal of gruel and hard bread I'd come to expect periodically. If I based it on the instinctive feeling of the moon rising, I would have estimated it came in the evening.

The guard who stepped up to the door of my cell wasn't the typical male who delivered our food, and his arms were empty of the questionable sustenance I both dreaded and craved.

"Up," he grunted, the keys to my cell dangling in his hands. He was the one who had waited for me in the throne room, who'd chained me up to await Mab's punishment: Malachi.

"I'm quite comfortable," I said, forcing a saccharine smile to my face as I leaned back on my elbows and lounged.

No matter where he meant to take me or for what, I knew well enough to know I didn't want to go. Caldris got to his feet on the other side of the dungeon, leaning forward to glare through the bars of his cage.

"I will haul you out if I must," Malachi argued, and I winced when I heard the sound of skin sizzling. A glance around his hulking form confirmed Caldris had touched the iron bars meant to contain him.

"Come on in and try then," I teased, trying to ignore the way Caldris seethed at the taunt.

I glanced toward the shades of Lozu and Monos, realizing they'd made themselves scarce when Malachi showed his face, disappearing into the spirit realm to avoid the male who would harm them if he was able.

Why couldn't the blasted gnome eat someone useful?

"Leave her alone, Malachi," Caldris growled, the warning echoing with power in spite of the iron around us. It couldn't quite hit in the same way it might have if it hadn't been for the presence of the metal, but mine had in spite of that.

What the fuck?

"But we're so looking forward to playing a little game with her. Mab wants to get to know her new daughter-in-law is all," Malachi said, finally slipping the key into the hole of my cell gate.

His flesh burned when he grabbed hold of the door, shoving it to the side and leaving a distinct line of red, marred muscle where his skin had once been. The color was so vibrant in the cell that seemed devoid of all life and color, and the blood dripped onto the floor, blending in with the dried, old stains of suffering that had become my home.

I pressed my hand into the stone I'd cracked, wrapping fingers around the sharp shards and lifting it from the dirt that protested my touch. Caldris narrowed his eyes on the movement, shaking his head subtly as he realized my intention. His feelings came through the bond, strangled and warbled but present, nonetheless.

A warning to play the long game, that a quick burst of violence wouldn't get me freedom. My own pride and arrogance at wanting to prove I *could* fight would only result in more difficult conditions for my eventual escape.

Imelda would tell me I was an idiot for fighting when my life wasn't directly at risk, her voice chiming in my head as clear as day. I swallowed, releasing the stone and getting to my feet slowly.

"Take me to your leader, faithful servant of darkness," I said, bowing my head forward mockingly.

He stepped aside, motioning me through the open cell door with a dramatic flourish. The tight smile on his face made it clear what he thought of my flippancy, but he didn't move to make me suffer for my blatant disrespect. I imagined he would leave that to his queen.

I approached the iron, glaring at the pair of shackles held in Malachi's grip. He held them out, presenting them to me as he stared at the hands clenched into fists at my sides. I lifted my arms, twisting them so that my palms faced the ceiling, then lowered my wrists into the shackles slowly. I stared at Malachi's face as he dropped his gaze to the shackles, then fastened them around my wrists. The hard swallow that made his Adam's apple bob gave away his nervousness. He wasn't all bravado in the way he wanted to appear when faced with something that had hurt his queen. He latched the first shackle, shifting his hands to the second one as my lips twitched into a smirk.

I clenched my fingers so that the tips of them touched his wrist, shifting forward quickly. "Boo," I whispered, finding too much pleasure in the way his body jolted and the shackle clattered as he hurried to lock it with nervous fingers.

"Fucking bitch," he muttered as he glanced up at my grinning face.

Malicious, cruel laughter filled the dungeon, and it took me far too long to recognize it. The chuckle was the ruination of everything that had once been innocent within me, a twisted creature that thrived on the promise of tormenting my enemies.

I raised my shackled hands to my chest, ignoring the burn on my wrists as the iron melted through my flesh. "I don't know how I will ever recover from such a grave insult to my character. That one stung right in the place where I do not care."

He dragged me forward by grabbing the chain, making my skin tingle with the added proximity to the iron gates as it very nearly brushed against my skin. I felt it like a hum echoing within me, as if it was as much a part of me as it was a repulsion. We strode past Caldris's cell, and my desire to remain with him made me pause in front of the cage that still contained him. His jaw clenched, his body taut as he warred with the idea that I would be out of his sight, away from his protection, when I faced Mab this time.

"Your boyfriend isn't coming with us, Pet," Malachi said, touching the palm of his bloodied hand against my lower back. He gave me a firm push forward, forcing me into movement as a growl rumbled out of Caldris at the contact.

"Keep your hands off my mate," Caldris warned, the promise of retribution humming in the threat. He might be contained for the moment, but the expression on his face promised that one day, Mab would be in need of his services. That one day he would be freed from his cage, and those who harmed me would be the first ones he sought revenge from.

"Don't worry, Caldris. It is not me who intends to play with her," Malachi said, a cruel, *stupid* smirk gracing his face. As if he could not resist the challenge waiting to come for him. The promise in my mate's eyes left no doubt that it would be painful when it did arrive.

I couldn't fucking wait for it.

Malachi guided me forward, and I allowed his hand to continue to touch the bare skin of my spine where my dress was split down the back. With every step we took, every breath he continued to have the luxury of inhaling, one thought repeated in my mind: *One day*.

One day I would take that hand and shove it down his own throat so that he suffocated on it.

We strode through the gate from the part of the dungeon that had become our home to find a narrow, winding staircase waiting for us on the other side. We passed a guard who refused to so much as look at me as we made our way around the bend at the bottom. The steps were steep enough that I had to wrestle the fabric of my dress into my shackled hands so I would not humiliate myself by doing something as mundane as tripping.

I held my head as high as I could as we ascended, the light from the windows at the top of the steps casting a dim glow into the dungeon. It wasn't the light of the sun that I glimpsed through the window, but the light of the twin moons of Alfheimr shining down upon the Court of Shadows.

The stairs never seemed to end, like we were ascending out of an endless, inescapable abyss. A guard waited at the top of the stairs, his hand grasping the hilt of his sword as he reached out with his other and inserted the key into the lock. He opened it, bowing his head like a gentleman, as if I wasn't covered in filth and hadn't been deprived of a bath for a straight week.

The hallway outside the entrance to the dungeons was crowded with people. The citizens of the Shadow Court lingered against the stone walls as I strode through the path they created in the center. I ignored the hushed whispers, the subtle judgment in their stares when their eyes clashed with mine for a few moments.

In this place, with Mab's people, I was the one who was unwanted.

Sconces lined the hallway, the bright amber glow of flame pulsing within them and illuminating the white stone statues of creatures—some Sidhe, some inhuman in appearance— placed on pillars beneath them. The ceiling overhead arched into a point, meeting at a wooden beam supporting the center. It had been carved into the ornate figure of a snake, winding its way through floral medallions where the support beams curved from floor to the apex of the ceiling.

There were no windows in this part of the palace, bathing it in the shroud of eternal darkness. Only the light of the candles offered any reprieve, and I greatly missed the light of the moon and stars shining down upon me as we walked through the crowd of people lining the blue stone walls.

Something wet splashed against my cheek as I walked, making me pause in my steps to raise my hand. The spit was warm against my fingers as I brushed it away, turning a glare to the man who'd been responsible for it.

"Keep walking, Pet," Malachi ordered, nudging his knee into the backs of my thighs. "You won't find any friends here should you do something foolish."

I turned to the male who'd spit at me, memorizing the sharp edges of his youthful, eternal face. His light hair was so blond it was nearly white, but it lacked the ashen quality of Caldris's. His eyes glimmered with a vibrant purple hue, the deep glare sinking inside me as I looked at his tense mouth.

My own twitched into a smile. "How brave you must feel to spit on a chained woman when surrounded by your friends. Let me assure you, boy," I said, smiling when he sucked in a ragged breath. I had no doubt he was older than me, but I didn't let that technicality keep me from forging on. "I do not need my magic to kill you."

I turned away from him suddenly, my steps continuing forward as I left him forgotten. One day, I'd remember to return the favor he'd shown me. I'd show him how it felt to be unwelcome just for existing.

I'd show them all.

5

Estrella

Malachi stopped us in front of an ornate door, reaching over my head and rapping his knuckles against its metal surface three times in quick succession. Someone on the other side pulled it open, and a male's face filled my vision. He looked over my shoulder at Malachi, then stepped to the side to allow us entry. I moved into the room slowly, my eyes scanning from side to side as I looked for the threat I knew must be lying in wait.

The walls were crafted in that same blue-tinted stone as the rest of the palace, and heavy brown curtains hung over what I presumed was the sole window in the room. They'd been drawn closed, keeping out any light that might have drifted into the room. To the left of the door sat a single bath. Small side tables carved from heavy, cherry-hued wood were placed sporadically around it. The bed frame was carved from the same wood and had four pillars which jutted toward the ceiling with pointed spikes meant for murder rather than functionality or practicality. A lone fireplace with light limestone lining the mantle waited just beside the bed as a fire blazed in the hearth.

"How are we to have a civilized meal with her smelling like death itself?" a woman asked.

I spun to look at the long table set up in the alcove to the other side of the door. The guard closed the door as I stared at the table, allowing my gaze to travel up from the female's feet to the dangerous beauty of her face. Mab's dark eyes snagged mine. Her lips twisted into a disgusting snarl, as if she hadn't been the very cause of my appearance.

"I would hate to inconvenience you," I said with a droll smile, glancing over my shoulder at where Malachi lurked. "Return me to my cell and I'll gladly fit right in with the smell of decay you've provided in such lovely accommodations."

"That mouth will be your downfall one of these days," Mab said, her voice quiet. While others may have mumbled these words, Mab whispered them threateningly. She didn't need to speak loudly in order for her message to be heard, not when she was the epitome of evil in the world. To mumble would be beneath her.

She raised her hand, plucking a ripe berry from a bowl on the table and pinching it between two long, black nails. "Bathe her," she instructed, placing the berry on her tongue as Malachi's hands grabbed my shoulders. He turned me away from where Mab sat, heading for a water basin with hot steam billowing up over the edge.

I shrugged his hands off me, swatting them away as he stopped beside the basin and waited. With the iron shackles on my wrists, I was limited in how much I could fight. My magic wouldn't answer my call, hovering just out of reach like a bitter torment.

Mab sighed behind me, as if my obstinance was futile. It didn't matter if I ended up bathed, I'd take a part of Malachi with me in the process.

"It doesn't need to be this way. You must long for a nice bath after your week in the dungeon. Get in, and we'll allow you to wash yourself at your leisure."

I swallowed, warring with my pride. I knew what the right choice would be for my health and my desire to not be touched. "I can't remove my dress," I said, raising my shackled hands in the hopes that I could gain even the slightest bit more power in this situation. Whatever game Mab was playing, whatever fool she thought me to be, this would never be a civilized meal.

She wanted something, and I very much wanted to keep it from her.

"Malachi," Mab said, waving her hand passively.

Malachi approached my side, removing a dagger from the sheath at his waist. The fabric of my dress tore down over my ass and thighs, leaving my undergarments exposed.

"Hold still, Pet. I would hate to cut you when I don't intend to," he said, the cruel twist of his lips displaying the truth to his words. He would cut me later on. He would bleed me. He would do everything in his power to break me.

I raised my wrists cooperatively, holding his gaze as I held my head high. I wouldn't show signs of bending as he stripped me from my clothes and did his best to humiliate me.

His dagger slid beneath the hem of my sleeve, cutting the fabric as he slid it up my forearm with painful slowness. The edge of the blade glided against my skin. His eyes held mine, making it very clear just how much damage he could do with a single flick of his wrist. He cut all the way to my shoulder, watching as that half of the dress fell to my waist.

I turned my gaze away, refusing to think of his stare upon my flesh and what Caldris would feel through our bond. Malachi stepped around my back, not touching me until he came to my other arm and repeated the process. When he cut through the final threads of the fabric, it fell to my feet.

I slipped out of my underwear, shoving them down my thighs and stepping into the scalding water of the basin. If the intent was to burn me alive to make sure I wouldn't carry a disease to the Queen of Air and Darkness, they'd met that goal. I lowered myself into the water, ignoring the way my flesh burned and grew pink beneath the heat. Malachi stood beside the basin, watching every move I made as I took the soap in hand and scrubbed the dirt from my body. The water changed color, becoming murky as I sank lower and scrubbed my hair.

"I was told Alfheimr had special products for washing hair that would make it sparkle with life," I said, glancing toward where Mab eyed me with disdain.

"You'll earn such luxuries in time if you behave," she said, continuing to eat the berries from the bowl on the table.

"I've never been very good at doing what I'm told," I said, dragging my fingers through the snarls in my hair as it floated on the surface of the water.

"Malachi," Mab said softly, and I barely had time to begin to scramble out of the water before his hands were pressing into the front of my shoulders. He shoved me down until water covered my face, then held me there, keeping me trapped beneath the surface. I stared up into the warped sight of his features as the water sloshed against the sides of the basin while I struggled.

My lungs burned with the need to breathe. Just when I thought I couldn't hold it for any longer, Malachi lifted me out of the water. I sputtered, desperately sucking back a deep lungful of air. He shoved me back down the moment I'd stolen that lone breath, forcing me beneath the surface so harshly that my head clattered against the metal of the basin.

I struggled, grasping his wrists with my chained hands and trying to escape his grip. But my body was weakened by the lack of nutrients in the food they'd given me in the dungeon, weighed down by the iron stealing what remained of my energy.

In one last bid for freedom, I shoved a single leg off the foot of the basin. Angling my body up and lowering my head deeper in the water, I watched Malachi's moment of confusion before my knee hooked around his throat. I used his surprise to pull him back, to shove him toward the opposite end of the bath until his hands left my shoulders and I was able to rise to the surface.

I pulled him lower until his spine struck the edge of the tub, his body twisting with the force of my leg. Air filled my lungs as I took greedy breaths, watching as Malachi crumpled to the floor. He got to his feet only a moment later, his expression murderous as he lunged for me.

"Enough," Mab said, raising a hand. I turned my eyes to her. "I believe you've made my point, Malachi."

"But my Queen…" Malachi trailed off, the implication obvious.

"What fun would it be if she just took your punishment lying down and begged for mercy? How dreadfully boring it would be to have my new plaything behave the same way everyone else in this forsaken court does," she said, smiling at me. Something lurked in her gaze that I knew I would come to dread.

"Set them free, and I'm sure a great many of your servants would be more than willing to give you the entertainment you seek," I said, dancing around the truth. If she wanted people to stand against her, then she shouldn't have bound them to her will.

"There is a difference between a plaything and an uprising. Fear not, Little Mouse, you'll be like them soon enough," she said, tapping a nail against her chin. "Even the brightest of lights fails to remain entertaining for long."

I swallowed, keeping my thoughts of the ferryman as far from any room Mab occupied as possible. I didn't think she could hear my thoughts, didn't know of any Fae who could do such a thing, but that didn't mean that they didn't exist.

What would she make of the Ferryman insinuating I was something creatures would use?

Malachi reached into the tub, forcefully pulling me from the water and dragging me out of the basin. He shoved a towel at me, and I hurriedly dried myself off as he grabbed a dress from the back of a nearby chair. I winced when he shoved it over my head, trying not to offer any physical sign of the comfort that came from no longer being nude. I wore no underwear beneath it, nothing to accompany it as he grabbed the two sides of the fabric that would make the sleeves and wrapped them around my arm. They secured around each one with ribbons, making my shackles irrelevant for the time being.

"Come and eat, Little Mouse," Mab commanded.

I turned my back on Malachi in favor of the bigger threat in the room. She perked up as I turned toward her, walking to the table slowly and taking the chair she'd pulled out on the other side of the small round table. I lowered myself into it slowly, keeping a wary eye on her as she chewed.

"You must be hungry."

"I'll live," I said, not daring to eat the food she offered. Even the food in the dungeon had been a great risk to eat, something I only indulged in when the hunger pangs in my stomach became too much to bear.

Everyone knew humans weren't to eat the food of the Fae, that it was a way to trap us within Alfheimr for the rest of our days. Eating food provided by Mab herself seemed like an even greater folly, increasing the potential risk of poisoning.

Mab tipped her head to the side, studying me curiously before her frown shifted into a scoff. "What is it they tell you about the Fae in the human realm?"

"That you're tricksters who will stop at nothing to get what you want," I answered, shrugging my shoulders as if it were inconsequential.

I'd already learned that I could trust nothing the Priestesses had taught us of the Fae. Some of what they'd said might have been rooted in truth, but the bias toward the Fae was undeniable and colored everything with their hatred.

"And you still believe this to be true when you are so clearly in love with your mate? I assure you, he is not immune to the ways of the Fae," she said, making Malachi laugh. I had no doubt he wasn't, not when he'd lied and manipulated me into falling in love with him in the first place.

"Just because I love him does not mean I do not see his wrongdoings. Caldris is far from perfect. I can, however, trust him with my life," I said, glancing toward the guard, who never seemed far. Malachi wouldn't leave Mab and me alone, as if our power imbalance wasn't enough on a good day, let alone with me shackled in irons.

"I've no intention of killing you. If I wanted you dead, I would choose a far more brutal method than poison. Poison is the way of cowards," she said, reaching over to the glass goblet at my side. She lifted it, taking a sip of the wine before placing it beside me again.

At least we agreed on one thing: poison was the way of those who wanted their killings to remain a secret.

Mab and I both wanted ours to be known to the world, wanted to wear our crimes like badges of honor.

"It is not poison I worry about, but what you might have done to it that could trap me within Alfheimr for the rest of my life," I admitted, taking the goblet in hand.

I glanced down at the wine, waiting for the response I knew she would have. She raised her head into something akin to respect, and then let out a sharp bark of laughter that hinted at the evil within her.

"Faerie food can trap a human on Faerie soil for a life-time, but I think you are forgetting one very important thing in your considerations of what may harm you," she said, lean-ing forward slightly. She rested her elbow on her knee, placing her chin in her hand as the leg crossed over the other one bounced. The delicate, cruel heel of her shoe glittered in the light, looking more like a weapon than footwear. "But you, Little Mouse, are not human."

The words struck me in the chest, rendering me unable to hide the flinch that made my wine slosh against the edges of the cup. I'd acknowledged it. I'd had to make my peace with the fact that no matter what I had become in my cycles of life, I hadn't originally been born into this world as a human.

None of that prepared me for the stark realization, for staring down my enemy and having her point out that my entire life as I remembered it had been a lie. I was not what I'd been born to believe, and all the things I'd learned about myself over the years were now irrelevant.

That meant I didn't know what was a weakness and what was a strength. It meant I had to fear things I didn't under-stand but not the things I'd always been taught to fear.

It meant I didn't know who I was any longer.

"Oh no, Sweetling. Had you not realized that already?" Mab asked, her tone mocking.

Clenching my jaw, I tried to fight the response bubbling up within me. I tried to combat the fury of being humiliated in a moment when I wanted to grieve for what I'd lost of myself.

"I realized I was not human weeks ago, but would you like to know what really solidified that knowledge?" I asked, lifting the goblet to my mouth. I took a sip of the wine, letting the bold flavors of it dance over my tongue as I swallowed and resisted the urge to go back for more in my thirst. "It was the moment I cut *you*. Listening to your people whisper about you, knowing some mortal girl could not bleed the Queen of Air and Darkness."

She dropped a hand to the edge of the table, her nails drumming a steady beat against the surface as she ground her teeth together. Her nostrils flared, and Malachi moved toward me until she held up her other hand to stay his attack.

"You did cut me. I'll give you that," she said, rolling her neck. As if the tension in her body was a physical sign of having to deal with me and my disrespect. "You would be a fool to think you can do it again now that I know not to underestimate you. You played your hand far too early in this game, and now you've only given me more power over you."

"I guess we'll find out whether or not that's true in time," I admitted, nodding thoughtfully. It very well may be, because despite my bravado, I wouldn't know if I was capable of defeating Mab until the moment I did it. The odds were not in my favor.

"I've offered you the chance to bathe, given you some of my best wine, and offered you a dinner the likes of which you've never seen, I suspect. Still, you sit there and openly

mock me, plotting my demise. What am I to do with that?"
she asked.

I set my wine down on the table, staring at the feast she'd
offered me. It was, in fact, greater than any meal I'd ever
known, but that wouldn't stop me from turning it down. Not
when it came with a cost to my soul. Not when I didn't know
what it was she expected as payment for such a kindness.

"You could tell me what it is you want and end the monotony of this game," I said, pursing my lips as I studied her.
"Pretending you are doing this out of the kindness of your
heart is futile when I've heard of your cruelty from the other
half of my soul. When I've seen it when you ordered me to be
chained and whipped for displeasing you. So, what is it that
you want from me, Mab?"

She heaved a sigh, impatience settling over her features. I
knew I was playing with fire, treading dangerous waters that
I had no hope to escape, but that wild thing living inside of me
couldn't seem to shut her fucking mouth. It was as if she saw
Mab as a threat, her beast rising up in challenge and wanting
to claim whatever shred of dominance she could find.

"You may think me cruel now, but I am the only thing
standing between you and rape. Your mate has made himself
a large list of enemies, and any one of them would use you to
get some shred of vengeance against him if I so much as muttered a word of approval," she said, nodding her head toward
Malachi. I expected the guard to step toward me, to show his
willingness to be the one to execute that order.

Instead, he stepped toward the door to the chambers,
pulling it open to reveal the broad form of a male standing just beyond the doorway, his features far too similar to
Malachi's. He stepped forward, then paused on the threshold,

only tearing his gaze away from me to respectfully bow his head to his queen.

"Thank you for joining us, Ophir. I had hoped our guest would not require any incentive, but it seems she needs a reminder of the fate that waits for her here without the benefit of my protection. Would you care to tell her the ways in which Caldris has wronged you?" Mab asked, folding her hands together and resting them in her lap as she waited.

"He killed my mate, three centuries past," Ophir admitted, his jaw clenched with his anger.

"And why did he do that?" I asked, because I was under no illusion that my mate was a good male. He did horrible things, but he usually had a good reason for that kind of anger.

"It doesn't matter," Ophir said, shaking his head in frustration. His body thrummed with his rage that I would dare to question whether or not Caldris had just cause to kill a woman. It wasn't as if female Fae were innocent, and Mab was proof of that. "She was good…"

"How good could she have been if she was mated to the likes of you?" I asked, tipping my head to the side and watching his body vibrate with his fury. "You are an errand boy for an evil queen who wants nothing more than to hold the world within her grasp. You are not innocent, and I'm sure your mate was just as fucking dangerous to the world as you are."

Mab interrupted, cutting off whatever reply Ophir might have had. "Do you want me to hurt you? Is that it? You think you'll be some kind of martyr? Your mate is the only one who cares about your pathetic life, and I own him. No one else will so much as think of you when you're gone," Mab said, drawing my attention away from Ophir. "Or is it that you think I will not allow him to have his way with you?"

"He can certainly try," I mumbled, readying my posture. Whatever the reason, Mab had planned ahead. I couldn't be certain if she intended Ophir to be a threat to force me into complacency, but I knew nothing good could come from giving her what she wanted from me.

"Close the door, Malachi. It seems our guest is in need of a reminder that she is no longer in Nothrek, where petty humans play foolish games. Members of the Shadow Court do not think twice about violations that can damage the soul for an eternity," Mab ordered.

The air changed, Ophir's body tensing as he undoubtedly waited for the command that would unleash him upon me. I would not go quietly into the night, waiting for Malachi to finish closing the door behind the other man.

"Would you like to tell her what you intend to do, Ophir?" Malachi asked, his cruel eyes glimmering as he twisted the key in the lock.

"I'm fairly certain my imagination works far more efficiently than anything he could conjure up with the rocks cracking together inside his skull," I said, pushing to my feet.

I waited, positioning myself to receive Ophir's first attack. At my size, the best thing I could do was study my opponent, to learn how he fought and how he moved. But I lacked energy due to the iron and lack of food, meaning I wouldn't have the kind of time I needed to do so. Ophir lunged, stretching his hands out as if he meant to wrap them around the front of my throat.

"I need her alive, Ophir," Mab ordered.

Her voice was almost muffled as I sank down into that deep pit within me. It seemed far more empty than normal, lacking the accompaniment of my magic that I'd grown so used to. It made me feel even more alone in the moments while I waited for Ophir to close the distance between us, time moving as if it had been caught in the slow-moving dials of time.

I twisted and grasped my wineglass by the stem, smashing the thick cup against the surface of the table. The sound of shattering glass reached my ear a moment later, and I spun quickly to stab the shard into the first part of Ophir I could reach.

It sank into his flesh just below his ear, the glass weapon protruding from his neck. He froze with his hands just shy of reaching my throat. Blood gathered at the tip of the glass, staining it red. The shard in the side of his neck behaved like a plug, stopping the flow from falling. He gritted his teeth and raised his hand to grasp the stem of what remained of the glass, pulling slowly until it came free of his flesh.

Blood pumped free, splattering down his shoulder to the floor beside him as he staggered for a moment. I twisted and grabbed one of the heavy bowls off the table, flinging the berries Mab had been enjoying across the room as I swung it in an arc toward the side of his face.

Ophir raised a hand and caught the heavy bowl, already recovering from his stab wound as it slowly began to heal. He clenched his fist with his grip on the dish, making the metal twist into something that no longer resembled a bowl at all. He released it suddenly, and I didn't hesitate to pull back and lower my aim, swinging lower the second time. I struck him in the balls. He bent forward with a wheeze; the breath forced from his lungs.

"Do my iron chains not weaken me enough for you to conquer?" I asked, lifting the bowl over my head.

He struck, swinging the hand that held the glass shard toward my face. Bending backward as quickly as I could, I barely managed to escape him taking my eye. I didn't care to discover if I would regrow such a thing the way the Fae could, but the shard cut a line across my cheek and the bridge of my nose.

"Alive, Ophir," Mab repeated, staring at the fight. She never bothered to vacate her seat, even with the proximity of our violence, as if the greatest entertainment in her life came from the pain and suffering of the people so close that she could touch them.

My skin burned lightly with the cut, but what shook the ground beneath me was not the pain. It was not enough to bring me to my knees, even as Ophir used my distraction to use his free hand to land a punch against the other side of my head. My head swam as I staggered to the side, and the furious roar of my mate echoed up through the layers of stone separating us.

It struck me deep in the chest, knocking me off-kilter until I had to scramble to get away from Ophir's next attempt to grab me. Never had I felt such unending rage, such mind-altering anger that stripped away everything humane. For my mate to feel my pain, to know I was in danger, and to be trapped within Mab's dungeons...

I pitied whoever let him out.

"I think we made him mad," Malachi said with a chuckle.

I grabbed Mab's goblet from her hand, hurling it at Malachi's face and grimacing when I missed only slightly. It crashed against the wall, what remained of her precious wine dripping down the stone.

"I was enjoying that," she pouted, tapping her nails against the wood of the table as I adjusted to the feel of Caldris's rage within me.

"Imagine how angry he'll be when he feels me tear you in two," Ophir said, stepping toward me slowly. I tried to block it, but the heavy thump of his fist struck me in the stomach. My muscles protested immediately from the force of the blow.

The one that came after nearly took me out. His fist cracked against the underside of my jaw so hard my teeth clacked together, and my skull throbbed. My knees gave out beneath me, sending me crumpling to the floor.

A hand came down upon my back, pushing me to the floor to take what was coming. I gathered what remained of my strength, pushing through the nausea and the spinning room, preparing myself for the only thing I could do to save myself from that fate.

I spun on my knees, getting to my feet as Ophir lowered himself behind me. His weight shifted forward as I spun away from his grip, my body no longer supporting him. I punched the back of both his knees, forcing them to cave in on him so that he dropped down in front of me.

I lifted my hands, the iron chains between my shackles swinging freely. I wrapped my iron chains across the front of his throat, pulling them taut as I placed my hip against his spine and pushed him forward to hold him there as I pulled my hands away.

He sputtered, fighting for breath as his hands rose to those chains. When he couldn't grasp them, couldn't seem to get his fingers beneath where the chains dug into his flesh and broke through the skin, he threw his hands into the air and reached behind him to try to grab me instead. All he found were my forearms, his nails shredding the skin there.

Still, I held.

Malachi moved to step forward, the look on his face communicating that they were more than just friends or allies. Their appearance was similar enough that I suspected brothers as I held his gaze, knowing that if he interfered, I wouldn't be able to do a thing about it.

Mab halted him with a raised hand. If I didn't already hate her, it might have been a moment of respect. She'd condemned me to this, to this battle and this fate; she would at least let me see it through.

I suspected it was all a test to see what I was capable of. Not my magic, but me as a living being. If I had a line I would not cross; if I would not murder and cause harm to save myself.

She wanted to know if I saw myself as the hero of my story, but I didn't.

I only saw myself as the villain of hers.

My face twisted as I fought back that beast rising inside of me, the part that came from my mate roaring out his rage in the dungeon. I pulled harder on the chains, my scream bouncing off the walls as I put all the strength I had into pulling on the chains that they'd used to try to contain me.

My arms burned with pain, echoing the fire that erupted up my throat with the hoarse sound. I pulled until I felt the life fade from his body, until the chain popped as if it had split in two. I looked down at the figure kneeling in front of me. Ophir's head rolled to the side, bouncing off my arm before it fell to the floor beside his still kneeling body.

I didn't stop to consider the amount of strength I'd possessed within my own body to make such a thing happen. I stared into the mess of flesh within his throat, at the muscles where they constricted and released, as if still trying to breathe. The chain dangling from my wrists was covered in blood and gore. It swung when I lifted my booted foot and kicked his body forward until it sprawled across the stone floor.

Malachi's eye twitched, and he took a step toward me with his hand on the hilt of his sword. He stopped with a flinch, raising that hand to his heart and digging his fingers into his chest. Looking toward Mab, I watched her outstretched hand squeeze until Malachi took an obedient step back like the *pet* he was.

Mab turned her attention from Malachi to me, lowering her hand with a smile. That smile raised the hair on my arms, a warning that I'd appealed to all the wrong sides of her.

She tossed her head back, and the Queen of Air and Darkness laughed.

6

Caldris

Heat filled my hands, the iron burned the skin from my body as I gripped the bars and pulled. They didn't budge, refusing to release me from the cage Mab and her twisted little minion had left me in. There was nothing I could do to reach my mate while her pain flooded the bond, her blood staining my soul.

I felt it drip down her face, felt her need to push it away in order to fight. I felt the lingering terror that she refused to even acknowledge to herself for fear of not defending herself against the threat that was coming for her.

The roar that tore itself from my throat felt more like a cave beast than a man, deep and calling to every wild part of me that existed beneath civility. I was not human, but that didn't mean I particularly enjoyed the reminder that I was one moment away from becoming more beast than Fae. The loss of my mate would be too much for me to bear, forcing me to descend into the feral madness that came with the loss of the half of my soul that I'd waited *centuries* to hold in my arms.

"Estrella!" I roared.

The sound echoed through the empty dungeon. Even the shades who had occupied Estrella's cell shuddered, retreating into the back corner to hide from my wrath. I pulled back from the iron bars, my lungs heaving with the force of my distress as I glared at them. I shifted to the back of my cell, turning my body slightly to the side and vaulting myself forward. I ran with all the speed I could possess in such a limited space, hurling my body at the bars.

They groaned beneath the force of it, the reinforced iron tempted to give way to my strength, but still they held. They kept me caged as they were designed to do, refusing to let me make my way to freedom. I could sense her as clear as day, feel her just a few floors directly above the dungeon. Mab hadn't chosen that location accidentally, placing Estrella in a place where she would be able to hear my struggles.

As if the way she could feel me wasn't torment enough when we were forcibly separated.

Given my centuries spent under Mab's control and imprisonment, I didn't need to be able to hear her words to know what she would use as a threat to get what she wanted. She would torture. She would allow my mate to be raped. She would do *whatever* it took to break Estrella's spirit so that she could take control of her.

I understood her game; the only thing I couldn't be certain of was the strategy behind it. She could play the short game, taking what she wanted and discarding Estrella when she had it.

Or she could play the long one, slowly manipulating my inexperienced, young mate, who didn't know any better than to fall for the games of the Fae. It was hardly Estrella's fault she only had two decades of life to arm her against a creature who had ruled for centuries.

Any threat Estrella could pose, Mab had probably already faced. She'd lived and learned and fought and surrendered.

She'd won the battles Estrella had yet to fight.

I growled, the sound vibrating against the iron as Monos took a step toward my cell. "You must calm yourself. The guards will come," she murmured softly, doing her best to appease the monster.

My lips pulled back into a snarl, revealing my teeth that I would have used to shred through her flesh in that moment if she'd had it. It didn't matter that I'd fought to try to spare her from the fate that awaited her. Not when my mate was in danger.

I shoved my weight into the iron bars once more, fury overwhelming me when the dungeon door opened. Three guards stepped into the space, standing in front of the bars and exchanging nervous glances among themselves. One more stepped into the dungeon, a syringe clutched in his hands. I was no stranger to the contents of it. The potion had been crafted by the witches Mab employed and contained flecks of iron, weakening a Fae from the inside.

It was the only way for Mab to control me, even when she wasn't nearby. The only way her guards could keep me complacent when she wasn't around to enforce her orders.

Estrella screamed, the shrill sound of her shriek making the hairs rise on my arms. The moment they opened the gate to my cell and all four guards stepped into it, I lunged. My claws went for their skin, for any part of their body I could reach as they grabbed me to restrain me. I couldn't access my magic, not with the iron surrounding me, but neither could they. So we grappled in a physical fight, tearing flesh from limbs. I dragged my black nails through the fleshy part of one of their eyes, not even bothering to pause to see who I'd maimed. They shoved me into the iron bars, and the skin along my back burned through my clothing as the one with the syringe got close enough to jab his needle into the side of my neck.

I gasped as heat flooded my body. Burning me from the inside out, searing me alive and making it so that my legs crumpled beneath me almost immediately.

It was a small dose, a precarious balance since too many iron flecks within the injection could kill a Fae, shred his heart in a way that was irreversible.

This didn't offer me the peace of that oblivion, nor burden me with the regret for taking Estrella with me into death thanks to our blood vow. It sent me plummeting to the floor in a useless heap. My mate struggled upstairs, her fight out of reach and my body rendered entirely useless.

My eyes drifted closed as I fought to keep them open for just a few more moments. Just a few precious seconds in the hopes that my mate would survive. I lingered in that space between life and death that ran parallel to the moments between being awake and falling asleep. Estrella's fight ended abruptly upstairs. Her body going slack with the end of her struggles and the death of her opponent tickled at my senses.

His figure hovered on the edge of my vision, waiting for me to take him to the ferryman so that he could pass into the afterlife. I wouldn't be there to help him, wouldn't place coins on his eyes even if I could. His spectral form carried his head in his hands, his face confused as it stared down at me from where he clutched it tightly.

What a shitty way to wander the world for eternity. He deserved nothing less.

I smiled when I felt her victory consume her, my lips tipping up in a sleepy grin with the satisfied beast that rose up within her.

My delirium rose as the place between life and death called my name, summoning me to the other side. "Ophir is dead. Long live the Queen," I mumbled, fading into the delirium of sleep

***

My head throbbed, a tandem beat echoing in my ears. As if living underwater, I existed between the planes of all I'd known.

I'd been to the edges of this place so many times that I recognized the feel of it, the emptiness that surrounded me calling to the part of me that had too long existed outside of the realm that waited to welcome me home.

Snow drifted through the air, the white of it stark against the night sky. A murky river lingered below me, the water supporting my weight as I pushed myself up onto my knees. My body felt fresh, like none of the hazards of my life nor the injuries I'd sustained could touch me here in this place of peace.

I lifted a hand to look at it. The fresh, unmottled skin stared back at me. My Fae Mark glimmered in the dim light of the stars shining above, the only thing to surround me as I pushed to my feet and stared around.

Had the guards injected me with too much iron? Was that why I couldn't feel Estrella through our bond?

I touched a hand to my chest, soothing the ache that accompanied the thought. To be severed from her was a fate worse than death itself, but we'd bound our lives together.

Without me…

She should have followed.

"Estrella?" I called, looking through the Void surrounding me. There was no one to be found, no mate to return my call as she drifted into the afterlife.

"She cannot hear you," a male voice said, forcing me to spin on my heel. He stood behind me, his body perfectly still as he watched me. Shock overcame me; it wasn't often that anyone snuck up on me with the Fae senses I'd honed over years of practice.

"Who are you? Why have you brought me here?" I asked, because the confirmation that Estrella was not with me meant I was not dead after all. No living being had any place being in the Void between realms. My presence here was a horrific abomination in itself.

"Keep her alive. No matter the cost," the male said. There was no trace of emotion to accompany the order, only the stark reality of the task I'd been given.

"She is my mate. Of course, I will keep her alive." I scoffed, my eye twitching as I considered the fact that maybe, just maybe, he meant someone other than Estrella. Could he mean Fallon?

The coincidences were too large to be ignored, with Estrella having been dragged before the ferryman in her slumber. Yet I still clung to the hope that whatever destiny the Moroi had woven, Estrella would exist just outside of them. That she'd be free to live a life not entangled in the fate of the world as we knew it, finding a path to happiness regardless of the impossibility of our depressing world.

"Your own arrogance will be your downfall," the male retorted, tipping his head to the side. "I will never understand why the Fates chose you for her."

"I've bound my life to hers. I've done everything I can to make sure she lives, because I cannot imagine my life without her. What more can I do?" I asked. Whatever the answer was, I would do it. Whatever the sacrifice, I would give it.

"You can stop behaving as if she is the weakling and you are the savior. You see the bond of your lives as a benefit to her, but that is because you assume that your life will be longer than hers. She is no longer human. The rules of Nothrek no longer apply to Estrella Barlowe. You would do well to remember that," he said, his jaw clenching in frustration. It was the first sign of any kind of emotion he showed, his head tipping to the side with a subtle, disgusted shake.

He turned his back on me, walking in the opposite direction as the stars at the edges of my vision went fuzzy.

"What is she?" I called, demanding the answer that would cure me of my ignorance so that I could help her.

He paused, looking over his shoulder with a creased brow. "You think you can be trusted with that information? You, who are a slave to Mab herself?" he asked, the words landing the blow he'd intended. "How could I expect you to save her when you cannot even save yourself?"

The stars faded, the walls they created shaking as the Void around me appeared to melt into nothingness. All illusion, a trick of the mind.

It wasn't the Void at all.

I turned my stare back to the male who had greeted me, the one who had spoken the harsh words. His form melted away as he watched me over his shoulder with gleaming golden eyes. He drifted into the night sky as it crumbled until his place was empty.

Only those golden eyes remained.

7

Estrella

I sat in the chair beside the fire, trying to warm my limbs. I couldn't stand to look at the trail of blood leading away from the table. Two of Mab's guards had come, grabbed Ophir's body by the feet, and dragged it out of the room. They left Malachi to carry the head of what I'd learned had been his brother, his face carrying the first traces of softness I'd ever seen.

That faded the moment our eyes clashed, the ire in his expression unparalleled.

He would be a problem if Mab couldn't control him; the wind of the vengeance he sought for his felled brother carrying my name on it. It didn't matter that it had been Ophir who'd attacked me or the fact that he'd done so under Mab's command.

I was the murderer. I was the one who needed to suffer.

I swallowed, turning my gaze back to the fire. The dress they'd put me in was stained with Ophir's blood, the metallic scent reaching up to torment my senses. I wanted nothing more than to strip off the fabric and burn it, but I didn't know if there was anything else I could wear in its place.

Mab lingered in her seat at the table, looking all too disgruntled that our conversation had been derailed by the show of violence. As if my rape wouldn't have made reaching an agreement impossible at any rate. The guards left us alone at a wave of Mab's slender hand, dismissing any threat I might have posed. The temptation to test her rose within me, but even I knew that with my magic crippled by the iron around my wrists, there was zero chance my explorations would end favorably for me.

"You've made your first enemy here," she said, sipping her wine dramatically as she stood. "That was not a wise decision."

"You're wrong. You were my first enemy here, and we were set to this rivalry before I'd ever set foot on the soil of Alfheimr. Your actions toward my mate for the entirety of his life have guaranteed that you will never find a friend in me," I explained, holding my head high as she took a few steps toward me. She stopped just out of reach, staring at the cut on my cheek and glancing down at my shackles.

"I do have to wonder. If I removed those shackles, would you heal your injuries as suddenly as in the throne room?" she asked, reaching out a hand. The sharp tip of her nail pressed into the cut on my cheek, separating the flesh until a fresh stream of blood trickled out. I pursed my lips, refusing to flinch back as she drew her finger away and took the tip of her nail into her mouth.

"Why don't you take them off, and we can find out together?" I proposed, raising an eyebrow in challenge.

Her lips tipped into a smile that surrounded her finger, and she finally withdrew it. Reaching forward to cup my cheeks in each of her hands, she tipped my head up to meet her gaze as she revealed teeth at the corners of her mouth that looked as if they'd been sharpened intentionally. "You taste like power, and I will know where it comes from by the time I am finished with you."

"I sincerely doubt either of us will like the answer very much once we have it," I said, wrenching my head away from her grip.

Her nails scraped along the skin of my cheeks, trying to hold on as I fought to get free. They tore through the skin, gathering beneath the tips of her talons.

"It doesn't need to be this way. You and I do not need to be enemies, Little Mouse," she said, and the term twisted into something akin to affection in her attempt to convince me that there was anything other than a rivalry with the most powerful Fae queen of all time in my future.

But the Fates had written my story already, and nothing I could do would change what was to come.

When they spoke, I would listen.

"And what of my mate, whom you have tortured for centuries? Am I supposed to ignore the harm done to him in order to become your ally?" I asked, rising to my feet and turning my back on her. That was not something I would ever be willing to do, even if I could bring myself to ignore the plights of the Fae. They'd never cared about me, so why should I care about them?

I did care about Caldris and Fallon, however, and both were presently imprisoned by Mab.

"Do you enjoy your place as a woman in this world? Trapped in the games of men and nothing more than a pawn for them to use and abuse so that they might get what they want in life? Do you think it is you whom your mate loves, or is it what being mated to you will *give* him?" she asked, a cold, bitter laugh escaping her. "Or do you want to be *free*?"

I glanced at her over my shoulder. "My freedom does not need to come at the cost of the freedom of another. There is no reason we cannot all be free to live our lives how we desire," I explained.

"He will take his part of your magic. He will grow stronger, and he will become King. Whether he manages to overthrow me and becomes King of the Shadow Court or he takes over as King of the Winter Court, he will place you as a pretty object at his side. You have no birthright here. You are not royal, and you do not stand to inherit a single throne. He is the son of the Queen of the Winter Court and the King of the Shadow Court. You are nothing compared to his succession," she said, stepping up to the door. She paused there, giving me time to absorb the words.

A pretty trophy at his side. I loved him and believed he loved me with everything he had.

But would that change the suffocation I was bound to feel being trapped as a figurehead without any authority? That had been the promise of the life I would have lived with Byron in Mistfell, but I had to believe Caldris wanted more for me.

"It is possible for a queen to have power. You rule over all of Faerie. Twyla commands the Winter Court…" I trailed off, not knowing enough of the other court royals to speak of their arrangements.

"I rule over Faerie because *I took it*. Twyla has her precious Winter Court because her mate and husband are both dead. If a male remained to steal her power, he would have. Why do you think she has not remarried since the death of her husband? Because she knows as well as I do that in spite of whatever pretty lies we tell ourselves to help us sleep at night, we are *nothing* compared to our male counterparts. Our world is not ready for women in power as peaceful rulers," she said, turning her back to the door.

She held my gaze as I twisted my body, preparing for the words that would come next. They hung between us, silent and deadly. Words that I knew I would never un-hear once she put them out into the open. It was something I wanted no part in but could never erase from the deepest parts of my worst fears.

She held out her hand, reaching toward me without ever taking a step. "You remind me of myself. Young and full of life, full of wrath and vengeance, desperate for the world to know the kind of pain you've survived. You can have all of those things, Little Mouse. All you need to do is take my hand."

I stared down at it, noting the way her fingers remained as pure and porcelain as the rest of her skin. Whatever magic she possessed, it didn't affect her physically in the same way mine did me. Imelda's fingers had the same night sky at the tips, the magic of the night bleeding into our skin.

"Where is Fallon?" I asked, tipping my head to the side. "Shouldn't you be concerned with improving your relationship with your daughter, or have you already given up the hope that she will be useful to you?"

"My daughter's name is Maeve," Mab said, clenching her jaw as she turned back to the door. She grasped the handle, twisting it and pulling it open so that she could step into the dimly lit hallway just beyond the threshold. A guard waited there, their presence never far. But it was the face beside him that made my heart stall.

Imelda stared back at me, the pure white of her hair gleaming in the firelight.

I shoved aside my relief at seeing Imelda unharmed, focusing on the other of our friends who could have been suffering in that very moment.

"If you hurt her…" I trailed off, staring into the back of Mab's skull. Whereas any normal being would have treasured the return of her long-lost daughter, Mab seemed to be disappointed by the reality of the person Fallon had become.

"I've no reason to hurt her so long as she proves herself useful. I did not lay with her father so that she could prove to be without magic. At some point or another, she'll have no choice but to let whatever waits within her free," Mab said.

Imelda's face twitched with anger at the harsh words. She shut it down as soon as the expression fluttered across her cheeks, forcing herself to remain impassive as Mab stepped into the hall.

"Heal the girl. She will remain chained in iron for the time being and needs the assistance."

Imelda stepped into the room, turning and nodding to the guard, who closed the door and gave us a few moments of privacy. She dropped the bag strapped across her shoulder down atop the table without preamble, turning to me and taking my face in her gentle hands. Her touch was like coming home, soft and soothing and gentle in all the ways Mab's touch had felt wrong.

"Estrella," she murmured softly, placing her hand around the back of my head and tugging me into her chest. When she pulled back, her eyes dropped to the blood smear on the floor where Ophir's body had been dragged out. She touched a thumb to my cheek, and I felt the skin shift as she pushed the two parts of my flesh back together.

She frowned, stepping back and looking over my body. She passed by the burns on my wrists where the iron rubbed against my raw skin, knowing that until the shackles were removed, there was absolutely nothing she could do for them.

"Is my mother safe?" I whispered, not wanting anyone to hear about her existence. Until I knew she was safely tucked away somewhere that Mab couldn't find her to use against me, no one within the walls of this cursed place could know of her existence.

Imelda nodded. "The Wild Hunt and I saw her to Twyla in the Winter Court. She's given her refuge, tucked her away from prying eyes as much as possible, and told her not to speak of you until you're free from Mab. The fewer people who know of her connection to you, the better off she'll be. If nothing else, she'll be free to live out the rest of her life comfortably, regardless of how long you're here. It's a better life than she had in Mistfell," she answered. The meaning of her words was clear, striking me in the chest like a lightning bolt.

Caldris had fought against Mab—been her prisoner for *lifetimes*. The odds of me escaping Mab before my human mother lived out the duration of her life were slim.

I would likely never see her again.

I'd known that was a distinct possibility when Brann and I escaped Mistfell originally. I'd had to come to terms with that knowledge. But to find my way back to her just to have her taken away from me all over again was a cruel fate I wouldn't have wished upon my enemy.

"That's good," I said, nodding through the pain. I had so many questions for her that she would never answer. About my father, about how Brann had come to be a part of our lives.

"Are you hurt anywhere else?" Imelda asked, running her hands over my arms and checking for signs of injury. They pressed into the tense muscles at the back of my shoulders, her scowl deepening when she found the lump on the back of my head. "*Gods*. The idiots have no concept of how precarious an injury to the head can be. Sit."

I moved to the chair I'd taken before, distinctly avoiding the place where Mab had sat. I had no desire to touch anything that belonged to her. Imelda took out her supplies, setting her mortar and pestle on the table as she rooted through the herbs she carried with her. She pulled out a pouch filled with something dried, dumping out the wine from a spare glass and putting the leaves into it. She poured water from a pitcher, stirring it quickly with a spoon. Pausing, she picked up the knife from beside my plate and pricked her finger with it. A single drop of blood fell into the goblet, splashing into the cold tea. Imelda's multicolored eyes drifted closed, and she waved her hand over the goblet in a slow, steady circle.

The Old Tongue fell from her lips, the words an incantation as the liquid spun within the goblet almost as if it held its own current. Steam billowed from the top of the cup, slowly rising until it kissed the palm of her hand. Imelda's eyes flung open. From my view, I could only see the white in her eye as it opened. A shining light pulsed for a single moment before her pupil faded back to its normal, lustrous shade.

"Drink," she ordered, and the stern look on her face left me little room to argue. I brought the cup to my mouth, letting the flavor pass over my tongue as it slid down my throat.

"Have you seen Fallon?" I asked as I handed back the cup.

She took it and placed it upon the table as she set to grinding fresh herbs in her mortar. She added water as needed, forming a paste of some sort.

She merely shook her head, focused on her work. Fallon was the smartest of all of us when it came to her ability to blend in and survive. She would be the least likely to anger Mab out of the three of us, minding her tongue when I seemed to be incapable of it.

"I don't suspect either of us will be allowed to see her any time soon. If Mab is trying to keep a close eye on her, she'll keep her locked away from you," Imelda answered.

Imelda slid the blade across her wrist, letting blood steadily drip into the mortar.

I gasped. "What are you doing?"

I vaulted to my feet, grabbing a cloth from the table and reaching for her wrist. She accepted it with a sad smile, wrapping it around her wound and tying it off in a way that showed me she'd done such things far too often.

"Head wounds are tricky beasts and can cause far more damage than we can see. This will make sure there are no lasting consequences for the damage done to you."

She stepped around me, the cloth at her wrist staining red from her blood.

"You'll bleed out."

"I am a witch, Estrella. I cannot die from a mortal wound," she explained, her fingers pressing against the bump at the back of my head. I winced, my entire head throbbing.

"But the witches on the beach..." I trailed off.

"Your snake strangled one, squeezed the life from her body. It was not the action of a natural snake, but one you enchanted to do your bidding. There is magic involved in such things, and only the magic of another creature or the complete draining of our own magic can end the life of a witch," she said, applying a thick coating of the paste to the bump. "Leave this on overnight and wash it in the morning. It should help with your headache and the swelling."

"Okay," I said, knowing I would follow her instructions. There wasn't a chance I would let her sacrifice and the pain she must feel from cutting herself be in vain.

She stepped around me to my front, applying what remained of the paste to the cut on my cheekbone. "Tell me what you know of the Fae," she said, staring down at me. Her mouth set into a hard line, and her lips pursed as she waited for my response. Her fingers were gentle despite the impatience on her face, carefully dabbing the poultice into the valley of my wound.

"That they're horrific creatures I should fear," I said, my tone rising incredulously. I couldn't turn away from her heated stare, the crescent upon her forehead keeping me bewitched.

Imelda rolled her eyes finally, dropping her fingers from my wound and wiping them upon a cloth she pulled from her pack. "The Fae operate under their own set of rules. Some of them will apply to you, others will not—now that we know you are not human in the least. As a Fae, do not say something three times unless you mean to hold true to your word. The law of three makes it binding, and the only way to break that vow is through death. The same goes for blood vows. They hold more meaning now and are unbreakable; you will owe a favor, and that is not something you ever want to owe anyone here," she said, her voice trailing off as she glanced toward the door.

She knew as well as I did that our time was limited before the guards snatched her away. I wanted to ask why she'd even come, but I didn't need to. She would go wherever Fallon and I went. Such was our bond; we were somehow connected in ways we didn't understand.

"The Fae can't lie," I said, adding another rule to her list. I supposed that must have applied to me now, leaving me incapable of muttering untruths.

"But they can dance around the truth in ways you may never realize until it is too late. Less is more. As you cannot lie, try not to speak at all. A hardship for you, I know," she said with a little smile.

My skin buzzed with warmth, the flesh slowly feeling as if it was beginning to heal. I had so many questions about the magic of the witches and how it compared to the magic of the Fae, why the witch's magic seemed capable of working through the blockade of the iron that kept my magic at bay.

"Never, ever give a Faerie your name. It gives them power over you. Withhold it as long as you can, though I doubt it will be possible to keep it a secret for long. One slip from Caldris, Fallon, or I, and your name will be known, but there is one rule we haven't discussed that you *must* abide," Imelda said as the sound of keys jangled just outside the door.

"What?" I asked, my voice a hurried whisper.

The key slid into the lock, and time seemed to slow as Imelda hurried to tell me the last rule.

"Never accept a gift from a Faerie, and if they give you one by force, do not, under any circumstances, thank them for it. It implies gratitude, and that is something they can use to call upon a debt in the future. If Mab gives you a gift, you are not to be grateful for it. You are to remain indifferent, even if she offers you water when you're dying of thirst. Do you understand?" Imelda said as the door opened.

She turned away from me, gathering up her supplies as the nameless guard stepped into the room. He looked me up and down as I got to my feet, assessing the threat I posed or could have posed. I knew the moment his logic warred with his fear, thinking me unimpressive at a glance, but I'd killed his immortal Faerie friend.

I smiled, forcing arrogance to my face in spite of the conflict warring within me. I had killed a man—brutally, in fact—and no matter that it was self-defense, I felt the stain of each death I caused upon my soul. I didn't *want* to become like the Fae, killing without remorse.

The day that I did would be the day I truly lost my humanity.

He huffed, turning his attention to Imelda. "Time's up, Witch," he said, stepping out of the doorway and waving a hand for Imelda to step through.

She slung her pack over her shoulder, barely glancing at me as she stepped through it and disappeared into the hallway. I knew the idea was to keep her distance from me. She couldn't claim not to care about Fallon, but I could be irrelevant to her.

It was better for her safety that way, but it did nothing to stem the hurt in my chest. My bond with Caldris had gone silent at some point during my fight to survive with Ophir, leaving me anxious. I'd only managed to keep my panic at bay with the commotion of others being in my room, not knowing who would be able to hear my thoughts. I didn't want to give them any information that wouldn't be safe to share inadvertently, and until I had a full lesson on all the capabilities of the Fae, I couldn't take that chance.

But now alone, I realized how quiet it was to be trapped alone inside my head. There'd been a time when I had lived for the solitude of those moments.

Now I just craved the feeling of my mate's annoyance grumbling away at me.

8

Caldris

The clearing of a throat woke me, and I knew before I opened my eyes who had come to torment me in my cell. My body felt weighted down, sluggish, and impossible to move. It took every bit of my energy to force my eyes to open, to stare up at the woman who could take everything from me if she wanted to.

"Where is my mate?" I asked, my voice hoarse.

Flames burned up my throat, the first hint at how long the iron had kept me unconscious. The fuzzy remnants of my dream hovered at the edges of my memory, threatening to consume me if I gave them the attention they needed. They slipped through my fingers as I forced my body to roll onto my side, pressing a palm into the stone beneath my body and trying to push to sit myself up.

"She's in far better condition than you at the moment," Mab said, crossing her arms over her chest as she stared down at me. She kept her distance from the iron bars, her nose wrinkling in disgust at the horrid, damp smell of death and decay that always consumed the dungeons. "Must you force me to lock you away down here? You know how much I hate being forced to subject myself to this stench."

"Sorry to inconvenience you, my Queen," I mumbled, dropping onto my back when my body wouldn't cooperate.

I couldn't force myself to sit, let alone stand. The iron had rendered me incapable of protecting my mate, as if the cage hadn't already done that. The snake wrapped around my heart was a sufficient cage in itself, forcing me to obey Mab's commands even when they went against everything I believed.

Estrella's relief pulsed down the bond, her sense of me returning as I awoke. I felt her worry—her fear for me—and guilt plagued me in response. To be so separated from all parts of me must have been devastating, and I wasn't sure I would survive it without having eyes upon her body to know that she still breathed.

"What must I do to earn your loyalty? Your mate will follow you, and I have no desire for us to be enemies. The three of us united in one cause—just think of it, Caldris," she said, her eyes alight. It was the closest thing I'd ever seen to hope on Mab's face, as if something she'd only dared to dream of was finally within her grasp.

"You want to see the Fae in chains," I said, the accusation ringing between us.

She'd never kept secrets, even when I was a child. She'd been clear and straight with me and my father, putting her desires into words.

"I want to see the Fae at peace with one another. I want to return to the days of Old, where the Fae took their rightful place as Gods among men. I want our courts to coexist without strife and wars between them. I do not want the Seelie and Unseelie Courts to return to the wars that nearly ruined them before you were born. You are too young to know the horrors of that time, but I remember them like they were yesterday," she said, the smile drifting from her face.

"You cannot imprison an entire race to ease your own fears. That makes you just as bad as the Fae who committed war crimes in the name of their court," I said, a cough racking its way out of my throat.

"I will do whatever I please, with or without your willing aid. Surely, you must know that you and your mate will be my weapons, regardless of what you wish for Alfheimr. Why not enjoy the luxury of standing at my side as a loyal ally? I could give the two of you the Winter Court to rule over. You could be *happy*. That is what I want for you," she explained.

The words felt like the first in a long line of deceptions. Never before had she bothered to manipulate me, because she knew she could get what she wanted from me, regardless. But Estrella was another beast entirely. Her magic was fully formed and waiting within her to fight.

Mab could not wrap a snake around her heart unless Estrella owed her a debt or agreed to it in some other way, and she would need to remove the iron shackles in order to do so. Her only option to bind my mate to her will was out of reach for the moment.

Except for going through me.

"You tainted my soul with your will long ago, and I've lost hope of anything but *Helhaim* waiting for me in the afterlife. But the soul of my mate is the most valuable thing in the world to me, and I will not aid you in condemning her to the same fate. Even your magic has boundaries, and I think it is high time for you to meet your match," I grumbled, tossing an arm up over my head. I managed to maneuver it beneath my skull, offering myself a pillow as I turned my head to meet Mab's annoyed stare.

"You think I would ever allow you to complete your mate bond with her so that you might become a challenge to me?" she asked.

A laugh erupted from her. It was all things cold and hollow, lacking all the warmth it should have possessed. It was so easy to forget that long ago, Mab had been the Princess of the Summer Court until the cursed gem had twisted her into this dark, cruel creature without a soul.

"I wasn't talking about me," I said, correcting her assumption. If I'd learned one thing about Mab in my centuries at her side, it was that she thought all men wanted power. They all wanted to use. They all wanted to be stronger than their female mate, because that was the way of males in the world.

I didn't care if Estrella was more powerful. I didn't care if she ruled over me, and I was the figurehead at her side. All I wanted was to stand beside her in all her glory.

All I wanted was to love her for eternity.

That meant loving all of her. The powerful parts of her that possessed magic so strong it coated my tongue. The sweet parts that were so unaccustomed to unconditional love that she looked at it suspiciously. The innocent flower that had been scorched by a hard life, and the female who rose from the ashes of it, ready to right the wrongs done to her.

That was love. Not whatever Mab thought love was.

"You think that girl is enough to challenge me?" she asked, huffing out a bark of laughter. She wanted to use Estrella, no doubt; but for Mab to truly fear Estrella, it would have required her to admit that there were beings out there stronger than her.

The Primordials had disappeared, leaving the Gods in charge of this place, and Mab had positioned herself at the forefront of them all. What could possibly challenge that?

Mab's smile broadened, her cruel sense of humor overtaking her features.

"It's been so long since we had any fun, Caldris. You stopped being entertaining centuries ago, but *this*?" she said, gesturing at my body where I lay prone. Where they'd had to inject me with iron in order to keep me from breaking down the walls of my iron cage to get to my mate. It had been centuries since I'd cared about anything long enough to provide Mab with a single emotion to use against me. "This side of you I could play with."

Mab's final words rattled in my head as I tried again to stand, but she'd already turned on her heel. Leaving me to my cage.

Leaving to do Gods know what with my mate.

Fuck.

9

Estrella

I sat with my knees curled into my chest, my back to the wall in the corner of the room. The stone grated against me even through the fabric of my dress. A bed waited for me to claim it as my own, but I couldn't force myself to lie upon it, couldn't bring myself to relax in a way that I knew would lead to falling asleep. Even after sitting propped in the corner for hours, my eyelids felt far too heavy for comfort. The vulnerability of sleep was a luxury I didn't have in this place, not with my wrists bound by shackles and my magic crippled.

My only defense came in the ability to physically protect myself. I might have been as strong as the Fae around me now, but that didn't mean I would be capable of overcoming an attack I didn't see coming. My only chance came in having my eyes open and senses alert for any who meant me harm.

I'd lost track of how many hours passed, never really knowing how many minutes or hours I'd lost to the faint vestiges of sleep that claimed me as I sat there waiting. It was only a matter of time before Mab returned with a new strategy to gain my cooperation. Threats hadn't worked. Being my friend hadn't worked.

Offering me the freedom I'd sought for so long hadn't worked to her advantage, either. No matter how much I might long for the freedom she promised, I wouldn't become a tyrant to achieve it. My freedom would not come at the cost of the freedom and lives of other innocent people.

I drifted again; my eyes fluttering shut for a few moments. Caldris's anger woke me. It pulsed down the bond like a ripple in the water. The threads between us pulled taut, forcing me to sit up straight and grab a candlestick off the bedside table. I wrapped my fingers around it, shucking the candle itself to the side and testing the weight of the silver.

I stood slowly, moving toward the door that I already knew was locked. I'd checked before retreating to my corner, hoping that the noise of the key being inserted would be enough to wake me if I stopped pacing long enough to drift between the realms of sleep and waking. My sense of my mate shifted along with him, his physical form moving through the dungeon. It seemed to strengthen as he grew nearer, and I pressed my ear to the door to listen for any sounds on the other side.

I couldn't know for sure if he moved because he'd escaped, or if Mab had other plans for the male that she'd proven she had no qualms about hurting time and time again.

I tested the knob on the door once more, twisting it from side to side and growling in frustration when it refused to turn. Banging the base of the candlestick against the solid door, I winced at the way the silver clanged against the filigree detailing lining the stone and wooden structure.

"Quiet, *Pet*," Malachi shouted from the other side, the menace in his voice forcing me back a step. "You do not want me to have to come in there to quiet you down myself without Mab around to protect you."

"Eager to lose your head, too?" I snapped, biting the tip of my tongue to refrain from allowing the insult to the memory of his brother to go any farther.

"You're either the bravest human I've ever met, or the fucking stupidest," he called.

I could almost hear the laughter in his voice. It wasn't the friendly sort; rather a mockery of everything light and humorous. I considered myself fortunate in that moment that he chose to be amused rather than to attack me, because I wasn't sure I was up to another physical fight for my life.

"I'm not a human at all," I reminded him, stepping away from the door and pacing back and forth in my room.

My mate was out there somewhere, and my only assurance of his wellbeing was the lack of pain I felt from his bond. It had faded in the hours since he awoke, as his body slowly managed to heal whatever damage had been done to him. It meant they must have removed his iron shackles at some point so that his body could function normally once more.

It was a privilege I wasn't likely to receive unless Mab put a snake around my heart as well.

His presence grew closer yet, until the commotion outside confirmed that, for whatever reason, they were bringing him to me. I braced myself for whatever pain and agony would be sure to follow our reunion, knowing without a doubt that it was not allowed out of the kindness of Mab's heart.

The key slid into the lock, the scraping of metal upon metal forcing my heart to accelerate. I watched the door in rapt fixation. The knob turned, forcing me to toss my candle stick to the side when the first face that appeared on the other side was *his*.

Caldris stared back at me, his hands at his sides as he stepped into the room slowly and took in his surroundings. Checking for traps, observing the different corners of the room before he finally allowed the full force of his gaze to fall upon mine once more.

"My star," he murmured, carefully avoiding my name. I didn't know if Mab knew my name already, but I was grateful for the show of some semblance of protection.

Whatever magic she possessed that would affect me on the inside, she needed my name to do it.

"Caelum," I said, glancing over his shoulder to where Mab stepped into the room. She averted her gaze, for all purposes seeming to give us a moment of privacy. Relief washed over me, his and mine blurring into one mass between us. I couldn't tell where mine ended and his began, the comfort of seeing one another mostly unharmed becoming almost blinding in intensity.

I rushed forward. Throwing my weight into his body, I allowed him to wrap me up in his arms. I cursed the shackles for another reason, having to keep them from touching his skin as carefully as I could manage. Where I might have thrown myself into his arms and allowed him to pick me up in the way I'd so often protested when we'd made our journey to the Hollow Mountains, I could only settle for his chin resting on my head and his hands on my back.

"Are you hurt?" he asked, finally pulling back to look me over.

The cut on my face had scabbed over, Imelda's paste creating a sort of wax that hardened to protect the injury from the elements. His thumb touched it gently, careful not to crack the surface as his nostrils flared and his jaw clenched.

"Who did this?" he asked me, the promise of retribution burning in his gaze. He would murder anyone who hurt me. He would make them feel every bit of pain I experienced tenfold.

Because I was his, and he was mine.

"No need to trouble yourself, darling. He's already dead," Mab said, light, youthful laughter coming from her as she traced the steps of the blood smear across the floor. Her shoes were black flat slippers today. She toed them off and sank her bare feet into the crusted blood as she danced over it.

Malachi winced; his fury evident on his face as he lingered in the open doorway. He only pulled his eyes away from mine when he moved out of the way for a servant to step into the room. She had scales on the side of her face, moving in a path down her neck. She brought a single bucket of water in with her, then rolled up her sleeves and dumped it into the basin the others had emptied and scrubbed after my bath the previous night. She waved her hands over it, circling them in a smooth, dance-like rhythm. The basin filled with water, her magic making it expand and grow until the tub was filled.

Another servant stepped into the room and deposited a fresh stack of clothes on the bed. There were two sets, one male and one female. The tunic and pants for Caldris were the black of night, devoid of all color. The dress chosen for me was the deepest green, the color of a snake's skin, in contrast to the black bedding it rested on.

"For you both to wear tomorrow," Mab answered as the servants fled the room.

With fresh clothes set out and a bath to clean ourselves, I turned a disbelieving stare to Mab.

"What happens tomorrow?" I asked, swallowing nervously as Caldris tightened his grip around my waist. He shifted us so that he could look at Mab, tucking me into his embrace as if he could protect me from the Queen of Air and Darkness.

As if either of us could protect ourselves from Mab right now.

Mab rolled her eyes in response, stepping farther into the room. She moved to the window, pulling the curtains open until the dim light from outside drifted in. I hadn't dared to open them, not knowing what I might find outside. I knew nothing of the Court of Shadows, having only awoken when I was already trapped within it, but the light hinted at a filtered sort of sunlight.

"Don't be disgusting," she muttered, shaking her head. "You've already disappointed me with your foolish attachment to one another. Don't make it worse by acting as if you cannot bear to be separated. Nobody enjoys codependency."

"Says the woman who slaughtered her own mate in his sleep after she bore her heir," Caldris said, offering the first hint of what had happened to Fallon's father. My heart constricted in my chest, knowing that she would have wanted to bridge that gap while she was stuck in Mab's clutches. For Mab to have killed him, he must have been even the slightest bit more decent than she was.

"That explains a lot," I muttered, thinking of how Caldris claimed that he was halfway into the madness that consumed a Fae when he couldn't reach his mate. Mab's other half of her soul wasn't just missing but dead, and by her own hand.

How much of her evil and the chaos she caused could be attributed to that?

"Mind your tongue," Mab hissed, and Caldris gritted his teeth as she turned a glare upon him. "Or I will remove it." The anger over her violence seemed out of character, whereas she would normally be proud of the death and carnage she caused. She hadn't felt even a modicum of guilt over Ophir's death or the fact that she'd been the cause of it, but the mention of her mate struck a chord.

She'd felt the bond, perhaps had even known love for a brief time.

And she'd chosen to rid herself of it anyway.

"You loved him," I said, the breath rushing out of my lungs with the realization.

Caldris stilled at my side, his stare turning to me. His disbelief coursed through our bond, communicating the fact that he didn't believe it to be possible. But I was more certain than I'd ever been of anything in my life, that the Queen of Air and Darkness had, in fact, felt for her mate before she killed him.

"Of course I did," Mab scoffed, shaking her head as she furrowed her brow. "But love is a weakness, and I would not allow anyone to use my bond with him against me. You would be far better off if you followed in my footsteps and killed your mate in his sleep, Little Mouse. I would not fault you for it. In fact, it would only strengthen my opinion of you. Killing that which you love the most is no easy task. It is perhaps the most difficult choice you will ever make."

Snuggling deeper into Caldris's chest, I let the feeling of him surrounding me comfort me. I couldn't imagine my life without him in it now that I'd accepted him, and the night I'd even *considered* stabbing him in the heart haunted me more than I cared to admit. To do so now would have been unimaginable, and I would have rather plunged that dagger into my own heart than his.

"It is the coward's choice," I said, looking up at my mate briefly. He held my gaze, his icy stare capturing mine as he leaned forward and touched his mouth to my forehead. I turned my attention back to Mab before I spoke. "You can hurt me. You can try to break me. But I will never give him up. I know what awaits is worth all the suffering you'll cause."

Mab's eyes drifted closed, and she nodded as she ran her tongue over her teeth. "I would be lying if I said I was not disappointed in your decision, but I will allow you to see your mate daily."

Caldris stilled at her words, confirming my suspicion. I drew my bottom lip between my teeth, considering a response.

"And what is it you expect in return?" Caldris asked, not bothering to dance around her Faerie games. She wanted something, and she was willing to compromise to get it. I was glad for the fact that we were on the same page, that my instincts where Mab was concerned seemed to be trustworthy.

"You will earn those visits. I wish to know what you are, and I believe you are just as lost as I am when it comes to that answer. We will uncover the truth together. All she needs to do is cooperate with my tests, and I will allow you to be waiting in her chambers when we finish at night," she explained, steepling her hands as she moved back toward the door.

"Tests?" I asked, the blood draining from my face as I tried not to imagine what that would entail. If the woman would whip me for merely saying her name, what would she resort to in order to uncover the truth she thought she could use to her advantage?

"No," Caldris growled, his grip on my waist tightening. His fingers dug into the fabric of my dress, bruising the flesh beneath it as he struggled to contain his need to protect me.

"No?" Mab asked, her tone turning playful as she took a few steps closer. She paused just in front of us, reaching out a hand. It was not me that her taloned finger reached out to touch, but the bare skin of my mate's forearm. A shudder rippled through his body at the contact, a dark tendril spreading over his golden skin like a web. "You could make it easier on all of us and just tell me what I want to know."

"I don't know what she is," Caldris said immediately, Mab's control over him tearing the words from his throat. He gritted his teeth against them, fighting back as I barely resisted the urge to grab Mab's hand and throw her off him.

"Then I'll have to figure it out for myself. How brutal these tests become will depend entirely on you and your mate," Mab said, removing her finger from Caldris and stepping away. She looked at me, raising her brows as if she waited for me to protest. I knew that nothing I did would stop her from getting answers, and nothing would prevent her from brutalizing me to do so.

"Use me instead. She's just as likely to respond to my pain as her own," Caldris said, making me snap my head to look at him. I shouldn't have been shocked that he would volunteer himself to suffer instead of me, not after all the times he'd chosen his own pain to protect me, but this was different.

"No," I said, ignoring Mab's twisted laughter in the background. I stared at my mate, refusing to allow him to make such a sacrifice. Pain was one thing, the guilt of knowing Caldris's pain was my fault was another.

"You two are so dreadfully predictable. If you both sacrifice yourselves for the other, who am I to play with?" she asked, lifting her finger to her face. She tapped that long, black nail against her cheek thoughtfully, studying us intently. "Perhaps both?" she asked, looking over at where Malachi waited in the doorway with his arms crossed over his chest.

"I like both," he agreed, a cruel smile lighting his face.

I leveled him with a glare, repeating the promise I'd made to kill him in my head and only pausing for a moment to question that humanity I wanted to cling to. That deep well within me seemed to throb with need, like it was thirsty for the blood of those who wanted to harm my mate.

I didn't want to think about that well, about the emptiness that lurked there waiting to strike.

Caldris's fingers turned to ice, freezing the fabric of my dress with his anger. I didn't look up to follow the path of his gaze, knowing instinctively that I would find it settled upon Malachi. Caldris was limited in what he could do to fight Mab, but Malachi was less of a hardship.

Mab interrupted the moment, drawing my attention back to her as she cleared her throat. "I meant every word when I said it did not need to be like this. I've no interest in being your enemy, Little Mouse. Not when we would be so much stronger united."

It might not have been a lie, but it *felt* like one. A lie by omission, at the very least. It was such a Faerie game to play that I snorted, shaking my head in annoyance.

"And what happens if I do not cooperate?" I asked, putting the reality out there for all of us to acknowledge. Caldris and I both knew that Mab's interest in me meant she could never know the truth of my magic.

I couldn't give her the bow with which she would launch the arrow that ruined the world.

"Then you will not see him. Perhaps if I grow tired of your antics, I will send him away or allow my companions to enjoy him as they once did. I do not suggest we explore that option if we can avoid it," she said, studying me as I nodded simply. It was no less than I'd expected, though her constant willingness to wield rape as a weapon only worsened my opinion of her. "What? No thank you for the kindness I have shown you? Where are your manners?"

"I know better than to thank a Faerie for anything. My human sensibilities will only get me into trouble here," I answered, causing her to raise a brow at me in a moment of respect. She turned toward the ornate door, allowing Malachi to lead the way.

"Enjoy your night together. We begin tomorrow, Little Mouse. I suspect it will not be pleasant for you." With those final words, she retreated through the door, leaving Malachi to lock us in together from the outside.

One night.

10

Caldris

Estrella turned to me the moment the lock finished turning, her eyes wide as she pressed closer into my chest. I wanted nothing more than to rip the shackles from her wrists, to allow her to heal the wounds they'd left behind. To bind her in such a way for a prolonged period of time was unnecessarily cruel, especially when Mab would need to release her from the irons if she wanted to explore Estrella's magic at all the next day.

My fingers coasted over the sharp edges of the iron, nearly brushing against her raw, burned skin.

"I'm sorry," I muttered, shaking my head. I couldn't believe I'd been foolish enough to think I could tuck her away before Mab learned of her existence. I'd failed to protect the one thing that was the most important to me in this world, and perhaps Mab was right in some ways.

Death would probably be the humane fate compared to what waited for us, and perhaps we were better off with Estrella killing me in my sleep. With our blood vow, she'd follow me into the Void.

"Don't," Estrella mumbled, touching her forehead to my chest. She drew in a deep breath, wincing when the scent of the dungeon filled her lungs. "You stink."

"I am the God of the Dead, Little One. Does my very nature make you uncomfortable?" I asked, smirking as I ran a hand through her hair.

She tipped her face up, giving me her eyes as a playful little smirk toyed at her mouth.

"We both know that you do not normally smell of the decay of death. I want you to smell like you when you take me to bed," she said, lifting her hands.

She grabbed the laces of my tunic, pulling them slowly until it untied, so she could carefully raise it above my head. She moved so cautiously; her fear potent in the air. She didn't want to hurt me, didn't want to cause me pain with the very shackles that burned her skin with every moment that passed.

For her to be imprisoned in such a cruel way while I did not experience any of the pain she suffered was a fate worse than the pain itself. I would have gladly borne it myself to save her from it.

I took her hands in mine, guiding them up to rest against my shoulders. My skin sizzled as the iron touched my chest, the chains draping over the top of my abdomen as Estrella fought against my grip.

"If you suffer, I suffer too. If you bleed, I bleed as well. If you die, then I will follow," I murmured, dropping my forehead to hers.

Tears flooded her eyes. Her chest racked with a strangled sob that she refused to release, the mask of strength she wore dropping for only a moment.

The walls inside her head came crashing down, the truth of her emotions flooding into me. Whether she crafted the barricades to protect herself or to protect me from her tumultuous emotions, I didn't know. I didn't think it mattered as I lowered my hands to untie the laces stretching up her arms. The fabric fell away from one side of her body, draping from the other arm as I moved my attention to it. The white of it was stained with the deep red of blood, hinting at what she'd done when I hadn't been there to protect her.

Estrella needed to keep her strength for when she was being watched, never allowing Mab to see her crumble beneath the weight of what was coming for her. She could only do that if she had a safe space with me, a place where she could be herself and reveal all the weaknesses. All the doubts and the worry, all the pain she would undoubtedly suffer.

"Caelum," she murmured, her eyes drifting closed as the wetness touched her cheeks.

"It's all right, Little One. I'm here now," I said, the words hanging between us. We both knew this night was limited, that it would end in the morning.

"I can't give her what she wants," Estrella said, shaking her head softly. Her face twisted with the pain of knowing that her own actions would lead to our separation once more, that this night would not be repeated tomorrow, for she would anger Mab all over again.

"No, you can't," I agreed as the fabric dropped down from the other side of her body.

It caught at her waist, the flare of her hips snagging the fabric and holding it up so that it didn't fall to the floor. Estrella dropped her hands to the laces of my trousers, unknotting them quickly and shoving them down my thighs with an urgency that took my breath away.

If I only had one night, I wanted to spend it inside of her. I wanted to be as connected to her as I possibly could while we had the chance, and it seemed my mate understood that driving need more than I could give her credit for.

She knelt at my feet, staring up at me through her lashes as she untied my boots and shucked them off my feet. She tore my pants off my legs, reminding me that her human sensibilities had likely fled. She was still human in upbringing, those notions of inappropriate behavior that I'd worked so hard to unravel still existing within her; but she was also something *other*.

A creature driven by her nature, with a mate bond to encourage her to claim what was hers.

I grasped her by the chin, staring down at her as she hesitated. If I'd already bathed, I'd have demanded she take my cock into her mouth while she knelt at my feet. I'd have used her to remind me that I was powerful in spite of my position in this court, letting her show me what she and I could be once we were free.

Instead, I ran my thumb over her cheek, lifting until she stood in front of me and watching as she shoved her dress off. She was nude beneath it, not so much as a pair of shoes on her feet to interrupt my view of her body. The faint pink stain of blood that had soaked through her dress tinted her stomach. The sight conjured a vision of her bathed in blood, her nude body covered from head to toe as she strolled through a field of bloodshed, her enemies lying dead at her feet.

Any normal male would not have craved the sight of it so much as I did. Yet, I wondered how much of what I saw was real, and how much of it was a vision from the Fates or the man whom I could no longer see in my memory.

A gift, a token of our future.

I hadn't wanted to corrupt Estrella, believing her to be my balance in a world that had long since tried to turn me into the villain of my story. But what did it mean if she was already corrupted? If she wasn't as innocent as I'd originally thought?

I swallowed, stepping away from my mate, knowing that I would love her until my dying breath. No matter what she did, who she was, or the crimes she might commit in her path of vengeance. Stepping into the tub, I turned back to look at Estrella as she watched me.

Her eyes locked onto mine, narrowing slightly as I settled into the warmth of the water. She tilted her head to the side, trying to understand my conflicting emotions as they trickled down the bond. There was something so animalistic about the movement, about the angle of her head as she slowly sauntered toward the tub.

A predator stalking her prey.

Our roles had undoubtedly reversed, with my mate staring at me as if I were something to be devoured. She watched me, her gaze trailing down my body in the water as I grabbed the cloth and ran it over my skin, washing away the stench and filth of the dungeons and the death that occurred within them.

"You're afraid of me," she murmured finally, blinking away the creature that had risen to the surface. Her head straightened as she crossed her arms over her chest, looking far too vulnerable all over again.

"Never, *min asteren*," I murmured, putting all the warmth I felt for her into the bond between us. Her bottom lip trembled as she nodded slightly, but there was no confidence in it. "I could never fear the other half of myself."

"Why not? I fear myself. What I am. What I might be capable of," she said, glancing down at her shackled hands. I could practically hear the loud thoughts echoing through her mind. Her questioning if the shackles were for her own benefit as well.

"Whatever you were born, you are not a monster now," I said, my voice softening as I reached out of the tub and held out a hand for her.

She accepted it, stepping into the bath with me and settling between my thighs to face the foot of the bath. Her back pressed into my torso, and I wrapped her up in my arms, raising her shackled wrists over our heads so that they could drape over the edge of the basin.

I looked over her shoulder, getting the perfect view of her body as it stretched out before me.

"I cut Mab," she said, her voice catching as she admitted it. She sniffled, drawing air into her lungs as she fought through the shock of saying those words out loud.

"You did," I agreed, nodding lightly. I kept her tucked tightly into my arms, holding her firm and warming her against the chill that swept over her despite the warm water.

"I killed a Fae male with my bare hands, all while chained in iron," she said, her hard swallow making her body move.

I was grateful she couldn't see my face, and I worked hard to keep my side of the bond quiet. She didn't need to stop and think about the wrath I felt at knowing someone had tried to hurt my mate, and that she'd been forced to defend herself alone.

That I hadn't been there to do it for her.

"You did," I agreed once again, running my hand over the skin resting above her heart. It thumped beneath my touch, a reassurance that she was still alive.

"Then how can I be anything other than a monster? Those are monstrous acts." She sighed, leaning her head back against my shoulder. I pressed my cheek into hers, reveling in the feeling of my skin against hers for the moment.

"Am I a monster for what I did to Calfalls? Even you and I would agree that was a monstrous act. I caused the death of thousands," I said, dipping the cloth into the water and raising it until it dripped onto Estrella's chest.

"You weren't yourself. They hurt you. What you did may have been wrong, but you didn't cut off a man's head with dull chains," she said, making the chains clank together behind my head. It was far easier to see the monster in the mirror than to see the ones who stared back at us, wearing the faces of the people we each loved. Estrella had learned that the hard way, vilifying herself for acts of self-defense because they were so against her nature.

As much as I joked about her violence, it was because I knew she would never hurt someone for the sake of it. She didn't find *joy* in death and slaughter, seeing it only as a means to an end if she wanted to survive a world that had proven harsher than winter to her.

"I just raised the dead and used them to reduce an entire city to ash," I said, chuckling against Estrella's spine.

She stilled. Her features twisted into a pout, her brow furrowing as her lips pursed adorably. She could not defend my actions while condemning hers.

"Sometimes, it is far easier to see the good in others than it is to see it in ourselves. Sometimes, the hardest thing to do is understand that while we are not perfect, the way we defend ourselves is not an indication of our character but purely of our will to live so that we might do the right thing when given the freedom to do so."

"I don't think we'll ever have that chance," she said, making my heart clench in my chest.

I wanted nothing more than to offer her the assurance she needed that we would one day find the freedom she so desperately craved. That I wanted to share with her more than anything. She had been a prisoner all her life, had never known true freedom.

As had I.

"Come whatever may, we will fight for our freedom," I said, rubbing the cloth along her skin. Goosebumps rose along her flesh, and her back arched into me when I dragged it over her breast, the sensitive tip hardening beneath my touch.

"Until chaos reigns," she murmured, turning her head to look at me from the very corner of her eye. Something dark flashed through it, a dark streak of gold reflecting off the night sky before it faded away just as quickly as it came.

I did my best not to acknowledge my surprise, not wanting to add to my mate's uncertainty about the things that marked her as different. In all my years, I'd encountered a great many beings.

None so strange as her.

"And eternity begins anew," I said, echoing the vows we'd taken to one another. We may not be able to complete our mate bond yet, but I would give her every part of me that I could in the meantime.

I brought my free hand toward the one holding the cloth, slashing the tip of one of my nails across the surface. A deep cut split my flesh, and blood trickled down to drop into the bath alongside us as I raised my wrist to Estrella's mouth.

"Drink," I ordered, watching as droplets of red landed on her chest.

"I doubt that I need your blood any longer. I am not human," she said with a sad sort of smile. It was bittersweet, as if she would miss the part of her that required my essence inside of her.

"Need it or not, you will take it, anyway. I like knowing that I'm inside of you in any way I can be. I like watching you drink me down and beg me for more," I explained, pressing my wrist to her lips. She parted them slightly, allowing the first drops to touch her tongue as a muffled groan tore free from her throat. She pressed her mouth tighter to my wrist, sealing her mouth around the wound and sucking at my skin. "Since I have no desire to finish inside your mouth tonight, my blood will have to do."

Estrella whimpered, her hips writhing within the water. I sensed her pleasure sliding down the bond between us, hardening my cock as she drew me inside her. I let her take more than I should have, hoping against hope that my blood could help sustain her through the tests Mab would force her to endure the next day. I wasn't yet used to the idea of my mate being the stronger of the two of us, of her ability to heal wounds caused by iron far more quickly than I.

If it meant I would see her safe, I would do whatever it took. Even if it left me weakened.

"Enough, Little One," I said finally, pulling my wrist away from her mouth.

She panted for breath; her mouth stained by my blood as she licked it clean. I dropped my hand between her thighs, touching the most intimate part of her, and she jolted against my touch. She was already wet, already aching as she pressed against my hand. Seeking more contact, more pressure, more everything.

"Take what you need," I told her, sliding my fingers down to press into her entrance. The heel of my palm ground against her clit as she moved her hips, grinding against my hand and using the movement to fuck herself with my fingers.

She whimpered as her thighs tightened around my touch, trapping my hand between them in a grip I couldn't have extricated myself from if I'd wanted to. She came, her pussy clamping down on my fingers as she took them deep.

I gave her a moment to come back to life, to find her energy once more after the force of her orgasm. Then I reached above my head, grasping her by the iron chains and removing them from the edge of the tub. I pushed them around to her front, helping her to her knees in front of me until we draped those chains over the edge of the basin on the other end.

The position left her ass in the air, her position on her knees putting it just above the surface of the water. I got to my knees behind her, slapping my palm down on the fleshy part of her ass and watching it bounce.

She turned her head to gasp at me, a glare on her face. It disappeared the moment I drove my cock inside her. Her pussy still quivered around me as I pushed in, stretching her with the first thrust. She couldn't take all of me, not right away, not until I worked her open slowly.

"Caldris," she whimpered, turning her head forward. She hung it, laying her forehead against the edge of the basin with her elbows braced against it beside her head.

I watched my cock disappear inside of her, thrusting slowly until I managed to bury myself within her. "This is going to be hard and fast, my star. You'd better hold on tight," I grumbled, fucking her so harshly that her knees slipped along the base of the bath.

She shifted, pressing her knees into the edge and forcing me to lower myself until she practically sat on my thighs. Wrapping a hand around her hip, I touched the space where my cock disappeared into her pussy, wrapping my fingers around my length and reveling in the feeling of us joined.

This was where I would spend the rest of my eternity if given the chance. Fuck the world and what it needed.

This was my home.

I fucked into her in sharp, shallow movements until her body started to move with mine. She bounced on my thighs, meeting me thrust for thrust in a frenzied need to claim what was ours. If I only had one night with her before she was taken from me once again, I would fuck her until she could still feel me the next morning.

This was only the beginning.

Water sloshed out the edges of the bath, splashing against the floor and leaving us with less warmth around us as we moved in harmony. I drove into her, chasing my orgasm as she whimpered with the approach of her own.

My fingers abandoned the place where we joined, drifting up to circle her clit.

Once.

Twice.

She came on the third stroke, her head tossing back and wet hair sending a spray of water cascading toward the ceiling. Her head struck my shoulder, giving me the perfect grip as I raised my hand and wrapped it around the front of her throat.

"Good girl," I murmured, squeezing her throat as her pussy squeezed my cock.

She tore my orgasm from me, forcing me to shutter my eyes as I fought the urge to roar out my release and continued to take her even as I filled her with my cum.

We sat there for a long time, catching our breath while I softened inside of her. I didn't need to be hard to enjoy the haven of her body.

The peace she offered transcended sex, giving me a few moments where it didn't feel like the fate of the world rested upon me and now my mate.

The one who seemed gifted with the threads of fate themselves.

11

Estrella

Mab sat upon her throne. A large crowd of her supporters gathered throughout the room as Malachi and a female guard ushered Caldris and me into the vast space. The members of Mab's court lingered at the edges of her dais, observing her as she waited for us to approach.

It felt like walking to my death. Like walking to what I knew would be an endless, miserable torment for me. A chair lurked off to the side, set there as if it had been forgotten until it would serve a purpose.

The Fae who had leered at me, the one who had spit upon me, stood closest to it, running his hands over the surface like it was something to be worshiped. A messenger darted past us as we made our way up the center of the room, hurrying to Mab's side. She grimaced at his lack of tact, ushering him forward when he hesitated just at the top of the steps. He leaned forward to whisper something that I couldn't hear as I placed my foot on the bottom step and lifted the hem of my dress as gracefully as I could manage.

Court life was not something that would ever appeal to me, too like the life Lord Byron had tried to force upon me. I couldn't breathe through the parallels in the lives I hadn't wanted, feeling plagued by the reality of my fate.

I wanted a quiet life with Caldris at my side and the ability to come and go as I pleased. We'd have just enough land to call home without entrapping us. I wanted to see Alfheimr, to know what made each of the Faerie Courts unique. I didn't know if that future included children. I could be entirely content to just have the love we shared. But none of it seemed possible. Even outside of our imprisonment with Mab, Caldris had titles and responsibilities to his people.

Those responsibilities included an heir, but this world was ugly and cruel. I didn't think I could ever bring a child into it, not while knowing the fate that child may face one day. The pain they would feel with the loss of those they loved. The pain I might feel if I ever lost *them*.

"Bring him to me," Mab ordered, waving her hand to the side.

Caldris grabbed my forearm, guiding me to the side of the dais as the messenger darted past us once more. He left through the doors of the throne room; the stone creaking as he heaved it open. I pressed into Caldris's side, turning to watch as a Fae Male stepped into the throne room.

He limped his way up the center column. The hushed whispers of Mab's court were the first confirmation that something truly horrific would happen to him if it hadn't already. His hands swung at his side, the motion jolting and uncoordinated as he fought to drag his injured foot over the stone floor. In another life, I'd have gone to meet him.

I'd have helped him as I'd so often helped my mother, understanding the pain of putting pressure on a limb that didn't want to bear your weight. But in this world, I felt trapped to the dais, watching as he struggled. Caldris's grip was tight on my arm, understanding my desire to help better than any other.

"You appear to be empty-handed," Mab said, pursing her lips as she stared at the male.

He nodded, his face pinching with pain as he paused at the bottom of the steps. I watched in horror as he grasped his leg by the thigh, forcibly lifting it up onto the first step. He grunted as his good foot followed, leaning his weight into his injury.

"Yes, my Queen," he said, taking the second step. He maneuvered his way up every stair, stopping finally in front of Mab. He collapsed at her feet, kneeling upon the stone as his breath left him in ragged, harsh gasps.

"And why have you not brought me what I asked for?" Mab asked, her fingers clenching around the arm of her throne.

Her cheeks hollowed out. Her mouth pinched in rage. Whatever it was that the male had failed to deliver, she wanted it more than she wanted to know what I was. Her eyes were wide, wild, and feral as she stared down at the male before her. It was the first hint I'd seen of the madness many had alluded to; the first sign that she had that within her.

The man turned his head up to her, his eyes filled with sorrow. It was the gaze of a man begging for forgiveness, for another chance. His first tear fell, splashing off the stone in front of his knees as he shook his head from side to side.

"They deemed me unworthy," he rasped.

Mab swallowed, nodding her head as she considered his words. "I did not ask you to return to me empty-handed. You should have remained in Tartarus until you were able to prove yourself worthy."

I looked at Caldris, silently questioning what she could have wanted from Tartarus. There wasn't much that I knew about the prison, only that it was the home of the most terrifying creatures of Faerie. The things that could not exist within our world without destroying it.

He shook his head silently, his vow to tell me about it later rippling down the bond between us. I gritted my teeth as I forced myself to stay silent, to stay out of business that wasn't mine. I felt more like Caldris in those moments than ever before, putting him before the male that I couldn't help.

I would burn the world if it meant saving him, sacrifice every shred of my dignity and morals if it meant he was unharmed.

The male sputtered, his hands trembling where he rested them upon his knees. "But the others are dead, my Queen. To stay is to die. There is no winning against them. They're—"

"A pity you thought the fate waiting for you here would be any kinder," Mab said, waving a hand as she turned away from him.

Impatience pulsed off of her, striking me in the chest as one of the guards stepped away from her side and unsheathed his sword. I gasped as he stepped up beside the man. I was no stranger to killing. No stranger to death and battle. This was purely cold-blooded murder, not a strategic death or self-defense.

This was no casualty of war.

"Shhh, my star. Keep quiet," Caldris said, his grip tightening on my forearm.

His fingers pressed into my skin, a warning in the touch as well as his words. I was in no place to interfere, and his meaning was clear.

I bit my tongue, clamping my teeth down on the fleshiest part and turning my head to bury my face against my mate's chest. The sword cut through the air, a distinct whistle as Mab's guard struck.

I stood by and did nothing, made no move to save the male. I hadn't owed him anything, aside from basic decency.

Those who lingered within the throne room didn't seem bothered in the slightest, going about their business as if death were irrelevant to them.

All it took for evil to flourish was for the good to do nothing.

Mab hadn't even done the job herself, instead ordering her man to handle her dirty work for her. The callousness of it all made me want to weep. I determined then and there that no matter what came of me, I would always kill my enemies myself.

I would not put the stain of that soul, of that death, onto another person. I would give them the dignity of being worthy of my time, more than a muttered command or the wave of a hand. There was honor in that, something the Queen of Air and Darkness seemed to have none of.

Mab's guards moved, grabbing the body and dragging it from the throne room. The name of the place she'd sent the male echoed in my head, the word a mantra that seared itself upon my soul.

Tartarus.

The Prison of the Gods.

There was no telling how many of the Gods had been locked in there, trapped in a magical place that no one seemed to know how to access. As a girl, I'd wondered who ruled the prison, who knew where the entrance was and who sentenced creatures to an eternity of suffering within its confines.

It seemed Mab at least knew where, and she knew how to send someone into it.

But what was locked within it that she wanted to remove?

"Get out," she muttered, her anger at being denied making her quiet voice echo through the silence of the room. "I said get out!" she yelled when nobody moved.

Caldris took me toward the doors, following the rush of people trying to escape the Queen's wrath before she could single them out as the target for her anger.

"Not you, Little Mouse," Mab said, the words crawling upon my skin. "You and I are going to play a little game." She flicked her hand, and Caldris stepped away from me. His movement was sluggish, as if he fought her for every step as he moved toward the dais and the chair that waited at the edge.

The legs of another chair screeched against the stone as Malachi dragged it over the floor, depositing it directly in front of Mab before he turned for me and held out a hand, as if he were a gentleman wanting to push in my chair for an evening meal.

Shit.

12

Estrella

Caldris sat in the chair at the edge of Mab's empty throne room, his posture tense as he watched Malachi guide me to the seat that waited in front of Mab. I held my head high as I approached it, longing for the moment when the shackles would be removed for whatever Mab's purpose was.

I would be useless if my magic was crippled, impossible to perform tests on to determine what I might be. My wrists ached with the constant abuse of the iron upon my skin, feeling as if they would wear down to the bone soon enough.

"Have a seat, Little Mouse," Mab said, waving a hand to the chair in front of her.

I stepped around the edge, lowering myself into the seat slowly. The arms were made from thick wood, the scratch marks of previous victims clawed into the surface a clue for what was coming. I paused, hovering just above the seat as I cast a glance toward her. I didn't want to think about what she might do to elicit such a response from me, but I swallowed and sat fully in the chair.

Caldris fidgeted in his seat, putting pressure on his feet as if he was about to stand. He grunted, his nails digging into the arms of his chair as he sat back. Mab's pointed stare, which was fixed on him, melted into a sinister smile.

Malachi stepped up beside me, a metal key grasped between his thumb and forefinger. He lifted one of my arms to the arm of the chair, unlocking it and opening the shackle until it dropped free. He shoved it onto the fabric of my dress so that it rested in my lap. The sight of my mangled flesh beneath it forced me to turn my head away. The blackened, burned skin looked like something from my worst nightmares.

As if I'd been engulfed in flames, my skin bubbled with blisters and wept blood. I stretched it, wincing at the pain the movement brought to my injured flesh. He reached beneath the arm of the chair, grasping two ends of a shackle I hadn't seen and pinning my hand to it. The iron sealed around my wrist once more, binding me to the chair as the too-familiar burn returned.

I looked from him to Mab, confusion overwhelming me as I tried to process what was happening. How was I to do any sort of magic with iron upon me?

"What are you doing?" I asked, elbowing Malachi as he stepped around me and reached for my other arm.

He pinned me down, releasing the shackle and using both of his hands to pin me still as Mab stood from her throne. She approached slowly, clasping the iron shackle from beneath the arm in her hands that were covered by black silk gloves. She lifted the two halves, wrapping them around my wrist and securing them together until I was pinned to the seat completely.

"I am many things, but I am not foolish enough to let you free until you and I come to an understanding," she said, smiling sadly as she returned to her chair. "Prove yourself to me. Prove that the mate you love so dearly will be enough motivation to keep you contained, and I will allow you to heal yourself. You will no longer suffer in irons, so long as you prove that my threat to him will suffice."

She clenched her hand into a fist. Caldris groaned in his chair, his head bowing forward. I could feel the way his heart convulsed, feel the slowing of its beat within me. Mine seemed to slow along with it, the echo of his life beating within my chest.

"What do you want?" I asked.

My lungs heaved with relief as she relaxed her hand. Her grip on his heart eased, allowing him to draw in a full breath finally. My own heart paused for a moment before it beat strongly, resuming a normal pace as if it too had been released.

"What is your name, Little Mouse? What am I to call the creature who perplexes us all?" she asked.

Imelda's words rang in my head, and I knew that she'd known. I didn't know how much time she'd spent in the Court of Shadows before coming to Nothrek, but she was no stranger to Mab's ways.

She'd known it would always lead to this.

I gritted my teeth, clenching my eyes closed as I forced myself to remain quiet. I didn't allow myself to look back at Caldris, not wanting to risk putting the idea into her head that he should suffer for my insolence. He was the one thing she could use to make me cooperate; the only force that would make me behave.

"I thought as much," Mab said, waving her hand until a web of shadows appeared within it.

They were sharp, spiky things as they writhed upon her hand, looking like the thorny vines of a rose but crafted from the inky black shadows of night itself. They spread, growing until they were too large to be contained by her palm. They climbed down to the ground, creeping along the stone until they wrapped themselves around the base of the chair. I watched in horror as they split into five pieces each, crawling up until they positioned themselves at the tip of each of my fingers.

"I will ask you again. What is your name?"

I sank my teeth into my tongue, the coppery, bitter taste of blood filling my mouth. The pointed ends of the thorns were as sharp as the needles I'd used to repair my own dresses, a weapon in their own right. I let my eyes close once more, not wanting to watch as they moved—not able to stomach seeing them disappear into my flesh.

Mab sighed. "Very well."

I flinched back as much as I could the moment the tip of the thorns touched my finger, sliding forward painfully slowly. The anticipation of the pain was as much a part of the torture as the pain itself. The thorns moved as if in slow motion as they slid beneath the curve of my nail. They found the tiny space between my nail and my flesh, slipping beneath like a wooden splinter.

A scream tore up my throat as they kept pressing forward, the hot, white pain of it sinking all the way down my nail bed. I sobbed as they withdrew, opening my eyes slowly to stare down at them. They glistened, the black too dark to show the color, but blood trickled down the tips of my fingers as I turned my glare up to Mab once more.

"What. Is. Your. Name?" she asked, gritting her teeth as I glared at her.

I forced myself to lift my head, holding her stare as I kept my lips clamped shut. I would not be my own downfall. I would not give her power over me by offering her my name.

She waved her hand, turning to look at Caldris in frustration. I followed her gaze, finding him shoving to his feet. "That's enough."

"Sit down, darling. The fun has only just begun," she said, smiling broadly as she turned to me.

Caldris fell into his seat, the command she'd issued leaving him no choice but to obey. The vines crept forward once again while I stared at him, sliding into the place beside the last intrusion they'd created. They lit a new path of fire inside of me, and I struggled through the urge to scream as I held his eyes.

His brow furrowed, his nostrils flaring as he tried to fight against Mab's command. His hand rose to his heart, his talons digging into the fabric of his black tunic and shredding it as if he would tear his heart from his chest. I tore my eyes away, bowing my head forward as the vines slid farther still.

I couldn't feel how far they went, had no knowledge beyond the pure agony lighting me in two as I screamed at the top of my lungs, giving Mab the satisfaction she wanted as she pulled them back.

My hands trembled. My fingers curled in on themselves as if they could find shelter from the vines that would come back for a third assault if I didn't give their master what she wanted. I raised my eyes to her once again, my chin bowed as a whimper escaped my throat.

"Give me your name, Little Mouse, and all the pain ends. I will allow you to heal your wounds and put you out of your misery," she said, her voice almost soft in spite of the fact that she was the one who would cause me pain.

I swallowed, gritting my teeth as I forced my fingers to flatten against the arm of the chair in a moment of defiance. Hiding the tremble in my lip, knowing what pain would follow, I bit out the words that would solidify my place as Mab's favorite victim.

"Fuck you," I growled.

The smile fled her face instantly, and her brow furrowed in surprise. She held out her hand, drawing her fingers in slowly, one by one. Her pinky curled in first, the vines that had assaulted my pinky fingers fleeing to return to their maker. Her ring finger came next, then her middle, and so on, until each of the vines returned to her and vanished within her grasp.

The Queen of Air and Darkness stepped forward, rounding to the back of my chair. She grasped the fabric of the dress she'd given me, tearing it open at the back until the cold air of the throne room touched my spine from my neck to the small of my back. I turned to look at her over my shoulder, holding perfectly still as she touched a single talon to one of the worst scars on my back.

"It is such a shame for you to be permanently marred by something you could so easily heal if it was done to you now," she said, drawing a line up to the top of the scar. My skin withered beneath her touch, feeling as if she dragged death itself over my flesh. "I wonder if they will return with your new flesh if I peel the skin from your bones?"

She sliced her claw against the top of the scar, creating a line of fire across my back as the warmth of blood trickled down from the deep wound. I winced, curling forward when she slid two nails inside of the gash, gripping my skin between her fingers and thumb. I couldn't stop the whimper that escaped or the tear that fell onto my cheek as I clenched my eyes closed.

She dragged my skin down, peeling it in a strip as my flesh tore, her talons slicing whatever skin resisted. The scream died in my throat, trapped there as I froze solid. There was nothing but the pain, nothing but the heat against the muscle and sinew in my back as she took my skin.

She paused for just a moment, a laugh brushing against my ear as she leaned forward. Her lips practically touched my temple, moving as she murmured to me.

"How much more do you think your mate can take before he intervenes and gives me what I want? You refuse because you think it will harm the precious world, but he doesn't care about the fucking world if it means you must suffer. He would burn it all and every living being within it to the ground if it meant you remained unscathed. You can defy me all you want, Little Mouse. But he will not," she said, then pulled on my skin so suddenly that it tore down to the small of my back. It hung from my body like a strip before she cut it at the base, tossing it to the side.

I couldn't bring myself to look at it, turning my gaze away from the strip of skin that belonged on my body. My breath came in ragged gasps, my lungs struggling to breathe past the overwhelming shock of pain. Mab cut her nail across the top of my back once more, and I sobbed as I forced myself not to speak. The cold air burned what remained of my flesh without my skin to act as a barrier.

"Stop," Caldris said, forcing me to snap my head to him.

I shook mine, muttering an order of my own. "Don't," I pleaded, my bottom lip trembling as his face softened. He knew my wishes; knew I would rather suffer than give her anything she could use against me one day.

He closed his eyes, sinking his teeth into his bottom lip as he doomed us all.

"Her name is Estrella," Caldris said, opening his eyes to hold my gaze.

There was no further trace of the shame he must have felt, only his sense of duty in protecting me clouding his judgment. I wanted to condemn him for it, to judge him for what he might have done.

But could I have sat there and watched Mab skin him alive when I could have put an end to it?

Love was our greatest weakness, and Mab had kept Caldris close intentionally.

"Her full name," Mab said, stepping away from my back. She patted the side of my face as she walked toward her throne, staining my cheek with my own blood.

"Estrella Barlowe," Caldris conceded, glancing between us.

"And where was she born?" Mab asked, pushing the boundaries of what Caldris would offer.

I realized with a start that she could have just asked him in the first place. That he wouldn't have been able to deny her the knowledge.

My suffering had been a show, a test to prove whether or not she could allow me free. It had been entirely unnecessary, but Mab enjoyed pain. She'd proven her point.

We were powerless in the face of her.

"Mistfell village, just beyond the Veil," my mate answered, standing from his chair smoothly. He approached me, stopping instantly when Mab held up a hand. "I gave you what you asked for. Now allow her to heal herself, my Queen." The words were torn from the deepest parts of him, an appeasement he didn't want to offer.

Every part of me recoiled from the honorific upon his lips when speaking to someone else. That deep, hollow thing within me rose up, struggling against the ties that bound her still. She thumped against my chest, teeth and claws scratching as if she meant to tear her way out of me.

There was only one person he should be calling his anything, only one woman who should be his queen.

"I should let her rot with her injuries. She did not answer my questions," Mab said, turning a chastising stare to me. "But I will reward your loyalty, Caldris. I'll allow her to heal herself, but she will not be permitted to spend the night in your arms. Hopefully, she will respect my kindness and pay it forward tomorrow."

"I reject your kindness. I want no gifts from you. I know what they'll cost," I said, staring at my mate. He'd doom us all with the favors Mab would collect on one day.

"Malachi," Mab said, ignoring my outburst.

I hung my head forward as the Fae male's gloved hands touched my left wrist, sliding the key into the lock and twisting. The shackle fell away, hanging from the arm of the chair as I flexed my throbbing fingers. I studied the lines in the stone floor, memorizing the way the cracks rippled across the surface. They spread like tributaries, stemming from one large river until each little crack faded into nothing.

The other shackle released, falling from my skin as a full, clean breath filled my lungs. The air was crisp, cool, as if I breathed it for the first time. My chest expanded with it, a rush of warmth flooding my body in the absence of the iron. A flicker of light shone in the corner of my eye, drawing my gaze to where my fingers glowed with a soft golden glimmer. The blood faded away, disintegrating into the air as the injuries healed.

I followed the path of light up my arm, watching the whites of my Fae Mark turn to gold. The rush of it moved beneath my skin, rolling forward like a wave within my blood. I watched the gold work a path from my fingers, up each swirl at my wrist as the burned, charred flesh mended itself slowly.

It continued up my arm, rolling into the side of my neck and filling my head with the rush of strength. My headache faded, the lingering effects of Malachi's assault in the bath vanishing as I rolled my neck in a circle.

I stood slowly as the flesh of my back healed, all too aware of the way Malachi stepped away from my side hurriedly. I felt him move, felt the cord of life where it kept him tethered to this world. The room shook as my feet pressed into the stone beneath me. Those cracks grew and spread like fissures upon the earth.

I opened my eyes, staring into Mab's shocked gaze as she kept her mouth pressed firmly into a line. She gathered shadows at her side; her worry and curiosity pulsing off her in waves. It tasted bitter on my tongue, coating the air with the stench of her fear. I wanted to feed on it, to turn it into ash and dust until nothing remained of the queen who shouldn't have been.

"You have something of mine," the creature within me murmured, and I could practically see the fuzzy, blurred form of her standing amid the stars. She was nothing but a silhouette in the darkness, a golden, glowing woman who was not meant to be contained.

She found freedom in the dark.

She and I remained separate, two minds within one body. I couldn't grasp her thoughts, couldn't wrap my fingers around the parts of her that she kept hidden from me just yet. I tried to sink into her, to connect in a way that might offer me some protection.

I took a single step forward, my skin tingling as I moved. Everything felt new, as if my entire being was remade all over again. Mab raised a hand in warning, her shadows dancing upon her palm. They were so dark compared to the single golden thread that spread across her chest. It was frayed at the end, extending toward that skull on her throne that I'd moved the day I woke up.

I raised a hand to play with it, to capture it between my fingers and pull and find out what I could do with the thread of a Goddess in my palm.

A horrible screech came from my throat. A band of iron wrapped around my neck.

I pulled away from Malachi where he'd stepped up behind me, the click of a lock snapping into place. It was too late to undo. The iron scalded my fingers as I raised a hand to try to pry it open. I could not find the lock itself, fumbling to free myself as Mab smirked at my struggle.

The beast within me recoiled, sinking back down into that hollow place where she slept. It wasn't safe for her to come out, I knew, but I missed the euphoria she filled me with. The knowledge that she would protect us at all costs.

"What the fuck was that?" Malachi asked, his very breathing irritating me as I turned a sharp glare to him.

My neck seemed to crack as I turned, a growl upon my lips proving that the beast had left a lingering stain of something *other* behind, even though she'd abandoned me.

"I have no idea," Mab admitted, taking a step forward.

Her feet brought her to stand before me, the perfect poise of a queen as she studied my face. Her clawed fingers touched my skin, rubbing over the top of my wrist where the iron had scalded me. "You should find your collar far more comfortable.

We lined the inside with cloth so it would not burn you, as I believe you'll be wearing it for some time."

"Take it off," I snarled, leaning forward to murmur the words so softly that I doubted anyone but Mab heard them. The wind seemed to carry them away, a threat from one female to another, a promise to repay all the wrongs done in blood.

"Welcome to the Court of Shadows, Estrella Barlowe," the Queen of Air and Darkness said, dropping her hand away from my wrist.

She spun on her heel, making her way to the massive stone doors at the end of the throne room. She paused just at the exit, turning to look at me over her shoulder. No one existed but the two of us, not Caldris or Malachi. We both knew they had become nothing but pawns in the games we would play with one another.

"We're going to have fun together, you and I."

The train of her dress trailed behind her as she stepped through the doors, and then she was gone.

13

Estrella

Malachi shoved open the door to my room, motioning for me to walk inside. The iron at my throat made my body sink heavily, even without the scalding burn touching my flesh directly. Compared to the moments where that creature had danced just beneath the surface of my skin, her magic coursing through my veins, the inevitable feeling of being completely powerless was a nightmare in itself. I wanted nothing more than to revel in that power again, to feel my body flood with the cold hollowness as it surged toward the surface.

Staring down at her felt like looking into a pit, a well of something unknown lurking inside of me. If I ventured deeper into that pit, I might never emerge again.

A woman stepped into the room, raising her hands to fill the bath with water for me. She deposited a bundle of clothing on the bed once more, standing in front of it with her hands clasped before her as Malachi tugged the door shut. Her clothing was finer than the servants who had tended to my bath previously, deep blue in color and adorned with delicate embroidery. The bodice of her corset glimmered with tiny stones set into the threading, and a cloak was clasped around her shoulders with a shimmering golden broach.

Her brown skin had warm undertones, her features kind as she smiled at me slightly. Her long hair was pulled away from her face, twisted into a complex braid that hung over her right shoulder to drape over her chest. She'd twisted ribbons and gems into the braid, making it shimmer as it caught the candlelight and speaking to a wealth I hadn't seen in the others so far.

"My name is Nila," she said, stepping toward me. She clasped her hands in front of her, pausing as I settled my gaze upon her hesitantly. The last servant hadn't lingered after doing her task, moving on quickly to the next guest she undoubtedly had to see to. "I am to be your lady-in-waiting at Queen Mab's request."

"I've no need for a lady of my own," I said, trying to keep my expression polite. "I'm fully capable of seeing to my own needs."

It wasn't her fault she'd been ordered to tend to me, but I couldn't shake the reminder of how Lord Byron treated his servants—how Lady Jacqueline behaved as if they were so far beneath her, they might as well have been the dogs. I had no desire to become like that.

"Be that as it may, our queen has sent me to assist you. Might I offer some advice?" Nila asked, tilting her head to the side as she raised her hands to the broach at the front of her cloak. She unclasped it, pulling the heavy fabric around her shoulders and draping it over one arm so that she could fold it neatly over the back of a chair.

"I've a feeling you will no matter how I answer that question," I said, stepping toward the table.

Fresh food had been laid upon it while I'd been tortured in the throne room, and now that the pain of such things had faded, I couldn't fight the grumbling in my stomach. Mab was right, I was not a human, and as such, Faerie rules probably didn't apply to me.

I needed to eat if I was going to maintain any sort of strength for what Mab would put me through. She'd proven today just what she was capable of, the pain she was willing to make me feel if I defied her. A shudder rippled down my back as if it remembered the feeling of my skin being torn from my body, and cold air kissed the skin through the tear in my dress.

In the end, I didn't know that it would matter. Nothrek would never be safe for me now, not with the way my ears tipped at the top and the magic marked upon my skin. I raised a single hand to touch the subtle point on my ears, wincing at the reminder of just how much I'd changed.

"Your life here will become much easier when you learn to just give her what it is she wants. Once she gets bored with you, you will no longer suffer under the pains of her attention," Nila said. She raised a single hand to her shoulder, brushing her hand down a long, thin scar that marred her bicep. It looked as if someone had carved her open with iron, taking a piece of flesh from her skin.

"You say that as if you're speaking from experience," I said, turning my attention to her.

I grabbed a piece of the flatbread off the table and tore a chunk from it. It was dense, coated in spices. Its delicious scent reached my nose, and it took all I had not to shove the entire thing into my mouth. Instead, I took a small bite and chewed delicately as Nila and I sized each other up. The buttery flavor of the flatbread coated my tongue in warm comfort, drawing a small groan from me as she watched.

"I grew up in the Summer Court. My father was an adviser to King Rheaghan and his closest confidante. I was barely two hundred when we came here with the King on a diplomatic mission to visit his sister. I became a curiosity to Mab when she claimed there was something inappropriate brewing between her brother and me. My father and Rheaghan both insisted that was not the case, and everyone knows the King is a rake and will not settle down until the day he finds his mate; but Mab decided to keep me here, regardless. Life became much simpler when I told her all about my feelings for Rheaghan and our stolen moments in the gardens when my father was away," Nila said, shaking her head as if she'd been foolish to allow such things.

I shouldn't have been surprised. Not when I knew the enigmatic power the Gods held, and how impossible it was to resist that.

"Why would you share those moments with him?" I asked, crossing my arms over my chest.

Something about the situation didn't feel accurate, as if I was missing the pieces of the story. If it was true, my opinion of Rheaghan would be even worse than it already was just for the fact that he was Mab's brother and had allowed her to become what she was today.

"Our moments in the gardens were innocent. Rheaghan liked to allow me the time to talk about the cactus flowers I enjoyed tending to. There was never anything inappropriate about them; he merely kept an eye on me when my father was unable. But Mab likes to see the worst in people. Give her just enough that she can make her assumptions, and she will gladly do so and leave you in peace, Princess," Nila said, stepping up to me.

She touched the ribbons tying my dress on my arms, unknotting the one at my elbow. Her fingers brushed over my Fae mark almost reverently, lingering upon the white lines specifically.

"I'm not a princess," I said, staring up into her dark eyes defiantly.

I didn't care what my connection to Caldris meant to these people—being a princess implied I would one day sit in a stuffy throne room and conduct business for the courts. I'd be more likely to run free through the meadows at night and avoid all sense of responsibility entirely, and I wouldn't apologize for it.

Nila ignored me, her brown eyes falling to the white mark upon my arm.

"Is it true they glowed gold when you healed yourself?" she asked, a bit of wonder leaking into her tone.

Being here, being different, it was everything I'd ever wanted to avoid. It was a reminder that I wasn't the same as those around me and that I probably never would be. I didn't want to be treated like the animals in the Royal Circus that traveled around Nothrek in the Spring. I didn't want to be gawked and leered at for the rest of my suddenly very, very long life—locked in a cage until it came time for the people of the kingdom to lay eyes upon me.

"And if they did? What difference would that make?" I asked, pulling my arm back away from her trailing fingers. I wrapped the arm back in the cloth, doing my best to retie the ribbons she'd loosened.

"Then I would say that is all the more reason that you need to be protected. The hands of the Fates themselves have woven themselves into your very existence. You being here cannot be a coincidence. You are meant for great things, Princess Estrella. I cannot wait to see the day when you realize it," she said, raising her other hand to untie the knots on my biceps all over again. She was persistent, but her fingers remained gentle, coaxing.

"I hardly think many in Mab's court care to see me safe," I said with a scoff, holding the fabric of my dress to my chest as she untied the final knot upon my shoulder. She stepped up to my other side, leaning over me as she began the process of freeing me from the confines of the simple dress, the back already torn to reveal more flesh than normal.

"You have more allies within this court than you have allowed yourself to see. Blending in has become necessary to our survival, but I assure you, we are here. Waiting for a chance to rise up and overthrow the queen who imprisons us," Nila said.

I looked up at her face, at the seriousness with which she studied me. She was far taller than me, ethereal in her height and stunningly beautiful in her poise. Her shoulders remained straight even as she bent at the waist, her posture flawless.

"Perhaps that day finally approaches." She stared at me meaningfully. Her deep brown eyes were wide and far-set, with charcoal lining them and accentuating the curve at the outer corner.

She finished with the knots, stepping toward the bath basin. She grasped a vial off one of the small, circular tables nearby, allowing a few drops of liquid to fall into the bath water. The steam rising from the warm water turned a deep purple hue, like the prettiest tone in the starlit sky.

"What is it?" I asked, stepping up beside the bath.

I peeked over the edge, staring down at the purple-tinted water in awe as I clutched my dress to my chest. Nila reached in, cupping a palmful of the jewel-toned water in her hand and raising it. She spread her fingers, letting it trail back into the basin.

It left a slight shimmer to her brown skin, making her sparkle like moonlight. She grasped my hand, touching the tips of her fingers against mine where they were painted black from my magic.

"You are a daughter of the night, Princess Estrella. It is time you experienced the luxuries of one." She picked up one of the round tables, setting it closer to the bath and lining the surface with a collection of other vials. "Think of it as armor. Court life is not an easy one. There are no swords to protect you here. There is no magic for you to defend yourself so long as you wear that collar. Allow me to help you embrace what you were always meant to be. Allow me to show you the pampered ways of the Fae. I promise you will take Mab's breath away the next time she sees you, as well as your mate. For entirely different reasons, but both are equal motivators in court life."

"I am surprised that Mab would waste her energy on things such as beauty," I said, reaching a hand in to touch the water. It was warm, the perfect temperature, and something about the texture of the water seemed to cling to my skin, moisturizing it even after the droplets fell from my hand. "Why bother when you have all the power in the world?"

"Because there is privilege in beauty. There is power in taking away the breath of your enemy so that they never see you ready to slit their throat, too fixated on the curve of your lip. There is strength in allowing yourself to appear fragile, all the while knowing that your pretty silken skirts hide a dagger that could carve the heart from a male's chest," she said, her lips curving into the sly smile of a woman who was well acquainted with such deceptions.

My eyes immediately dropped to her thighs, to what might be hidden beneath her dress. She'd been alone with me, had me at her mercy, and never moved to harm me. That was a first in the Court of Shadows.

"I've never been very good at playing the games of court," I said.

I released the fabric at my chest. With the back torn, it fluttered to the floor at my feet into a pool of fabric. I fought to ignore the fact that I was nude with a stranger once again. The Fae were far more comfortable with their bodies, unbothered by nudity in the way humans were, and I would do my best to embrace it in spite of my upbringing.

Instead of a protest to the truth of her words, my statement was far more a warning. Her attempts to turn me into a beauty to rival hers would likely fail, because there was more to beauty than a bath. The confidence to carry such things was another story, the ability to manipulate with a smile and seduce with a single glance. I possessed none of those things.

"Well then, it's a good thing that the Fates have blessed you with a good teacher," she said, holding out a hand to me from the other side of the basin.

I hesitated only a moment, holding her gaze as she ignored the vulnerability of my nudity. Then I drew in a shaky breath, feeling as if I was about to walk to my death.

I took her hand, hoping I wasn't making a mistake.

14

Caldris

The lighting in Mab's throne room was even dimmer than usual that night when I strode through the heavy doors. People lingered about the room, chatting in small groups as they sipped wine from crystal goblets. Mab lazed about on her throne, looking far too bored for a queen who had a room of followers at her disposal.

Fury pulsed in my veins. They stood just to the side of where my mate's blood stained the dais, acting as if her suffering was irrelevant. Mab had bled her. She'd *skinned* her while I'd watched, and I'd been trapped, unable to do anything.

I'd never felt more helpless. Never wanted to rip out Mab's throat more than in the moments when she'd buried her claws in Estrella's flesh. I would never forget the sound of it tearing from her body, never stop hearing the sound of her screams echoing through the throne room. She'd taken the pain, suffered through it, and managed to remain strong despite knowing it would come again. But I hadn't been able to bear the pain in her eyes, the tremble in her body as she suffered.

I hadn't been able to listen to another pained whimper, another broken sound escaping her lips before she could stop it as Mab gripped her flesh all over again.

I'd been weak, and I feared we would all pay the consequences for it.

The Fae at Mab's side were her closest companions. A small group of half a dozen males and females, constantly lingering and providing her with the latest gossip from throughout the court. I refused to make eye contact with the one who frequently requested my company. Mab had not granted it in centuries, denying her friend the continued pleasure of my body. I didn't know if it was because my body had purely stopped reacting to such violations, or if it was because Mab grew bored with my lack of response to the abuse.

All I knew was that I was grateful for it, and that the timing had coincided with the moment I'd first felt Estrella come to life. It had been the mate bond snapping into place between us that made my body no longer any more interested than my mind.

Estrella had saved me, long before she'd ever known of my existence.

"You summoned me, my Queen?" I asked, kneeling at the foot of her dais.

I was almost grateful for the way lowering myself to my knee meant I could no longer see where Estrella's blood stained the floor. I didn't know if I could remain impassive while laying eyes upon it, but the scent of her blood rushing through my senses was enough to remind me. My nostrils flared as I forced my jaw to relax, hanging my head forward and parting my lips slightly so that I could breathe through my mouth instead of my nose.

The steps spread out in front of me, and Mab gazed down as her body perked up at the thought of finally having whatever form of entertainment she'd decided upon for the night. With the mate bond public knowledge, the laws of Faerie prevented her from ordering me to perform any form of sexual favors. Even Mab herself couldn't violate the witches' edict or the way it had tangled and twisted with the magic of Alfheimr.

The consequences were swift, outside the realm of one being or entity. To do so was to suffer the wrath of an entire ancient coven.

"I am bored, Caldris," she said, standing from her chair to approach the steps. "It has long been time for you to perform your duties and provide my court with entertainment." She swept out a hand, making the onlookers cheer with her proclamation.

I gritted my teeth against my rage, the memory of all the times I'd been forced to participate in acts for the entertainment of her court rushing through me. Not all who inhabited the Court of Shadows were evil, but those who were deserved no less than being exterminated and sent to Helheim where they belonged.

"What is it my Queen wishes me to do?" I asked, raising my head.

I kept my face neutral, the disdain I felt for her carefully hidden behind a mask. I had no doubt that Mab could feel it, that she knew exactly how I and so many others felt about her hold over us. If I thought it possible, I'd have cut my chest open and torn her snake from my still-beating heart so that I could kill her as painfully as possible—or die trying.

"I'm feeling generous, so I will allow you to choose," she said, her face caught with an aesthetically pleasing smile that never ended well for anyone.

Her boredom was bad enough, but when she thought she was feeling 'kind' was when the true cruelty she was capable of reared its head. She would make me choose between two impossible forms of suffering, and when I suffered, she would make me feel as if it was my fault and not hers.

Because I'd chosen it in the end.

"Will it be pleasure or pain?" Mab turned her head to the side, holding out a hand. Lady Malazan, Mab's lady-in-waiting, walked to her side slowly. Her caution was notable, her face a careful mask even as her eyes lit with hope. She looked down at where I knelt, and I had spent far too much time with her to not hear her voice in my head.

How pretty a God looks on his knees for me.

I suppressed my shudder, turning my stare back to Mab. "I have a mate," I reminded her, raising a brow. My relief for it was instant, knowing that of all the ways Mab could harm me, *this* was at least safe.

"I cannot force you to enjoy the body of another, but that doesn't mean you cannot lie there and allow Malazan to take what she wishes from you," Mab said, shrugging her shoulders. "She's been such a dutiful companion these last centuries. Surely, we can reward such behavior." *Reward.* My body, my *cock*, was not a reward for anyone but Estrella. I seethed, talons protruding from my fingertips as I dug them into the stone at my side.

"I will never be disloyal to my mate," I said, holding her stare.

Mab's mouth twisted into a pout. She didn't truly care if I lay beaten and bloody on her floor or if Malazan rode my cock until it felt raw, only seeking the option that would torment me more in the long run. Betraying the woman I loved was the worst choice, but even she could not force me to do such a thing against my will when I had a mate of my own, and I would never allow it.

"Even if she does not make the same choice when I choose her to entertain my court next?" Mab asked, raising a brow.

She smirked, as if she knew what the thought of Estrella having to make such a choice would do to me. I couldn't bear the possibility of another man moving within her, of her body being violated in such a way, but to be responsible for her making the choice of pain that would tear her in two was no better.

"Even then. *Always*," I answered, knowing that if Estrella was faced with the same choice, her decision would not sway my own. She could choose to pleasure another male; she could choose pain, and I would not blame her for either, if it came to that. The choices she made under duress were not hers.

I would love her until chaos reigned, no matter what or who tried to come between us. I would gladly suffer the pain of a thousand knives rather than allow another woman to touch me in the way that only Estrella had the right to. I'd suffered without her for centuries, never knowing the touch of the female who would change me.

I'd never do anything to hurt her, gladly taking the pain upon myself instead.

Mab sighed and scoffed. "Feel free to go first, Malazan. He's denied you all over again," she said as she turned back to her throne. She dropped into it, her face twisted into a pout as she placed her head in her hands and prepared to watch.

I bowed my head forward as Malazan lifted her skirts delicately, making her way down the steps until she stopped just in front of me. She raised the layers of silk and lace, pulling her iron knife from the sheath strapped to her thigh. She placed the edge of the blade beneath my chin, light laughter escaping her as my skin burned with the contact. She lifted, dragging my stare to meet hers.

"I should castrate you for your rejection," she said, glaring down at me. "It is a shame that your cock will grow back. My vengeance would be depriving your mate of that piece of flesh I am sure she loves all too much."

I didn't answer, staring up at her wordlessly and waiting for her to unleash her wrath upon me. Women like Malazan were not easily rejected, especially not with the status she'd gained at Mab's side.

"Do you have nothing to say for yourself? No apology to sweetly murmur to me to excuse your rejection? Many males would kill to be in your place, I'll have you know," she said, her lips twisting into the slightest hint of a pout.

To live for centuries and still require the reassurance of a male companion was a particularly sad trait, and in anyone less despicable, I might have felt pity.

But not for her. "So fuck one of them," I said, my face remaining deadpan as I wished she would just get it over with.

Her blade bit into my throat, slicing across it in her rage as fire tore through my flesh. Malazan's lips twisted, her cruelty on full display as she drew her blade back. She struck again, stabbing it forward until it sank into the top of my shoulder. The blade cut through the flesh above my collarbone at the same time her other fist cracked against the side of my face.

And the pain began.

15

I walked through the halls, the soles of my shoes clicking against the stone slowly. There'd been a flash of pain from Caldris the night before, a sharp burst of it across his throat. Walking to where Mab had summoned me felt like the worst torture after my bond with Caldris fell silent, the distinct vision of him slamming the window between us shut erupting in my head. I felt confident he'd done it intentionally, that he'd purposefully chosen to suffer alone rather than allowing me to try to bring him some comfort in his suffering.

It was little comfort when the bond remained silent hours later.

Nila had taught me how to walk in the impractical heeled shoes that added to my height, forcing me to pace back and forth until I was fully comfortable. Malachi lingered at my back, and I could feel his impatience as he waited for me to walk faster.

I hurried for no one when I was likely to fall flat on my ass, smirking when I thought of how frustrated he must have found the train of my dress. It forced him to either walk at my side like an equal or keep more distance than normal, lest he risk stepping upon the fabric. The light pink silk dragged over the dark stone behind me. Tiny bursts of light shimmered when the golden beads sewn into the fabric caught the glow of the torches.

The dress was backless, leaving the scars upon my back open to his gaze as I moved. The half where Mab had torn the skin from my body was smooth, unblemished by the physical reminder of what Lord Byron and the High Priestess had done to me all those years ago, but the other side remained marked by the signs of my suffering.

Nila had insisted on it, stating that I could not show them any weakness. Not when it meant they would use it against me, and the vulnerability and shame I felt about my scars would prove to be a weakness.

I would not be the product of what was done to me. I would not reduce myself to a victim when I stood stronger than I'd ever been, while Lord Byron rotted upon the ground in Mistfell. I may be a prisoner still, but I breathed.

That was more than I could say for him.

The fabric covered my breasts, curving toward my belly button on one side with only ribbons wrapping around my torso to connect to the other. The dress hung off my shoulders, draping with light, sheer sleeves that hung around my elbows and fell to the floor beside the skirts. The opposite side of the ribbons split up my thigh, revealing a line of leg as I moved.

Nila had lined my eyes in kohl, making the green of them stand out more. With my hair pulled back away from my face and braided in random sections, I felt like a different woman. Even with the gold circlet resting upon my head and the delicate color of my gown, I didn't feel as vulnerable as I'd anticipated.

I felt like a woman, but I needed to embrace the fact that femininity did not equal weakness. That it was only the standards men placed upon us that made us believe the two were mutually exclusive.

The guards outside the throne room stared at me for a moment too long when they caught sight of me. I kept my

chin raised and my gaze planted firmly upon the doors separating me from my newest torment. They opened slowly as the
three guards heaved them open from the outside. Mab's court
waited as I stepped through the threshold, Malachi following
behind me, with Nila trailing us. She drifted off into the crowd
as I approached the dais, blending in to avoid Mab's attention
as she said my allies often would.

They existed just on the outskirts of her notice, gathering information that they might use if ever there came
a time when someone was strong enough to challenge the
Queen of Air and Darkness. Mab spoke to one of her companions, laughing as the woman cleaned blood from her
blade.

The stain upon the stone floor was still wet in spots where
the blood pooled. The puddle was broad enough that I had no
doubt that whoever had been injured in such a way would be
guaranteed to be dead if they had been a human. I swallowed
as the scent of my mate washed over me. I would know the
smell of his blood anywhere. It thrummed through my veins
in response to the way it had been spilled.

Both women turned their gaze to me slowly, their posture changing as I stopped at the foot of the steps. The hem
of my dress touched Caldris's blood, staining it as I stopped
there and swallowed. My eyes landed on Mab's, understanding flashing between us. She knew that I knew, and we found
ourselves at an impasse, waiting for the other to discuss the
reality of what she must have done to my mate in that very
spot the night prior.

The woman at Mab's side sized me up, dragging her gaze
over my body in a way that felt far too familiar, given that
we'd never met.

"Estrella," Mab said with a smile. She rose to her feet, taking a step away from her throne to look down upon me more fully. "What a delightful surprise to see you enjoying the luxuries court life can provide. I can only imagine what a stark contrast it has been to experience such things after your life in Nothrek."

"It is certainly different," I said, recalling the feel of the oiled, sparkling water on my skin. I would not give her the faintest hint of appreciation, choosing my words carefully and keeping my voice blank.

"So this is the one?" the woman at her side said, stepping forward.

She made her way down the steps, stopping at the last one and waiting just in front of me. She would have towered over me even if she hadn't stood upon a stair, but the added height difference made me feel smaller than I was.

"Yes, Malazan. This is Caldris's not-so-human mate," Mab agreed, watching our interaction.

I glanced over Malazan's shoulder, finding Mab's lips tipped into a smirk. Whatever game I'd stepped into, whatever knowledge I was lacking, this woman clearly had a reason to hate me. Her eyes heated with disdain as she studied me, stepping down the final step and making her way around me. She made sure to step upon the fabric of my train, tearing it slightly as she went.

She hummed, reaching out with a hand to capture a single lock of my dark hair. Her own blonde hair shimmered in the candlelight as she stepped before me once more, her skin matching in fairness.

"I suppose you can only do so much to dress up a pig." She turned her back on me, making her way back up the dais as the crowd chuckled.

A wave of insecurity filled me, leaving me feeling once again like an intruder in a land of pompous luxury. I would never fit in there, but as much as I wanted to find a place to call home, I didn't want it to be this place bathed in cruelty. Nila's words rang in my ears—her warning that this was exactly what they would do.

Women did not insult the attractiveness of those they thought beneath them. They insulted those they perceived to be a threat, wielding their own insecurity as a weapon against them.

"How long have you desired my mate for yourself?" I asked, making Malazan freeze in place.

The air around her went still, a chill creeping out from her as she spun with that unnatural speed only the Fae possessed. Hatred blazed in her eyes as I held her gaze.

"I have had your mate far more times than I care to count," she said, the words dripping from her mouth like venom.

I waited for the moment when pain came from the admission, but Caldris's past had stopped having the power to hurt me once I acknowledged how he felt about me. Nameless women in his past didn't matter, because no sex could compare to the bond we shared.

They were nothing but a distant memory, no longer a threat to us or my confidence in our relationship. I could not continue to punish him for his conquests or bed partners before I'd even been born, and there was freedom in no longer allowing them to have any power over me.

"You and half the realm, it seems. But it is me who will share his bed for the rest of his days. You are one of countless others who will never again know the way his body feels, and you never knew the truth of *him*. He lives within me, his soul as much a part of me as mine," I said, pausing as I delivered the final blow to her confidence.

I might not have done it if I hadn't known she would already be my enemy, but nothing I could say or do would change my fate where her jealousy was concerned. I smiled sadly, my eyes filling with pity. "You are nothing to him, whereas I am his entire world. Dressed up pig or not."

"You insolent, little shit—" Malazan snarled, spinning to face me fully as she took a step in my direction.

"This conversation grows tiresome," Mab said, the words making Malazan hesitate in her hurry to get to me. "It is not your bond to Caldris that interests me, and I should like to get to know the parts of you that are not connected to him. Take off her collar, Malachi."

"But my Queen—"

She turned a glare to him.

"Estrella, your mate is severely weakened and injured at this moment. You will never harm me more quickly than I can end his life, and with him out of your sight, you won't have any warning before I kill him. Harm me, or even attempt it, and you will be alone in this world. Do you understand?"

I ground my teeth together, toying with the idea of trying to decipher any deception to her words. There was none to be found, at least not easily, and I'd already known as much from the pain I'd felt the night before.

"What have you done to him?" I asked, gritting my teeth as I shifted my feet.

His blood coated the bottom of my shoes, making it feel as if he was still with me, even when I could not sense him. I'd know if he was gone from this world, but why did he continue to shield me from him?

"I think it pertinent that you worry more about yourself for now. Caldris is still alive for the moment. That's all you need to know. Understood?" Mab said.

"Yes," I hissed, bowing my head forward as Malachi swept my hair over my shoulders.

He grasped the back of the collar, the click of the hidden lock separating as he opened the heavy iron. He drew it away from my neck, guiding it away from the front of my throat. My eyes closed as I breathed deeply, feeling warmth flood my Fae Mark. I turned my head toward it, opening my eyes slowly as I stretched my arm, reveling in the way the golden light shimmered like stars.

Raising a stare at Malazan, I watched her flinch back the moment my eyes met hers. I could only imagine what she saw, wondering if the same thing filled them as it had that night in Blackwater when I'd banished the stars from the sky.

"What is she?" she asked Mab, her voice a breathless whisper.

"I have every intention of finding out," Mab said as Malachi brought me the chair from the day before.

I glared down at the iron shackles hanging from the arms, wondering if she'd freed me for only a few moments to make her grand show to her court. She didn't banish them as she had before, allowing them to stay and watch as I walked around the side of the chair and lowered myself into it.

Mab stared at me in silence, and I couldn't shake the knowledge that we were waiting for something. That whatever came would be even worse than before.

A single snake slithered across the throne room floor, making its way to my feet and rising onto its tail to stare at me.

"I want to know what's inside that pretty head of yours, Little Mouse. Unfortunately, I cannot rely on you to just do the easy thing and tell me."

The snake wrapped around my ankle, slithering over my skin as it climbed up my leg and settled in my lap. I swallowed back my nerves, fearing snakes for the first time in as long as I could remember.

This one looked at me as if I was something to devour, as if it was entirely under Mab's control. The temptation to test who it would obey was strong within me, but I shoved it down. Some secrets were better left in the dark, and I had to protect mine to the best of my ability.

He climbed up my arm, wrapping around my bicep until his mouth lay against my shoulder and his tongue flicked out to tease my neck. His eyes connected with mine, leaving me with no doubt that he knew what I was. That wherever my affinity for snakes came from, he recognized me as being like him.

Still, his teeth sank into the flesh of my neck. Blinding pain followed the puncture wounds, the heat of his venom filling my veins. Reaching up to grasp him, I moved to tear him away from my throat.

"Ah, ah, ah," Mab warned with a tsk. Her voice turned mocking, her eyes clouding over like a snake on the verge of shedding her skin. "I would hate for Caldris to pay the price of your insolence."

"You would hate no such thing," I hissed.

I lowered my hand to the arm of the chair and gripped it to keep myself from tearing the snake free. The heat spread, filling my head with a grogginess that felt unfamiliar. I couldn't shake the dream-like state it induced, couldn't break free from the mist swirling in my mind. The throne room disappeared until only a room filled with steam in the night sky remained.

Mab stood on the other side of it, her voice carrying across the emptiness that lay between us as she spoke.

"What are you?" she asked, the command pulsing up through my body from the point where her snake had sunk its teeth into me.

In the same way the snakes controlled her victims, binding them to her will, that very venom existed within me for the moment. I felt her will pressing down on me as I gritted my teeth, molten lava following when I didn't answer quickly enough.

"I don't know!" I screamed, bowing my head forward as the snake adjusted his bite to get his fangs even deeper. I was still screaming when the mist faded to a moving portrait in my mind. There was only the faint vision of Mab beyond it, her eyes glowing with an eerie white.

The day at Blackwater filled my head, the moments where the moon and stars had faded from the sky replaying like a memory. Whatever power the snakes gave Mab, as the scene played out, her eyes moved as if she was watching it in her head. My fingers twitched in response, the memory of that all-consuming rage washing over me as if I was back on the bridge once again, discovering the lifeless body of a human boy who had been entirely innocent and died for *nothing*.

There were no golden threads hiding in the mist. There was nothing for me to grasp onto to unleash that rage as my Fae Mark glittered in the dim lighting.

Mab didn't seem appeased by the memory she'd brought forth, making the rest of my journey toward Alfheimr skim through my head quickly as she searched for the answers I couldn't provide.

I fought, struggling against the hands moving through my memories, rifling through them as if they were hers to command. An eternity seemed to pass, my blood boiling with the venom her snake kept within me. She rifled through weeks of memories, flashing across them quickly. She paused every moment Caldris stared down at me with affection, noting the love he showed, and I could practically hear her planning to use it against him.

If love was weakness, then what Caldris felt for me would be his ruin.

She paused when she found the blight dying in the snow, her eyes widening as I approached. I reached out with shimmering fingers to touch the feathers of the bird, his eyes glowing with gold once more as if it recognized me.

"Through death comes life." My voice echoed through the mist between us.

The white in Mab's stare faded suddenly as she reared back. Her snake released my neck finally, the mist around me fading slowly as the venom no longer pumped through my veins, stagnating within and leaving me weak.

I rolled my head to the side, finding Mab standing before me and staring down at me. Her mouth was hidden by the hand she'd raised to worry her bottom lip between her talon-like nails, shredding the skin that healed as soon as it bled.

"Did you find your answer?" I asked, my head filled with a dull, throbbing ache.

Having her rifle through my memories wasn't pleasant in the slightest, and I could only feel gratitude that the ferryman and the mysterious golden-eyed man had stayed out of her sight—that she'd stopped before she uncovered them.

I had a feeling they would provide more answers than my life ever could.

"Nothing possible," she said, brushing her hands down the front of her dress.

I felt like death warmed over, like I might collapse from the pressure remaining in my head while she was perfectly poised.

"Then why stop?"

"The mind is a delicate thing," she answered, stepping forward until she waited just beside my chair. "To push too hard would be to break it, and I don't desire that for you."

"Yet," I said, continuing her words in the only natural course. She might not have spoken the threat aloud, but it lingered there, waiting for me.

"I've no desire to see you become useless, Estrella," Mab said, a smirk playing on her lips. "You're worth far more to me, alive and bound." She stepped around the edge of my chair, making her way toward the massive doors to the throne room. "Come. We'll be late for dinner, and I would hate for you to miss it."

***

My body sagged as I followed at Mab's heels. All attempts at the composure Nila had tried to instill in me had fled with the venom making me sway on my feet. The velvet of Mab's gown trailed over the blue limestone at her feet, creating a line that I focused on as I walked behind her. Malachi caught me when I stumbled to the side, a hand bracing at my elbow.

I jerked away from the touch sluggishly, shifting myself off balance as I tumbled to the opposite side of the hallway. My hand landed upon one of the statues lining the walls, the figure of a woman standing atop a pillar staring down at me as I turned my gaze up to look at her face.

"Her name was Sarilda. She was the Goddess of War, before I killed her in her sleep," Mab explained, appearing at my side.

I turned to face her slowly, my vision dancing as the hallway swayed. The vision of two of them flashed before me, making me sick to my stomach as Mab placed a steadying arm beneath mine.

"Why would you kill her?" I asked.

The statue depicted a woman with long hair, her body encased in armor and a shield and sword in her hands. I supposed the real question wasn't why she'd killed her, but why she'd done it in such a cowardly way.

Mab paused, staring up at the statue of the Goddess with a curve to her lips. It was almost a genuine smile, as close to respect as I'd ever seen on her face.

"She was loyal to Alastor, Twyla's late husband. She is one Goddess I would not have stood a chance against in a fair battle. So while we were in the Autumn Court for *Mabon*, I slipped a drop of serpent's venom into her wine at dinner, and then I crept into her room while she slept it off, and I cut her heart from her chest and fed it to my snake."

"You have no sense of honor, do you?" I asked, shaking my head.

It only served to make me stumble, and my hatred over the fact that Mab was the sole thing keeping me standing grew. I adjusted my grip on the statue, holding onto her more tightly than before.

"Surely, you've noticed the statues that line the halls of Tar Mesa? Each one of them represents a God, a Goddess, a creature, or a Sidhe that I have slaughtered in my quest for power."

She stretched her hand across the front of my face, touching a black nail to the bottom of my jaw and using it to turn my languid head to face her.

"I have been playing this game for longer than you've been alive, Estrella. You cannot win. I like to think Sarilda and I might have been an incredible team had circumstances been different. Instead, she is dead, her magic wasted. But there is still time for you and me to change our path. This world will never give us what we deserve. We must take it."

"I will never become the very thing that I hate," I said, my words slurring as I stared up at the statue of Sarilda.

I imagined she might have felt similarly if Mab had given her the choice. I imagined that was precisely why she hadn't.

"Why put them on display like this?" I asked, my thoughts sluggish.

I needed sleep, but Mab's warning about how she'd slain Sarilda in her sleep meant it wouldn't come easily when I could finally find my way to my bed. I choked back my dread of such things, focusing on staying awake on my feet and not collapsing to the limestone in a puddle.

My gaze turned upward as I waited for her answer, finding the metal chandeliers descended from the ceiling. One hung in a circle above me, making me feel like I existed within it as the stack of candles got smaller in a cone shape toward the wooden beam above my head.

"Why would I not? Bodies rot, but these trophies last forever. They serve as a reminder to all who walk these halls—of what happens to those who oppose me."

She gripped my elbow with her free hand, using the hook of hers within mine and her hand upon mine to guide me away from the statue of Sarilda. I kicked off the heeled shoes Nila had dressed me in, toeing them to the side as I walked. Mab didn't comment as I forced my bare feet across the cold stone, letting that ground me more fully.

In my haze, I barely registered the fact that she walked with me at her side. Not as a victim trailing behind her, but assisting me as an equal for a moment, as if she wanted me to experience what life here could be in my venom-induced stupor.

"Why are you helping me?" I grumbled, glancing over my shoulder to where Malachi looked disgusted by my place at his queen's side, certain he would be more than willing to drag me across the stone. I turned my eyes forward and focused on putting one foot in front of the other.

"Maeve was meant to be my heir," she said, her nails gripping into my arm just a little too tightly. They indented the skin, leaving curved marks behind when she realized what she'd done and loosed her grip just enough.

"Fallon," I corrected instinctively.

She continued as if I hadn't spoken at all, ignoring the insolence she was growing far too used to. "But she doesn't possess a drop of magic in her blood. There's not a single trace of me in her."

I shifted at her side as she stopped outside a single wooden door. It wasn't as ornate as some of the others at court. Iron details stretched across the vertical wooden planks in the shape of a massive, curved M.

"You hardly need an heir if you never intend to step down from your reign," I said.

The observation hung between us as she glanced down at me. I kept my eyes forward, ignoring her pointed stare on the side of my face. I didn't dare ask where Fallon was, what Mab had done with her if she was such a disappointment. In my stupor, there was nothing I could have done to help her, anyway.

It was a battle for another day, a question for when I was confident I could understand the answer. It felt as if all the admissions of this walk would slip through my fingers by morning, lost to the haze of the venom circulating in my blood.

"An heir is not only a necessity, but a symbol of stability. In the event that something does happen to me, it will reassure my loyal followers that there is someone who will take my place. Someone strong enough to fill my shoes and keep hold of the kingdom in the same way I have," she said, waiting for me to look at her.

I swallowed, my hand trembling as I finally turned to meet her stare.

"I would have considered naming you my heir if I thought you would proceed as I have, but you've made it very clear you have no intention of doing so. *That* is what you reject at every opportunity. The ability to rule over the world that sought to break you. But it's not meant to be, so I suspect I will have to try again one day."

"But you killed your mate," I objected, comforted by the knowledge that she could not produce a second heir without him. The witch's curse had done more than just limit all the Fae from producing more than one child. It had made it so that she had condemned herself to her *one* chance at an heir she deemed worthy.

"I don't need the child to be my blood, just for it to be strong enough to take my place and for it to be at my disposal from a young enough age that I can mold it to my image," she said, pausing as a gleeful smile transformed her face.

There was only a moment of hesitation before she turned a sly glance my way, making everything inside of me freeze to solid ice beneath the weight of it—the horrid intent washing over me.

"Perhaps I will allow you and Caldris to complete your bond one day. Just imagine it, the child you would bear with the God of the Dead." She sighed, reveling in the horrified gasp that erupted from me.

Everything in me raged, the revelation angering that monster that lurked within me. She rose up in fury, and ice so cold it burned flooded a path through my veins. I felt it move through me, felt it slowly begin to burn away the remaining traces of venom in a path that stemmed from my center and reached each of my limbs as they thrummed with golden light.

"I have no intention of having children," I said.

Her words solidified that truth. I would not bring a child into this world, not until Mab and her evils were gone from it.

I held her stare as her nostrils flared and she stared down into my eyes, her malice slithering through me. "And I would sooner burn this world to ash than ever allow you to lay eyes upon any child of mine."

"We shall see. The Fates work in mysterious ways. You are here for a reason," she said, abandoning her hold on my elbow to grasp the door handle. "If they want you to have a child, you will have one. No matter what precautions you take to prevent it."

Unless we didn't complete our bond.

The thought danced in my head; but doing so was the only chance of freedom. It was our only chance at being whole and one in the way I wanted more than anything. In the way Caldris had dreamed of for centuries.

I couldn't deny him that.

Mab pulled open the door, revealing a room lit only by a few candles spread throughout the room and the light of the twin moons shining in the window. They were curved into crescents that night, gleaming in the distance. The Court of Shadows was carved into one of the rolling Faerie hills of Tar Mesa, and the valleys between them were filled with white sand that seemed to glow beneath the light of the moons shining above. The other hills were formed out of white rock, pale and gleaming and rounded, but the Fae had carved the symbols of the Primordials into the sides: the stars and the sun, mountains and the ocean, belladonna and skulls. Like a rolling sea of white rock and sand, it was everything light, whereas I'd expected nothing but inky black and shadows.

I'd heard legends of the Fae existing within the hills and mountains in Nothrek before the time of the Veil, but I found it difficult to believe that anyone would knowingly choose to exist in the darkness forever.

"You cannot have shadows without the light," Mab said, stepping around me to approach the seat at the head of the table.

Sidhe surrounded it, their plates empty as they waited, and their wine goblets full as they sipped and chatted aimlessly. Silence descended the moment they looked up and found Mab staring back at them. The entire room rose to bow or curtsy for the Queen of Air and Darkness as she moved to her seat.

She took it gracefully, glancing around the long, rectangular surface crafted from the finest wood and giving a brief nod. They moved to sit immediately, their gaze snagged on her and stayed planted there.

I had no choice but to take the place at her side, sandwiched between her and Malachi, where he moved in synchronization with her. I glanced around the table, seeking out the bright, shocking blue eyes that would give me any level of comfort in a room surrounded by my enemies.

Caldris was nowhere to be found, and my thoughts immediately went to searching for him down the bond once again. I felt the vaguest sense of him nearby, felt his steady heartbeat, but couldn't seem to place him beyond the mere fact that he lived. I searched the table for Fallon next, not finding her either as I settled more fully into my chair.

I picked up the metal goblet beside my plate, staring down into the ruby liquid inside and placing it beneath my nose so that I could smell it.

"We've discussed this, Little Mouse. Our food cannot trap you here if you are not human," Mab said, drawing a sip of her own wine.

"I was more concerned with what might be hiding within it," I said, taking a quick sip of the sweet drink.

The berries and grapes washed over my tongue, that slightly bitter flavor hitting the back of my palate as I braved a second taste. Each swallow went down hard, my body revolting against the potential venom after Mab's story in the hall.

Two Fae women made their way around the room, depositing food onto the plates in front of us. Tiny white pumpkins filled with some sort of cream-based soup sat upon my plate, a fried meat crumbled across the surface.

"Eat. You'll need your energy," Mab commanded ominously, picking up the spoon beside her plate and dipping it into the soup.

I did as ordered; my hunger finally becoming too much for me to resist. I wouldn't thank her for feeding me, but her tests and prodding and torture had long since begun to take their toll. I couldn't fight back if I was half-starved.

I raised my spoon, dunking it into the soup cautiously and forcing myself to take a careful bite despite my hunger. Even after all these weeks, the Priestess and Lord Byron's commands about manners rang in my head. A constant reminder that I would be beaten if I abandoned such formalities in my haste to just eat. I was no stranger to hunger, having become well-familiarized with it in my years spent working in Mistfell.

The cream of the soup was pleasing, thick and flavored with a subtle hint of cheese as I ate it spoonful by spoonful. Around the table, small talk resumed as the Fae ate, but I ignored them in favor of making quick work of my meal. I wanted to eat my fill and return to my rooms as quickly as I could.

I sputtered as a hand touched my thigh. The thin fabric of my dress did next to nothing to keep the violation from sinking inside of me. My spoon clattered against my plate as I dropped it, turning an incredulous look to Malachi, who smiled at me as he leaned in. Turning my head away, I flinched back from the feeling of his lips brushing against my jaw. The faintest bite of his teeth touched my skin, hard and threatening, as I chanced a concerned glace toward his queen.

"He wants to fuck you," Mab said with a shrug, bringing another sip of wine to her mouth as I did the same. The wine went down hard as I swallowed, fighting back the urge to vomit up my dinner. "And they want to watch." She nodded to the table, to all the guests who I realized were watching Malachi rub his nose against my jaw.

It felt like a tease, like he meant it to be affectionate. But he and I both knew it was a deception; we both knew how much he hated me for killing his brother.

Fucking me wasn't about sex. It wasn't about my body or any sort of desire. It was about violating me, about having the part of me his brother hadn't successfully taken.

"That didn't work out so well the last time," I snarled, leveling him with a glare.

His eyes were hard as he stared back at me, his mouth twisting into a cruel smile.

"This is a formal event. He won't be attempting to achieve that in the same manner his brother did. All you need to do is say yes, and he'll make it feel good for you. He'll lay you out upon the table, and your pleasure will become our dessert," Mab said as Malachi slid his hand higher on my leg.

His fingers brushed against the highest part of my thigh, making me reach down to still his hand with a tight squeeze. I dug my nails into his hand, relishing the feeling of his blood beneath them as I broke skin.

"And if I say no?" I asked, pursing my lips. Saying yes would never be an option, not when the thought of anyone but my mate touching me made me both murderous and sick to my stomach.

Mab shrugged. "Then he'll hurt you. Dinner requires entertainment, wouldn't you say? As the new Fae to join our table, it is only natural that you should provide it tonight."

She stared back at me, her will pressing down on me. She wanted to command me to allow myself to be violated, and I suspected it had even less to do with me than I'd originally expected. Allowing myself to be violated would punish Caldris. It would hurt him and break him.

Silence passed between us as she waited for my answer, as the table of Fae I didn't know watched and waited for the answer I would give.

"I will never willingly allow anyone to touch me who is not Caldris. You know that," I said, raising my chin to her in defiance.

Malachi sighed, lifting his hand from my thigh. He pulled a dagger from his sheath, cutting the fabric of my dress sleeve and tearing it off my body as the shimmering feeling of magic coated the air.

The last time I'd felt something similar, Caldris had revealed himself at the battle in Calfalls, dropping his glamour for the first time. I glanced around the room, looking away from Malachi as he pressed the tip of his blade into my wrist. As I watched, Mab waved a hand toward a male on her other side. The glamour faded off him, disappearing into wisps of shadows that floated away. My mate's eyes stared back at me; the other Fae male having vanished as the glamour melted away to reveal him.

"You two are dreadfully boring, always choosing loyalty," Mab said, the faintest hint of a pout in her voice.

"Then perhaps you should move on from this tedious game," I said, wincing as Malachi slid his blade beneath my skin.

He cut through it carefully, making a circle around my entire wrist as I bled onto the white plate beneath me.

"Perhaps we should cut the bond from your skin. Will you still be Fae Marked if we do?" Malachi asked.

He slid the flat edge of the blade into the gash he'd cut in my skin, slowly fileting it off my wrist. Nausea swirled in my gut. The bright, searing pain of his blade sent a ripple of fire straight to my head. My arm felt as if it were on fire, the agony so intense that my vision went white.

I gritted my teeth, swallowing against the pain and refusing to scream as my skin was folded over itself and he made quick work of taking it in a layer back toward my elbow.

"It will grow back," I said, my voice hitching with a pained moan.

Caldris remained silent on the other side of the table, his hands gripping it tightly. He would have fought Malachi had Mab allowed him to move. I could feel the fight in him, his interest in defying that command and the bond that kept him still.

I forced myself to smile at him through my pain, though I was certain it was more of a grimace. My eyes rolled back into my head as the knife carved closer to my elbow.

The vision that burst through my mind was of the night sky surrounding me, that void where I'd seen the golden eyed man. But it wasn't him who waited for me in the flash of that moment. My mate's face stared back at me in shock as he spun through the darkness.

I slammed back into my own body a moment later, Malachi's voice hitting me over the ringing in my ears. He was oblivious to the shocked stare I turned to Caldris, to the open-mouthed expression he gave back to me as the pain returned in a single breath and tore it from my lungs.

"A shame. You look prettier without it," Malachi said, cutting the loose piece of skin free from my arm.

He dropped it to the plate before me. The wet sound of my skin slapped against the plate on impact as he wiped the knife on my upper arm. I howled in pain, staring at the revealed flesh and trying not to vomit. Sweat slicked my brow, cold rushing up my spine as I hung my head forward and sobbed.

A scream tore itself from my lungs once more. In the moment when I thought I couldn't take any more, when I would pass out from the pain, the wound pulsed with a golden chill, and my skin healed over my flesh once again, my Fae mark untainted.

I smiled in relief as Malachi glared at it, my features drooping with exhaustion.

16

Caldris

I strode down the stairs, passing the doorway to the dungeons that had housed Estrella and me for a week. Pushing on the hidden spot on the wall, I watched as the single panel of limestone retracted into the wall. The wall groaned as it slid against the floor; the part hidden beneath the alcove of the stairs retreating and sliding to the side to reveal the passageway to the dungeons of the forgotten.

I grabbed a torch off the wall as the door slid back into place behind me, sealing me into the depths and darkness of Tar Mesa. I stepped out of the entryway and into the place that rivaled Helheim itself.

The ceilings in this part of the palace were high, carved beneath the ground of the rolling hills of Faerie itself. My father's statue emerged from the wall at my right, half his face revealing the skeletal form of his true nature. This was the place where the Court of Shadows imprisoned humans, where they went to waste away until they died, and he and Mab had modeled it after the entrance to Helheim.

It was a mockery for his statue to be here, for the woman who had slain him to put it in the one place in Alfheimr that mimicked the place of his true dominion.

The skeletal form cut a line down the center of his nose; the other half of the stone carved into a smooth, polished surface of his skin. The skin he so often wore when ruling over his court, before his wife had taken over. Before she'd been furious to find her husband had a mate, and that she was the Queen of the Winter Court.

The two of them together would have proven unstoppable at the time, and Mab would have been forced to return to her brother in the Summer Court. She had no claim over my father's court outside of their marriage, and the moment that dissolved, she stood to lose everything.

Everything she had fought to achieve. Everything she had killed for.

In one of my father's hands, he held the exact replica of the sword that was normally strapped across my back. The one remaining part of him I was allowed to carry. Mab had stripped it from me when I returned to court to save Estrella in that throne room.

I hadn't seen my favored weapon since. I doubted I would until the moment she needed to send me away from her court on whatever mundane mission suited her fancy.

In my father's other hand, he clutched the head of a cyclops by the hair. The enormity of it always stole the breath from my lungs, grateful that the remaining of their kind had long ago been locked within the confines of Tartarus. Its eye was still open, centered in his massive forehead, even though Sephtis had severed his head from his shoulders. The skin around that eye it was folded, creased with wrinkles that seemed to follow a path from his enormous pointed ears. The rest of his mouth was occupied by a massive mouth, his rotting lips peeled back to reveal a wide line of jagged teeth. His mouth was twisted into a hysterical smile to accompany the fact that the cyclops were always laughing.

Laughing as they brought their feet down upon the Sidhe, crushing them beneath legs as thick as trees. Moss grew off their backs, fading into thin black hairs that trailed up their necks and stopped just below their heads. The cyclops' tongue protruded from his open mouth, ready to catch his next prey and make a morsel out of him.

I turned away, determined not to dwell on the fact that my father had never been given the privilege of meeting my mate. He'd never know what it was to see me happy, to know that the love he could never hold for himself had rested within my arms.

That she would do it all over again, and that I would do whatever it took to make sure that was our norm.

The walkway was smooth until it dropped off the side, plunging into the depths below. The valley was filled with smoke, the result of the fires burning to keep the prison warm. It was too hot, nearly suffocating as I made my way to the crude steps carved into the cliff face. The rocks shifted as I stepped down them, hurrying as quickly as I dared and only casting a brief glance over the edge.

Mab waited at the bottom, turning her pale face to look up at me as I continued down the steps. She'd summoned me to do my duty, to deliver the souls of her prisoners into the afterlife, but I hadn't stopped to consider who she might have housed in the worst part of her prison.

There was no iron down here, nothing to prevent a Fae from escaping. The cells found in this part of Tar Mesa were intended for the lesser beings, the ones who weren't strong enough to escape regular shackles and chains.

The bodies of Mab's latest slaughter lay spread throughout the ante chamber, scattered around the fire at the center. The dirt floor had long since turned to mud, the blood of her victims soaking into the ground beneath my feet as I stepped off the last of the stone steps.

There were nearly a dozen dead, but the crying from the narrow passage told me that the cells were still far from empty.

"Don't look at me like that," Mab said, rolling her eyes toward the ceiling. I didn't know why she bothered. We both knew she couldn't see past the cloud of smoke that lingered at the mouth of the valley. "This wouldn't have been necessary if that mate of yours wasn't so infuriatingly *good*."

"My mate would never have wanted this," I snapped, sighing as I realized where Mab had found the humans to slaughter. They were some of what remained of the group who joined us on our journey, what remained of Adelphia's companions and those who had welcomed Estrella to join them in their revelry before the Veil fell.

The children of the witches who had left to try to find her when Brann had stolen her from the rebellion in the night.

"Exactly! Her humanity makes her weak when she could be powerful beyond our wildest dreams. Instead, she worries over the lives of creatures that will die in the blink of an immortal eye. Their lives are so short, nothing in the wheel of time. Why does she care what happens to these irrelevant creatures?" Mab asked, pressing the toe of a black boot against the hand of the closest corpse. The man didn't twitch, his throat ripped out by Mab's shadows, the gaping hole still bleeding.

Mab's undertaker waited against the wall, leaning against the stone and holding the three-pronged pitchfork he would use to shove the corpses into the flames the moment I left with their souls. There would be no careful burial, no return to the earth for those who died in this place.

It was perhaps the worst of all of Mab's crimes against them.

Drawing my coin purse from my pocket, I pulled two pieces of gold out and squatted beside the first corpse. The man stared at the ceiling, his eyes blank and unseeing as I deposited the first coin onto his eye, pressing it deeper into the socket so that it might stay long enough for me to see his soul to the ferryman. I tucked the other into my pocket, tethering the soul to my being as he appeared to me.

Barely there, he swayed in the breeze that came off the river entrance as I proceeded to repeat the process with the other prisoners.

"Because every life matters. Every soul matters in this world. I doubt you care what my mate thinks of others, but I could tell you exactly why I think she infuriates you so."

I moved to the next body, placing a golden coin upon the woman's eye as I turned to look over my shoulder at Mab. Her lips pursed, her tongue running over her teeth as she rolled her eyes.

"And why is that, my darling stepson?"

"Because Estrella is living proof that you can be both powerful *and* kind. She is your reminder that you didn't need to sacrifice your soul to be granted the power you have. After ruling for centuries, Estrella is your penance. She has the potential to be everything you have fought to become, everything you have clawed your way through life to achieve. She has been given that for merely existing, and where your people hate you for what you have forced yourself to become..." I paused, watching as Mab's eye twitched. It was the subtlest sign that I'd struck a nerve, that I'd been correct in my assumption.

No matter how many centuries Mab had lived, everyone held onto the insecurities that plagued them as a child. Mab remembered how it felt to be second best, to be the dark child to her brother's golden light.

Just. Like. Estrella.

"They will love her until their dying breath," I finished, watching a shudder work through her body. As if the chill of my words crept up her neck, forcing her to acknowledge the truth of them.

"Perhaps I'll kill her first," she said, her voice cold as she snapped at me.

I continued my work, depositing my golden coins before I finished and stood before her.

"Maybe you will. If you were smart, you probably would," I admitted, and it was a small comfort that if Estrella left this world, I would go with her. Our blood vow worked in the best of ways, ensuring that I would never be without her. "I felt her horror when she was with you. Knew it didn't relate to pain for once. It didn't take much for me to comprehend what you might have said that would elicit such a reaction from the woman I love. I know her, but even beyond that, I know you. I have spent centuries watching you collect children, watching you prey on the weak. You cannot get what you want from her if she is dead."

"And what is it I want so desperately that I would allow her to live?" Mab asked, lacing her fingers together as I took a single step toward the souls waiting to go into the canal. To float down the river while I rowed my boat to where the ferryman waited at the entry to the Void. The Styx flowed just outside the cavern, waiting to take us there.

"Our child," I said, a smile curving my lips as her mouth dropped open in dismay.

I may not have been able to speak to my mate, I may not have been able to hear her direct thoughts until the moment when our bond would be completed, but I knew her better than she knew herself.

"You want to bind our child to your will. Children are malleable. You could mold him or her into your image."

"You are my greatest failure. I hope you know that," Mab snapped.

I grinned at the reality that she'd been unable to break me the way she had so many others. That I hadn't changed to suit her purposes.

"I take great pride in that," I said, turning my back on her as I walked to the canal.

A lone rowboat waited for me; a single, double-sided oar placed within the boat. I stepped in, watching as the souls of the dead followed down the steps into the river. They floated in the water, lingering just beneath the surface as their transparent forms almost blended in.

Pushing off the stone with my oar, I rowed myself into the center of the canal and let the current lead me out. The ride was smooth, the water a slow glide as it guided me out from the cavern that housed the worst of Mab's crimes. The fire behind me burned brighter, embers flashing through the air as the Undertaker shoved the first of the human bodies into the flames.

Only when I emerged from the cavern did I draw in a full breath, the fresh air filling my lungs as the boat curved around the river bend. I sailed down-river in silence, left to only my thoughts as the rolling white hills passed me by.

Two centaurs filled their cups in the river, their heads jolting back when my boat came into view. In the distance, the entrance to the Void came into view. Two identical figures loomed overhead, carved into the white marble of the hillside where the river disappeared beneath them. They were an exact replica of the ferryman, cloaked in shadows with hoods that draped down over his forehead. Their arms crossed as they raised them toward one another, swords arching toward the sky.

At their center, two black doors were carved into the limestone of the hill. They were foreboding, unforgiving as they remained shut tight. Only water filtered through the cracks between them.

The ferryman's boat lay across the narrowest part of the river, bones and skulls hanging off the side as he paced from one side to the other. It was no coincidence that Tar Mesa was located so close to the entrance of the afterlife, not with my father's ties to it as the God of the Underworld. It was his job to protect the sanctity of such things, to make sure that the two realms did not bleed into one another.

This was where he'd chosen to lay his head at night. Where he'd decided to position himself so that he could do his duties.

I passed between two of the rolling hills, the white sandstone cracking as it fell into the river. The Ferryman looked up as I approached, stopping his pacing, and those golden eyes landed upon me. Estrella's memory, and the knowledge that this creature I had known for centuries had somehow played a part in the raising of my mate, haunted me.

Had he known that all this time? That each and every day I came to him, waiting for her, he knew exactly who she was? My boat stopped just before his; my oar easing into the water to hold it still as I stood.

Something arched between us, a newfound knowledge that hadn't been there before. At some point, I might have considered the ferryman very close to a friend.

"Some secrets are better left in the dark," I said, grasping the coins from my pocket. I let them fall through my fingers, tumbling into the bottom of his boat as he stared at me.

The souls I'd brought passed by his boat finally, waiting at the entrance to the Void. The river behind the doors gleamed with gold as they opened slowly, allowing the souls to continue in their voyage. The ferryman picked up his oar, prepared to usher them to the Void beyond and deliver them to The Father and The Mother if it was their time.

"Do you love her?"

The ferryman stilled, turning back to face me for a moment. Something almost human passed over the gaunt face that remained unnaturally still.

"Your mate is… unique," he said finally, his voice inhumanly low.

"That doesn't answer my question," I said, wanting the answer for the benefit of Estrella.

She'd mourned her father, spent a life grieving for him. If she was nothing more than a duty to the ferryman, a service to the Fates, then she deserved to know the truth. She deserved the opportunity to carve him from her heart once and for all.

The ferryman cast his eyes to the sky, following the path his pet blight cut through the air. The bird landed upon his shoulder, staring back at him with golden eyes as the ferryman nodded finally.

"We did, but that love will not save her from what the Fates have in store," he said ominously, turning his back on me to signal the end of the conversation.

He rowed his boat through the doors to the Void, and the blight's eerie golden stare held mine until the gates closed behind them.

17

Estrella

Three days passed.

Three days of healing, of recovering from the snake's venom in my veins. The worst of the effects had worn off days prior, but the mental fog and exhaustion lingered. Mab left me in peace, likely knowing exactly what consequences the venom could wreak upon a body. It felt like a test, as if she wanted to see exactly how quickly my body could work through it, but the iron collar at my throat slowed everything to a standstill when Malachi had returned me to my rooms that night.

So I slept, and I slept. Until Mab grew tired of waiting, and Nila arrived to prepare me for the day. The blouse and skirt she selected were far more casual than usual.

Nila and I entered the throne room in the middle of the day, with Malachi at our backs. I'd expected it to be empty save for Mab, but the floor to ceiling windows that bordered the edge of the hall were thrown open, casting the bright light of the sun gleaming off the white sand into the space. Fae I'd never seen worked in tandem, grasping the heavy chains from hooks on the wall and lowering the cages from the ceiling.

The stone floor was now littered with the bodies of Mab's victims. Other Fae worked to pull what remained of the mangled, rotting corpses from those cages to lay them upon the floor. They worked in near silence, the melancholy of such a task pulsing off each of them in waves.

At the back of the throne room, the tallest Fae I'd ever seen stretched toward the ceiling. He dragged a wet cloth over the stone ceiling, cleaning the dirt from it and leaving the rock lighter somehow. I didn't want to think about what manner of debris had coated the porous surface, or what I inhaled every time I set foot in the room where Mab held court.

The body of the Fae female was humanoid. A dark sweep of feathered wings covered the back of the blood-red jumpsuit she wore. Her hair was parted down the middle, flowing in silver cascades along the feathers of those great wings as she scrubbed. She spun as if she felt me staring, and her silver eyes glinted maliciously as they landed on me.

I swallowed, staggering forward when Malachi placed a single hand on my shoulder and shoved me forward. "Get to work."

Nila took my hand, guiding me into the fray, while Malachi lurked by the doors, watching as we moved toward Fallon and Imelda. They were already working to remove Adelphia from the cage that held her remains. Her charred flesh stuck to the metal frame, melted to the ore as if she'd been set on fire right where she hung.

They looked up as I bent forward, leaning into the confines of the cage so that I could pull each strand of hair that remained out of the blood matted to the metal while they worked.

"She decided you needed to be useful in some way too, I suppose?" Fallon asked, breathing through her mouth as she pressed a hand against Adelphia's charred shoulder and *shoved*. The burnt flesh crackled, and then it tore from the rest of Adelphia's body in a strip. Fallon gagged.

"I don't know," I admitted, glancing toward Nila, who nodded as she and Imelda worked on the other side of the cage.

Glancing around the throne room as I worked, I shoved aside the stench of rot and decay as I grasped one of the rags from a bucket of water.

Or rather, what had been water at one point. Dark, inky swirls of blood and gore floated within it now, the clarity and pureness of the water itself long gone in the time the Fae here had been at work cleaning.

I started at the top of the greasy cage, trying not to think of the burned fat and flesh and blood that made the surface rough and uneven. The rag was too soft. I pressed into the cage with all the strength in my body, and the metal groaned as it bent, then gave way beneath me.

A gnome appeared at my side, a spiked, bristled brush in his hands. It was almost as large as he was, the spikes as sharp as any weapon the Mist Guard possessed in their armory. He lifted it up for me.

Accepting it from his hands, I smiled down at him and tried not to think of Lozu and his desire to eat me.

I nodded instead of thanking him as I knelt in front of him.

The blood and gore upon the stone stained the chartreuse skirt Nila had dressed me in. The skirt reminded me vaguely of the pea-green dress I'd worn when I'd escaped Mistfell. It seemed so long ago, like I'd been an entirely different person then.

"It is a pleasure, Princess. We watched you," he said, looking over his shoulder as two other gnomes stepped up behind him. Lozu lingered behind them, his spirit as corporeal as a body despite its translucence as he stared at me beneath the sweep of his hat across his forehead. "You did not object when you were given work beneath your status. You stepped into the fray like you belong."

I smiled softly as he approached my knee, hauling himself up onto it so that he could come to stand in my palm. "Only a ruler who does not deserve her people would think that she is better than them." I stood, allowing him to come to stand upon the cage.

He picked up the rag I'd been using, wiping down the surface with water so that I could follow the path he created and scrub at it with the harsh brush. Bits of burnt flesh scraped from the cage, some dropping to the floor, others flying into my face as I closed my mouth and focused on my work. A gag swelled in my throat, making my tongue feel heavy in my mouth as I fought it back. I would not appear weak—would not seem disgusted by the manner of this work—not when so many in this room had undoubtedly been forced to do worse.

"You must have very different rulers in Nothrek than we have here," he said.

I considered how well he spoke. Lozu's language had been stilted at times, his use of it less advanced. As if summoned, the shade of my dungeon companion stepped into the cage with Adelphia's body. He set to work, picking up the pieces of her that were large enough chunks to be carried out and laying them atop her torso.

"What makes you say that?" I asked, scrubbing each and every one of the bars where they met at the top of the cage. I didn't want to think of how thick the debris would become when I moved lower, of what might shift or change when we hauled Adelphia's body out.

Of the gore that would cover the cage beneath her.

"You have a very different perception of a ruler than we do," he admitted, leaning forward to run his tongue up one of the uncleaned bars. His tongue peeked out from behind those sharp, menacing teeth, dragging over the metal slowly as he breathed deep. When he pulled it away, it was filled with tiny chunks of burnt flesh, the red somehow deeper in hue from the tint of blood.

I ignored it, barely disguising my shudder. "The man who ruled me had me beaten if I did not curtsy deep enough. So, no; I think the humans and the Fae have far more in common than the Queen or my Lord would have wanted us to believe," I said with a scoff, turning to look at Fallon and Imelda as they reached into the cage. They grasped Adelphia by what remained of her legs, pulling her out slowly as pieces of flesh sloughed off. "Cruelty is not solely a Fae trait nor a human trait. It lives in all of us."

"Even you?" the gnome asked, forcing me to level him with a meaningful stare for a moment before I abandoned my brush and moved to help my friends.

"Especially me," I said, glancing toward where Malachi had abandoned his post at the entrance to the throne room. He held a short whip in his hand, cracking it against the floor when creatures did not clean fast enough or work hard enough for his liking.

Everything inside me hardened, tensed, at the sight of that whip—the familiar crack of it through the air making my spine go rigid.

I shoved it down, that beast within me trying to rise to the surface. She met the collar around my neck, snarling and acting as if she could claw her way through it from the inside out as she paced. I dropped the brush beside me, moving to the center of my friends, where they struggled to keep down the bile that rose in their throats.

Reaching into the cage, I slid an arm beneath Adelphia's waist. Something wet and sticky coated my hand as I did, seeping into the fabric of my blouse as I bent over and slipped into the cage. Just far enough to slide my hand around the back of her neck, cradling her head as I pulled her toward the front. Imelda and Fallon grabbed her ankles once again, pulling smoothly to help as I stabilized her upper body and kept the rot from tearing her in two.

When her waist and below were out of the cage, I stepped over her carefully to get out. Using my grip on her, I took her with me as the scent of her death penetrated my lungs. It settled inside of me, making everything inside of me recoil as I got to my feet. Taking her weight with me, bearing it in my arms, I cradled her with her knees draped over my elbow and her head tipped back over the other.

I walked slowly, passing by Fae as I took her to the side of the throne room. There was already a line of bodies piled up there, discarded with as much tenderness as one could give to the rotting corpses that were missing entire chunks. Imelda and Fallon's eyes felt heavy on my back, the two women knowing that while I hadn't known Adelphia well, she'd been the beginning of this journey for me.

She'd been the one to welcome me to something other than the way I'd been raised. She'd been the first to show me that something existed outside the firm control of the High Priest, and that it was *okay* to question everything I'd been taught.

I lowered myself to the floor as I set her down gently, removing my gore-covered arms from beneath her body. My hands raised of their own accord in the same way I'd seen Caldris do for Melian, gently touching her eyelid and closing it so that those unseeing, fogged-over eyes no longer stared at the ceiling.

I hung my head forward, closing my own eyes as I watched her for a moment. Waiting for breath to fill her lungs, for one of the miracles of Faerie to occur.

No movement met my gaze, not even the slightest hitch of breath. I hadn't expected anything less, knew she was too far gone for even the magic that ran through these lands to touch her.

I stood, spinning slowly as my skirts swept against the surface of the stone. My arms were covered in gore, the blood having soaked my sleeves as I raised my head slowly.

The stare of countless Fae met me. I stumbled to a stop, looking from one side of the throne room to the other as my nerves peaked. I didn't know the name of most of the creatures staring back at me, and the ones I did...

They'd been the legends of stories that had driven me to my parents' bed as a girl, the nightmares that made me afraid of the dark until I found comfort in the night.

Eyes of red. Teeth so large, they were closer to tusks. Wrinkled and taut skin.

I heaved a sigh, raising my chin as I took the first step toward Imelda and Fallon. Imelda met my eyes, hers communicating something silently. I held that gaze as I strode forward, keeping my face impassive.

Inside, the swirling in my gut was a mess. The creature within me rose, filling my lungs with her breath. Something in my back cracked, as if she wanted to escape the confines of my body, pushing my spine straighter. Pulling my shoulders back tighter as whispers sounded from the other end of the throne room.

My heart pounded in my chest, as I held that multicolored gaze from Imelda. A bead of sweat dripped down the back of my neck, the precipice of the moment making that creature turn my blood into icy fire.

I took the first step forward, ignoring the pulsing dread coursing through me. That distinct feeling that things had shifted in the moments I'd seen to Adelphia's body. The Fae closest to me shimmered in the shadows in my peripheral vision.

Her face was just two eyes and the slit of a nose, her mouth hidden entirely as her hair fell like feathers to the floor. The red stare of a predator landed on my face, studying me intently as I strode forward. When I moved to pass her, she shifted her weight, slipping one of her feet behind the other and lowering ever-so-slightly as she bowed her head forward.

My lungs seized.

Still, I held Imelda's gaze as I strode forward, the Fae lining up beside me to form a hallway of sorts.

They bowed their heads, leaving me to stride toward Imelda. Even the gnomes dropped their eyes to the floor and kneeled. Imelda smiled lightly, turning her gaze away from me finally to look over at Fallon. My friend, my *sister* without blood, nodded lightly, her lips twisting into a bittersweet smile as she lowered her head into the subtlest of bows.

The remaining air rushed out of my lungs, leaving me gaping as my lips spread into a shocked expression. Imelda bowed her head forward. The last remaining elder of the Lunar Coven and Mab's heir bowing before me stole every thought from my head.

I didn't know what had caused it. I didn't know what I'd done.

Only that part of me wished I could undo it—wished to make them all stop looking at me as if I was something they'd waited for.

Where was my mate?

I pushed down the thread of our bond, only a surge of pride welling in response to my terror. He was no help, no reassurance that they'd forget this moment by morning.

Asshole, I thought, wishing that the bond was more than just the surge of feelings between us. Even that seemed to grow more and more muted with every day I spent in my collar, as if the magic of our mate bond couldn't survive the constant suppression.

I strode past Imelda and Fallon, going to the place where I'd been scrubbing at the cage before everything went still. In the distant other side of the throne room, I was vaguely aware of Malachi barking orders. They reached me in a haze, as if they existed outside the bubble that I'd sunken into in the moment when that first Fae lowered their head.

I picked up my brush, putting all my strength into scrubbing away at that cage. It felt like melting away the wall surrounding me, like every brush of those bristles over the cage mended a tiny piece of the miniscule, bloodstained pieces of my heart.

As if being seen by the creatures I'd once feared no longer terrified me.

But somehow set me free.

Imelda came to my side as the gnome dripped blood-stained water upon the cage for me to scrub. I didn't even know his name, but my throat felt too raw, too hoarse from the emotion choking me, to even ask.

"They see themselves in you," Imelda said, picking up her own rag as she set to helping to clean the cage.

Fallon stepped to the other side, her hazel stare meeting mine as she smiled sadly. I wondered for a brief moment what it must have been like to *know* she was meant to be the heir to this.

And to defect to me, anyway.

"You know what it is to go without. I see it in your eyes. It's a need, a hunger that never fades," the gnome said, reaching out a tiny hand to stop the brush from scrubbing. The bristles pricked his skin, the wounds seeming too large on his hand. "Not many Sidhe would treat a human with the reverence you just showed. Even less would deign to speak to a gnome. Let alone a Sidhe who is the mate of a prince."

His hand left the brush, and I resumed my cleaning. My gaze fixated on the bristles against the metal, on the crystal-clear task in front of me that did not involve the complications of those around me.

"You've given them hope," he said, his voice going distant as he looked out at the throne room and the Faeries who had resumed their work. "That is not something the Llaidhe have had in a very long time, Princess."

"The *Llaidh*e?" I asked, turning to look into the bulbous nose and eyes I could not see. Something in that word scratched beneath the surface, plucking at the scars that lingered there.

"What did you think they called those of us who are Fae but not Sidhe? We are the Llaidhe," he said, his voice hardening at the end.

"The worthless," I said, my jaw clenching as fury made every muscle in my body tense.

That part of me that refused to go back to sleep grumbled, her rage rising at the word from the Old Tongue that I'd never heard used in such a way.

That word would be the first thing I struck from existence if given the chance.

The gnome nodded, his beard twitching with the movement. I could have sworn his lips twisted into a cruel smile, the promise of retribution lurking within it. "You didn't know—"

The whip cracked.

Everybody within the throne room stilled, waiting for the moment of impact. The resulting scream came from the dais. My head turned to follow it.

Feathers floated through the air, drifting toward the stone floor as the giant Faerie crumpled forward. Her hand shot out, catching herself against the very wall she'd been cleaning when I last looked to her.

Malachi stood behind her, swinging his arm back once more. The whip lashed forward, striking against the center of those beautiful wings.

More feathers of ebony drifted through the sunlight as they glistened in the dimming rays coming through the windows.

The other Fae went silent, stepping away, leaving her to the suffering Malachi seemed intent to inflict. I took a step forward, pausing only when Fallon reached out and grasped my arm. She shook her head, the movement a subtle plea.

The whip cracked again; the sound striking me deep within the well. The memories struck me again, the sound of the cane swinging through the air enough to make everything in me freeze. The pleasure coating Malachi's voice as he tossed his head back and laughed was nothing like the silent disapproval of Lord Byron as they broke my skin.

But those beautiful wings tore open the same as flesh, deep lashes cutting through her until blue blood dripped down the wings and onto her red jumpsuit.

I yanked my hand out of Fallon's grip, striding forward as fast as my feet could carry me through the carnage.

These people had suffered enough.

They'd suffered for centuries.

While Malachi got off on their pain. I stepped in front of the giant Faerie, my body feeling painfully small as she dropped to her knees behind me. The throne room shook with her weight, but I held my ground even as Malachi stumbled to the side.

His head tilted to the side as he looked at me, as he took in the fact that I stood between him and his fun. The scent of the faerie's blood washed over me, thick and cool and smelling like the hearth on a winter's night. Her wings shuddered behind me, the sound of those feathers fluttering as she tried to move.

"Move." There was no question in Malachi's order, no hesitation. As if I were the dog and he were the master.

I stood, not so much as twitching when he drew his arm back and snapped the whip for effect. I did not flinch.

I knew the pain of the whip well, knew what my skin would look like when it tore it in two.

"Princess," the Faerie behind me said, her voice soft. There was an urgency in it, a plea for me to leave her.

I would not.

Malachi glared, our standoff coming to a pause as he considered his options. A glance around the room showed the rest of the Fae had closed ranks. They'd moved closer to watch. To whip me would be to make me a martyr, to make me the female who took a beating meant for someone *less*. I knew the moment that realization dawned on him, the trap I'd unintentionally set.

"Take off her collar, pet," someone in the crowd called. A soft murmur of agreement came throughout the room. "Let us see who is still standing when you fight someone who can fight back!"

Tilting my head to the side, I raised my brows in a challenge. A grin played at my lips, because Malachi and I both knew who would emerge victorious from such a fight. He swallowed, winding his whip back around his arm.

"Get back to work," he barked, stepping away from me.

The Faerie behind me shoved to her feet and moved to stand beside me, the bottom tip of one of those magnificent wings brushing against my shoulder.

Thank you, the touch seemed to say.

I brushed one of the ebony feathers with a finger.

You're welcome.

***

Sweat slicked my brow in spite of the chill of winter, the full sun beating down upon the white salt at my feet. The rock beneath the salt and sand and pebbles was firm, nearly impossible to crack as I shoved the pointed tip of the shovel down into it over and over again. The Fae all around me did the same, digging through the impossible hardness of the rock to create shallow graves for those we'd pulled from the cages in the throne room. Adelphia's body had been wrapped in the thinnest of shrouds, a mercy that Malachi rolled his eyes at but allowed when the other Fae went through the motions of a proper burial for those unfortunate souls.

"It's more than many here receive," Imelda said, her soft words carrying upon the wind that blew salt into my eyes. I swallowed as the giant Fae female with the wings, Elli, swung her pickaxe into the ground just in front of me. She hadn't left my side since I'd stepped in front of her, assisting me with the tasks that exhausted me far more quickly than I wanted them to. The immortal strength, the unending power, it seemed to linger just out of reach, thanks to that venom.

I had no doubt that was intentional.

The rock crumbled beneath her blow, leaving me to shovel the shards of it out of the way. The grave formed before my eyes, and it wasn't me but Elli who reached down to pick up Adelphia and lay her body in the hole in the rock.

Imelda stepped up beside me, depositing two golden coins into my hand before she made her way around to the others, who prepared to bury nameless Faeries and humans alike. Tears stung my eyes as Imelda pressed her own coins into the hands of those she passed, aiding the souls of the fallen in their passage to the Void.

I lowered myself into the shallow grave, Elli's hand reaching out to steady me. My own touched hers, barely a baby's grip on her pinky, as I stepped down into the small space beside Adelphia's head. I pressed a coin into each of her eyes, resting them atop the lids I had closed forever.

The first tear fell as I stared down at the woman who had been one of my first friends in a changing world.

"May The Mother guide you peacefully to the meadows of Folkvangr," I said, running a hand over the shroud that covered the worst of the damage to her hair—to her head.

Elli helped me out of the grave, scooping up piles of rock and salt and sand with her bare hands and loading it into the grave.

My friend disappeared from view, returned to the earth so that her body could become something else even as her soul moved on—as she found peace in the afterlife.

My blood burned, begging for me to let my wrath loose upon the world. I turned, looking back to where Malachi watched me, his hands shoved into the pockets of his trousers.

He read the promise in my eyes, the weight of my stare.

I turned away, Elli and Fallon following at my heels as I helped the closest Fae with the grave they dug. My hands bled as I pulled stone out of the way, scraping myself upon the rocks.

The earth seemed to tremble; the ground seemed to shift.

As if it too recognized the monster that simmered in my blood.

18

Estrella

Caldris waited atop the hills above Tar Mesa two days later, the tallest of those undulating masses of curved rock and salt seeming unending as we hiked up the steep side. A male I didn't know well enough to name led the way. Malachi followed at my back as we proceeded in silence.

I hadn't seen my mate in days, hadn't been allowed to visit with him in the time in which Mab spent preparing for the solstice. I'd heard whispers of the coming celebration when Malachi took Nila and me on walks throughout the palace, 'exercising my legs', he'd joked, as if I were no more dog than Fae. I missed Fenrir desperately, but I didn't dare to imply that I cared about the three wolves who had tackled their way into my heart.

Not when Mab could use them against me too. If my love was a weakness to her, then the fewer creatures I revealed my love for, the better. I trusted that Caldris had made sure they were safe, that they'd been able to survive this court and the delicate scheming for the entirety of their lives before I arrived.

They'd continue to do so now that I was here.

A familiar smirk claimed Caldris's face, his eyes softening in the way that I'd come to recognize he reserved for me and only me. His mother hadn't received the same affection, that same indication of the love that thrummed along the thread between us.

Only me.

I sighed, my shoulders slumping with relief. I hadn't even paused to consider the tension in them, the way my body coiled tighter and tighter with every moment that passed in which I was kept away from him. It wasn't natural to have that distance now that I'd accepted what he was to me. I wanted to live the rest of my life held within the safe haven of his arms. He was the only being in this world who had ever managed to make me feel protected without suffocating me. The only one who encouraged me to accept the parts of me that terrified others.

The only one who loved me, monster and all.

The jagged pieces of my heart found a home in his, our souls interlocking.

A male I didn't recognize stopped at his side, but I didn't pause before I stepped into the arms that Caldris spread in perfect time, our bodies moving like two halves of one whole. Those muscular arms closed around me immediately, clamping me against his chest so tightly that I felt like I may never breathe again.

But his scent filled my lungs, the smell of *home* settling inside my soul. When he finally spoke, the gruff words torn from a hoarse throat, it was only to murmur a quiet, "my star." They weren't the purposeful declarations of love he'd given to convince me of his love for me, but the weight of those words settled in me all the same.

The thread between us pulled taut when Malachi grasped my shoulder, tugging me back out of Caldris's grip. Then his other hand went to the collar at my throat. He gripped it, wrapping his hand around the iron as if the burning of his flesh mattered little to him.

The male I didn't know stepped between Caldris and me, his silver eyes holding mine as I snarled. He only grinned, something deep and dark lingering in that stare as he studied me. It wasn't the same as the malicious smile I'd come to recognize in Mab and her loyal children; rather, genuine amusement at the feral agitation that existed within me when being forcibly separated from the mate I wanted to take to bed.

"It has been a long time since I was able to observe the nature of a mate bond," he said, a chuckle leaving his throat.

Caldris's gaze remained pinned on Malachi, on the male who held my collar in his grip, instead of the one who approached me slowly.

"So this is the mate of our mighty Caldris."

Reaching up with a single hand, he grasped my chin between two fingers. His hold was firm enough to tip my face up to meet his stare where he towered over me. His height was so similar to that of my mate that I had to look up, and up, and up to meet his eyes. The green of his eyes glittered like emeralds as he studied me, the smirk fading off his face as he seemed to try to peer inside my soul.

The beast stirred under my skin, pacing as her coldness swept behind my eyes. The male blinked as if he could see it, then that smirk returned. He finally took a step back and slapped Caldris on the shoulder. My mate shifted with the touch, shooting an eye roll toward the male who stood beside him. The casualness in that gesture settled the nervous part of me in our interaction.

"Estrella, this is my cousin Soren," Caldris said, introducing the male.

"The God of Twilight at your service, Princess," Soren said, waving his hand in the flourish of a bow. His eyes held mine as he dipped low, that smirk that was so like my mate's playing at his mouth.

"Cousin?" I asked. I hadn't stopped to consider that Caldris might have had family beyond his mother—a foolish and ignorant thought, considering the centuries of life separating our births.

"My father's nephew," Caldris admitted, sliding his hands into the pockets of his trousers. There was something so ashamed about the gesture, the fact that I knew so little of his life washing over both of us at the same time.

It didn't matter, I told myself.

All that mattered was how much I loved him. The family that may or may not work for Mab was secondary to that.

"Are you quite finished?" Malachi growled at my back, tightening his grip on my collar and tugging it back until it dug into the front of my throat. A growl worked its way up my throat, and my head turned so I could bare my teeth at him.

Soren waved a hand, unbothered by Malachi's impatience, as he stepped away from Caldris's side. "Mab would like you to know that the blight are observing your every move and will report to her far faster than you can make any attempt to save your mate's life, should you decide to misbehave. You are not to leave Malachi's nor my sight while aiding Caldris with the task given to you to assist in the preparations for the Solstice," he said, glancing over my shoulder to Malachi. "Did I get everything? I covered the usual doom and gloom, yes?"

Malachi grunted, his distaste for Soren evident in every motion of his body as he jerked me closer toward him. His hand pressed into the magic of the lock of my collar, the mechanism hissing with air as it dropped and separated.

Malachi was quick to snatch it up, wrapping it within a piece of cloth he pulled from his fur-lined cloak and tucking it into the pocket.

"Get to work," he grunted, nodding his head toward the crest of the hilltop.

Caldris held out a hand for me, and I was left to step toward him as my power rushed in my veins. With each step, it filled me. With each step, the creature within me rose to the surface, the golden threads of fate lingering in every direction I looked.

"What is it we're meant to do?" I asked tentatively as Caldris entwined his fingers with mine. Every place we touched felt whole.

We reached the top of the hill, looking down into the valley formed between the three closest hillsides. The rock was jagged, the very beginnings of steps carved into them as a group of a dozen Sidhe worked at the bottom of the valley. Their hands moved, their bodies slicked with sweat as they motioned and directed as needed. The magic they possessed was limited, a grueling process as they reshaped the landscape of the valley slowly, piece by piece.

I didn't know how long they'd been working, but the crude, bare beginnings of an arena and seating cut into the stone had begun to take shape. I glanced down at my hands, wondering if they thought I possessed that power. But where the threads hung from the sky, hung from the Fae themselves, nothing emerged from the dirt and rock beneath our feet.

Caldris released my hand, guiding me to the front of his body. His arms wrapped around me from behind, cocooning me in his warmth as he turned us away from the makeshift arena in the valley. The sun lingered to my right, shining upon our sides and nearly blinding that eye as it reflected off the surface of the white stone.

But I savored the feeling of it upon my skin, having spent so much time in mostly darkness. Caldris outstretched one of his hands, and I felt the moment he closed his eyes. With me in his arms, he used that single hand pointed toward the ground. Sparks of white left his palm, the snowflakes drifting forward to land on the ground in front of us.

Higher and higher the snow rose, the pile forming the shape of a pillar as Caldris gave himself to that power that existed within him. He created something from nothing, because the magic wasn't just something that was a part of our world. It was something that lived in him, that had made its home beneath his skin.

He blew out a single, shallow breath, and the winds of winter rose through the hilltops in answer. It blew against his pile of snow, sending it billowing toward the river that flowed in the distance.

All that remained when the wind settled was a pillar of ice, standing tall and stretching toward the sky as if it had always been there.

He raised his foot, dropping it down upon the earth beneath us. The rock froze to ice, sending a ripple through the hillside. Malachi and Soren stumbled, slipping on the newly frozen surface as the hill stopped quaking. Cracks spread through the ice like fissures, arcing toward the spot beside the pillar Caldris had already formed. Carving in an x to mark the spot, my mate swept the hair off my shoulder and pulled my hood back so that he could press his lips to the skin behind my ear.

"Create another," he murmured, the words a quiet challenge.

I shuddered, the feeling of that breath on my skin making things tighten low in my body as my mate chuckled knowingly.

I raised a hand, finding the threads flowing off his newly crafted ice and wrapping them around my finger. It came easily, the cold filling my palm as those icy tendrils wrapped me in their embrace.

"I didn't say to use what I'd created. I said to create one," Caldris scolded, laying his hand atop mine. The thread unwound from my fingers, leaving me gaping as I looked at him over my shoulder.

"I can't," I protested. I'd never been able to create from nothing, only to take what already existed and mold it to my will.

"If you rely too much on what is around you, you'll never be able to defend yourself if your opponent controls the situation. Anyone who learns about that weakness will deprive you of the cold and the snow; they'll make sure there are no bodies for you to animate," he said, keeping his words quiet as Soren distracted Malachi with endless conversation from a few paces away. They watched the workers in the valley, the ones who possessed the power to change the ground itself.

"Those Summer Fae in the valley need to have something to change in order to access their magic. They are Sidhe; their magic is limited. But yours is as endless as the depths of my love for you." He raised a hand to my chest, pressing the flat side of his palm against the skin over my heart.

"How do I create from nothing?" I asked, covering his hand with mine. I yielded to that love he spoke of, feeling it pulse through me as his lips moved over the skin of my neck.

"You summon it from within. You've wasted far too much of your life looking for answers in the world around you when you've had them within you all along. Nothing around you can tell you what you are, *min asteren*. Only you can make that choice," he said.

His hand pressed more firmly into my chest, grounding me as he loosed a single sigh, and with that sigh, he released a wave of power that crashed through the hills.

I thought I'd seen the worst of his magic that night in the clearing when he'd summoned a storm great enough to bury the world in snow. I believed I'd seen the worst of it when he slayed his enemies where they stood, making his way to me with the whisper of death surrounding him—shadows melting from his body as if they could not be contained.

I'd known nothing.

The ground quaked beneath him—matching the rhythm of his heartbeat as Malachi finally turned a shocked glance toward us. My heart beat in tandem with his as I let my eyes drift closed, sinking into the feeling of his power as it washed over my skin. As the cold and inky shadows of his magic wrapped me in their embrace, shielding me from the worst of the wind as it whipped around us.

I drew in a breath, the scent of fresh snow and wintergreen filling my lungs. It struck something deep inside me, kindling a flame that had long since waited to be awoken. I felt it slide along the thread between us, turning it to ice as the power waited for one of us to grasp it. He'd given me an influx of it, a taste of what was at my disposal, sending it coursing down our bond so that all I needed to do was reach out and grasp it.

I raised a hand with eyes still closed to the world around us. Cold leaked out of me, pouring from that hand as if it needed the release. As if Caldris had filled our bond with so much of the winter that it needed to escape, to wreak havoc upon those around us.

"Open your eyes, my star," he murmured, and I flung them open suddenly.

It was not the soft, billowing snowfall that Caldris had summoned when he'd built the first tower that I saw when I opened them, but a solid block of ice as it rose from the rock in front of me. The rock split, cracking to allow for the ice as it stretched toward the sky.

Whereas his creation had been gentle, a stunning process to watch that alluded to centuries of practice with honing his gifts, mine was a crude, violent birthing of ice. It tore from the rock as if the world itself had not wanted to release it, stretching toward the sky until it stopped at the precise moment it reached the same height as Caldris's.

Twin pillars of ice stared back at us as his power settled as quickly as it had risen, retreating to its master and filling him with it once again.

He released my chest, taking my hand in his as the warmth of his body refilled my chilled palms. Soren's eyes were heavy on the side of my face as I turned to face Caldris, his observation feeling far too significant for my taste.

"Was that really necessary?" Malachi asked, his clothing ruffling as if he'd needed to brush snow off his cloak.

I didn't bother turning to look at him as Caldris leaned in, touching his lips to mine in what started as the gentlest murmur of a kiss. He deepened it only when I moaned into his mouth, that surge of power within me making me want more.

More of him. More of his magic.

More of everything.

The creature within me felt starved for him—desperate to shred the leather and armor that covered his body. He grinned as that need pulsed between us, thrumming down the bond before he regrettably pulled away.

"There are two more waiting for you," Malachi ordered with a sneer.

Caldris merely took my hand in his, stepping up to my side as he waved a hand. Shadows appeared in front of us, a vortex of darkness and death and all the things most people avoided.

Caldris stepped into it, guiding me into the portal he'd summoned. It swallowed me whole as Caldris guided me through the eternal darkness, the world that existed just beyond ours. The shapes and figures in the realm we'd just left existed just outside the shadows, their light filtering through when I really looked.

Then it was over, my feet stood upon solid land on the other side of the valley.

I looked back at the distance we'd crossed as time slowed, the cavern where the Summer Court Fae worked behind me rather than in front of me suddenly.

Malachi glared at my mate as he summoned a ball of flame to surround him. He disappeared into it a moment later, then the brush of heat struck against my cheek as he appeared at my side within seconds.

"I don't know what I did to give you the impression you were permitted to shadow walk with her," he said, shrugging his shoulders and adjusting his clothing.

"I don't know what I did to make you think I care," Caldris said, his voice entirely deadpan as he faced forward, Malachi all but an afterthought.

He used his grip on my hand to tug me forward, curling himself around me as Soren appeared at our sides. The air around him was a thrumming mix of purples and golds, like the last vestiges of the sun on the horizon as it faded away into a glimmer.

His eyes landed on mine, that wicked stare probing into me in a glance that felt endless, eternal. Caldris's arms tightened around my waist, a silent warning to accompany the growl that I felt rumble down the thread between us.

"Are you fond of my cousin, Little One?" he asked.

The barest hint of a laugh escaped my throat, coating the words meant to tease. "He's very pretty," I said, tilting my head to the side as Soren's lips twitched with the hint of a smile.

He shook his head, his shaggy mid-length, deep brown hair falling about his ears in layers to cover the distinct point of his ears. His body was slightly narrower than Caldris's, but I didn't doubt the definition that would be packed into his frame. He moved like a warrior, every slight shift in his body feeling intentional, economical. The swords crossed at his back only added to the deadly nature of him. If I'd met him a year prior and not been able to see the otherness that lingered in his features, I'd have been attracted to him.

But now, with my love and mate bond with Caldris, there was nothing but a distant, objective recognition of that beauty.

"Do me a favor, Princess. Don't compliment me ever again. I prefer my head on my shoulders," he said, his voice tinted with amusement as he looked above my head at his cousin.

I turned in Caldris's arms, pressing tighter to him as I stared up at him. His icy gaze never left his cousin, never once turned down to me until I reached up to cup his cheek. I tilted his head, pulling him down to me slowly as I stretched up onto my toes. Pressing my lips to his, I murmured the finishing thought to my statement. "Perhaps Fallon will like him."

The harshness in those features softened, the thread between us relaxing as he continued to glare at me. "Don't toy with me," he warned, the menace in those words only serving to make me press my lips into a tight line to refrain from laughing.

"Mated males have killed for less," Soren said, attempting to be the voice of reason.

"You'd like that, though, wouldn't you?" Caldris asked, tucking a strand of hair behind my ear. "You and your violent tendencies would just love to see me murder a male because you think he's *pretty*."

"If you're looking for people to kill on my behalf," I said, glancing toward where Malachi observed the interaction impatiently.

The tension on his face hinted at his displeasure at how long it was taking us to finish our task, but he hadn't yet reached the point where he was ready to brave Caldris's wrath by interrupting our first moments together in days.

"I'd be happy to provide a list," I said, noting the slight tick of Malachi's eyebrow.

The threat hadn't gone unnoticed.

"Don't worry, my star," Caldris said, following my gaze to the other man. "I already have one of my own, and I suspect they are fascinatingly similar."

I suspected he was right.

He stretched out his power, freezing the surface of the rock and marking it where the next pillar needed to be placed. These two would go in the West, I realized, with the others placed to the East of the arena.

"Now, create a pillar without me sending that surge of winter down our bond. It's there. All you need to do is summon it to your will," Caldris said, the teacher returning as Malachi took a step closer to us.

Our window was fading, our time limited. As much as we'd rather just enjoy the time we had together, neither of us was oblivious to the rare opportunity we'd been given.

If we were to have any opportunity to escape, any chance at freedom, then the best thing we could do is make sure I was ready. Hone my skills, so that I could rely on every ounce of magic I had at my disposal.

I nodded, spinning in his arms to face that marker. I closed my eyes, searching inside of me for the place where our mating bond stemmed. For the place where that thread connected to my soul. I tugged on it, trying to pull the magic of winter away from Caldris.

Closer to me.

It came, spreading along the thread and turning it to ice between us. Only when it was a breath from my fingertips did it stop, shuddering to a halt as if there were some kind of barrier in the way.

I pulled again. The winter retreated back a pulse, as if it could sense that I was not its owner.

"Keep trying," Caldris said, his hands soft and gentle upon my waist. He rubbed his thumb over my dress in soothing circles, working to calm me so that I could relax into that touch.

"Would you hurry up?" a male voice asked, forcing my eyes to fling open.

I glanced over at where Malachi stood. In the time since I'd closed my eyes, lost to my focus and ignoring everything around me with the assurance that Caldris would protect me from any threats, another Fae had stepped up to Malachi's side.

I recognized him. Knew that purple gaze and the cruel twist of his lips.

Caldris felt me tense, felt the rigid stance to my body as the male laughed at my failure.

"Tell me," he said simply, his anger rippling down the thread of our bond.

The proximity always made our feelings more intense, always flooded me with every emotion that flickered through him. I couldn't help but feel his rage settle in me, as I was reminded of that day this Fae had spit on me as I left the dungeon.

"He spit on me as I walked past one day," I said, remembering the slimy, thick feeling of it when I'd wiped it away from my face.

Caldris merely hummed thoughtfully, but it didn't change the fact that the purple-eyed male froze in place. The promise of bloodshed came down the bond as I watched the male recognize the threat for what it was.

I smiled, letting my eyes drift closed once more. I settled into that feeling of vengeance, into our united goal of seeing those who'd wronged us dead. I stroked the thread between us, running gentle, loving fingers over it as I coaxed it to do what I wanted.

As I caressed it into recognizing me for who I was. Not a slave to the bond, but one of two masters of it.

It rippled, the cold of winter filling my lungs in a sudden rush. I thrust out my hands, flinging my eyes open as ice rose from the ground and soared toward the sky.

The male was no longer smiling when I turned to look at him once more.

19

Caldris

Haakon stumbled through the halls in the dead of night. There wasn't another soul to bear witness as he got farther from the throne room and those who lingered there, drinking and fucking and playing the silly games that occupied their time.

He was half-drunk on Faerie wine, the unusual chill to the dark passageways slipping right over his heated skin as I trailed behind him. It was a slow, delayed sort of stalk, forcing me to keep to the shadows as I summoned them to my side. Cloaking myself in them, making sure that anyone who did happen to pass wouldn't see me, should it come to it.

I wouldn't allow anyone to derail my fun, to stop me from doing what needed to be done. Estrella had suffered at the hands of the one Fae I couldn't protect her from, but this Sidhe had spit upon her.

Him, I could kill.

He turned right in the halls, heading toward the area that housed his rooms. When he rounded the corner, he took it too hard, stumbling into the wall. The torch lining the passageway nearly struck him in the face. If I hadn't already turned them upside down, he might have burned his flesh in his stupor.

Relief flashed over his face, his body sagging as he laughed lightly to himself.

Shoving off the wall, he continued the long, arduous walk to his room. He halted mid-step, his weight shifting forward and nearly sending him toppling over himself as he looked down the hallway.

Each and every torch lining the hallway to his room had been turned upside down, the eternal flames crawling over the torches as the fire attempted to right itself.

"What in the Gods…" he trailed off, taking another step forward.

His pace quickened.

On and on he went, his body shuddering with each inverted torch. I kept to the shadows, flipping a single golden coin in my hand. On that coin, an inverted torch had been etched.

It was the same coin I pressed into the eyes of the dead, the same kind that I often handed to the ferryman to deliver a soul to the Void safely.

A life ended.

A flame extinguished.

Haakon turned another corner in the hallways, the lights of the inverted flames casting shadows through the hall as I crept behind him. The only sound of my stalking was the noise of that coin flipping over and over through the air.

He spun, searching for me. The shadows clung to me, blending me into the darkness. I raised my hand, sending those shadows prowling through the hallway.

They smothered the flames, each one winking out in a procession as Haakon spun forward suddenly. He ran, stumbling over his own feet as the torches close to me went dark. The darkness traveled in a line up the hallway. He couldn't run fast enough to escape the total blackness that filled Tar Mesa.

It overtook his path to his room. His fingers fumbled with the keys to his door as he darted glances over his shoulder.

I summoned the darkness to my fingertips, circling them and stepping into the shadow realm as time slowed for me. He lingered at the door as I stepped out of the shadows on the other side, catching it with my palm when it crashed open. He tore it away from me, slamming it closed and locking it from the inside as he backed away slowly.

His lungs heaved from his panic—not from exertion. A disbelieving chuckle escaped him as he realized he'd made it to what he presumed to be the safety of his room. It wasn't often that members of Mab's court violated the sanctity of bedrooms without an invitation. We knew the chaos doing so could unleash upon us all.

I welcomed any to try to get to me in my sleep.

I stepped out of the shadows, waving a hand to use them to create a pocket of protected darkness around his room. He panicked, lunging for the door as those shadows rose, trapping him and shoving him back.

He sprawled across the floor, raising a hand in his panic.

"Wait! Please," he begged, his face twisting as he tried to think of a way to convince me not to take his head.

I prowled forward. "Get up," I ordered.

I had no interest in killing a man where he lay, wanting him on his feet when I took his body and broke it. He fumbled, getting to his feet with that hand still outstretched, as if he could make me stop.

As if it were a barrier that could do anything to subvert its fate of being cut off.

"I can help you," he said, his voice trembling as I took another step. I didn't bother with any weapons, didn't need them as I approached. "I can spy on the other Sidhe for you. Feed you information from Mab's court."

"I've no need for twisted lies from the mouth that spat on my mate. Do you think I take kindly to those who treat my future queen as if she is dirty?" I asked, my head tilting to the side.

My mate's pleasure echoed down the bond, as if she could sense that I was on the verge of granting her the revenge she was due.

"Mab won't allow this," he said, spitting all over himself as he sputtered and backed away another step. The desk opposite the door rattled as he stepped into it, knocking the candelabra sideways until the fire licked at the top of the wood.

He scrambled to right it, standing it straight once more.

"Your first mistake was thinking Mab cares about you. You are nothing to her, just as you are nothing to my mate. Your tongue will make a lovely gift, though," I growled.

He reached up with trembling fingers, touching them to his mouth in horror.

"Please," he begged once more.

I struck, my hand shooting forward to collide with his face. Bone cracked beneath my fist. His mouth splayed open as teeth flew through the air. I grasped the slime of his tongue in my hand, yanking it back so suddenly that the flesh severed.

Blood poured from his mouth, and his terrorized gaze dropped to the pink muscle in my grip, at where I held the tongue I'd torn from his face.

"I would take the time to warn you about picking fights with someone's mate next time," I said, raising a leg and slamming the bottom of my boot down on top of his knee.

He crumpled, leaving me to stare down at him where he knelt, waiting for the killing blow.

I thrust my hand into his chest, grabbing his heart and tearing it free from his rib cage. It beat within my hand.

Once. His body dropped to the floor, tilting sideways to sprawl as he stared forward, unseeing.

Twice. I pocketed my coin.

Silence.

***

I emerged from the shadow realm just outside Estrella's room. Malachi protested as I flung open the door, moving far too slowly to prevent me from stepping into my mate's space. I found her seated at her vanity with Nila brushing her hair behind her. I raised a finger to my lips, turning back to Malachi. If he kept quiet, no one needed to know how he'd failed to keep me from seeing Estrella without Mab's permission. The other male crossed his arms over his chest, glaring at me as he jerked his head toward the door. "Five minutes and then get out," he grumbled, his lips twisting with rage.

Estrella moved toward me, sliding her legs clad only in a silken night dress around the stool she sat on. She walked with quiet, nimble feet, approaching me as I held out the mass of tongue and heart held within my grasp.

I didn't speak a word as I handed them to her. Her delicate fingers wrapped around the bloodied organs, studying them intently as the thick fluid ran down her hand and onto her wrists.

She looked up at me through dark lashes, her lips tipping into the hint of a smile so wicked it nearly brought tears to my eyes.

This was the mate I'd waited centuries for. A queen of death and carnage.

I smiled, watching as she tipped her head back as a silent laugh shook her chest. She lifted onto her toes, pressing her lips to mine as I summoned the shadows to return me to my room.

Her love surged down the bond, warming me as I returned to the empty rooms that missed her presence.

Soon.

***

My door crashed against the wall when it flew open the next morning.

"Have you lost your mind?" Mab demanded, stepping over the threshold to enter my room.

Holding up a single finger, I finished reading the sentence in my book, lifted the metal bookmark off the dining table, then slid it between the pages carefully.

I set it down, standing slowly to face the incredulous, outraged face of the Queen of Air and Darkness as she seethed. My leather tunic was open at my chest, the buckles undone in the privacy of my room. I gave Mab a lazy, unenthusiastic smile as I grasped the lowest buckle, hiding the lowest of my abdominal muscles and pulling the two sides together tightly.

"Nice to see you as always, my Queen," I said, my sarcasm evident in my tone.

Her eyes dropped to my chest, sending a ripple of disgust through me as my fingers moved a bit faster to hide my skin. I turned toward the mirror leaning against the wall, the ornate silver detailing of it an ample distraction from the stepmother who would ogle an ogre if he were pretty enough.

"Don't play games with me," she hissed.

She raised her hand high, dropping the heart and tongue she held clasped within it onto the table. The heart rolled lopsidedly over the surface, coming to a stop against the weathered pages of my book in a way that made me sigh in frustration.

"Whose is it?"

The demand washed over me, lacking the force that the command needed to do anything but drive my frustration higher.

"No one important," I returned with a shrug, stepping away from the mirror once my leathers were secured. I paused at the table, flicking the heart to the side with a sneer of disgust.

My heart clenched in my chest. Her snake wound itself tighter as she squeezed her hand, black nails digging into her own flesh hard enough to bleed.

"Whose. Is. It?" she repeated, and the lack of a heartbeat made my knees buckle.

I caught myself with two palms on the table, calming my rage as Estrella's concern pulsed down the bond. "Haakon," I growled, my upper lip peeling back to reveal teeth.

That hand relaxed, dropping to her side as she rolled her eyes. "And what did he do to our dear Estrella?" she asked, crossing her arms over her chest.

I'd meant it when I told Haakon that his first mistake was thinking that he, a common Sidhe, meant anything to Mab. She only cared about those who could be useful to her, and his use was severely limited. He had no connections that assisted her—barely any magic to his name.

I got my legs underneath me more fully, my heart pounding as if it could make up for those moments when it hadn't been able to so much as twitch.

"He spit on her," I said, leveling her with a glare.

"Well, that is certainly distasteful," she said, stepping far-ther into my room. She ran her talons over my favorite chair, claws digging into the leather of the cushion.

Distasteful.

As if she hadn't ordered my mate to be skinned alive.

"Is this really how you want to spend your time? Hunting down any male who so much as looks at Estrella the wrong way?" Mab asked, approaching where I stood.

She ran a finger over the dark circle on the back of my hand, and shadows rose from within it as if she'd summoned them. They shrouded my hand, making it disappear into the darkness as if they themselves wanted to retreat from Mab's attention.

Disgust rippled through me, my hatred for her hands on my skin making me shudder. "Yes. Yes, it is," I said simply, pulling my hand away the moment her eyes met mine.

She pursed her lips, considering me and whatever punish-ment she might have for my insolence. For murdering a mem-ber of her court, regardless of if she cared if he lived or not.

Whatever she came up with, it would be worth the pain.

"If you're not going to behave, perhaps you should join Davorin. He leaves at first light to meet our guests and help them navigate the plains safely," she said, latching onto the only punishment that would deter me from doing something again soon. To send me away, even for a day or two, and leave Estrella behind.

"I'll pass," I muttered, holding her gaze. I'd take the tor-ture. I'd take a public lashing.

But Mab only grinned. "I don't remember asking."

20

Estrella

My robe swished against the stone floor, the blue jarring against the sheer white of it as Malachi forcibly guided me through the halls. We passed countless numbers of those statues, the faces I couldn't unsee staring back at me now that I knew what they were.

Victims of Mab's conquest and thirst for power.

Countless eyes peered down at me, gazing at my only half-hidden skin. The sear of Malachi's palm against the space between my neck and shoulder felt like a brand, a stain upon my soul. Caldris's rage thrummed down the thread between us; the reaction delayed.

I'd felt him go away, felt his end of our thread of fate get farther and farther from me with the passage of time the day before. My only comfort came when I'd finally risen from a night of tossing and turning, my sense of him growing closer once again.

"I can walk on my own," I snapped, attempting to shrug off his hold.

Nila trailed behind us, summoned to join the impromptu journey. I'd barely risen out of bed at the crack of dawn, tossing my robe over my thin, silken nightgown, when Malachi barged through the door and demanded I come immediately.

"Then hurry it up, or I will carry you. I think I'll enjoy your ass in my face far more than you will," he returned.

I turned to glare at him, a brutal growl rumbling through my throat.

"Such a feral little mouse," he said, a grin lighting his face as he shoved me forward once more.

That hand would make a beautiful trophy, and I almost wished he hadn't smelled the blood of the other male's tongue and heart tucked under my bed days prior.

I could have had a nice collection by the time Caldris and I killed everyone on our list. I'd already decided that he needed to die, but I debated which parts of him I would keep and which parts I would feed to the cwn annwn when given the chance.

The doors he stopped me in front of were different. The light shone through the carved metal without any wood to ground it. Snakes wound themselves through them, inky tendrils of darkness blending alongside them. Malachi reached over my head and pushed them open.

We stepped into an anteroom. Light poured in through the sole window that occupied most of a wall. It glinted off the muted red and gold tones spread throughout. Malachi stepped around me and grasped the knocker for the inner door.

"Come in," Mab called, her voice muffled behind the door.

Malachi pushed it open, stepping into the room first before he looked back at me and waited expectantly. I took a single step forward, pausing when I laid eyes upon the ornate bedframe carved from solid gold on the back wall. A thin veil of fabric hung in a circle around it, forming a canopy of shimmering gray.

Mab's bath was a massive square set into the floor itself. It was filled with water, the entire surface covered in rose petals as she lounged against the wall of it. Sunlight streamed in the windows, half-blocked by that same curling metal, casting shadows throughout the room and keeping it dimly lit. Pillars of curled metal arched throughout the room, curving toward the ceiling to separate the designated spaces: bedroom, bath, dining, and sitting areas. Her rooms were easily three to four times the size of mine, and far larger than the cottage I'd called home in Mistfell.

Mab's arms draped along the edge of the bath, the water covering up to the base of her neck. Nila walked into the room behind me, making herself as small as possible against the wall. It wasn't typical that my handmaid was dragged along with me whenever Mab summoned me to torment.

"Good morning, Estrella," Mab said, trailing a black nail along the stone. The sound echoed through me, the high pitch making me shudder.

"Good morning," I said, grimacing through the sound. It was faint, barely even there. As a human, it might not have registered at all, but as a Fae, it was agonizing.

"I'm sure you've realized by now that your mate has left," she said, leveling me with that dark, empty stare. There was a challenge in the words as she probed me for weakness, testing me to see how easily I could be swayed to believe whatever illusion she tried to paint with her half-truths.

"He would never have left me willingly," I said, lifting my chin.

Malachi walked to the sitting room to the left. He lowered himself into a chair, kicking his feet out in front of him as he made himself at home. He'd clearly spent far too much time in this space, in Mab's personal quarters, to be anything but intimately familiar with her.

I swallowed down the surge of nausea that rose within me.

"I've sent him to greet the coming royals for the Winter Solstice," Mab said, her mouth twitching with annoyance at my assurance in our mate bond—at my confidence in his love for me. Over and over again, he would have sacrificed himself to save me if he had the barest hint that it would do any good.

He never would have left me here unless she made him.

"And when will he return?" I asked, trying not to think about the fact that she was naked in the water. I didn't want to see beneath her dress, didn't want to see the fair skin that I knew wouldn't show a hint of any of the suffering she'd inflicted upon others.

I wanted her body to be mangled. I wanted it to be scarred in the ways she had scarred my mate.

I wanted to taste her suffering on my tongue and see the signs that she, too, had known pain—anything less was an injustice I blamed the Fates for. I sent a silent curse to haunt them.

"Tomorrow, I suspect," she answered.

She moved forward in the bath, her body shifting as she stood from what I presumed was a seat. Her hands swirled absently through the roses on the surface of the water.

"Has anyone told you what to expect of the Solstice?"

"Few people tell me anything here," I said, honesty ringing in the words.

Nila informed me of what she dared, giving me bits and pieces of information that she didn't think would get her in trouble. We were never sure if there were prying ears, if Malachi or any of the guards who relieved him at night would attempt to listen to every conversation we had in the supposed privacy of my room.

"Once, the Solstice was a way to celebrate the return of the sun," she said, her eyes going distant as she looked toward one of the windows lining the room. As if she could see the very court that should have been the happiest to see the solstice occur, and what it meant for the slow, subtle shift of power toward the Summer Court.

Her brother's court. The court where she'd been born and raised.

"What is it now?" I asked, fidgeting slightly at having to draw her attention back to me.

I didn't want the force of that gaze on me, but I didn't want to waste my time standing in her rooms as she bathed. Better she get through whatever she needed to say, setting me free so I could go about my day of idle lounging and waiting for my mate to return.

"The Shadow Court mourns the darkness. Other courts may celebrate with dancing and revelry. We grieve with blood and death," she explained, her lips curving with pure malice.

I swallowed, biting back the sharp retort that it didn't sound any different from daily life within Tar Mesa.

If Mab thought the events of the solstice were special, then I didn't want to consider what that meant for the people living here. For those coming to visit, forced to join in the grieving by the queen they didn't want.

"It sounds absolutely lovely. Am I to assume I'll be tucked away in my rooms and miss out on the joy of those celebrations?" I asked.

It was pathetic when someone who used to sneak out looked forward to being locked in her rooms in the way I'd once hated more than anything.

Malachi stood at Mab's slow nod, stepping up behind me and removing the collar from my throat. I drew in a steady breath, letting the power of Alfheimr flow into me and through me once again as he moved to the table and set the collar upon the surface.

Mab walked toward me, ascending the shallow staircase within her bath until water sluiced off her skin. Rose petals glided against the fairness of her flesh, dropping back into the bath as her body was revealed. Mab was unbothered by her nudity, moving slowly as she approached me. I kept my eyes on her face, refusing to so much as glance at the unblemished body I wanted to maim.

"You will wear what you are told, be where you are told, and behave as I dictate."

I swallowed. That sounded like I wouldn't be allowed to remain in the confines of my room. Sounded as if I would need to be an active participant in something I wanted nothing to do with.

I opened my mouth, my smart reply dying in my throat when she raised a hand to silence me. I bit the inside of my cheek to keep from cursing her out.

"For every moment you disobey me, I will pick a random Fae Marked from my keep, and I will make you choose between their life and your mate's. We both know what choice you will make, and all the courts will watch as I slaughter them. Most Fae Marked, I imagine, will have their Fae using the solstice as an opportunity to get within the walls of Tar Mesa to plead for their mate to return home with them. You will be responsible for the severing of souls, and for the fact that they will watch it happen *helplessly.*"

My jaw clenched as the threat struck me in the chest, sinking inside that hollow part of me that rose in fury. To sever a mate bond was unforgivable, whether the Fae Marked desired the bond or not. There'd been a time when I would have wanted to be freed; where I would have welcomed that death rather than be taken.

I'd been a fool, refusing to recognize the completion that waited for me if I only let it consume me.

"You'll lose your leverage over the Fae if you kill their mates," I argued, swallowing down my anger.

I couldn't fight, not with Nila so close and so vulnerable. Malachi, as if he could sense the coming tension, had moved closer to her. He took up position at her side as I watched, his shoulder bumping against hers as she gulped.

Her eyes connected with mine, a plea in them that I couldn't ignore. My poor behavior wouldn't lead to my own suffering, but *hers*.

"I warned you that your heart is your greatest weakness," Mab said, a cunning smile transforming her face. She touched a single nail to the Fae Mark where it swirled over my heart. The ink retracted and writhed away from her touch as if it hated her as much as I did.

"No matter how I hurt you physically, you've not broken," she said, turning and striding back into the bath. She resumed her position, staring at me as I gaped down at her. "Let's see what guilt does to that *goodness* in your heart, Little Mouse. Perhaps that is the path to breaking you."

"What do you want from me?" I asked, my control snapping as I glared down at her. "I don't *know* what I am. I cannot give you what I don't have."

She studied me, her lips spreading to reveal gleaming white teeth as she leaned forward in the water. She radiated calmness, grasping a flower petal in her hand. She crushed it within her grip.

"I want you bound," she said, the words striking me in the chest.

I pursed my lips, having considered and wondered why she hadn't just bound me in the way she had Caldris.

"Then why aren't I?" I asked, tilting my head to the side. I hadn't been able to ask Caldris about it in the time we'd spent in Tar Mesa—about how he'd come to be bound.

"The magic of the binding is complex," she said, pursing her lips as she studied me. "You have to be willing. Children are much easier to manipulate into accepting it. A few days without food will have them begging for scraps, more willing to accept anything I offer as payment for that food. But you, you would sooner die than bind yourself to me for eternity. I need you *broken* first."

The creature in me recoiled, staring out through my eyes at the threat only Mab could pose. What would it take for me to bind myself?

The creature within me hissed her disdain, her voice a slither.

Never, it said.

My morals might not have mattered as she pounded against my chest, striking against the cage of my flesh. Mab looked at my chest, her head tilting to the side as if she could see the creature attempting to escape my body.

My good heart wouldn't matter if she took over. I knew it as well as I knew my own name.

"Interesting," Mab purred, her eyes lifting to mine once again. "Very interesting."

I stood, silent, not daring to open my mouth. I wouldn't risk the truth that could pour out, or that she would see my deception as I danced around it. Nobody, not even Caldris, knew the extent of the thing that paced within me. The way she occasionally made it known that she would claw through me to escape, if only she could.

"Get in the bath, Estrella," Mab said, leaning back as she stared at me. I didn't move, refusing to be naked with the female I wanted to be nothing like. "It is time to get you ready to be presented to the kings and queens of the courts."

"Nila can see to that," I answered, glancing toward my handmaid.

She gasped as Malachi grasped her by the hair, wrenching her head back so that he could touch the edge of his blade to her throat.

I stilled, turning back to Mab. "Call off your dog."

"Get in the bath," she repeated, eying my chest as if she could see my heart beating.

I grimaced, shucking off my robe and letting it drop to the stone floor. My silken nightgown followed, pooling on top of my robe as I stepped out of the fabric. My breasts tightened in the cold, and I attempted to ignore the way Mab's gaze dragged over my body.

I stepped into the water, slowly descending the steps until I sat upon the edge of the seat on a side perpendicular to Mab.

She raised her gaze to my face. "We have our work cut out for us," she said, the brutal words leaving no doubt that she found me lacking. "Do have a seat, Nila. We'll be here a while."

Four women stepped in from the anteroom as if they'd been waiting, baskets of soaps, lotions, and all manner of devices clutched in their hands. One moved to Mab, tending to her upkeep as the others all studied me and sighed.

I snarled, feeling more animal than Fae.

They got to work anyway.

21

Caldris

Azra whinnied as we led the group in the direction of Tar Mesa. He'd been unsettled since we'd left the morning before, not liking the distance between Estrella and me any more than I did. The gathering of Fae accompanying us from the other courts was far larger than it had been in previous years, and it had horrified me to discover how many of them came solely for the reason that Mab had refused to release their mates prior to the Solstice.

They had to hope they'd be permitted to leave with them, take them back to their home courts. Not for the first time, I wondered where Mab had tucked them. I'd searched in all her typical hiding places, not finding them in any of the dungeons or holding cells that were typically used. She took no chances with her possession of them, not daring to risk the fact that I might have tried to smuggle them out and scatter them to the wind.

Davorin was on the other side of the group, leaving the royals to lead the procession of their people on horseback behind us. By some horrific misfortune, the Summer and Autumn Courts had lined up next to one another, leaving their kings to a quiet standoff for the entirety of our return journey.

Aderyn had inserted herself between them, flanking her husband, Kahlo, as if she could be enough of a barrier between him and Rheaghan. For all the centuries I'd known them, they'd been at one another's throats. I'd never dared to ask where their hatred for one another had begun, and I suspected they didn't even remember.

"We'll arrive before nightfall," I said.

Rheaghan nodded in agreement. I didn't dislike the male, despite the role he'd played in Mab's rise to power—his tolerance for her antics allowing her to become too powerful to stop. He'd wanted to see the best in her, remember the sister who hadn't been pure evil.

I couldn't fault him for that, but I did place some of the responsibility for the carnage that followed upon his head. Even still, as much as I blamed him, I knew he blamed himself far more. He'd never step out of the shadow of his inaction—or forgive himself for what his love had brought upon Alfheimr.

So we rode on, seeking out the mate who I knew waited eagerly for my return. It thrummed down our bond, a steady, comforting beat to remind me that she was alive, at the very least.

There'd been no pain in the time since I'd left—only worry and rage. Both were emotions I could handle, neither indicating that she'd been harmed in my absence.

"I heard rumor you found your mate," Rheaghan said, the words cautious as he rode at my side.

I nodded my confirmation, turning to look at him in warning. "Your sister has developed an unhealthy obsession with her," I said.

He swallowed and hung his head in shame. "That is unfortunate," he said, keeping his voice soft. "Yet even still, I feel I must congratulate you on the mating. To find one's completion is worth celebrating." He nodded, his gaze going distant as the rolling hills of Tar Mesa came into view ahead of us.

"Your mate will come someday, Rheaghan," I said, feeling that within my very being.

His own Fae Mark scrawled up his neck, the red twining flames upon his skin and shifting with shades of orange and yellow mixed in. I understood the impossible wait he must have endured, knowing that while mine had been miserable, his was even longer.

As one of the original gods, he'd been waiting an eternity.

"Or perhaps the primordials decided he did not deserve a mate for his crimes against all of us," Kahlo said, his reluctant, tenuous alliance with Mab keeping him from outright hostility. The God of Beasts would not have been my first choice for an enemy.

Rheaghan didn't so much as flinch at the harsh words. "At least I've had the decency not to string an innocent woman along in a sham of a marriage for the sake of politics. I do not see your mate anywhere either, Kahlo; so perhaps you've been shunned the same as I."

"Enough," I warned with a roll of my eyes.

For immortal beings, sometimes the feuds between us felt no better than the tantrums of children. We approached Tar Mesa too slowly for my liking; then the horses would require stabling and care when we finally arrived.

It would be hours yet before I could see for myself that my mate was indeed safe.

When we escaped, I'd keep her locked in the bedroom with me for weeks to make up for the agony of our separation. I'd run my mouth over every injury she'd suffered, until only the pleasure of my touch remained in her mind.

One day.

22

Estrella

Nila prepared me for the next evening as I stood in front of my wardrobe, staring into the mass of fabric and dresses waiting there. I'd never worn pants prior to spending time with the Resistance, and yet I couldn't help but long for the security they offered. With Mab's propensity for wielding sex as a weapon, I would have felt moderately better having something to cover myself—particularly after the exposure of the day before and everything that had been plucked, scrubbed, and shaped on my body while she watched.

The gown Nila pulled from the wardrobe was a deep teal, the color of the depths of a cove. It was embroidered with beading, white gems sewn into the fabric in a stunning pattern that accentuated the waist. There were no sleeves. The fabric merely rested against the shoulder in thin straps, leaving the chest open. Another piece of fabric hung about the hanger, a collar of sorts that I had to hope would conceal the iron at my neck.

"The Princess of the Winter Court will not look like a prisoner when we welcome the royals from the other courts," Nila said, running her fingers over the delicate pieces of fabric that draped down from the collar and would hang over my arms like sleeves.

I stripped off the silk robe I'd dressed in while I dried from my bath, allowing Nila to style my hair as she saw fit. She helped me into the dress, carefully doing her best to avoid touching my iron collar as she clasped the beaded material over the top of it.

I winced as she pulled the laces of my dress tight, pressing my breasts into my chest forcefully until it felt like I couldn't breathe.

"I think the collar is less painful," I wheezed, touching a hand to my chest as I glanced down at the swell that peeked out above the low scoop of the neckline.

"Don't be dramatic, Princess," Nila said with a chuckle. She knew as well as I did that it simply wasn't true, but that didn't change the fact that I couldn't breathe.

"You haven't told me what to expect during the Solstice. I think I should have some idea of what I'm walking into," I said.

Nila sighed, fluffing the fabric drapery to hang over the top of my shoulders and down my arms. "There will be Seven Events, all culminating in the Tithe," she said, her voice dropping low as if even in the Court of Shadows, the subject of such was forbidden.

"The Tithe?" I asked, turning to look away from the massive mirror that hung on the wall opposite the windows of my chambers.

"In order to keep the boundary between the court and Tartarus in place, the Fae must pay a sacrifice to the Primordial Ubel in order for him to agree to uphold it," she explained, staring down at me as she nodded. She dropped to her knees in front of me, placing the heeled shoes upon my feet one by one as I stared down at her.

My emotions were unpredictable on the best of days, but the word sacrifice would always send a flash of panic through me. I'd lost my father to such a notion, and nearly lost my life. If Caldris hadn't broken through the Veil when he had, I would already be dead. My life given to the power of something that I no longer believed should have continued to exist; something that was always meant to fail so that Fallon and I, or both of us, could end up exactly where we were now.

It all seemed so... pointless in the end.

"What does that have to do with the courts?" I asked as she fiddled with my hair and placed a silver circlet upon my head.

"I do hope Twyla has received word of your existence. She should bring your crown with her if she is aware, and that would be far more befitting of your station," Nila said, carefully evading the subject.

I ignored the panicked thump of my heart in my chest, the horror of wearing a true crown. I thought of Caldris's spiked silver crown that bled shadows upon the earth, wondering just how heavy the metal of it had to be. His amusement pulsed down the bond, as if he couldn't wait for the day my discomfort became reality.

I swallowed, shaking off the dread I felt over the forced acknowledgement of my status in this world. I hadn't asked for any of it, but it seemed I'd been born to receive gifts I'd never wanted.

Or maybe they were a curse when it all came down to it.

"The Tithe, Nila," I said, reminding the Fae woman of the topic at hand. My dread couldn't be stopped, but I could focus on what was to come that night and do my best to prepare for it.

"We sacrifice seven lives to Tartarus every seven years. It is necessary, else things slip through the wards containing the prisoners of Tartarus. It has been... difficult since the Veil was constructed. We've gone far too long without paying a Tithe, and this will be the first Solstice since the Veil fell—"

"What does the Veil have to do with the sacrifices? Do you mean to tell me that the Fae sacrifice humans to Tartarus?" I asked, my outrage only growing.

Humans had been sacrificed to the Veil for over a century. Humans were sacrificed to Tartarus even longer. It never stopped amazing me just how little any of the creatures in this world valued human life—as if our ability to reincarnate changed any of the heartbreak left behind for loved ones to experience.

"Changelings, yes," Nila admitted. "The Fae once took their place in the human realm, so their families never know they're missing at the time. It is better to avoid mass panic as a general rule, and the person disappears eventually over the course of the year. It's gradual, so the humans never realize their loved ones were taken all at once. With the Veil down, the practice will resume."

"The courts are bringing human Changelings to sacrifice?" I asked, hanging my head forward. If any of them were a loved one of mine, I would bring down the entire court before I allowed them to die.

"Six of them. Mab has also selected one of her own," Nila said.

I sighed. "Why seven? There are five courts," I answered.

"Seven is a magical number to the Fae and witches alike. So each Tithe year, two of the courts must present two sacrifices instead of one. They rotate. This year it will be the Winter Court and Summer Court, Twyla and Rheaghan."

"I think I'll stay here tonight," I said, shaking my head in disgust. I didn't want my first memory of Caldris's mother to be her participation in such a brutal ritual.

"The sacrifice will not happen tonight, Princess. It is a thirteen-day long ritual, with a great many factors to be considered. Mab will expect to show you off as her new prize to the other court royals, a trophy of her reign. She will not take kindly to you remaining in your room, and I imagine you will be forced to attend one way or another," Nila explained, stepping back and making her way to the door of my chambers.

She tugged it open, revealing Malachi waiting on the other side. His eyes tracked down to my arm, to the unblemished mark of my mate bond upon my freshly grown skin. There was a promise in his eyes, a malicious intent to see how far he could push it the next time Mab allowed him to try to take my mate bond from me.

I had a feeling I may be lacking an arm the next time.

I glared back at him in challenge as I brushed past him and into the hallway. Nila traipsed behind me, doing her best to arrange the train of my gown appropriately. The beading and gems glimmered in the candlelight as I took a few steps forward, heading toward the dining hall that waited beside the throne room.

"Aren't you coming? You shouldn't keep Mab's prize pig waiting," I said, turning to look at Malachi over my shoulder.

His lips twitched in something like a moment of amusement, but he shut it down immediately. He caught up with me with a slow amble, making sure to let me know that he didn't rush for anyone but his master.

"One of these days, she'll allow me to tear you limb from limb. I greatly look forward to the way you'll scream. That is the only use I have for your mouth."

"And one of these days, I'll cut off your cock and feed it to you, Malachi. I have no interest in your screams," I said, tilting my head to stare up at him through my lashes as I smiled sweetly. "Only your silence."

He clenched his jaw, turning his gaze forward as we made our way down the hall. The doors to the dining room were already open, the enormous table filled with Fae.

I followed behind him as Nila gave one last adjustment to my train before skittering out of sight.

"Crown Princess Estrella of the Winter Court and the Court of Shadows," Malachi said, making the Fae in the room fall silent. "Mate of Crown Prince Caldris Arawn."

Caldris turned from where he sat in silence, pushing out his chair so that he could stand slowly. He'd abandoned his usual armor in favor of a pair of black trousers that hugged the muscles of his thighs. His dress tunic was the same deep teal as my gown, like the deepest color of frozen oceans, with a black jacket draped over his shoulders that struggled to contain the muscles of his broad chest and biceps.

He stepped around the table, coming to a stop in front of me as the room stayed quiet. I felt every pair of eyes fall upon us as Caldris ignored Malachi entirely and grasped my hand within his. He leaned down, pressing his mouth to the back of my hand.

"You are more beautiful than all the stars in the sky, *min asteren*," he said, his voice dropping low as he held my gaze.

It was only after I smiled up at him that he let his gaze travel down my gown, taking in the subtle curves that had only begun to fill with more access to food.

Even though Mab liked to torment me, she fed me well. It was the first time in my life that I had more food than I could ever eat, and my body began to show the signs of ample nourishment. Even my face had begun to fill out, my cheeks looking less hollow when I glanced into the mirror.

"*Min anam,*" I murmured, drawing his gaze back to mine. I raised the hand he gripped to cup his cheek, watching as his eyes shuttered the moment I touched him. *My soul.*

Being separated from him was more than just an emotional toll. My body felt the loss of his presence the moment he was drawn away, the moment his skin left mine. As if my body needed to spend every waking moment wrapped within his embrace. If he felt even a fraction of that, then I understood the pain.

And the relief that came when the touch finally returned.

"Bring her, Caldris," Mab ordered.

My mate tensed in place. The grip on his heart made his body physically react as he turned, using my hand to guide me to the vacant seat between his and the end of the table where Mab had placed herself.

"We've saved you a spot, Little Mouse."

"I wouldn't presume to take a seat that surely should have been given to a court royal," I said, glancing around the table to find any who might desire the place of what Mab doubtlessly considered an honor.

"Nonsense, you are the guest of honor. All the courts are curious about you," Mab said, waving her hand dismissively.

She dropped her gaze, pausing at the sight of the embellished fabric covering my throat. Her lips twisted into a smile as she stood, approaching me and stopping directly in front of me. She dragged a black nail over the front of the fabric, tearing one of the gems from it so that it fell to the floor in a sound that echoed through the silent dining hall.

"Let them see you for what you are."

With those words, she pulled the fabric from my neck to reveal the iron collar and the raw skin peeking out from beneath it. She tossed it to the side, sending the glittering teal fabric fluttering to the floor. I thought she meant to remove the collar itself as well, to put my oddness on display for all to see as the evening's entertainment, but she left it.

She didn't mean for them to see me. She meant for them to see me as her prisoner.

I raised my chin as surprised gasps filled the room, turning my stare toward the table and the watchful eyes.

"Sister, what is the meaning of this?"

A male stood on the opposite side of the table, pushing his chair back as he glared at Mab. I knew who he must have been just from the things Caldris had said about Mab and where she'd come from.

Rheaghan stepped around the side of the table. "Why would you need to torment a human mate in such a way?" he asked, stopping beside his sister. He reached up to touch the iron, as if he needed the confirmation that it truly was made of iron and not a deception.

"Who said anything about her being human?" Mab asked, grasping her brother by the wrist. She pulled his hand away as he studied her in anger.

"She's afraid to play with me when she doesn't have me under control in one way or another," I said, smirking at him as the hush in the room went entirely still.

Caldris shifted behind me, trying to wedge himself between us as Mab lashed out with a clawed hand. Her hand bounced off his armor as he shielded me, tucking me behind him as Mab met his rage-filled stare with the hollowness of hers.

"Aside, now," she commanded, sweeping a nail across the front of his throat.

Blood trickled free from the wound as the bond forced him to step back, his chest sagging forward as his legs obeyed against his will.

The moment he was clear, Mab latched a hand around the front of my throat. The sound of her skin sizzling as the bottom of her hand touched the collar was loud in the silent hall. Her nails dug into the side of my neck, breaking through the skin as I grimaced up at her and fought for the breath she kept me from taking.

"You would do well to remember that you are nothing," she hissed, leaning in to speak the words as venomously as a snake. "I have lived for centuries. I am a Goddess who rules over other Gods. Whatever you are is insignificant compared to that."

I smiled through the pain burning my lungs, wheezing as I spoke the taunt that would push all the limits. "Then prove me wrong."

"Estrella," Caldris barked, the warning in my name nearly making me regret my outburst. I could survive my own suffering and pain, but I didn't want to him to suffer with me.

Mab stilled, glancing at her brother from the corner of her eye. He watched me, his brow quirking as he studied me for a moment before leveling his sister with an expectant glance.

"The girl does have a point."

Mab released my neck as suddenly as she'd grasped it, letting air fill my lungs once more. Caldris heaved a sigh of relief when I was freed, his chest moving as if the air being trapped outside of me had affected him as well.

"Remove it then," Mab said, waving a hand toward Caldris.

I dropped my stare down to the hand that still bore the signs of the iron, the burns that had not yet healed. She healed the effects of iron at the same rate as Caldris, one more tally in the box of differences between us.

Once, it had seemed unfathomable that I wouldn't be her daughter with the similarities that existed, but now it seemed like the differences became more and more staggering with every day that passed.

My mate raised his hands, stepping up behind me and glaring at Malachi. Caldris brushed my hair over one shoulder, revealing the locking mechanism on the back of the collar. Malachi moved behind me to assist, the magic within the collar recognizing his touch before he backed away.

Caldris grasped the collar even as he burned, dropping it unceremoniously upon the dining table. Mab glared at it in distaste, as if it was an affront to her table setting.

I closed my eyes as the familiar warmth wrapped me in its embrace, winding its way up my Fae mark until it could settle upon my damaged throat. I opened them to the faint golden glow I'd become accustomed to, staring at Rheaghan where he stood directly in front of me.

He jolted back a step as he met my gaze, the movement barely noticeable to any who weren't watching him closely. "What in the Gods..." he asked, tilting his head to the side. He took another step closer, glancing at Caldris in question as he stopped and raised a hand. His fingers lingered, hovering just off my skin as he waited for my mate's permission to touch me.

Caldris studied him for a moment before he nodded, but it was what Rheaghan did in the next moment that made him different from all the other males I'd encountered in my life.

"May I?" he asked me.

The simple question struck me in the chest. I couldn't remember a time when a man hadn't just taken what he wanted, touched without thought or permission. I stared up at him in confusion, taking in the way his dark hair hung just past his ears and was as sleek as Mab's.

His face was twisted with curiosity, but there was no mistaking the arresting beauty in the lines of his face or his piercing, light green eyes.

I nodded my assent, unable to find the words to thank him for taking such care. It was such a simple thing, such an obvious courtesy that should have been afforded at every opportunity. But I stood in the middle of the dining hall as he touched gentle fingers to my throat, fighting back tears that scalded the back of my eyes.

Rheaghan looked at Caldris's hands as my mate placed one upon my shoulder in silent support, the burns on his skin remaining even though mine were gone. He curled a brow as he drew his fingers back, rounding on his sister, who dropped into her chair as if she were bored with the evening already.

"You've been keeping secrets, sister."

"I often do," she said, grasping her goblet of wine and swirling it as she leaned back into her chair.

Rheaghan returned to his seat, eyeing the place between him and Mab that remained empty. "Are we waiting for another secret? I'd heard a rumor that my niece had finally returned to Alfheimr. Where is she?" he asked.

Caldris pulled out my chair for me as I prepared to lower myself into it, freezing in place as Fallon stepped into the dining hall. Her hair wasn't in the braids I'd come to recognize her by, the chestnut of it draping over her shoulders alongside the gauzy, taupe fabric of her dress. It was nearly translucent as it wrapped around her throat and then draped off her shoulders, revealing a deep line of cleavage that I knew made her uncomfortable. There was a slit that went high up her thigh, revealing a line of fair skin that matched her mother's.

Side-stepping the chair Caldris had pulled out for me, I moved toward Fallon at the same time her eyes fell upon me. She hurried forward, dashing away from the guard next to her and crashing into me. I clutched her in my arms, overwhelmed with relief that she'd remained unharmed since the last time we'd seen one another.

"Come and sit, Maeve," Mab ordered, lifting a foot to kick the chair on her other side out.

"My name is Fallon," Fallon returned, glaring at her mother as she released my arms and stepped away. I wanted nothing more than to follow after her, to interrogate her about what harm her mother might have caused in the time we'd been separated.

"You are my daughter. Your name is whatever I say it is," Mab said with a smile as Fallon took her seat.

Her guard stepped up behind her, pushing her chair in neatly as Mab reached over and grasped her hand in hers. The grip was too tight, the subtle wince on Fallon's face making my blood boil.

Caldris came up beside me, grasping my hand in his, pulling me back to my seat as if he could sense the growing tension within me.

"She's a big girl," he whispered as we passed the chairs of other Fae and returned to the seats Mab had designated for us.

I lowered myself into my pulled-out seat, allowing my mate to push in my chair as he leaned down and pressed a kiss to my cheek.

"You two know each other, I take it. What a small world," Rheaghan mused, turning to the niece who sat beside him.

"We made the journey back to Alfheimr together after the Wild Hunt collected us," I said, taking the attention from Fallon. She remained pinned by her mother's glare, withering in her place as the rest of the room turned away from her embarrassment.

"And what, pray tell, was a non-human doing in Nothrek for all this time?" Rhaeghan asked me, taking a sip of his wine.

"Mostly dying, I think," I said, making him sputter into his goblet. Amusement tipped my lips up despite the tension surrounding the table as Sidhe delivered food to the center of it.

Rheaghan studied me carefully, a smile making his lips spread as he nodded his head and carefully placed his wine goblet upon the table. "I like her."

"I'm so pleased," Mab said, a subtle roll of her eyes giving her away as she leaned back from the table and sipped her wine. "I do so love it when you grow fond of my playthings and want me to treat them properly."

"Perhaps it wouldn't hurt you to treat your equals with respect rather than torment, Mother. Just a thought," Fallon said, staring down at her plate as Rheaghan took it upon himself to fill it with food for her.

"She is not the equal to the Queen of Air and Darkness," Malachi said with a snort, condemning the thought that I was worth more than dirt beneath his shoe.

"Politically, she stands to inherit the Winter Court alongside her mate. I should think that would make her an equal, or near enough, under any normal circumstances. The courts once coexisted peacefully from my understanding, before the wars broke out," Fallon said, taking a sip of her wine.

Even in her protest of the status quo, she somehow managed to do it more diplomatically than I.

Mab was saved from needing to respond to her daughter's unwanted suggestion when another Fae at the table spoke up.

"I would like to ask when you intend to release my son from his servitude so that he may take over his rightful place as the heir to Catancia. Not all of us wish to rule eternally, my Queen," a woman said, the pale, silvery color of her hair being the only similarity between her and Caldris.

Her eyes fell upon Caldris, and the two of them shared a brief, silent exchange. Her skin was darker than his, brown whereas his was golden. Her lips were painted with red, her eyes more angular than her son's.

"You may take him with you when you depart for Catancia after the Tithe," Mab acquiesced with a cunning smile, turning her stare away from Twyla until it fell upon me. "But Estrella stays with me."

"Sister," Rheaghan said, interjecting before Caldris grasped his hand in mine and raised them, resting our bound hands upon the surface.

"You cannot expect me to leave her here," he said, gritting his teeth as he stared at the woman who was determined to ruin everything.

"Caldris…" I said, my voice trailing off. He'd suffered for centuries, been a prisoner for his entire life. If the opportunity for freedom was within his grasp…

"No," he said, the one word shutting down any protest I might have shown.

"Of course, I don't," Mab said with a laugh, leaning forward to take a piece of cheese off her plate and take a bite from it. "But it is nice to taunt you with the possibility of freedom. There was a time when you would have done anything for it."

"Not this."

"You overstep, Mab. These games cross a line," Rheaghan said, scolding his sister as he glanced over at us.

"That seems to be the norm for her, does it not?" I asked, glaring at her.

"You are a prisoner. Remember your place and, for once, remain silent," Mab ordered, spearing me with a glare.

"Funny. Even as a prisoner, she has more queenly tact than you ever did, dear sister," Rheaghan said, slicing through the meat he'd placed upon his plate and taking a bite. The rest of the table sipped their wine, remaining silent as the two siblings had a stare-down.

However Mab had become the Queen of Air and Darkness, I suspected she'd stepped upon her family to do it.

23

Caldris

I tucked Estrella tightly against my side, keeping her close as we walked out of the dining hall with the rest of the court royals, Mab, and her guards. Estrella hadn't had the chance to interact with most of them, the mood of the dinner dropping even lower after Rheaghan shunned his sister.

I liked it when Rheagan stood up to Mab. He was the only person she would occasionally tolerate an insult from aside from Estrella, but when she didn't retaliate straight away it usually meant violence was on the horizon.

I'd do whatever I could to not let Estrella be the victim of Mab's rage, even knowing that it was often outside of my control. I'd shield her from harm, but even I knew I could do *nothing* if Mab truly wanted to hurt her.

I had to hope she wouldn't be the convenient outlet for her rage. She'd already suffered enough and would continue to suffer throughout our time spent in the Court of Shadows. Mab had shown how cruel she could be when made me choose between the only two things I'd ever wanted in my life.

But if I had to choose between Estrella and my freedom, I would always choose her.

"Where are we going?" Estrella asked, looking up at me as we walked in a procession toward the doors that led outside the palace.

The doors to the mountain took six Fae to operate, turning locking mechanisms and gears until they wound open.

They towered over us as we approached, the creaking of the gears echoing loudly through the foyer to the palace as we paused before them.

"Outside," I said, grimacing as I glanced down at Estrella's bare arms.

While Tar Mesa wasn't as cold as the Winter Court and the land outside the rolling hills was characterized by barren landscape and salt-filled deserts, it was still far too cold for her to be exposed to the harsh winds.

Cursing, I shrugged off my jacket and wrapped it around her shoulders as the first breeze blew through the crack in the doors. The white salt outside blew in, drifting over the dark stone floors and spreading between the feet of the royals in front of us.

Many of the royals led the way as they approached those slowly opening doors, well acquainted with where the sacrifices would be kept until the Tithe. I didn't relish Estrella's reaction, knowing she would condemn me as much as she despised the lot of us for the crimes we committed against the humans in order to keep the things locked up in Tartarus. I couldn't expect her to understand, not until she had to partake in her first hunt, and she witnessed the kind of monsters that lurked within it.

Mab trailed behind us, Fallon at her side as the younger girl tried to escape her mother's notice. She would undoubtedly hear of Mab's dissatisfaction later on, when they were alone and she could give her an earful without appearing bothered to the Fae she considered her enemies.

I ignored her, knowing that I could hardly help myself when we were trapped within the Court of Shadows. Helping

Estrella had to come first over helping Fallon, even if my mate would have wanted something different.

Estrella snuggled deeper into my jacket, wrapping it tight and covering her entire torso in it. Whatever she was, her innate power didn't make her comfortable in the cold. Was she descended from a creature of the Summer Court? Something that lived on the coast of the Crystal Sea?

The thought had merit, and for a moment I wished I could trust Rheaghan enough to ask. But he was unpredictable at best in the way he loved his sister, often caving to her desires and ambitions in the interest of keeping the peace — in the interest of not losing the only remaining bond he had left.

Estrella and I followed behind Rheaghan as he strolled forward to follow the group ahead of him.

"What happens outside?" Estrella asked as I held her close.

Rheaghan rounded the corner first, the group of others far enough ahead that we lost sight of them in the blowing salt. Estrella lifted my jacket, using it to shield her face against the onslaught as I tucked myself against her back and guided her with my body.

I knew the way to the pens far too well for my liking. The rooms were carved into the side of the mountain where human Changelings were kept until they could be sacrificed.

"What do you know of the Tithe?" I asked, hoping to perhaps have a few moments to prepare Estrella for the coming reality.

I suspected her handmaid had told her something, giving her at least a basic idea of the reality that was coming. I had to hope so, because I couldn't guarantee that she wouldn't do something foolish to interfere if she wasn't prepared. As much as I doubted Mab would have intentionally done Estrella any kindness whatsoever, Nila had been an excellent choice for Estrella's handmaid.

Maybe she'd done it to use against her. Maybe she'd done it to test Nila's loyalty. But Estrella could have had the misfortune of someone like Malazan as her handmaid, and I shuddered to think of how quickly Estrella would have slit her throat if given half a chance.

We came closer to the entrance to the pens, the first of the royals reaching it ahead of us. Time was running out to make her understand what was coming. While I might not have agreed with humans being chosen against their will, I would never speak out against it. Not when my mate was present, not when her life and her body could be used against me. As wrong as it might have been, I would have killed every last human in Nothrek if it meant saving her and protecting her from harm.

If that made me their villain, then I would gladly play that part.

"I know about the sacrifices," Estrella said, the grimace in her voice reaching me even though I could not see her face.

We approached the much smaller doors to the pens, making our way inside and out of the brutal elements of the Shadow Court. Some areas were more lush; the Cove was as beautiful as any of the beaches of the Summer Court, but the area directly surrounding the capital was far from it.

Estrella dropped my jacket to hang from her shoulder as we stepped inside, shaking it off until the floor was covered in salt.

The pens were lower, settled into a pit in the center of the room as we all stood around the edge. Estrella glanced down, studying the humans who huddled in a mass in the center of the pit.

"What is this?" she asked, looking at me as she moved closer to the edge.

"This is where Mab keeps the sacrifices until the time comes for them to be given to Tartarus," I explained.

They'd be taken care of to the best of the Sidhe's ability, well fed and kept safe in the interim, even if they weren't given the comforts they should have been. There were no beds within the pit, nothing but sand and rock walls to surround them.

How far we'd fallen from the old days.

Prior to Mab taking over the Faerie courts, prior to the war with the humans, those who were sacrificed to the Tithe had volunteered for the honor. They'd been human and Fae alike, beings who grew tired of living or were ill in ways the healers and witches of Alfheimr couldn't help. Humans who were approaching death in old age.

It hadn't been a perfect system, but it hadn't involved the regular, ritualistic murder of seven people.

"They're treated terribly in their final weeks of life," Estrella said, shaking her head sadly.

Her anguish wafted off her in waves, to the point that I didn't need our bond to sense her feelings. Her bleeding, broken heart would be the end of her one day, making her do things for creatures who didn't deserve her loyalty.

I would do everything in my power to protect her from the consequences of such care, to save her from those who would use it against her, but sometimes I wished she could harden herself in the way that came with centuries of witnessing life and death.

But I loved the joy that lit her face when she uncovered a new wonder, and in the same breath knew I would miss the *newness* that existed within her when she'd seen it all and lived through it all.

"Why didn't they just sacrifice the Fae during the years that the Veil meant they couldn't find Changelings? I can't imagine Mab has any hesitation in killing her enemies. She could have used that as an opportunity," Estrella said.

She was right. "Mab doesn't kill often. She'd much rather torment her enemies for an eternity than give them the peace that comes with death. When she does kill, it's usually in a moment of blind rage. She isn't methodical about it, otherwise she would have been wise to keep Fae locked in the dungeon until the next Tithe. There will be consequences for the fact that so much of the boundary has been weakened. Aside from the creatures that have escaped and terrorized the courts already, I cannot imagine Ubel will be pleased that he's been denied the souls he was promised."

"What do you think will happen?"

"We have to sacrifice a more powerful soul to the magic alongside the humans as an apology for the lack of payment these last years," I explained, heaving a sigh as I tried not to think about the possibility of either of us being chosen to pay the price.

I could fight. I could survive the battle if it meant I would be there to protect Estrella. But if Mab decided to treat her like one of the Gods, I wasn't certain she was strong enough to protect herself. Her magic was strong, and she was good with a sword, but there was a difference between fighting humans and fighting the Gods themselves.

"A Sidhe?" she asked, swallowing as she stared at me.

She knew the answer to that, knew that the life of a Sidhe wouldn't be enough to make up for *centuries* of missing souls.

"Mab summoned the remaining Gods here because she has determined that we will all fight to the death. Whoever is deemed to be the weakest of us will be given to Tartarus on the day the holly tree burns to ash," I said, grasping her by the chin and turning her to face me. I cupped her cheek as I stared down at her, leaning forward to touch my forehead to hers.

"But you—"

"It won't be me," I vowed. I wouldn't allow anything to take me from her.

Especially not something as permanent as death.

I looked up as Mab stepped up beside us, her dark eyes gleaming as she undoubtedly read the realization on Estrella's face. "Don't worry, Little Mouse. Whatever you are, you're no God. I've no interest in your soul."

Estrella's chest quaked with the slightest sign of her relief, filling me with agony. Of all the ways to die, of all the ways for her to fear she might lose me, *this* would be the most traumatic for her.

It was a curse, as if the sacrifice was hunting her through her life, waiting to claim the soul that was promised. But I was the God of the Dead, and I would not bow to death.

Estrella stepped closer to the edge, moving away from Mab. I nearly reached out to pull her back, fearing how close she came to that sudden drop. To imply she was so fragile that the drop into the pit would hurt her would have been an insult to who she was—what she'd become.

Even if it was my own selfishness that drove me to my desire, I couldn't act on it. Not when she would condemn me for what she saw if she thought I'd had any part in it.

Her body stilled, her frame going rigid, as she stared down into the seven people within the pit. None of them so much as glanced up at her, huddled in their fearful group and pretending that the Gods hadn't come to look down upon them.

"*No.*" The word was a single command as she spun back to look at me in shock.

There, at the center of the seven, was one of the people she'd thought never to see again. She might have hated my mate for her part in the fall of the Resistance—likely would have even killed Estrella herself if given the opportunity, but still Estrella's heart bled for what was to come.

The moment her gaze landed on mine, I knew she understood that I had known. Known, and kept it from her.

"I thought you would be pleased to see your old friend," Mab said.

Fallon hung her head in shame where I saw her to the right, her body sagging in a way that I knew she'd also known of Skye's presence in the seven sacrifices.

"Fallon certainly was when they were reunited, though I can't say the same for the human now that Fallon is Fae."

"How did you even know about her?" Estrella asked, her hurt-filled eyes finally leaving mine. There'd been a plea there, begging me to intercede, begging me to tell her it wasn't true.

I would not interfere on behalf of one human life—especially not one who'd been cruel to Estrella and looked at her as if she was the devil herself. Not when interfering would put Estrella in harm's way.

Mab was indifferent to Estrella's plea, shrugging her shoulders as she glanced toward her daughter. Fallon appeared as if she wanted to shrink into the rock walls themselves, refusing to meet Estrella's eyes as her attention turned toward her.

"Fallon's memory was filled with images of people in the Resistance when I sorted through it, looking for traces of magic. I brought her here thinking she might serve as an incentive for Fallon," Mab said, and Estrella spun forward to look down upon the human woman.

I knew the moment she recognized the gash across Skye's cheek, the way she held herself across the middle, as if she could barely support her weight. The signs of brutality ran deep, though Skye did her best to disguise them.

"Pick someone else," Estrella said, wincing as soon as she spoke the words. She knew as well as I could that she couldn't subject someone else to Mab's cruelty.

That she could never make that choice.

"Give me a name," Mab said, a serpentine smile transforming her mouth. She *knew* what she'd done. She knew this was the first way to stain Estrella's soul.

To break her.

The choice would kill her, end all the good parts of her that remained.

"I forbid it," I growled, the command echoing down the bond. I put every ounce of myself into it, watching the moment it struck Estrella in the chest. It came with a sort of bleak understanding as the magic washed over her.

Still, her lips peeled back in a snarl, her hatred of being told what to do battling with the fact that she knew it was for her own good. If she truly desired it, she could fight the command. She could fight the way the bond made those words *meaningful*.

It was something I intended to use very rarely, especially given the fact I couldn't be sure who would win if we resorted to an all-out battle of wills.

I smiled, softening the harsh expression I'd adopted when I sent the command. Begging her to see—to understand that I would only command her when she was in danger. She could tolerate the pain, but the hit to her goodness would destroy her from the inside out.

Estrella's snarl faltered, melting away as she studied me. Slowly, she nodded, stepping into my embrace when I held out my arms.

"Such a bore," Mab drawled, rolling her eyes to the ceiling as she stepped away to find someone else to torment over the choice they'd made. I pulled my mate in a little tighter, holding her a little harder, knowing I'd played my part in condemning Skye to death.

If it saved Estrella's soul, I would shoulder the weight of that decision every day.

24

Estrella

Caldris guided me up to my chambers, with Malachi at our backs. He'd been granted the opportunity to spend the night with me, and I had no doubt that it was meant to be another torturous moment.

That we were meant to spend the night knowing the coming days would be filled with death and blood, or what would have been death if the opponents had been human, anyway. It was a slow, delicious torture. Knowing that this night could very well be one of our last together if he was chosen as the sacrifice.

I supposed, in a way, every moment Caldris and I shared had been the same, that our entire relationship had been precarious and riddled with danger. The knowledge of that did nothing to calm my queasy stomach as I moved to the window. Nila had pulled back the curtains, leaving the white sands visible to me just outside the window.

"Is there anything I can do for you, Princess?" Nila asked, coming over to stand beside me. She didn't touch me as I stared out at the white sand, shaking my head subtly.

"Will you draw her a bath please, Nila?" Caldris asked, his voice tempered.

I turned to find him staring at me, his eyes soft as he turned them to my handmaid.

"Of course," she said, nodding as she hurried to do his bidding.

"I don't want a bath," I protested, flinching away when Caldris wrapped his arms around me.

He touched his fingers to the unblemished part of my throat, where Mab hadn't replaced my collar for the night. I couldn't help but wonder if Rheaghan held more influence over her than I'd initially suspected. If his protest of my treatment had actually made a difference, perhaps there was a way that could be used to our advantage.

Fallon was his niece. If he had any kind of loyalty to her...

I turned in my mate's arms, facing the window once again. His fingers dropped to the laces at the back of my gown, loosening them until air filled my lungs slowly. It was easy to forget how much the corset had restricted my breathing once I'd adjusted to having less, but the sudden shift made me vow to never wear another.

The loosened fabric and boning shifted away from my skin, gaping at the front as I slid the narrow straps down my arms. It caught at my waist, the fitted waistline taking some maneuvering as I shimmied it down my thighs.

I headed for my bed, stepping out of my heels as I raised my feet to get over the pile of fabric. Caldris moved with me, scooping me up and carrying me away from the monstrous, comfortable bed to lower me into the warm water of the bath.

I glared up at him, crossing my arms over my chest as I settled into the basin, and he lowered his fingers to the laces on his tunic. "I said I didn't want a bath."

"You're cold," he said, as if my chilled skin was explanation enough.

"The furs on the bed would have been plenty to warm me," I snapped, shifting as he stripped off his clothes and moved into the water on the opposite side of me.

Nila peeked her head out from the little room where she stored any supplies she might need, getting an eyeful of my mate's ass as he moved. Caldris was unbothered, settling himself into the tub and turning to look at the blushing Sidhe woman with a kind smile as she spoke.

"Will you be needing anything else, my Princess?" she asked, bowing her head.

I couldn't fault her entirely, knowing that Caldris's presence was almost too much for me to bear sometimes. Even when he was clothed, he cut a formidable figure, but when he was naked and the corded lines of his muscle were open to view…

"That will be all tonight, Nila. Thank you," I said, channeling that same calm authority that Caldris had used with her.

She might have been tending to my needs, but that didn't mean she couldn't be treated with kindness while still trying to find a way to maintain boundaries.

Those seemed important suddenly when I was nude in the tub with my mate; our evening activities greatly foreshadowed.

"I have to be able to look at her in the morning, you know," I mumbled as she scurried from the room, closing the door behind her quickly to limit the view she afforded to Malachi, who seemed to guard my door at all times of the day and night.

"Are you ashamed of me, *min asteren*?" Caldris asked, cocking his head to the side in that arrogant way of his. "Does it bring you shame for your handmaid to know that I plan to spend my night inside of you?"

"It isn't shame," I pouted, sinking lower into the water as my cheeks heated.

"I think it is. It may not be because of me, but rather because of you. You were raised to believe that sex was shameful, and no matter how many times I fuck you in front of an audience, I cannot seem to rid you of that notion. Sex is beautiful. It is not something that must be enjoyed in private and quietly behind closed doors. You are my mate, and the drive to have me inside of you is something normal that should be embraced," he explained, smirking as he leaned forward and touched a thumb to my lips. The next words were a taunt, meant to dampen my foul mood, but Mab's threat rang in my ears. "How else will you give me my heirs one day?"

I sputtered, choking on my own breath as I sat up straighter and glared at him. "Don't go there."

Caldris laughed, snagging my bottom lip as he trailed his thumb over my chin and down the front of my throat. His touch continued, sliding through the valley between my breasts as he touched a flat palm to the slight swell of my stomach.

"Don't worry. We will not be bringing a baby into this world until we've fixed it for them, as much as I would love to see you swell with my child."

"I thought Fae pregnancies were incredibly rare?" I asked, swallowing back my nerves at the prospect of becoming a mother. I wasn't certain I even wanted that, let alone to be discussing the possibility of it so soon, and there was no part of me that would even consider it until Mab was dead.

In Nothrek, there were teas that could be taken to prevent unwanted pregnancies. The Ladies of the Night took them daily. If a Fae pregnancy wasn't impossible, I would take those until the day I died if need be, rather than see my child bound to Mab as Caldris had been.

"They are. I've never heard of a pregnancy occurring within the first century of a completed mate bond, and that is not for lack of trying," Caldris said with a chuckle. "We've not yet even completed our bond and children cannot happen until we do. You have plenty of time to decide how you would like to proceed in regard to children."

"To decide?" I asked, sinking my teeth into my bottom lip as Caldris trailed his hand lower. It drifted over my lower stomach, teasing the flesh at the top of my pussy as my legs spread instinctively.

"Greedy little thing," Caldris murmured with a tsk, tapping his fingers against me and sending a jolt of pleasure through my body. "Yes, to decide, my star. If you decide you don't want children, I'll not force it."

"But you want them," I said, fighting back the surge of pleasure gathering in my stomach. He coaxed his fingers against me, watching as my back arched in response to his touch.

"I do, but I want you more. If they are not a part of our future, I'll be content with having you happy at my side. You're young, and your thoughts may change with time and stability. But even if they don't, that will be okay," he said, sliding a finger inside of me. "In the meantime, I will spend every opportunity showing you how much I love you."

He lifted me out of the water, forcing me to scramble to grip the edges of the bath as he deposited me into it.

"You would do that for me?" I asked, adjusting my legs as he used his hands at my hips to guide me down onto his length.

He slid inside me slowly, filling me as I tossed my head back in pleasure. Raising a single hand to grasp me by my hair, he tilted me forward until he caught my eyes with his piercing gaze.

"My star, I would plunge the world into eternal darkness if it meant one more moment with you like this. Nothing else matters."

"Until chaos reigns," I murmured, our bond warming beneath the words. The vow pulsed between us, a reminder of the way we'd bound our lives to one another.

At the time, it had seemed like Caldris would die along with me, but now... Now who knew what it meant?

All I knew was the way he moved inside me, the way he surrounded me, and his warmth sinking into me, chasing away the chill that the sight of the sacrifices had left me with.

He echoed my words, murmuring them against my mouth as he kissed me. "Until chaos reigns."

***

I lay in his arms, my head resting on his chest in the moments following our latest round of lovemaking.

"When you said I was cold..." I trailed off, thinking of the warmth that now seemed to flow through me, to surround me in ways that were more than just the furs Caldris had covered us with as we settled down to sleep for a few precious hours.

"I meant you," he confirmed, trailing his fingers over my arm with a gentleness that never ceased to take my breath away.

I'd seen the brutality he was capable of, the way he could tear a man from limb to limb if he so desired. He grasped a dagger off the nightstand, sliding the edge of the blade against his wrist.

Blood dripped upon the dark sheets, slipping out of him as he pressed the wound to my mouth. I parted my lips, letting his essence wash over my tongue. The flavor drew a moan from me, a desire for more. I wrapped my hand around his arm and held him steady. It had been too long since he'd fed the obsession he'd created, since he made me desire more of him.

When he drew away, the wound healed while I watched, and I ran my tongue over my teeth. Whatever had remained of that cold place within me, the place where I withdrew to when things got hard, he chased away with the closeness that came to our bond when he was inside me in all the ways possible.

"I love knowing you're filled with me in as many ways as possible," he said, his voice a soft whisper against my skin.

I flushed, turning to hide my faint smile in his chest as I took the dagger from his hand. I healed faster than him. I healed wounds made by iron almost immediately once the iron was removed. Who was to say he wouldn't benefit from *my* blood now?

I dragged the blade over my wrist, ignoring the bite of pain as Caldris stared down at it in shock.

"What are you doing?"

"I'm not human, *min anam*. Do the Sidhe who bond to one another share their blood equally, or do they have a power imbalance and only pass it one way?" I asked, in genuine curiosity.

"They share it equally, but you are not Sidhe, Estrella. I do not know what you are, but the Sidhe have little magic. Without knowing, there is a risk in blood sharing," he said, but even as he spoke the words, he eyed the blood dripping from my wound onto his chest.

"It's your choice," I said, pursing my lips as I considered it.

It would always be his choice. He'd lived for centuries, *an eternity*, where choice had been taken from him. Where he'd been forced to do things, to tolerate the touch of others, against his will. I would never take that from him.

There were doubtlessly things that I wouldn't understand for a long time about the Fae, but that didn't mean I couldn't give him the option. The wound started to heal, those golden threads working to knit my flesh back together as Caldris made his choice.

He grasped my arm delicately, raising my wrist to his mouth. Heat spread through me the moment his lips touched my skin, a tingle pulsing through me. As if his essence slid into the wound, penetrating my blood. He groaned, the sound trailing into the depths of a growl as he sealed his mouth around my wrist more fully and pulled my arm tighter to his face.

"Fuck," I said, wincing as he drank from me in deep pulls.

Something slithered through the white of his Fae mark, a golden shimmer working the way through the snow as it writhed on his skin. I stared at it in wonder for a moment, turning my attention back to him as he continued to take my blood. It was longer than I usually took from him, more time passing as he took deep swallows of me into him.

"Caldris," I said softly, touching my free hand to his cheek.

His eyes flew open, glowing with golden light as he stared up at me. I flinched back, trying to take my wrist with me. He held fast, refusing to release me as he rolled me beneath him in a sudden, unnaturally fast movement. His hips slid between my legs, his cock nestling against me as he rocked his hips with a groan.

I stilled, watching him to see how I should move forward. While he was rougher, his body unhinged as if the thought of losing my bleeding wound was too much for him to bear, the man that lingered behind those foreign golden eyes was my mate. He was still Caldris, waiting for me to give him permission to take what he needed.

I may not have understood where the urgency came from or what my blood had done to him, but I still felt his love and desire for *me* pulsing down the bond between us.

That was what drove me to spread my legs wider, reaching between our bodies with my free hand and guiding him until his head notched against my entrance. It was the permission he needed when he couldn't seem to grasp the ability to communicate with words.

Driving inside of me, he filled the part of me he'd already claimed twice that evening. He held my wrist to his mouth, his other hand planted against the mattress beside my head as I wrapped my legs around his hips and took him deep.

"That's enough," I murmured, drawing my wrist away from his mouth.

He let it go this time, our bodies remaining united as he stared at my wrist and the blood that trickled from the wound. It healed over as he watched, his attention turning back to my face when the source of my blood no longer tormented him.

His golden gaze upon me was eerie, somehow so different from the mate I knew, and somehow *more* him than ever before. He dropped both hands to my hips, pinning me to the bed as he pulled free from my pussy and stared down at the space between my legs.

He pressed his hand against me, feeling how wet I was for him and sliding his fingers into me before he pulled them free. He flipped me to my stomach quickly, my body thumping against the mattress. His movements remained fast, frenzied, as he drove back inside of me.

A hand buried in the hair at the back of my head, wrapping it around his fist so that he could use it to pull me back so that my body arched for him.

"You taste like the night sky, *min asteren*," he groaned, forcing me to my knees so that he could fuck me as he yanked me backward and whispered in my ear. "Like raw, untouched power. Like ice running through my veins with the cool sweetness of twilight berries."

Ice would have flooded my veins at the reminder, but the heat of his cock driving through me kept the daemons at bay.

"What *are* you?" he asked, his frustration echoing through the cadence of his voice.

He touched his lips to the pulse thrumming up the side of my neck, as if he could feel my blood flowing and wanted to be as close to it as possible. He touched a wet finger to the *other* part of me. The one that remained untouched.

I flinched away, jolting forward as he held me steady. "I don't think—"

"Relax, my star. It will hurt less if you do," he murmured, massaging the ring gently.

He worked my body into relaxing for him, angling his hips so that his cock dragged over that sensitive part inside me and worked me toward an orgasm.

I whimpered as it approached, as his finger coaxed me to open for him until he slid inside. My body burned, feeling as if it had been lit aflame from the inside as he fucked me, making shallow thrusts with his finger in time with his cock.

"If you're going to take me here, you'll need to practice."

There was a bite of laughter in his voice, something raw and powerful as I held his golden stare over my shoulder. The lights shimmered, traces of his blue eyes appearing through the glittering dust of power.

"Caldris," I murmured.

"That's right, my star. Fucking come for me," he said, driving deep.

I shattered, seeing the stars that had become my namesake as my eyes rolled back in my head. He groaned as I squeezed down around him, thrusting into me and striking the end of me as he came.

The heat of his climax filled me, searing my insides as he dropped his head forward and paused to catch his breath.

I collapsed onto the bed, exhaustion claiming my body. We'd need to have a conversation in the morning when I could form a coherent thought, but for now, I drifted off.

Because what the *fuck?*

25

Estrella

The Winter Solstice was meant to be a celebration that the darkening of the days had ended. That the longer days and warmer weather would be coming soon enough. It was meant to be a time of celebration, not melancholy.

I got the impression the same was true for the rest of the Faerie courts as the Gods shuffled their way through the darkened, candlelit halls of Tar Mesa in front of us. Caldris strode at my side, his head held high even as he remained quiet.

I'd never been to this part of the palace, ventured this far into the earth of the rolling Faerie hills that comprised the landscape of the capital of the Shadow Court. Even in the brief time I'd spent outside, even in the moments I glimpsed the terrain outside through my bedroom window, all I saw for miles was the distinct rolling and rocky hills covered in jagged stone.

We ventured down, and the gradual slope of the hallway gave way to a rugged staircase. The sconces on the wall lit the way, the Summer Fae waving her hand casually as she came upon them.

"This feels wrong," I said, glancing over my shoulder as we walked.

Malachi met my gaze, lifting his brow at me as if I meant to run away. The very air in this place was tense, as if it lacked anything living; as if only death existed within the narrow passage.

"*Cradthail non Beathor* isn't something to be taken lightly. It is said that this is where life first began. That this is the place where Khaos stood when he created the moons and stars in the sky, when he created life itself, and the Void for all souls when they die," my mate said, leaning down to murmur the words against the top of my head as we made our way down the steps carefully.

The Cradle of Life.

I grasped the skirt of my gown in my hands, the red fabric fading into a taupe color as it approached the stone floors. It wrapped around my chest, binding my breasts and leaving my stomach bare to the distinctive chill in the air that I couldn't seem to place.

"It smells like death," I said, contradicting his words about it being the cradle of life. It didn't *feel* like anything living had touched this place in centuries.

"Mab has forbidden any from entering the Cove since the construction of the Veil. This is where the Shadow Fae complete their mate bond, and without human mates…"

"There's been no reason to come here," I said, understanding dawning upon me.

Whether it was the Cove itself that smelled of death or merely the passage of time, I didn't know.

Mab led the procession, pausing at the foot of the stairs. The passage was just dark enough that it was difficult to see through the small group of us crammed into the narrow path, but I watched as she raised her hands above her head. She grasped the crown, lifting it from her dark hair as the air seemed to ripple around us.

The others seemed unfazed, unflinching as she bowed her head forward and held the crown out in front of her. The mist swirling in front of her faded, swaying in a breeze before it vanished entirely. The dark gem placed at the center gleamed. Candlelight playing off the surface, snagging my attention.

The passageway faded into the background, and the image of a woman with gleaming green eyes shone back at me from the center of the gem. Her hair writhed in the shadows, her lips twisted into a scowl as she pinned me in place. There was a slash across her neck, a deep, jagged wound that seeped blood as if someone had severed her head from her body and then sewn her back together once more.

Only when Mab raised her crown to her head did the connection sever. Caldris nudged me forward as if he was completely, blissfully unaware of the woman I'd seen trapped within the gem. Unaware of the woman staring through from the other side, robed in darkness and bathed in serpents.

I shook off my disorientation, stumbling forward at his urging and trying to make sense of what I'd seen. But as we approached the opening at the bottom of the passageway, I stared into the lushest forest I'd ever seen. The waters of the Cove glimmered like the brightest turquoise I'd ever seen, surrounded by pink sand and small rodent-like animals that carefully dug through it.

They scurried into the woods as our party of the Gods stepped into the clearing, disappearing into the tree line that surrounded the Cove on three sides. The trees were taller than any I'd ever seen, enormous, towering things that created a shaded canopy. A glimpse through them was rare, the inside of the Faerie hill looking like white limestone as it curved overhead to protect the Cove.

The Cove waters drew me forward, compelling me to approach their depths. My insides *burned*, that hollow within me shifting as if the creature could rear her head, sensing what was close. I stepped forward as if in a trance, the sounds of the Gods around me fading into the background. They existed as if I were in a bubble, only the glimmer of the water penetrating it. The rising deep called to me, summoning me toward them as if they pulled at that golden thread that existed within me.

Come home.

The voice was the whisper of a caress, slithering across my skin. Another step brought me closer to it, the pleasure in the woman's voice sliding over me like a warm embrace. Her voice was a song, a melody that begged me to join in and become part of the music of the Cove.

But Caldris gripped my hand tightly and shook his head. The bubble surrounding me burst, the sudden penetration of sound making me stagger as I blinked rapidly up at him. He tilted his head to the side, reaching up to cup my cheek with a silent question in his stare.

My mouth dropped open to answer, to ask what he felt when he looked at the waters themselves, and if he heard the music too, but I couldn't seem to find the words to describe that haunting melody.

I couldn't find the words to explain why I felt as if my soul had been torn in two—that part of me belonged to him, my mate and other half, but the rest of me...

The rest of me belonged to those still waters.

The others veered into the treeline, disappearing into the lush forest and the massive palm leaves that hung low. One of Mab's personal guards held the leaves back, revealing a path that was slightly traveled in comparison to the rugged, natural overgrowth of the rest of the trees.

"I want to see the water," I said, my legs refusing to move as Caldris tried to follow.

I glanced back at the Cove, wishing for that connection to snap into place once more. I craved the beauty of that song, the feeling of belonging that had washed over me—consumed me—the moment I heard it.

"As pretty as it may be, stay away from the Cove," Caldris commanded, stepping onto the path through the trees.

He gripped my hand more fully, pulling until I had no choice but to follow him. I couldn't tear my eyes off the Cove itself, even as the glimmering waters disappeared when we stepped into the forested path. The leaves blocked it out, the ferns stealing the view.

Emptiness settled inside me with every step, that creature within me sinking deeper into the well than she'd ever existed before. She paced in a circle, settling down with a huff of disappointment.

I tried to focus on the sounds of the birds chirping overhead, on the natural sounds of beauty in a place I'd thought condemned by death. The rotting smell of natural decay existed here as well, all a part of the cycle of life, but the clean air and scent of flowers in the air overpowered it.

"But why?" I asked, shaking my head as if I could rid my memory of that feeling of completion that had awaited me in the waters.

"The Cove is the entrance to Tartarus," Caldris explained, following behind his mother and the rest of the Gods.

She walked slowly in front of us, keeping her head turned forward as if she was ignoring us. I got the distinct impression she lingered close so that she could be with her son, even if she couldn't risk speaking to him directly.

Hearing his voice.

Feeling his presence.

We walked in silence, the feeling of the Cove calling to me. In spite of the fact that it was simply a hole in the ground, that there was no ocean or current to justify it, I swore I heard the waves lapping against the shore. I swore I felt the ebb and flow of the water striking against my soul, summoning me to the depths of the place I shouldn't dare to go. It was a prison that housed the worst creatures in the world, that housed some of the Gods themselves.

There would be no escape for me.

"Why is it called a cove when there is no ocean?" I asked, earning a chuckle from Rheaghan where he strode at Twyla's side in front of us.

"There was an ocean once," he said, looking at the hillside that now surrounded it. "Peri, the Primordial of Mountains, cut it off from the sea when the Cove became the entrance to Tartarus, so that no unsuspecting sailors could sail in and become trapped."

I tripped over a tree root as we walked, my dress snagging on one of the branches jutting into the path. Caldris caught me as I stumbled, his concerned glance fixed on me as I pulled on my dress to free the fabric. It served two purposes, both to ease my embarrassment at being clumsy and to distract from the probing stare of my mate.

I knew he could feel how unsettled I was, that he could feel my nerves and that pulsing thrum of the tide washing over my heart that no one else seemed to hear. I squatted down to free my dress when it didn't come loose, coming face to face with the smallest of creatures. She was the size of a mouse, the fur on her body the color of moss. Blue eyes gleamed back at me as she stared up at me, her tiny front paws clawing at the taupe fabric of my dress at the bottom.

She had a cute button of a nose, and the tiniest antlers rested upon the top of her head.

"What are you?" I asked, lowering to my knees.

She twitched her nose as she stared up at me, glaring at my hand and baring her teeth as I held it out like I might pet her. She snapped her long, skinny tail through the air, the spiked edges pointed as they came down upon my flesh and drew tiny pinpricks of blood.

"It's a wolpertinger," Caldris explained, eyeing the sharp teeth she bared as he spoke.

"I don't want to hurt you," I said, grasping the fabric of my dress where she didn't seem to want to let go, despite her lack of fondness for my attention. I tore a small piece from the bottom, letting her keep the part that she clung to as her mouth closed and she hid her teeth once more.

"That wasn't wise," Caldris said, sighing as he held out a hand for me to take.

I failed to see how a tiny scrap of fabric would matter to me in the end. I had a feeling the wolpertinger needed it more than I did.

"Why not?"

"They're greedy little creatures. If they think you'll provide them with the things they need, they'll never leave you alone," he answered, chuckling beneath his breath. "Once she tells all her friends about the woman who gave her a nice blanket, you'll have all of them raiding your wardrobe."

"They're just clothes," I said, thinking about how nice a scrap of soft, warm fabric must be after centuries of no people being allowed within the Cove.

"We'll see if you still feel that way when they find their way to your room next time," Caldris said.

We paused as the forest opened up, and a clearing emerged in front of us. The others made a circle around a tree at the center of the clearing. The holly tree was even larger than the others in the forest. The trunk was bigger than a man, wide with deep roots that spread through the clearing. It jutted up into the sky, moonlight streaming down through a hole in the Faerie hill until it reached the free air outside. Mab stepped forward; her face drawn tight as she stood before the great tree.

"Seven days of light in the dead of winter," she said, nodding to the Summer Court Fae who wielded fire.

The woman stepped forward, holding out her hand and summoning fire to her palm. Mab held out a torch she'd grabbed from the side of the tree trunk itself, the metal rusted from the passage of time. Turning to the Summer Fae, she held it out and watched as the other lit the flame.

The fire made Mab's fair skin seem to shine in the darkness, and I took a step forward against my own will. Caldris wrapped his arms around my shoulders from behind, crossing them over my chest and pinning my back to his front.

"It will be all right. I promise," he murmured.

"She can't possibly mean to—"

"The ritual of the burning tree is sacred to the Court of Shadows, and this tree has been alive for longer than I have. It will be reborn soon enough," he explained, holding me steady through my wince as Mab raised the torch above her head.

"Seven souls to pay the tithe," Mab said as the flames licked the low-hanging leaves. They caught fire, the branches seeming to glow with golden light as the flames spread through the tree.

It rolled up to the top; the flames lighting the branches and each of the leaves. But even as they burned, they didn't change. They didn't dissolve to ash or blacken. The burning tree lit the clearing like the beacon of a sun.

"We mourn the loss of the darkest night, welcoming the time of the sun," Mab said as she returned the torch to the holder. A few pieces of bark fell away from the trunk as she scraped it.

The first of the leaves fell upon the ground, burning as it floated free.

Seven days.

26

Estrella

That haunting voice called my name—the sounds of each syllable resonating like a song in the wind.

Estrelllaaa.

The vision of the woman from Mab's gleaming jeweled crown appeared before me. Her brown skin shone in the light of the twin moons overhead as her full lips formed my name. The voice stretched across the dark void between us as she took the first step to close that gap.

"Come home, Estrella," she said.

She crossed the distance suddenly, as if that single step had moved her across an entire world. A flash and then she was in front of me, her deep green and gold hair writhing upon her head.

It took me longer than I cared to admit to realize it wasn't hair that sprouted from her scalp, but the living bodies of snakes. They bared their teeth at me, their green hued scales the same color as her shining eyes.

As the leather and armor she wore upon her breast.

"My mate is my home," I whispered to her, unable to tear my gaze off those eyes.

I swallowed, tears pooling in my eyes as I felt something click into place. Fear tore at me like phantom talons, sending my heartbeat racing until it flooded my own hearing.

There was nothing outside of our stare, nothing existed but that moment of connection.

"Take what is yours and come home," she said.

The memory of that gleaming black gem, of the crown Mab didn't deserve to wear, flashed through my head. The rage followed—the illogical drive to tear it from her skull and make it mine. I couldn't shake those thoughts, couldn't get that unending pit of rage to go back to sleep within me.

It was a fire, consuming my every thought, as I took a single step away from the woman in front of me. Her snakes slithered closer, reaching out with fangs descended—

* * *

A phantom touch brushed against my cheek. I turned my head to the side, thrashing away from the mouth of the snake. These ones wouldn't obey me. I knew with every bone in my body. That woman, she owned them.

My power was but a fraction of what existed within her.

"My star," a man said.

Hands grasped my arms, pinning me down as I tossed from side to side. I couldn't get away, couldn't break free from the confines of the grip holding me. Panic flooded me, the thought of being trapped beneath the snakes waiting to devour me—

"Wake up."

Love tugged at my center, pulling me from the depths of despair. *A dream*, I realized with a start. I gasped as I took a real breath, the fear fading away as my eyes flung open to find my mate staring back at me.

"Just a dream," he reassured, confirming my realization.

My body felt slicked with sweat, my hair a tangled mess about my head. But Caldris didn't care, leaning down to touch his mouth to mine in a sweet caress.

"A dream," I echoed, nodding my head as his forehead pressed into mine.

He sighed, his lips pressing into a thin line as he stared at me. Waiting for the shadows to clear, for the worst of the terror to fade, he watched me.

"Do you want to talk about it?" he asked, rolling onto his side.

His weight left mine. The body he'd used to pin me down so that I couldn't hurt him, or myself, pressing into mine as I turned to face him and buried my face in his chest.

I shook my head, unable to form the words to describe what I'd seen. Something about her felt private, like she was my secret to bear for the time being. I'd tell him when I knew what she was, who she was, to me.

When I knew why she'd decided to haunt my dreams, and whether or not I'd crafted her from my imagination. The things I'd felt, the things I'd seen, since arriving in Alfheimr had begun to take their toll.

Had I imagined her face in the gem? Had some part of me broken beneath the pain?

"I'm broken," I murmured, feeling Caldris's arms tighten around me.

He pulled back, his eyes meeting mine as the first tear slid free from my eye. It fell onto the pillow as he leaned forward, kissing the top of my head.

"I think we all are, in our own ways," he said, the words a soft assurance. He didn't try to convince me that regardless of whatever I'd dreamt, I wasn't broken. He didn't try to heal me.

He just held me, loved me—jagged, broken pieces and all.

"I love you," I said softly, snuggling into his chest as he pulled me tighter.

His scent filled my lungs, the steady throbbing of his heart reminding me of home. *This* was where I belonged, not the Cove that called to me even now.

"And I love you, *min asteren*. Now sleep. I'll be here to watch over you," he returned, the soothing calm of his voice allowing me to let my eyes drift closed.

"You can't protect me from the monsters in my own head," I said, my voice sluggish as the pull of sleep called me back.

There was silence for a moment, his chin coming to rest above mine as we shared a pillow. Then, in my final moments before sleep claimed me, the soft, gruff voice of the male I loved said, "Watch me."

***

Mab pushed for me to use my power the next day, for me to summon the part of me that sparked with gold every time she bled me. But something inside me had withered, shrunk that day when we left the Cove, lingering behind as if it would keep that part of my soul for itself.

I struggled with nightmares during the night, with visions of the woman in the jewel atop Mab's head, the overwhelming rage consuming me with the desire to strip it from her head. I couldn't shake those thoughts, couldn't have summoned the power I didn't understand even if I wanted to. Before, using it had seemed instinctive, coming to me with extreme emotion or the need to protect myself from the harm others would do to me.

Now all I could do was suffer as Mab allowed Malachi to carve into my skin with iron, to bleed upon the chair she strapped me to in order to confine me. Pain was no longer a motivator. My fear had abandoned me. I knew it was only a matter of time before Mab held true to her promise to hurt someone else, to use the mates against me.

Nila dressed me in leather pants after helping me clean up from my morning torture, drawing a raised brow from me. She kept her head turned down as one of Mab's men summoned Caldris for some mundane job that day. She wasn't her usual reassuring self as she worked, pulling my dark hair back into a complex braid that draped over one shoulder.

"I'm not going to like this very much, am I?" I asked, heaving a sigh.

She jolted, her stare finally raising to meet mine. She merely shook her head, returning to her braiding in silence as I watched in the mirror. Her fingers shook, her hands trembling and causing her have to start entire sections of my braid over again.

Fuck.

***

Nila walked me away from the throne room, where I usually spent my time in Mab's company. The halls in this part of Tar Mesa were broader than the passageway to the Cove had been, a path far more traveled, even though I had never ventured this way. Gratefully so, considering the unusual number of Fae who traveled through them at the same time as us, whispering among themselves as Nila and Malachi guided me through the crowd gathering for the first of the seven events that would mark the Winter Solstice.

The latter pushed people out of the way, clearing a path for Nila and me to stride through.

"Where are they all going?" I asked, swallowing through the lump rising in my throat.

For the first time since the Cove, it felt like something reached inside me and strummed fear into my heart. The numbness the Cove had left me with faded away, leaving me unprotected against whatever horror I would face that day. The creature within me stirred at last, as if she herself could scent the danger. None of the others walking through the crowd were dressed so casually, none were prepared for battle.

I swallowed down the surge of nausea that rose in my gut.

"The same place we are," Malachi said, turning back to sneer at me.

Satisfaction pulsed off him in waves, a horrific reminder of whatever I was about to face. He'd stopped taking joy from tormenting me with iron blades, not getting the reaction he wanted out of me. For him to be pleased with my fate did not bode well for me.

"Mab has summoned you to the Labyrinth," Nila whispered, the reverent, fearful tone to her voice crawling up my skin. It set goosebumps along my flesh, raising the hair on the back of my neck with the chill she created.

"The Labyrinth," I said, echoing her words.

I knew what one was, of course, having heard of the legends of the King's infamous Labyrinth at the palace in Ineburn City. A twisted maze of rose bushes meant to make it impossible to find the correct path to the palace; it served as protection for the royals tucked safely within. Only a select few knew the way through the path.

"I'll cut it down if I must, to find my way through."

"It isn't the maze itself that you should fear," Nila said, shaking her head sadly. "It's the Minotaur who calls it home.

I can't remember the last time someone came out alive when they were selected for the Labyrinth."

I swallowed, not liking the sound of that. I'd hardly been exposed to any of the Fae creatures of Alfheimr aside from the Sidhe, hardly experienced even a hint of the horrors I'd heard legends of.

I suspected that was about to change.

We strode in silence as we came to a set of smaller metal doors. They still took two Fae warriors to haul open, allowing us to pass through as the crowd tried to swallow us whole. Outside, the white sand whipped through the air, barreling against the hedges tucked into the valley. All around the valley were the rolling hills of Tar Mesa. Windows were thrown open to allow the Fae within a view down into the maze. I knew if we continued to the east, we would come to the arena we'd carved into the stone of the next valley and the ice pillars Caldris and I had crafted.

Where we stood, though, only an enormous maze existed within the valley before me. The hedges were the vivid green of nature that I never could have found in Nothrek. An intricate, zigzagging path cut through them.

Malachi led us down into the chasm to the Queen of Air and Darkness, where she waited just outside the entrance to the Labyrinth. A creature stood at her side, towering over her. He was easily twice her size, with a humanoid body packed with muscle. His shoulders were broader than a Sidhe, his neck thick and corded as it curved up toward his face. The head that rested upon his shoulders was that of a bull. His massive horns curved out the side of his temples to stretch toward the sky. His feet were hooved and large enough that the ground seemed to shake as he shifted his weight at Mab's side.

Caldris knelt before them, his hands chained behind his back with iron. His face was beaten, and the blade of an iron sword was pressed against his throat as one of Mab's men kept him still. My jaw clenched at the sight of his swollen eye and the bruising that surrounded it—the gash that cut across his cheekbone. I raised my chin, a vein pulsing in my temple with that surge of anger. As my heart beat faster, the creature within me snarled.

Malachi guided me forward, leaving Nila behind to avoid the wrath of the creature waiting for me. I felt the moment the Minotaur settled his gaze upon me. His eerie black eyes captured mine, his head tilting to the side as he huffed out a sharp breath.

"You promised me something to eat. This is barely a snack," he said, turning his attention to Mab. His nose twitched, the hoop piercing shifting with the movement.

She smirked. "Maybe. But if she loses, you can eat him too," she said, turning her gaze down to where Caldris knelt.

It shouldn't have mattered, because if I died, Caldris would follow. He would likely even be gone before the Minotaur finished devouring me, but the thought of desecrating his body—my body—in such a way made me clench my fists. Talons protruded from my fingers, my own nails shifting and curving as they extended.

"Then let us fight together. If we both suffer the fate of this battle, surely the Minotaur can handle two Fae," my mate argued, leaning into the blade at his throat as if he meant to stand. His face remained the portrait of calm, but I felt the echo of his heart beating in time with mine. I felt his fear, his panic, that the Minotaur might not be a fight I could survive.

"So that you can use your magic to protect her? I think not. The entire purpose of this exercise is to force Estrella to do what she refuses. Perhaps some survival instincts will be enough to push through her stubbornness," Mab said.

She leveled me with a glare, her reference to my inability to perform that morning perfectly clear. I wondered if it had always been me who would have been sent into the Labyrinth, or if she'd changed her mind after my failures that day.

"I'm not refusing to use my magic," I argued, shrugging my shoulders. "I can't touch it anymore. It just isn't there."

Whether that was because of my own doing, I didn't know. I didn't know if I'd pushed it down so far within me that even I couldn't find it, or if the Cove had done something to me. But my instincts told me it was a bit of both—that I needed to protect the knowledge of what I could do for a little while longer. The hands of Fate were playing with the spinning wheel, maneuvering the pieces into place before my bloodline could be revealed, but the Cove *had* shifted something in me—awakened something—only to plunge it into the depths of slumber.

The Minotaur walked to the first entrance to the Labyrinth as Malachi led me to the second entrance. I swallowed, struggling to control my breathing. I couldn't let them know how terrified I was to go into that maze without my magic, couldn't let them see that fear to use against me. I looked at him expectantly, waiting for a weapon to be given to me. The Minotaur held a massive double-sided axe in his hand, the blades bigger than my head.

Surely, I would at least get a knife.

Malachi smirked as he stepped away, leaving me weaponless as he returned to the queen, who had grown tired of my games. My eyes shuttered closed for a brief moment before I forced them to open and shoved my fear down.

Fear would do nothing but get me killed. Panic would force me to make mistakes I couldn't survive.

"The first one to reach the center of the maze wins," Mab said, smiling at me viciously as an ugly laugh bubbled up her throat. I couldn't decide if she truly thought I would die in that maze, or if she was expecting a fantastic show.

I didn't know if she cared either way.

"If he wins, he gets to eat me. What do I get if I win?" I asked, flinching back from her amusement.

She exchanged a knowing glance with Malazan as she appeared at the queen's side, laying a hand on the top of Caldris's shoulder. I tensed, my gaze narrowing in on that touch as Caldris stilled beneath it.

Disgust rippled down the thread between us, his shame an echo of what I'd hoped to make him never feel again. What they'd forced him to do wasn't his fault, and I focused my attention on his face, willing him to see that I did not blame or judge him for those actions in his past. They'd taken from him, and if I survived that maze, I would be sure to take *back*.

His gaze softened as I held it, understanding and love spilling over his features.

"You get to live," Mab said, interrupting the moment with a chuckle. As if it was ridiculous for me to expect anything more than that—as if my life was the most valuable bargaining piece she had.

But it wasn't.

"If you want me to play your game, you're going to have to do better than that," I said, keeping my words careful. I crossed my arms over my chest in challenge, watching as her eyes narrowed at my body language.

"What is it you want, Little Mouse? I have given you every luxury—"

I cut her off, braving her outrage as the crowds of Fae watched our interaction from above—their ears perked, as if they could hear every word. "I want to complete my mate bond with Caldris. I want to be given access to the Cove, so that we can finally unite ourselves as one."

I would deal with the potential consequence of pregnancy once it was done, seeking out the remedies necessary to prevent it. We could not sever her bond over Caldris and challenge her until we completed our bond, and I was *done* with watching them abuse him—with watching those he despised lay their hands upon him like he was a thing without will.

Mab pursed her lips as she considered my terms. She couldn't say no, not when I'd laid down the challenge so publicly. To do so would imply she believed I could win this battle, that I would stand a chance of beating the Minotaur.

I would, if I could use my magic. If I could access that part of me that saw the threads of life, severing the Minotaur's and ending him without ever laying a hand upon him.

I shuddered to think of what it would take to bring that part to the surface, and I would avoid it at all costs. The golden threads connected to Caldris's magic were still there when I passed by water, and I'd learned to pull from our bond.

But he was weakened by the iron—his magic a dull throb where it normally shone brightly. I had to hope it would be enough for me to use either of those things in the Labyrinth, that the bones of his previous victims might litter the ground to form an army.

"I'll need more than a victory to agree to those terms. I'll need my Minotaur's head laid at my feet," Mab said.

I swallowed, disappointment flooding through me. Reaching the center first would have meant merely outrunning him. Delaying him long enough to reach it first.

Killing him...

Shit.

"Deal," I said, pushing aside my fear in favor of the opportunity it presented.

Caldris met my gaze, his eyes wide with fear as he pushed against the blade at his throat. The iron cut into his skin, forcing him to wince back for a moment before he tried to struggle against his iron bonds.

"Estrella," he whispered, horror coating his voice as the Minotaur stomped his hooves and glared at me.

I nodded silently to my mate, turning my attention away from him to face my opponent.

A moment of understanding flashed between us.

Only one of us would leave the Labyrinth alive.

27

Estrella

I sprinted forward the moment Mab's guard announced the start, using my smaller size to my advantage as I sprinted through the pathway. The Minotaur knew the way; he knew the paths that would connect us and allow him to reach me sooner.

He knew how to get to the center.

There was nothing within the Labyrinth but the unending maze of hedges. Their leaves and brambles jutted up out of nowhere, forcing me to slow enough to round the sharp corners. I didn't hesitate in my decisions, keeping left and then right as I allowed some sort of instinct to guide me forward. I couldn't be sure where it came from or how I knew the way, but a voice whispered in the back of my mind with every turn I took.

If I'd hoped to find the remains of the Minotaur's victims, I was sorely mistaken. He'd either eaten them—bones and all—or removed the remnants of their bodies from the Labyrinth.

The sound of snapping branches reached me first. My heart pounded in my chest, jumping into my throat as I snapped my head to the side. An axe cut through the hedge to my right, the gleaming silver of the metal shining against all that green.

Time slowed to a crawl as those hedges were cleaved in half. The axe came straight for my face.

My feet stopped. I skidded along the dirt.

Throwing my weight to the ground, the leather of my pants protected me from the thorns and rocks as the axe cut the hedge away. I landed on my knees—bending my back and flattening myself to the ground. The axe swept through the air above me, narrowly cutting through just above my head. The wind from the motion blew across my face.

The Minotaur appeared on the other side, raising a leg to step over what remained of the hedge. I would have had to climb over it to escape, but his height allowed him to traverse it with ease. Those enormous hooves thumped against the ground; his legs oddly bent.

Slowing him down, I realized. He might have had the advantage of knowing the Labyrinth by memory, but I would have speed on my side, at least.

He stepped into the path as I sprawled on my back, scurrying backward as he took a step forward. I slipped in the mud beneath me—the ground suddenly slick. The coppery tang of it surrounded me as I hurried backward on my hands and kicked my feet.

To my right, blood trickled out of the hedges, the branches bleeding from where he'd cut them down as if they'd been alive. I stared at them in horror, at the roses that wilted as they died. They bled upon the dirt, as if they'd trapped the life and death of his victims within them. The Minotaur's hooves hit the wet earth, the mud squelching as he sank into it ever-so-slightly.

It was enough.

"Use your magic, you foolish child!" Mab screamed, her voice cutting through the air.

I glanced above to where she stood on the hillside, looking down into the maze. She was a blur, a single dot in the landscape of Fae surrounding us. The Minotaur approached slowly, watching me, mindful of my every move.

Waiting for me to do something, for me to fight instead of cower. I'd had such bravado outside the Labyrinth itself, making that deal with its master, only to stare up at my death within moments.

The golden threads of Caldris's magic reached out to me, the gleaming, shimmering liquid of the blood from the hedges providing moisture upon the ground. I grasped onto one, pulling it toward me as the familiar comfort of my mate's cold surrounded us. Wrapping it around my hand and claiming it as mine, I turned a glare back at the Minotaur and thrust my hand toward the ground.

My palm collided with the wet earth. My hand sunk into the mud. The wet, sucking sound erupted through the silence, and the Minotaur paused. I sank my hand as far as I could, only stopping when I found the dry dirt beneath the surface mud. Turning my full attention back to the Minotaur, I watched as ice spread from my hand and created a halo beneath my body. It spread toward him—the blood-soaked ground turning to ice beneath his feet.

His hooves couldn't grip, slipping to the side as he grunted, and his breaths left him in puffs of white upon the air. I used the opportunity to race forward, hurrying to my feet. I fumbled on the ice as I moved, forcing my body to keep going anyway as I slipped and made myself small.

My hands covered my head, prepared for the worst. All it would take was a single moment of coordination on his part— one swing of his axe—

I slid between his parted legs.

Dissolving the ice on the other side of him, I ran across the dirt and put as much distance between us as I could. I'd need a weapon of some kind, *anything* that could be used against him, if I wanted to kill him. If not, getting to the center and surviving would have to be enough.

I'd fight the battle for completing our bond another day if need be.

My feet pounded against the dirt so hard that I clenched my jaw to stop my teeth from grinding against one another. I flexed my fingers at my side, knowing that I could only outrun him for so long. There had to be another choice, another way to escape.

I cast my eyes from one side of the path to the other, frantically searching for anything I could use to my advantage.

There was *nothing* but hedges and thorns.

His roar rang through the air as I ran, swerving around a bend to the right and hurrying. I knew the moment he got himself off the ice I'd created. His heavy hoof steps echoed through my bones as they thudded against the ground. The entire pathway shook as he came closer, leaving me scrambling to decide which way to go.

My breaths rattled as they escaped me, the air in front of my face turning white with the warmth of it in the cold air. I couldn't blink as my legs trembled beneath me. It wasn't exhaustion that made them weak, but the strong press of fear that darted down my spine.

I glanced over at the hedge beside me, grimacing in frustration as I did the only thing I could. I grasped one of the lower branches, wedging my body into the hedge itself.

The thorns and branches cut my skin, and blood leaked down my arms and my face as the branches seemed to sway toward me. They wanted more, desired my blood as if it was the nourishment that kept them alive. I forced myself to climb, to put one foot on a branch and push myself up. Using those swaying branches to my advantage, I got higher and higher until I could see over the top. I pulled myself free, draping my body along the top of the hedge that was so neatly trimmed into a straight line.

I kept as low as I could as I rose up just enough to see— keeping myself hidden and silent as I looked through the Labyrinth and tried to make sense of the maze. Searching for the center, I grimaced when I found it in the distance.

I hadn't even run through a tiny portion of the maze. Too many turns remained for me to keep track once I lost the bearings of the view. I couldn't walk along the top of the Labyrinth without the Minotaur cutting it down.

I turned, my eyes flashing toward Caldris where he knelt in the dirt. I felt the weight of his eyes upon me, the distant echo of the bond trying to settle me through my panic. His calm spiraled up the thread, striking into my chest and forcing me to slow my breathing and *think*.

I flattened myself against the top of the hedge once more as the Minotaur emerged beside me. Covering my mouth with my hand to silence my panting breaths, I peered over the edge as he stomped through the path.

His pace slowed, as if he could sense me. He looked from side to side, waiting for me to reveal myself in the path.

"Come out, come out, wherever you are," he said, his deep voice reaching the top of the hedge.

He stopped suddenly, his snout flaring as he turned to the hedge where I lay. He took a step closer, breathing deeply and smelling me.

"It will only hurt for a second, sweet blood." His fur-covered hand reached out, touching the hedge. His hand came away stained with blood, *my* blood, I realized in horror.

He raised that hand to his mouth, his long tongue darting out to lick a path up his hand and take my blood into his mouth. He shuddered; his eyes glowing golden as I hurried to act in desperation. If his reaction was anything like Caldris's had been...

His eyes rose to the top of the hedge, seeking the owner of the blood as I leapt from the top. I screamed as I twisted my body in the air, letting instinct guide me as I settled my legs around the back of his neck and squeezed his throat. I tucked myself into his head tightly as he reached for me, claws scraping against my legs and my back. One of my hands wrapped around his horn, holding on for my life. The moment he threw me to the ground would be the moment I died.

I reached around to his face, grasping the ring that protruded from the nostrils of his snout in both my hands. He roared as I pulled, burying my face into the back of his head as I screamed with the effort of trying to tear it through his flesh.

My back tore beneath his claws, a deep wound setting my skin on fire. Healing was almost instant, though. My body worked to fix the damage he caused as quickly as he could cause it.

"*Estrella!*" Caldris roared, the anguish of his voice striking me in the chest as he undoubtedly *felt* my pain.

I screamed again as I settled into our bond, channeling what remained of my mate's strength as I pulled. It filled me, the muscles in my forearms hardening as if they'd become his.

The piercing came free suddenly, the gush of blood following to cover my hands and the Minotaur's chest as he yelped. I twisted my grip on the piercing as he fought to get me off him, maneuvering the sharp part of it toward his face.

I jabbed it into the fleshy part of his eye as he howled, tossing his head back in an attempt to dislodge me. Holding steady, I did it again until blood trickled down from his ruined eyeball.

The beast raised his hands to his ruined eye, pressing them against his flesh as he finally bucked me off. I fell with a thump. My breath left me for a moment as pain shot through my torso. I writhed on the ground, pressing a hand to my chest as he spun and searched for me with his remaining eye.

I gasped as air finally returned, filling me with an ache as well as relief.

The Minotaur's hoof touched my foot, making me jolt back as he lunged for me on the ground. I wasn't fast enough to get away—only to avoid him landing on me. His weight slammed down on the ground beside me and narrowly missed me. With his blind eye facing me, he was quick to rummage around as he turned. He found me, and his hands made quick work of groping along my flesh until he found my throat.

I tried to breathe through his grip, getting no air as he squeezed with all his might. His remaining eye glared at me, the gold shimmering as I gasped for breath.

My ears rang. I sank into the bond, the thread glowing and fading with golden light in time with my struggle. Caldris roared down it, his silent fury radiating toward me. My exhaustion made my limbs sluggish.

I was so tired.

Don't you fucking dare.

The voice came from nowhere and everywhere at once, surrounding me in a quiet, steely embrace that smelled of winter nights and evenings by the hearth. He was the shadows beneath the moon on the coldest of nights, and the comforting embrace of a lover after sunset.

Get up, my star. Get. Up.

My arms slid along the ground beneath me, fumbling for purchase, for any remaining strength. Darkness flickered at the edges of my vision as the Minotaur leaned in, coming close enough for me to reach. His tongue snaked out of his mouth, dragging over the blood on my cheek.

"I'm going to savor you, sweet blood. Been a long time since I had one of—"

I thrust forward with the sharp edge of his nose ring, stabbing him in the other eye. Where before I'd settled for multiple, shallow wounds, I thrust hard and deep, twisting the piercing in his eye and lodging it deep. Blood dripped down onto me, staining me with the stench of dark magic.

I pushed through, yanking the piercing back and taking what remained of his eye with it. I gagged as he finally released my throat. Breath returned to my lungs suddenly, flooding my sight with the return of light. He screamed, a high-pitched bleat which echoed up the path in the Labyrinth as that mighty jowl opened wide, preparing to swallow me whole.

I pressed two hands against his chest, holding him back as he snapped at me, and his rotten breath wafted across my face. Maneuvering my leg between his, I raised it sharply into his groin and reveled in the pained hiss that left his snout.

"*Get. Off. Me!*" I yelled, shoving him back.

It took every bit of force remaining in my body to roll him over to his back, to free myself and hurry to my feet despite how battered my body felt. His hoof connected with my face as I scrambled. My nose cracked beneath the force of the blow, and my blood poured upon the ground at my feet.

I thrust a hand into it, grabbing a ball of mud and forcing Caldris's magic into it. The mud shifted to ice, a jagged, solid ball. I raised it in my arms and threw myself atop his body. I brought the sharp end down on his face, plunging it into his snout as his fist struck my face.

I saw stars, my vision swimming as I reared back and swayed. He got to his feet as I fought for my balance, reaching blindly for the axe he'd dropped at some point in our scuffle.

I shook off my dizziness, racing forward to meet him as he stumbled around to find it. I cracked my elbow across his face, knocking him to the side, then wrapped my hands around the hilt of the axe.

My body dragged forward with the weight of it, sagging with the effort as I tried to summon *anything* from that well of cold within me. It didn't answer, remaining silent as if I didn't need the help. Tears stung my eyes as I glanced over my shoulder, using both arms to drag the axe closer to where the Minotaur stumbled toward me. His nose twitched, the hole I'd made pumping fresh blood as he scented me.

I paused in front of him, watching as his body stilled, as if he knew exactly what was coming.

"Don't worry," I murmured, kicking out and wrapping one of my legs around the back of his knee.

I pulled it toward me, shifting his weight beneath him. He fell to his knees, and I cracked my foot against his face until he fell backward. Dragging his axe the final distance, I paused beside his head as his chest drew in a final breath.

"It will only hurt for a moment," I wheezed.

I raised the axe over my head with a scream—swinging it down as every muscle in my body throbbed.

It cut through his flesh and the bones in his neck in one clean line, imbedding into the mud beneath his body until I pulled it free and pressed it into the dirt to lean against. I fell to my knees beside his body, exhaustion stealing over me.

Grasping his head by the horn, I dragged the heavy thing back toward the entrance to the maze. It bumped along the surface of the ground, my arms too tired to lift it as it left a dark trail of blood. The roots from the hedges reached out, slithering into the pool beneath his body and what I left in my wake. They consumed the blood, drinking it down as if it was water within the ground.

I stumbled as I walked, my wounds healing over but the tiredness taking everything from me.

All magic had a price.

I emerged from the Labyrinth to silence. My eyes were fixed on Mab's face as I dropped the Minotaur head between us. "The next time you think to pit one of your pets against me for a game, do it knowing it will not be me who dies."

The Fae observers cheered, celebrating the bloodshed as if it was the greatest entertainment they could have asked for.

"You didn't use your magic," Mab said, lifting a brow as if she cared very little for the creature she'd used to kill her enemies when they displeased her.

"I didn't need it," I said with a grimace as Mab's guard allowed Caldris to get to his feet.

He stepped up beside me, his eyes searching the side of my face. I refused to look at him, refused to acknowledge what he would see there.

I hated thinking of what I was becoming. Of what Mab was forcing me to do to survive.

"You made a deal. Allow us to complete our mate bond."

Mab studied me, her lips twisting into a smirk. "In time," she said, the trickery of a Faerie deal hanging between us.

While she would need to allow it eventually, we would all live long lives naturally. She had all the time in the world before she had to do it, because I'd made a fool's mistake and not been specific enough.

I glared at her as Caldris led me away, seeming to warn me to fight that battle another day. Blood dripped off me as I walked, staining the dirt and stone beneath us as we made our way back to my rooms.

Mine. The Minotaur's. It hardly mattered now.

"He called me sweet blood. Said it had been a long time since he'd tasted one," I said, my words a whisper between us. I didn't dare speak louder, dreading the thought of one of Mab's spies hearing our interaction. Caldris stilled, glancing back at the Minotaur head upon the ground as if it could offer more explanation. "What does that mean?"

"I don't know," Caldris said, but as his stare landed upon mine, I knew we were both thinking of what had happened when he'd taken my blood. We hadn't dared to allow it again, worrying about the repercussions of such a thing.

His reaction had surprised him, and I had to imagine it was more intense than a normal Fae male consuming the blood of his mate for the first time.

The Minotaur had wanted more, too.

I stared down at the blood on my hands, raising them in the light cast by the twin moons through the window at my side in the hallways. The blood shimmered with the faintest golden light as I moved my hands back and forth. I doubted anyone would notice, doubted it was obvious enough for anyone to see unless they looked for it, but I glanced back at the Labyrinth nervously, anyway.

"Mab can't know," Caldris whispered.

I nodded. He wrapped me in his arms, and we hurried to my room and the bath Nila would draw for me.

We needed to wash the evidence away, rid me of any sign that my blood was different. If drinking it did something, if there was something to be gained from it, she would use it to become more powerful.

And I would die before I allowed that to happen.

"Caldris," I started, wincing back from the glare he aimed at me as we came to a stop outside the door to my chambers.

"Say it, and I will bend you over and fuck you until you forget how to speak, *min asteren*. Don't even think it," he growled, his voice a warning. I had a feeling the fucking would only be the beginning of my punishment if I dared to disobey him. "Don't ever think to ask that of me."

I swallowed, nodding.

Even though I knew he was wrong.

28

Estrella

I felt like a walking corpse later that day, like my body was far too heavy to function. Pulling on Caldris's magic had never taken that much from me before, so I suspected it had more to do with the physical exertion of fighting a creature twice my size than anything. But my magic had begun to stir in my veins once again—the faintest whisper of it awakening after the trauma of the Labyrinth.

Malachi led me down to the throne room. The hall was oddly empty as we stepped in. Mab stood with two other people, and only one of them I recognized. Fallon hung her head forward, worrying the bridge of her nose between her fingers.

The male who stood across from her couldn't seem to take his eyes off her, studying her intently in a way that made the hair raise upon my arms. His deep auburn hair hung around his shoulders in waves, his brown eyes cold and unyielding as he shifted his gaze to me.

I forced my chin high, even though I wanted to collapse into a puddle on the throne room floor, only stopping when I stood opposite Mab, with Fallon to one side and the stranger to the other.

"You summoned me?" I asked, my insolence showing in my refusal to bow.

Mab didn't pause, unbothered by my lack of formality. I knew there would come a day when she tired of our games, but I hadn't reached the point where I ceased to be entertaining yet.

Soon enough.

"I tire of having two incompetent children beneath my roof. You cannot seem to summon the magic that we both know you possess, magic that would make you *useful*. Maeve cannot seem to summon *any* magic at all. Both are unacceptable to me," Mab said, running her tongue over her teeth in dissatisfaction.

"Her name is Fallon," I corrected, staring down the woman who seemed to refuse to accept that her daughter was not the child she'd birthed. That she'd had centuries and lives for her soul to grow into her own person, not just possessing the traits her mother wanted to instill in her. "But I fail to see what you would like either of us to do. Magic cannot be forced. If it does not come when summoned, then perhaps we are not fit to control it."

Mab sneered as she huffed a laugh. "I might have believed that to be true if I hadn't heard rumors of all the things you've done. If I hadn't *seen* them in your memories and for myself, Little Mouse." Her voice was low and soft, a quiet reprimand for my assertion that was as close to a lie as any Faerie could come. We both knew that while unwieldy, my power responded when it needed to protect someone I loved.

I ignored the challenge in her dark stare. "I think I have proven myself to be more than a mouse," I said, smiling sweetly. I could still feel the stain of the Minotaur's blood upon my skin. Could still feel the way he had nearly choked the life out of me.

Yet as promised, only one of us had left that Labyrinth alive, and it hadn't been him.

"Occasionally, the mouse's bite carries a deadly disease. But it is still just a mouse, at the end of the day," Mab said, making me clench my jaw at the insult. It drove me further into that well, into the determination to have a hand in her demise when the time came.

"What do you want from us?" I asked, glancing to where Fallon looked as if she might be sick. I had no doubt she already knew of Mab's plans, but I would do anything within my power to see her safely protected from harm.

She wasn't helpless, but she was far too sweet to be broken. Far too kind to suffer the worst of Mab.

"I only have the energy to invest my time into one of you. You will determine which of you remains here with me," Mab said, waving a hand as if it was inconsequential.

I glanced toward Fallon hopefully, knowing that if it was the opportunity to free her from Mab, then we would take it.

"Will the one who does not stay go free?" I asked, feeling the catch in Mab's conditions. Something didn't add up, and I could only picture the dungeon calling my name all over again.

"Of course not," Mab said with a cruel laugh. "Etan is in need of a wife, and he is owed one for the loyalty he has shown me during my brother's reign as king. Whoever does not remain with me shall be betrothed to him and return to the Summer Court with him after the Solstice."

My ears rang, the sound of water rushing through them as I tried to understand her words. "I have a mate," I said, turning a cautious glance toward Etan. He shifted, as if the idea of taking another man's mate made him uncomfortable as well.

"It is adorable that you think I care about such trivialities. Political marriages happen all the time. Caldris will learn to share you and remember his place," Mab said, dismissing the thought of it being an issue.

I gave her a small smile. "I somehow doubt that," I said with a scoff, thinking of all the people Caldris would kill to reach me when he found out. But I couldn't leave Fallon to that fate. Turning my head, I found her face twisted with sadness.

"It's okay, Estrella," she said, her eyes filling with water. I knew she would make the sacrifice, that she would give herself to save me from the agony of being taken from Caldris.

I shook my head, pursing my lips to fight back the sting of tears. I couldn't do it. Couldn't condemn her to a marriage to a man she didn't love. That had always been my destiny. I had been prepared to survive it—when she hadn't.

"Whoever displays the magic I wish to see first will stay here with me," Mab said, interrupting the moment.

"And if neither of us do?" I asked, prepared to simply refuse to make the choice. If I didn't summon my magic…

"Then I'll marry the other one of you off to one of my other allies. Perhaps a far crueler one than Etan. I have done you a kindness in selecting him. He is not a cruel man and will not be a cruel husband. He is distant but will see that your needs are met. I would tolerate nothing less for my daughter," Mab said, turning to Fallon with a knowing stare. "Even if she does not obey me."

Mab knew without a doubt that Fallon would be the one she sent to this marriage, that I would remain behind. She knew and was willing to sacrifice her own daughter to force my hand.

Fallon stepped forward, standing between Mab and me as she took my hands in hers. She ran her thumb over the circle on the back of my hand, stroking the Fae mark there delicately, as if she could summon my bond to the surface. Her palm touched the white teardrop of our blood vow, sending a rush of magic through my hand.

"It's okay," she said, her hand trailing up the white marks on my forearm. A trail of warmth followed, as if our connection and bond could bring forth the magic I'd suppressed.

I shook my head again. "I can't," I protested.

"You can," she said, touching her forehead to mine. She leaned forward, her eyes spearing mine as my lip trembled. "It is you. It's the most terrifying part of you, but it's also the most beautiful. All you have to do is let it out."

"It's not that simple," I said, resisting the urge to look at Mab.

Fallon took my hand, turning me away from her and guiding me out of the throne room. I was vaguely aware of Mab and Etan following behind us, of the fact that Mab allowed us to make our way outside the palace of Tar Mesa.

"She cannot use you for evil if you do not allow it. Knowledge is power, but do you really think anything she does is stronger than you?" Fallon asked, her voice a low murmur. "You have lived in fear of what you are. You have suffered the pain of suppressing yourself to protect the world. When will you learn that you are not our destruction, Estrella? You are our savior."

My knees buckled beneath me as we stepped outside, the moons shining high in the sky above us. Fallon stepped back with a nod, releasing my hands as I turned my stare down at them.

"I'm not strong enough for this."

"Then lean on the people who love you. Take what you need from us," she said, raising a hand. The golden thread I recognized as our bond thrummed between us, glowing steadily as I opened my eyes to that part of me once again.

I nodded, letting my eyes drift closed as I drew a deep breath in. Air filled my lungs, the scent of the night sky becoming part of me as I tried to sink into that hollow—into the place of rage where I'd gone when the boy had died in Blackwater.

It didn't feel cold this time. Instead, I was filled with the warmth of Fallon's words and the promises I hoped she had the opportunity to keep. I sank into it, gasping as the warmth surrounded me, and threw my eyes open to stare up at the sky. The golden threads hung from the moon, dangling from the stars as I looked up at them. I turned my head to the side as I studied them, looking up at the moons and remembering the prophecy of the two moons that had been whispered in my ear.

A gentle murmur. A reminder of two women, standing side by side to give light in the darkness.

I raised my hand, stroking the end of one of the threads with gentle fingers. Coiling it around my pointer finger, I drew it into my palm. I was all too aware of Mab's eyes on me, of the way she studied me. My cheeks felt wet with tears. Allowing my magic to touch me, feeling it upon my skin, I realized why it had always felt so hollow.

It was abandoned. Forgotten. Feared.

When all it wanted was love.

But how could I have loved it when I, myself, didn't understand what that love meant? It wasn't until Caldris made me see. It wasn't until Fallon stood by me and made a vow to protect one another. It wasn't until Imelda confessed the truth of my brother, of her place in my life, and witnessing the way she loved Fallon with everything she had… and feeling that love extend to me.

I closed my palm, pressing my fingers against it slowly. One of the moons disappeared from the sky, vanishing into the darkness as I watched. I reached up with my other hand as Mab gasped, waving it in a circle and gathering the threads into one mass. I pressed them into my palm, forcing the night sky into darkness. The moon vanished.

The sky faded to black.

Only the light of the fires hanging from the doorway to the palace of Tar Mesa illuminated us where we stood.

"Impossible," Mab whispered, taking a step toward me.

I turned my stare to her, unflinching, when she stopped in front of me and raised her hands to cup my cheeks. She stared down at my eyes in something mixed between horror and awe, running a thumb through the tears on my cheeks.

"And yet here I am," I murmured, drawing back from her. I released the threads, tossing them back into the sky so that they could reclaim their rightful place. "Did that give you the answers you were so desperate for?"

"You can see the threads of Fate," Mab said, her voice filled with awe as she stared down at my hands. "That is how you summon."

I didn't deny it, my shock at her knowing about them too potent for me to respond. "You see them too?" I asked with a swallow.

"I see… shadows of them. Whispers on the wind occasionally, but I can never grasp them. I'm not — " She paused, clearing her throat as the closest thing to emotion I'd ever seen from her seemed to clog it.

"You're not what?" I asked, feeling closer than ever to the answers I wasn't sure I wanted. I swallowed, glancing at Fallon as she took a step closer, hesitating only so she didn't interrupt the moment.

Mab clenched her jaw, and I could already imagine the strategy working through her head. How she would navigate the new information.

"A Primordial."

29

Caldris

Estrella stumbled into her chambers. Her face was bewildered, and she appeared half-drunk. There were dark circles beneath her eyes, her exhaustion written into every part of her face.

I abandoned my pacing, rushing toward her to catch her in time for her to collapse. Her emotions were too intense to understand, her confusion and terror potent.

"Estrella, what's wrong?" I asked, lifting her into my arms. I'd felt her panic—her fear—after she'd been summoned by Mab, but there was never any pain to accompany it. None of Mab's usual tricks.

I settled her back on the bed, draping my body alongside hers and trying to chase away the chill that seemed to cling to her skin. The iron collar lay against her throat, whatever had happened that night condemning her to the suffering of it once more. She stared up at the ceiling, her eyes almost unseeing. If her chest hadn't risen and fallen with her strangled breathing, I might have thought she lingered at death's door.

"*Min asteren*," I murmured, cupping her cheek and turning her gaze to mine.

"The threads," she whispered, her bottom lip trembling as tears gathered in her eyes.

"What about them?" I asked, running my nose along hers.

She sighed, wrapping her arms around me finally as she returned from that cold place that seemed to claim her when things got rough.

"The Primordials used them to create the world. That's how they channel magic, Caldris," she said, shaking her head from side to side as her features twisted. "Mab thinks I'm a Primordial."

"No," I said, shaking my head sadly. "That isn't possible. I spent centuries of life feeling you *die*. You cannot possibly be a Primordial. When a Primordial leaves this plane, their magic follows. If you were a Primordial, whatever magic you channel would not have returned with you. It would have been lost to this world, because it isn't channeled from the world around you. It comes from you, and you would not have that magic any longer."

I leaned over her, begging her to see the truth in my words. The death of a Primordial was a rare, tragic thing, but my mate could not be one of them.

"Then how do I see the threads?" Estrella asked, her voice laced with confusion. She went on to explain how Mab had come to learn of her ability to see the threads, to the choice she'd given my mate.

To be married to a man who was not me... Mab was foolish not to know that I would burn everything to the ground. She would have no choice but to kill me, because there was *nothing* that would stop me from protecting Estrella from the torment of that.

Mab saw glimmers of them, but I didn't know another God who did. I'd never realized she saw them, never knew she could even hint at the power of the Primordials or that the threads were how they functioned. My own parents had both been Gods, with my magic being the unusual consequence of a mate bond between two Gods.

As if I was meant to exist, crafted by the hands of the Fates themselves.

I wondered how much of that related to my mate, how much of it might have been the way they seemed to maneuver her through time and space. She'd always been meant to be here, and even though she was suffering at the hands of the one woman I wanted to murder more than anyone, I had to wonder if she was *exactly* where the Fates wanted her to be.

If whatever was coming would be the change for the greater good. If it would be the driving event that finally freed all of Alfheimr from Mab's clutches.

"Mab will not allow us to complete our mate bond if she can find ways to get around that vow," I said, wrapping my mate in my arms.

She turned to her side, facing me as she turned hazy green eyes up to my blue. I wished I could chase away the fear that lingered in them, to remind her that she was capable of anything and everything if she only put her mind to it.

"Because she fears you'll break your bond once you're stronger," she said, nodding as she sank her teeth into the corner of her mouth in thought.

I could practically see the gears turning, see the way she thought over the turn of events and searched for a new solution. The problem solver in her wouldn't just let things lie, instead determined to manipulate and change until she had her desired outcome.

"It was never about me," I sighed, the realization forcing a scoff from my lungs.

All my life, people and Fae alike had feared me and treated me as a terrifying God. All my life, I'd been told of the things I could achieve if I could only be freed. I was who I had to be in order to stand at Estrella's side. In order to reach her and protect her, to guard and guide her on her journey.

"I am here for you. I am here to help you reach your full potential and to give *you* the boost you need to fight. Mab will not stop us from bonding to keep me complacent. She'll do it to keep you controlled. She'll do it to keep you small when you are meant for so much more."

"Stop," Estrella murmured, her expression shutting down as she reached the end of her tolerance.

She might have come a long way since her escape from Mistfell, but she was still the girl who didn't dare to act on her dreams. She was still the one who was beaten if she didn't behave exactly as they told her to. She didn't dare to dream in splendor. Instead, she chose to tailor her dreams to her reality, managing her expectations. She limited herself before anyone could ever tell her no.

"I am going to love every moment of watching your journey, Estrella Barlowe," I murmured, touching a thumb to her tense bottom lip. It softened in response, allowing me to lean down and touch my lips to hers. "And when you've finished molding the world to your desire, I'm going to have a portrait of your creation hung on the walls of Catancia. I'll make you stand before it, make you look at what you've done—and I will be the first of many to tell you *I told you so*."

She closed her eyes, pressing her forehead to my chest as she hid her face from me. A lesser being would buckle under the weight of all that pressure.

But Estrella would rise like the stars in the evening sky.

30

Estrella

The air blew through the valley at the front of Tar Mesa, whipping along the eternal salt field that led to the rolling hills. Malachi nudged me forward, forcing me to take another step. One of Mab's guards tossed me a bow and a quiver of arrows, leaving me little choice but to catch them. I fumbled to get a grip, slinging the quiver over my shoulder and grasping the bow.

I'd never held one before and knew I would be absolutely useless with it. Hunting had been forbidden in Mistfell. Only those with permits were allowed to kill the animals in the woods surrounding the village.

"What am I supposed to do with this?" I grumbled, approaching the rest of the crowd.

Every God was there, knives and swords and bows and arrows strapped to them. The God of Twilight approached a table covered in weapons, pursing his lips as he selected from what remained. He chose a long dagger with a silver handle. The metal curved and knitted together like writhing snakes. At the top of the hilt was a crescent moon, the points of it sharp enough to bleed if I swung it wrong.

He approached, kneeling at my feet as stunned silence reached my ears. The only sound came from behind me, the deep growl of a voice I would recognize anywhere, as Soren raised his hands and wrapped the straps of the sheath around my thigh, pulling the buckle tight enough that the dagger wouldn't slip. His pale silver eyes held mine as he fed the end of the leather strap through the loop, securing it finally.

"Take your hands off my mate, cousin," Caldris barked, stepping up behind me.

Soren's hands left my thigh suddenly, and the male pushed to his feet, turning his back on us as he approached the table once more.

"Do you know how to use a sword?" he asked me, ignoring my mate's possessive irritation.

"Better than I know how to use a bow," I answered, my lips quirking up at the corners. His playfulness with his cousin didn't feel slimy; it didn't feel like he actually had any interest in me—only in rattling my mate.

Caldris snatched the sword and sheath from Soren's grip as he approached, wrapping it around my waist. His fingers brushed over the waistband of the leather trousers Nila had dressed me in. The faint scales of armor at my sides and over my chest and arms jangled as he touched me.

They were so much heavier than I'd ever imagined them being, so much more weighted than Caldris made them seem. A circlet hung over my forehead, peeking out from beneath the smokey gray hood that concealed most of my hair.

"Why do I need all these weapons, exactly?" I asked.

Malachi brushed that hood back, and I went rigid beneath his touch, hating the feeling of his skin on mine. His fingers wound into my hair, removing the collar from my neck. I drew in a deep breath, spinning to look at him.

Weapons and magic at my disposal. It seemed like I would not particularly enjoy any of the festivities for the day.

Mab stepped to the front, her eyes on me as she spoke. "Welcome to the Hunt," she said.

The other Gods nodded their heads. From the Goddess of the Harvest to the God of the Sun, all were present as they readied themselves for the hunt.

But what were we hunting?

"One by one, you will be brought to a remote corner of the Pillars," Mab said, her voice dropping low. The others knew the place she spoke of, were clearly familiar with the Pillars in a way I could never be. "There, you must hunt down something that has escaped from Tartarus and bring its head so we can return them to where they belong and appease the prison."

I swallowed, leaning into Caldris. I didn't like the thought of being separated from him—of fighting some horrific monster that was terrifying even to the Fae. He wrapped an arm around my waist, holding me close as if Mab would take pity on me and allow me to be partnered with my mate.

Aderyn, The Goddess of the Harvest and Queen of the Autumn Court, stepped up to one of Mab's elite guards, the ones who never spoke and always lingered at the edges of her space. The male raised his hand, summoning the shadows to do his bidding. Taking her arm, he guided her into the shadow realm, and they disappeared as we watched.

"How will I know if something has escaped Tartarus or if it's just another creature of Faerie?" I asked, staring at Mab as her lips spread into a joyful grin.

"The creatures have made the Pillars into their home. It is their safe haven, their hunting grounds. If you find something *alive*, the odds are likely that it has escaped from Tartarus," she explained, holding out a hand for me. I didn't leave Caldris's side, remaining with him and ignoring that extended hand. "Come, Estrella. Consider this your chance to prove yourself."

"I would have thought I'd already done that with the Minotaur," I snapped. I stepped away from Caldris's side, anyway, holding my chin high as I prepared for certain death.

"All you proved with the Minotaur is that you and Caldris have a solid bond and his magic flows through you. I wonder how much of yours is in his veins?" I turned to look back at Caldris, watching as his lips parted ever so slightly.

He glanced down at my hands, at the fingers I used to touch the threads before his gaze drifted to his own.

It was the last thing I saw before Mab brought me into the shadows.

***

The bow in my hand felt strange, harsh, and unforgiving. There was something brutal about killing my prey before they could ever reach me to engage in battle—about taking away their fighting chance.

The leather pants and tunic covered my body as I crept through the Pillars of the Court of Shadows surrounding Tar Mesa. The ground beneath my feet was an odd mix of grass and rock, the steps jagged as I continued down the pathway through the trees. They were barren of leaves in the area Mab had dropped me in, as if nature itself had died when the creatures took over the Pillars.

The wind howled through the trees, sending a scattering of snow over the path. I stepped through it cautiously, slinging the bow over my shoulder as I walked. I couldn't help but wonder if I was really hunting for anything.

Or if I was merely being hunted.

There was tension in the air, and I should have been more afraid of it. I should have given into the urge to be cautious. But my bones rattled with the magic simmering in my blood—with the knowledge that for once, I was free from prying eyes. My throat was un-collared. There was no iron to prevent me from touching the surface of that deep well.

The creature who lurked beneath the surface of my skin rose to greet me, opening her golden eyes as she took control of my limbs. I looked to the surface, thinking of Caldris's lesson in summoning my own magic.

In creating, rather than shaping, whatever already existed.

Closing my eyes, I paused in the clearing. Cupping my hands, I thought of the way the threads of the stars felt when I grasped them between my fingers.

They were warm—the surface smooth like silk. But the stars themselves were rough and molten, like a giant burning flame held trapped within the cold of the night sky. I focused all that energy into my palms, embracing the feeling of fire against my skin as a wave of cold air brushed against my face.

I opened my eyes slowly, peering down at the orb of light that floated above my palm. It was smaller than my hand, glowing with the golden light of fate in the dark of the woods.

I smiled, a laugh bubbling up from my throat. I curled my hands around it, imagining the light dimming to a soft glow. Shadows wrapped around the surface, encasing it in a dark film around the curves of the ball. I let it free, watching as it floated through the forest.

It didn't rise to the sky above; instead, it floated ahead of me to light a path. I formed another, allowing it to rise and hover beside the other. They cast a warm glow upon the otherwise gloomy forest as that strange, otherworldly laugh spilled free from me once again.

I ran forward, delighting in the way they followed me, as if tethered to my soul. The path through the woods curved in a circle as I cast out one tiny star after another. I sprinted, dancing and spinning as I went, reveling in the feeling of magic upon my skin.

Reveling in the way I felt whole, my soul lighter than ever before.

Even the terrifying creature within me laughed, her smile illuminating the darkened corners of my heart. I leapt from one rock to the other, jumping over a crevice in the ground as my newly immortal body sang.

Freedom raced in my veins as a tear fell down my cheek, the moment so unlike anything I'd ever dared to dream of. I might have had to go back to my cage when it was all said and done, but for a single, bittersweet moment, I tasted the air on my tongue. I tasted the sharp crispness of moving where I wanted. Doing what I wanted.

Touching everything I passed.

Caldris's joy echoed my own, thrumming down the thread to strike me in the chest. His response to my own happiness—to my moment of freedom—echoing my own elation.

I spun around a corner, coming to a stop as I approached a pillar. It jutted into the sky, a single flat slab of stone. There was nothing around it but the steps leading up, the surrounding ground in the clearing just as haunted and dead as the rest of the forest.

Symbols had been carved into the surface as I approached, then made my way up the half-dozen steps. The stars cast an eerie golden glow upon the marks I didn't recognize as

I reached the top of the steps, but I would have sworn they glowed from within as I stretched out with a single hand.

I was only a breath from touching the surface when lightning cracked through the air somewhere behind me. I spun, turning so sharply I nearly tripped over my own feet. My dagger was in my hand before I finished my rotation, finding glowing eyes of gold staring down at me from above.

They shone down from the ebony face of a horse, situated to the side of a single horn wrapped in blue light. It was twice as tall as any normal horse.

I shifted the dagger in my hand, but something kept me from stabbing it forward. Stopped me from slaying the creature where it stood.

I studied those eyes, only noting the pulse of blue light beneath his black hair in a distracted way. He flapped massive, feathered wings of black, shifting the air toward me and forcing me to stumble backward.

I caught myself, my hand touching the pillar behind me. A rush of warmth filled my hands, and the creature and I both turned to look at the symbols that glowed. They spread out from my palm, moving farther and farther up the pillar as if I were the apex of power.

I drew back suddenly, stepping closer to the creature in front of me. He made no move to harm me, tilting his head to the side as he leaned forward.

His hoof touched the bottom step, his head raising so that the end of his muzzle could press against my chest. It twitched over my armor as he smelled me.

I drew in a deep breath, shuddering as I sheathed the dagger in my hand. He didn't miss the movement, watching me carefully as I reached out with that now empty palm.

I let my eyes fall closed as I stretched forward slowly, lingering just shy of touching. I couldn't force myself to close the distance, couldn't risk losing my hand. Fear thrummed through me, sending my heart pounding in my chest.

Stupid. So fucking stupid.

He closed the distance, leaning his head forward until he pressed against my open palm. My breath fled in a single sigh as my eyes flew open, finding his golden gaze gleaming down at me. There was a hint of amusement there, something far too human for a horse. He stepped back, moving away slowly as lightning cracked through the sky. It moved beneath his skin, as if it originated from him when he raised his horn to the sky.

I followed him as if in a trance, making my way down the steps.

He lowered himself, leaning onto a front leg that he bent. The other straightened in front of him, his head hanging forward into a bow.

I gaped at him, not understanding as I walked forward slowly. His wings lowered to the ground, feathers spreading across the grass and rock. The sight of them drew me forward, tickling at the vestiges of a memory.

The arrow thudding into his withers snapped me out of the moment. He reared back with a neigh, lightning erupting from his horn as I darted forward.

Another arrow came, heading straight for his neck. I drew my sword, arcing it through the air to deflect. The arrow bounced off as I grasped the one still planted in his withers and *pulled.*

The horse screamed as I tore it free, his furious golden eyes snapping to mine as Mab and her guards emerged from the tree line.

"Go," I ordered, shoving at the horse's side. I pushed against the point of his shoulder, shoving him away from the threat.

He whinnied, flapping those massive wings and taking to the skies. I watched in horror as Mab's arrows flew for him, falling just short as they brushed against his tail.

"Stupid, foolish girl!" the Queen of Air and Darkness grunted. She strode forward, one of her arrows in her hand as she stabbed it down toward me.

Not a hit meant to kill, but to maim.

It came for my cheek, striking against a golden boundary that sent her spiraling backward. Lightning cracked through the sky once more, a reminder of the creature that had once stood in this spot.

Mab collided with the ground, lying upon it before she pushed to her feet and began to prowl toward me once more.

"I do not suggest that, sister," Rheaghan said, stepping out of the tree line. "The *aonnaigh* showed itself to her. Even you are not fool enough to harm her after that."

Mab scoffed, turning on her heel as Rheaghan came closer. I sheathed my sword as Mab disappeared into the tree line to go hunt something else, allowing the God of the Sun to take my hand.

"Let's find your mate, and find you something to kill," he said, guiding me toward the woods.

I summoned a star to my free hand, allowing it to drift in front of us and lead the way. The others had faded in my panic to save the horse—the *aonnaigh*.

"What's the *aonnaigh*?" I asked, stepping over a particularly large root from a tree. My soul felt heavy, such a contrast to the lightness that had claimed me when I frolicked through the woods in my semblance of freedom.

How quickly the cage walls had come crashing down, watching the winged horse fly to freedom while I remained.

"A creature crafted from the darkness itself. All the stories state that Khaos crafted it from the night sky to be a gift for his wife, Nyx, when he created her from the stars. He meant it to belong to the one true queen," Rheaghan explained, guiding me forward.

"The one true queen of what?"

The woods seemed less alive than they had when I'd danced through them earlier. Whether it was the near death of such a beautiful creature, or the shift toward danger, I couldn't know.

Rheaghan's stare felt heavy on the side of my face as we walked. "Everything."

I swallowed past the implication in those words, wondering if I really wanted to face the reality they may present. That thread in the center of my chest pulled, as if Caldris knew I was looking for him. I could imagine his smile while he engaged in battle with some horror of Tartarus—feel his teasing thread of humor pulse down the bond.

"Then why would it show itself to me?" I asked.

"The Primordials have been missing for centuries. Perhaps they've hidden themselves within human vessels," Rheaghan said as he swept a tree branch out of the way. He'd clearly been speaking with his sister following the revelation of the night before—her accusation that I was something *impossible*.

Caldris stood in between the trees, his armor and leather covered in blood. Already at his side, three creatures lay in pieces, the heads severed from their bodies. They were similar to the arachni that haunted the caves in Mistfell, but their bodies were even larger.

They were larger than I—their legs standing tall even as their bodies collapsed upon them. One shrieked, charging for my mate as he swept the legs out from under it with a clean cut of his sword.

The legs flung through the air as he shoved his hand up, snapping through flesh to grasp the creature's heart and pull it free. It was still pumping blood upon the ground when the creature collapsed at my mate's feet, the God of the Dead turning to strike me with a brutal smile.

Blood was splashed all over his face, adding to the brutality of his features. Only the gleam of his white teeth shone from beneath all that red as my star floated toward him, guiding me forward. I reached him, flinching slightly when the warm press of his blood-soaked hand touched my cheek.

We didn't speak of the creature that had shown itself to me, or Rheaghan's theory that I was somehow the embodiment of Nyx. Caldris reached down, grasping two of the spiders by the head, cracking their necks, and wrenching them in a circular motion until they came free. Then he opened the shadows, allowing Rheaghan to walk through first with one of the spider's heads.

We followed.

31

Estrella

My room was too quiet after Nila left that night. My magic thrummed through my veins, the collar absent from my throat. After Mab's presentation of the creatures to Tartarus, she'd only leveled me with a glare and a warning.

Escape attempts would only result in Caldris's suffering and the death of human mates.

It was a rare moment of understanding between us. Mab didn't *want* to keep my magic suppressed, because if she did, we would never come to know what I was capable of.

And she would never be able to use that magic to her advantage if we didn't know about it.

I had so rarely engaged with it when I wasn't in a moment of fear, when instinct wasn't driving me to protect myself.

I settled deep into myself, standing in the center of my room. The fire roared in the hearth to my left, but I let my eyes drop closed and stared into that chasm of power. The monster waiting there cracked an eye open, lifting her head off her paws and purring in delight as I took a deep breath.

Darkness swirled around her as I raised my arms, holding out two flat palms in front of me. I thought of the depths of night—of the new moon and a cloudy sky. I needed a walkway, a passage to reach the other half of me. The memory of the shadow realm formed in my mind as the creature within me sighed, raising a single talon to gift me with the magic I requested. I became the shadows she held within her, melting into the night that formed at my palms.

My nightgown swirled around me, blowing back from the subtle night wind that passed through my room.

I opened my eyes.

The edges of the shadow realm were twisted, gnarled, and writhing like the leafless trees of the Pillars as I stepped forward, putting my first foot into the walkway. A wall of darkness blocked my path, pressing back into me as if it could lock me within my rooms. Pushing forward, I touched a single finger to the wall.

It pushed back, shoving at me with the loud howl of furious winds filling my passageway. The darkness swirled furiously, shifting from the quiet, peaceful night I'd summoned to my aid to a raging storm of black.

I thought of the moons in the sky, of light in that darkness. *Of love.*

The stardust upon my fingers glowed with gold that spread throughout the barrier in front of me. Mab's magic pressed down on me, her raging, hollow emptiness that was devoid of all life. In those moments, I felt exactly what I had seen in her stare that first day in the throne room.

Nothing.

Dark wind howled through the shadow realm, pushing me back toward the entrance to the passage. The tendrils of shadows felt like claws as they dragged over my skin, wrapping around me and squeezing. I saw the madness within Mab, the fate that cursed crown upon her head had condemned her to.

Within that storm of darkness was only the thirst for power—hungry and insatiable. It was never satisfied, never content as it tore through my skin and bled me, taking anything it could.

I refused to give into that, to allow that nightmare to win. I sank not into the monster inside of me, but to the thread that connected me to Caldris. Focusing on that pulsing warmth — on that love — I shoved back at the shadows surrounding me.

Stardust flickered through the boundary that tried to keep me in, a ripple spreading through it as the shadows melted away. They turned liquid beneath the starlight, fading away. I pulled my magic back ever-so-slightly, stepping through the now pass-able barrier and turning to watch as it reformed behind me.

I needed to come and go as I pleased, but I didn't want to dissolve whatever magic Mab had placed around my room. I willed it to strengthen, to not allow any others to walk into my room or suspect that I could leave, but to always recognize me and my magic.

It reformed, the twisted shadows knitting themselves back together as I turned and made my way toward my mate. I could see the real realm through the barrier they formed, but I continued forward as it sped past me. Four steps was all it took to reach Caldris's bedroom. I'd never been there, never even known where they kept him, but the thread that connected to my very soul guided me toward him, regardless.

He was alone as I approached; an ancient book opened on the arm of the chair where he sat. His tunic was half untied, the laces loose and hanging down his chest. I stepped out of the shadow realm, putting the first of my slippered feet against the blue stone floor.

He jumped to his feet; his hand curled to summon the shadows that he would use to defend himself against any intruder.

I pressed a finger to my mouth as I smiled — a warning to be quiet as I stepped up to him.

Tucking a strand of hair behind my ear, he grinned. "I see you figured out the shadow walk," he said, his voice amused as those full lips curled.

"So it would seem," I whispered, leaning up onto my toes so that he could grace my lips with a kiss.

"Only you, *min asteren*, could summon the shadow realm so easily. It took me decades to master. Others take centuries if they ever manage," Caldris explained, reaching down to take my hands. "Particularly when your room is shielded against such things. She'll know you broke through her shields."

"I didn't break them," I said, my lips twitching. "Just altered them to allow me to pass."

"Devious little thing," he said, his voice twisting with pain and affection as he looked toward his door. "You won't be so lucky with the shields she's put around Tar Mesa. You cannot shadow walk out of the palace, so we'll have to sneak you out the doors the normal way, then you can go from there." He left me, going to his wardrobe and rummaging around for a cloak as he eyed my nightgown in distaste. "You could have at least dressed before you came and been better prepared."

"I'm not running," I argued, turning to face him as I crossed my arms over my chest.

He froze in his rifling, turning to look at me over his shoulder. His hands still lingered on the clothes where they hung, his blue eyes flashing with rage. "Yes, you are."

"What would be the point exactly? You'll remain here, and we will have no chance of freeing you if we are not together. She'll punish you and send you to drag me back, and then they'll know that I can shadow walk out of my room whenever I feel like it if I do not wear that collar. We'll lose our advantage, and for *what*?" I snapped, flinching back when he spun so suddenly, he revealed the predator waiting within *him*. I wondered if he had that monster, that creature he saw when he looked inward, or if it was merely the way I imagined my power. My own fear of it that created that imagery.

Just as I saw the window from my childhood bedroom at the center of our bond, shutting us off from one another or letting our feelings flow freely to one another.

"The point," he said, his mouth twisting into a snarl, "is that you would be free, and she wouldn't be able to harm you. If you can walk through Mab's shields, then you can shield yourself against our bond. I'll never be able to find you."

"It is offensive that you think I would just walk away from here and leave you to suffer. Is that what you think of me?" I asked, scoffing as my own anger rose.

"You tried to kill me in my sleep," he said shortly, the words drifting into a chuckle at the end.

"So dramatic," I purred, smiling as my gaze slid down his body. He raised a brow at me, as if to remind me that was exactly what happened. "I didn't do it." I rolled my eyes to the side, pursing my lips as I fought my own rising laughter at the incredulous look on his face.

"You didn't do it," he said, his nostrils flaring as his chest shook with silent laughter.

"How could I kill you when you whispered such pretty words to me?" I asked, my words far lighter than I felt inside.

Even with the laughter shaking his chest, that sadness lurked in his eyes as he watched me, stepping toward me. He stopped just in front of me but made no move to touch me as he blew out a breath.

"I want more for you. I have lived for centuries, and *this* is all I've known. These walls and the cage wrapped around my heart have overshadowed my entire existence. Before you were born, I used to go to the hilltop and stare up at the stars," he said, raising a hand to capture my chin between two fingers.

I smiled sheepishly. "I didn't mean I needed more declarations of love," I said in an attempt to lessen his intensity.

"Quiet, *min asteren*," he said, the command soft but not lacking in authority.

I clamped my mouth shut, blinking up at him as he captured his bottom lip between his teeth.

"I wondered why I existed, if this is all there was for me. There had to be a reason my parents came together against the odds. There needed to be a reason I was a God when it went against the natural order of things. What good did that power do me when I was taken before I could speak?"

"Caldris," I protested, trying to turn my gaze away from him.

He held me still, pinning me with that icy intensity as cold crept up my spine. The room filled with the vestiges of his power. From the corner of my eye, I caught frost sliding along the walls.

"You are my reason, Estrella," he said.

I pinched my eyes closed to fight the torrent of emotions surging down the bond. The love that struck me in the chest, that poured off him in the silence where he stared down at me, waiting for me to open my eyes, was unfathomable.

"You are my reason for every breath. The reason every day I have spent as a prisoner has been worth it. Because it brought me to you." He leaned forward, touching his forehead to mine as his head shifted to the side. Pain twisted his face, his thumb stroking over my jaw as he willed me to see. His voice broke as he murmured the next words, the sacrifice he would make for me. "That is why you have to go. I cannot let this be for nothing."

"I'm not going to leave you," I said softly, tailoring my voice to the difficulty he'd had in making the concession. In choosing to set me free while he lived a life of captivity, knowing full well he may never see me again.

He dropped his hand, stepping away as his body tensed. I turned from him, striding back toward his bed. This hadn't been what I'd wanted when I came to him tonight.

"They thought it was me who could rise up to fight Mab, but it isn't. If it hasn't happened for centuries, it isn't going to now. You are Alfheimr's only hope for salvation—"

"Then let it burn!" I snapped, whirling around to glare at him.

My chest heaved with my heavy breaths as his shocked stare met mine. Never before had I spoken the traitorous thoughts in my head; had I told him just how much I was willing to ruin my soul for him.

"What good is it if it doesn't have you?"

He blinked at me rapidly, as if he couldn't quite believe the words I'd spoken. I'd always wanted to save every life. To protect the weak from those who sought to break them.

"You don't mean that," he said finally, raising his brows as he shook his head subtly.

"I didn't understand when you said you would let the world die if it meant I could survive the wreckage. I hadn't let myself love you... not like this," I explained, stepping toward him slowly. My bottom lip trembled, this confession feeling different from all the others. "But I do now."

I reached up, cupping his cheek as he stared down at me. "I would sacrifice *everyone* if it meant I had you," I said, pulling his face down so that I could brush my lips against his. "So do not ever ask me to leave you. Never again."

He sighed as he pinched his brow between two fingers. "My star…"

"Don't," I said, making my way to his bed.

I brushed off the emotion clogging my heart, shoving it down to salvage what I could of our night together. With my ability to shadow walk, I hoped they wouldn't be limited any longer, but I had no control over when Mab collared me—or when she didn't.

I would take what I could when it came to the male who stared at me in disbelief. I dropped down onto the edge of the bed, pulling my nightgown up inch by inch so that my calves showed as I crossed my legs.

"We both know I'm not leaving."

My mate's eyes dropped to the exposed flesh, his head tilting to the side as that animalistic desire spread over his face and washed away all traces of sadness.

"We could spend the night arguing about something you will not change my mind about, or we could…"

"You escaped the prison of your room because you wanted my cock?" he asked, but his feet had already moved, bringing him closer. He paused in front of me, staring down at me as he reached out with a single hand. His thumb stroked my cheek, making a single sweep over my skin as he curled his fingers beneath my chin.

"Not just your cock," I said, nearly breathless. He'd barely touched me, barely even shifted his attention away from our argument. But even still, heat gathered between my thighs. "I want your mouth too."

That stunning face spread into a grin. "I've created a monster."

He plunged his mouth down onto mine, his lips so firm against my own that I groaned into him. He devoured it, swallowing the sound with a growl of his own as his hands fisted my nightgown—shoving it farther up my thighs and lifting me from the bed just enough to reveal the bare curve of my ass against his sheets.

"I'm *your* monster," I said as he pulled back, the words quietly torn from the depths of me and an echo of what he'd once said to me. It felt like an admission—like telling him my deepest secret of the creature who lingered there. I'd tried not to look too closely at her, at the mix of scales and darkness and flesh that comprised her very being. She wasn't human, but she wasn't an animal either.

And though her eyes were larger and gleamed with golden light…

Her face was mine.

My mate's expression softened, and he leaned forward to touch a far more gentle kiss to my mouth. It was the kind of kiss that nearly broke me—that spoke to the shattered pieces he saw that no one else could find.

"I have lived for centuries, my star. *Centuries.* And you are the furthest thing from a monster I have ever met."

I sighed, even as the creature within me settled into the warmth of his words. "You don't see what's inside me." I was tempted to look away, to hide the shame of the parts he hadn't seen—the parts that terrified me.

But I forced myself to meet his gaze as he leaned forward, touching his forehead to mine as his faint breath washed over me and surrounded me in the scent of snow and wintergreen. "I see all of you, Estrella. There is nothing left that you can hide from me, and there is no corner of you I do not love with every thread of my being," he murmured, his eyes so intent on mine that I forgot how to breathe.

I swallowed, letting his love wash away the shadows that threatened to consume me. "Is it always like this?" I asked, my voice the faintest murmur.

It seemed impossible to imagine that anyone could love someone as fully as he loved me, that other people existed out there—still kept from the completion that came with knowing their mate.

"I don't think so," he said, immediately understanding what I meant. He knew that I couldn't get enough of his hands on me, of his eyes on mine, and his feelings surging through the thread that tethered us. "But not all males worship their females. Some only expect it from them."

As if to prove his point, he leaned forward to touch his mouth to my jaw. He trailed those sinful lips over my skin, curving them around to the side of my neck as I arched for him. Brushing the straps of my nightgown down over the curve of my shoulders, he allowed the silk to drop to my waist so that my breasts were revealed to the chilled air.

The fire burned higher in the hearth as he sent a soft winter breeze to it, stoking the flames. It reached my skin in perfect time as he trailed that mouth over my breast, slowly easing himself to his knees. He wrapped his mouth around my nipple, biting it sharply before he continued down.

Skimming over the fabric of my nightgown, he placed his hands beneath my ass and pulled so that I tumbled back to the bed. Tugging me down to the edge, he spread my thighs around his head, draping my legs over his shoulders as he touched his mouth to me.

I pushed up onto my hands, staring down at him where he dragged his tongue through me. The sight of that beautiful, wicked face between my legs drew a moan from me. Caldris chuckled into my flesh, the rumble of it sending vibrations shooting through me as I grasped him by the hair.

I'd never get used to having a God on his knees for me.

His ashen silver strands glided through my fingers as I gripped, shoving him closer and demanding more. He obliged, using tongue and teeth to bring pleasure to every part of me as I whimpered.

Remembering what he'd said about what it was to fuck a God, I held him there even when he tried to pull away. When he tried to leave me at the edge of ecstasy, always preferring when I found my climax with him inside me.

I held him tight, reveling in the way he smiled into my pussy.

"Tonight, I want to be *your* God," I said, my voice breaking off into a breathless chuckle.

He slid his fingers inside me in answer, his growl of approval surging through me as he wrapped his mouth around that sensitive part and worshiped it with his tongue.

I shattered, pressing my arm into my mouth to stifle my cry. The God of the Dead licked me through it, his touches feather-light against my too sensitive skin as my breathing calmed.

He rose over me, shifting me higher on the bed so that he could settle his hips between my thighs. His face was a breath from mine, his eyes pinning me still as he slowly slid inside me.

"You are always my Goddess, *min asteren*. I worship at your altar with every breath—every moment of my existence," he said, blue eyes blazing with intent. "Not only because you are my mate and the Fates determined we were made for one another, but because I love *you*. The person you have become is a sight to behold, and I am privileged to stand at your side as you embark on your journey."

I surged up, capturing his mouth with mine. The words were too much—striking that sensitive, vulnerable part of me that *wondered*. Wondered if I was worth it—if I could ever live up to the vision he had of me and my potential.

He allowed me to silence him with my mouth, to crash my lips against his so harshly that it was a collision of tongue and lips and teeth. My lip bled beneath him as he pressed me back down, pinning me with his hands at my hips and sliding himself through the tender, swollen tissue of my pussy.

All gentleness was lost, all trace of emotion gone from his face as I wrapped my legs around his hips, pulling him deeper still. Our hips moved in tune with one another as I thrust up to meet him.

It was a battering of bodies—a battering of souls clashing against one another. My claws dug into his back, shredding his tunic as the monster within me rose to the surface. But Caldris met her gaze where she stared out from behind my eyes, then grinned at her as his own beast rose within him.

I felt the surge of darkness pulse off him, felt my monster purr in delight as my body clenched around him in answer. Caldris laughed, the sound a dark, mangled thing that spoke of possession and ownership rather than joy.

"That's my good girl," he murmured, pressing a hand against the front of my throat.

I snarled, baring tongue and teeth as that hand settled over the most vulnerable part of me. The creature within me lashed out, striking at him so harshly that I felt her move beneath my skin. He hoisted my legs higher as he rose over me, pinning me to the bed with that hand at my throat. He knelt between my legs, fucking me with deep, sharp thrusts as my legs spread to accommodate him.

I clawed at his forearm, tearing through the skin there. He didn't make any move to choke me, to harm me as he pinned me and fucked me. His blue eyes blazed as he held my furious gaze.

"I wondered when you would come out to play with me again," he murmured.

The image of that night in the bath after the boy on the bridge surged through me, reminding me of the cold creature who had possessed my body.

Was that what had happened? Was she the same monster who lingered within me now?

I bucked up, my body not entirely my own as she writhed within me. She didn't like our throat being vulnerable, wanted to wrap her teeth around his and force him into submission. The cold was gone from her now, replaced by the fury of a thousand flames.

Caldris pushed me back, pinning me to the bed beneath him once again. His cock stroked over that spot inside me, sending my eyes rolling back in my head even as the creature tried to focus.

"You're mine," he growled, baring his teeth as he stared down at me.

The ghost of a vision flashed over his face, half of it consumed by a skeleton as his own monster showed itself.

I swallowed down my fear, the trepidation I felt when staring at the creature within the God of the Dead. At the monster behind the beautiful face. But my creature wasn't afraid. She used my mouth, my throat, to emit something between a purr and a growl as Caldris kept fucking me.

Whatever he saw there made him smile; whatever that sound meant made him lean forward, daring my teeth to kiss me.

And instead of snapping and spitting and raging, the creature within me embraced him. We welcomed him deeper, welcomed him into our body and our soul.

Caldris pounded us into the mattress, his thrusts turning harsh and frenzied. I didn't remember a time when he'd fucked me like this, as if he'd been waiting for that monster to rise to share it with me.

His eyes glowed blue, flashing between that and the shadows of a dark night beneath the moon as he approached his orgasm. He took me with him, forcing my head to the side so that he could lay his mouth upon the side of my neck.

My creature purred as he sank his teeth into our flesh, grinding them into our skin. I went lax even as I felt myself bruise beneath the grip of those teeth, the claim that they possessed. But my body clenched around him, the bite shoving me into my orgasm as he groaned into my skin and followed.

We lay there for a few moments as the monsters settled, and there was blood on Caldris's mouth when he pulled back. His lips were twisted with the warning of a growl, waiting for me to fight the claim he'd just laid upon my monster and me.

His voice was more rumble than word when he spoke finally.

"Mine."

32

Estrella

The cages were empty where they hung from the ceiling of Mab's throne room, but one of the Summer Court Faeries had lit them on fire. The metal burned even though it was impossible, casting a golden glow down on the room as the flames stayed inside the bars of each cage. The Llaidhe had hung dark draperies of fabric, sweeping from one side of the throne room to the other.

The effect was ominous, sinking into that darkness everyone feared. The music that the troubadours played upon the stage near Mab's throne pulsed through the room as bodies moved in the twining of a dance that I recognized.

A jolt of disbelief struck me in the chest, with the realization that the very dances I'd been tormented into memorizing by the Priestess had been taken from the Fae. We'd stolen the culture and heritage straight from the very things we claimed to hate.

I scanned the gathered group of Gods, searching for the tall frame of my mate and his silver hair that would gleam in the firelight. There was no trace of him in the crowd as I made my way toward the center, hoping to catch even a glimpse of him.

Malachi watched my every move, seeming unwilling to allow me out of his sight, even at an event where I was meant to mingle. Mab wanted me to be sociable, had given me orders through Malachi to make myself welcomed among the Gods. I had no doubt it was so that she could watch my every move and interaction or use me to gather information for her down the line.

With Mab, there was always an ulterior motive.

Rheaghan approached me where I stood in the center, his light green eyes entertained. There was nothing sexual about the assessing stare he swept from my feet up to my face. The maroon of my gown was thin, the fabric breezy as it swept to the side to reveal a line of thigh. The top half of the dress was carved into sharp points that glimmered with gems, cut out to reveal lines of cleavage and breast that barely covered the necessary bits.

"I've not yet seen your mate, Princess," Rheaghan said, lowering his head into the slightest of bows.

I returned the gesture, making sure to drop my curtsy lower than he had. As the King of the Summer Court, he far outranked me. I could show my manners when it didn't involve showing deference to Mab herself.

I felt her eyes on my back as Rheaghan's wide mouth spread into a grin of satisfaction. "Now, where did a human girl learn to curtsy like that?" he asked, holding out a hand for me.

I took it, rising smoothly until my feet were properly underneath me once more.

Rheaghan studied the markings on my fingers, running his thumb across the teardrop mark from my blood oath with Fallon.

"I was groomed to be the Lady of my village one day," I said simply, swallowing as I thought of sharing the rest of the story. Of how gruesome that grooming had been.

Rheaghan must have read the unspoken words, his smile faltering as he nodded his understanding. "My niece has a mark just like this," he said instead of answering.

Holding his stare, I didn't offer the information he sought. He hadn't asked.

His lips twitched as if he knew exactly what sort of game I was playing. The Fae couldn't lie, but I wouldn't tell him the details of my oath with Fallon. He and his sister, for whatever reason, had some sort of bond. Even if I didn't understand how the male who radiated sunshine could still love the sister who wanted to plunge the world into darkness.

"Dance with me," he said, using the hand that clutched mine to guide me into position. He lifted it to place his palm facing toward me, allowing me to slide my fingers until they pressed against his.

"What makes you think I know this dance?" I asked, waiting as the song came to an end. There was a lull in the music as the troubadours prepared for the next song, leaving us to stare at one another in challenge.

"I think you know far more than you let on, Princess Estrella," he said as the music started.

I would never get used to people calling me princess, but I didn't protest, knowing it would fall on deaf ears.

The violin struck first, the chords of notes floating through the room as Rheaghan led me into the dance. He circled us, our steps slow and methodical—two opponents assessing one another before a battle. In this case, our battle was a dance floor. In a few days' time, it may very well be the arena.

We moved in harmony as I went through the steps that had been beaten into me as a girl. The perfectly timed movements were an echo of the other Fae moving around me, leaving me to be swept into the dance in ways I'd never been able to before.

There was no punishment for a hand that wasn't perfectly positioned, or a leg that didn't extend straight enough. There was only the joy that came from feeling the music sink into my bones, driving each of my movements with more fluidity than years of practice had provided to me. My only distraction came in the way I watched the throne room doors, waiting for my mate to arrive.

Rheaghan placed his hands on my waist, lifting me and spinning me in time with the others. It forced my attention back to him, to our dance, to find his mouth set in a tight line.

"I suspect he may be a few moments late this evening," Rheaghan said, answering the unspoken question of where Caldris was. It wasn't like him to miss any moment of time we could be spending together—under Mab's watchful eye or not.

"Dare I ask why that might be?" I asked, staring up into the piercing light green of his eyes. The sun-kissed color of his skin seemed so at odds with the coldness of the throne room as he held my gaze.

He glanced toward Mab upon her throne as we danced, our bodies moving from one song to the next as more and more of the Fae arrived in the throne room. He leaned closer, moving our bodies so that they very nearly touched so that his words could be soft. We lost eye contact as he towered over me, everything in me going taut with the sudden tension in his body.

"Did you really believe my sister suddenly stopped torturing you out of the kindness of her heart?" he asked, and my heart plummeted into my stomach.

"Of course not. She threatened to murder human mates if I didn't behave," I said, sinking my teeth into the inside of my cheek. It had seemed too simple, and I'd waited for the other shoe to drop. But if she wasn't getting anywhere with hurting me physically, it made sense to punish me using others.

"And has she?" Rheaghan asked, tilting his head to the side in question. He wrinkled his nose ever-so-slightly, the only hint of his judgment for me having believed her story. Suddenly faced with the reality of how naïve I had been, I grimaced.

"No, she hasn't," I said, swallowing as I glanced toward her throne.

She watched those dancing on the floor that had been cleaned by the Llaidhe, her chin raised high as if she were above her people.

Above the Gods themselves.

"She wouldn't want to kill a mate for every time you defy her. She'll save that for the moments when you embarrass her so much that she has no choice but to punish you publicly," Rheaghan answered, his knowledge of his sister's behavior coming through in every word he spoke. He'd had centuries to get to know her, her actions and motivations and weaknesses.

If he could be turned against his own flesh and blood, he'd be a valuable asset.

"Then what has she done to punish me in the meantime?" I asked.

We both knew I'd defied her in small ways, challenged her verbally without ever crossing the line. But for the Queen of Air and Darkness to have not retaliated against me physically, who was bearing the cost of those moments?

"Your mate is not one to sit idly by while you suffer. He cannot save you from Mab's violence, not when she can kill him with only a thought. That does not mean he has not spent the entirety of your time in Tar Mesa negotiating for the end of your suffering," Rheaghan said, sweeping the rug out from under me.

I stumbled our dance. He caught me, making the misstep look intentional. "What... what did he offer her?" I asked. My breath shuddered. My ears rang, nearly drowning out the sound of Rheaghan's words.

"Estrella—" Rheaghan started, interrupting me as my anger—my horror—rose.

What had Caldris done?

The male was insufferable, incapable of listening to what I might want. My throat felt too dry, my words caught on the lump in my throat.

Rheaghan pulled me closer, plastering my chest against his torso as he held me tight enough to suffocate. It was a makeshift hug, soothing as his free hand trailed up my spine in a light, comforting touch.

"What. Did. He. Give. Her?" I demanded, slowly enunciating the words as I ground my jaw.

The joy of the music had left me, the movements feeling suddenly hollow. That creature inside me rose, and I felt her dance behind my eyes as I stared up at Rheaghan. A flash of gold flitted across his skin as he pinched lips together and sighed out his nose.

The God of the Sun hesitated as his chest dropped. "He took your place. For every defiance, he is summoned to Mab's rooms so that she and Malazan might use him to punish you."

Nausea churned in my gut. *Malazan.* If she'd violated him....

Rheaghan read the tension in my body, shaking his head subtly. "The torture is not sexual in nature. The mate bond forbids such a thing, and my sister is no fool as to tempt the wrath of the Fates. But sex and violence are not so far apart for Malazan. The latter is merely her form of foreplay, so after she's done with him, she is in the habit of making Caldris watch as she fucks another one of Mab's children. The guilt of that alone is worse than the physical pain."

The throne room disappeared, swept out from under me. There was no music, no dancing around me. Only the memory of watching Lord Byron fuck the Ladies of the Night—watching them service him. At the time, I hadn't known he was exposing me to the things he liked—the things he would expect of me one day. It hadn't made it easier to deal with.

I was going to be sick.

"Breathe," Rheaghan murmured, that soothing hand working to keep my nausea at bay.

"I haven't felt his pain through the mate bond," I said, shaking my head. It wasn't possible. If Caldris had been suffering, I would have felt it.

"He's had centuries to master closing himself off from those around him. Closing himself off from you is another part of that. I imagine you've discovered hints of how to do it. Is it so hard to imagine he can do the same with you? That he would do it to protect you?" Rheaghan asked, his voice quiet.

Anger rushed through me, a sudden, vicious need to make them *bleed* coursing through my veins. The monster within me roared, having connected with his so intimately only the night before—all while he was feeding me yet another lie.

"What does Mab gain from this? If she wants to punish me, then surely, I need to know about it."

Rheaghan's voice became monotone, resignation leaking from him as he pulled back to stare down at me. "You're thinking too short term. Mab is *always* playing the long game. Her greatest interest lies in driving a wedge between you and Caldris. If she can control the narrative, determine *when* you learn of the suffering you've caused and the secret he's kept from you…"

"She can make me lose my trust in him," I said, running my tongue over my teeth.

My feet still moved in the habit of the dance, but my mind was on the queen sitting on the throne. I was too busy imagining all the ways I would kill her and her friend for what they'd done.

"Especially given that Caldris has been in a room while a woman he's been intimate with has gotten naked and fucked someone while he's made to watch—"

"He wasn't intimate with her," I snapped, my tone leaving no room for argument. "She raped him, and she violated him. There is no intimacy in that."

Rheaghan studied me for a moment before he nodded, conceding my point. "Fair enough."

I sighed, resisting the urge to hang my head as I tried not to let on what I knew. I didn't know what to do with the new information, but for once I needed to think it through. "I don't understand why he would keep this from me."

"It was the only way my sister would agree to the deal. The devastation on your face was always her end goal. She cannot break you when you two stand united against her, but if she can convince you that you're alone, she could stand a chance," he explained, spinning me in a circle as the music shifted to something more upbeat. He leaned in again when I came around to face him once more. "Play the long game if you want to win. Cunning over wrath."

I chewed the inside of my cheek and cleared my throat. "Why are you telling me all of this?" I asked, a knot forming in my belly. If it was a lie, all one of Mab's games, behaving rashly could be playing into her trap. I listened intently, tilting my head to the side as I waited for his response.

"I've made my fair share of mistakes with my sister. Don't think I am unaware that I could have stopped all of this," he said, swallowing as his face and neck became unnaturally still. His feet continued to move to the rhythm of the dance, as if they were enchanted in the way the humans would be if allowed to attend. "I didn't, and now Alfheimr has suffered because of me. I just want a chance to make it right."

"And if that means your sister has to die? What will you do then?" I asked, probing further. I needed him to say the words. Especially after Mab had tricked me with our deal at the Labyrinth, I couldn't allow any vague half-measures to interfere in what could be—what needed to be.

He huffed a laugh, glancing toward the fires burning in the cages above us. "Gods know I am not strong enough to do it myself, but I won't get in the way when the time comes. There can be no peace with Mab on the throne. I want there to be peace again, no matter the cost."

I nodded slowly, taking in his response. I didn't know what to make of it, would need time to decide—time that I didn't have in that moment.

Rheaghan's eyes swept toward the doors to the throne room where my mate entered with a slow gait, his eyes tracking over the crowd as he searched for me. Malazan strode by his side, another male next to her as she waved him off. She turned to my mate, smiling up at him in what I knew now was victory.

My jaw clenched as Rheaghan touched my face, turning my gaze back to his. "Long game, Estrella. You know nothing of Caldris's deal. *Dance*," he murmured, guiding me through the motions.

"Why should I pretend I know nothing and allow it to continue?" I asked, my fury rising all over again as Malazan took Caldris by the hand and guided him to the middle of the dance floor. My mate kept her at a distance, scowling as their hands touched, and searched for me.

I turned my attention away from him, focusing on Rheaghan even though I wanted nothing more than to kill Malazan where she stood.

"Because if you do not know, no one will suspect you when she turns up dead. I look forward to playing the game with you, Princess."

He spun me, releasing my hand as I turned in three rapid circles. The troubadours swept into the next song immediately as another pair of hands caught me. They settled upon my waist, guiding me into the start of a dance I wasn't familiar with. I looked up into his amaryllis eyes, distracted by that faint hint of pink at the center of the pale silver.

"Estrella," Soren said, his gaze turning knowing. "You look as if you are ready to sever heads from shoulders. As much as I am certain my cousin would enjoy the sight, those games are much better done in private." His black hair shone in the firelight, illuminating the subtle hints of purple that streaked through it.

I nodded, forcing a smile to my face as I let my body fall loose. I tried to find that place where I'd sunk down into the music with Rheaghan—feeling it move within me. For his part, Soren shifted our dance whenever needed to make sure I didn't need to watch my mate dance with his abuser.

"He's a big boy," Soren said softly, his gaze soft and encouraging, despite the harshness of the words.

My mate might have been capable of defending himself under normal circumstances, but this was the one place where he couldn't. Where that woman could lay hands on him, and he would know that as she cut his skin or bled him, she'd save that memory to then fuck another male.

I wanted to riot. I wanted blood and death and *vengeance*.

"Revenge comes to those who wait. Let her have this night," Soren said, leaning in to whisper in my ear. My body went solid, the feeling of eyes on my spine—watching the contact. "She has no idea it will be her last, does she?"

There was a smirk in his voice, a challenge for me to get past my own anger. To know that I would take care of her in time. I smiled, my lips spreading wider than they had in weeks. Laughter tumbled free, staring at the male who may have been under Mab's command, but worked to undermine her all the same.

How many of them were there?

"Enjoy your evening," he said, smiling knowingly as he spun me into the arms of the next dance partner.

The male who caught me stared down at me with indigo eyes that shone out from a stern face set into skin the color of crushed autumn leaves. It danced with a myriad of colors, warmth radiating off the subtle brown hues. His copper hair fell to just above his shoulder in slight waves, thick and shining.

I swallowed as he backed me up a step in our dance, not hesitating to place his hand on my waist to guide me through the music that increased in tempo from the previous song.

"I don't believe we've met," I said, swallowing back my nerves as I forced myself to smile up at him.

The power I'd come to associate with the Gods pulsed off him. It spoke to something related to nature coating my skin. His felt like the familiar rush of the harvest—like foliage and decayed leaves upon the ground.

"My name is Kahlo, Estrella. I am the King of the Autumn Court and the God of Beasts," he said, his head tipping to the side in that way that was purely Fae. More animal than man. He dropped our hands lower, only holding me with a few fingers as he studied me.

"Ah," I said, glancing toward where the Queen of the Autumn Court danced with another male. She smiled up at him, her face lit in ways that defied the mood of the Tithe.

I guessed mine hadn't been much different when I first danced with Rheaghan, feeling the joy of the music. "Shouldn't you be dancing with your wife?" I asked, pursing my lips as I raised a brow at him.

He chuckled, the deep sound sliding across my skin. "Let her have her fun. She is my wife, not my mate. We each enjoy the company of others," he said.

I swallowed as my cheeks flushed, opening my mouth to speak when Kahlo spun me out of turn. I kept my feet beneath me, rising up onto my toes until I danced into a familiar embrace.

Caldris wrapped one arm around me as he caught my hand with his in the other.

"Having fun, Little One?" he growled, seamlessly guiding me into the movements of the dance.

I turned to look back at Kahlo, finding him striding away and leaving me to my mate. I forced myself to quiet my concerns and my anger over all that he'd kept from me, turning back to stare up into Caldris's icy gaze.

"Jealous?" I asked, sinking my teeth into my bottom lip.

His gaze dropped to it immediately, a groan rattling in his chest. He spun me to face the opposite direction, pressing his body close to mine—closer than was necessary or appropriate for the dance—as I crossed my arms over my stomach and held one of his hands in each.

His warmth sank into my spine, soothing the frayed edges his secret had caused. "Always," he murmured, his breath brushing over my neck. My eyes met Malazan's where she danced with the other male who had entered with them—her stare fixated on where my mate melded himself to my body.

I swayed as I spun back to face Caldris, cutting her off from my view and deeming her unworthy of my attention. His eyes gleamed as he stared down at me, and it was then that I saw the hollowness I'd missed.

The agony in that stare as he looked at me, knowing that he was keeping secrets and contributing to my future pain. I sighed, reaching up to cup his cheek and draw him down to me.

"I forgive you," I whispered, stretching up onto my toes to touch my lips to his.

He'd sacrificed himself—given his own body and pain—to protect me from the same. No matter the consequence of that, the least I could do was forgive him for doing everything in his power to protect me.

I'd deal with those who deserved my ire later, but for now, I allowed my mate to wrap me in his embrace and guide me through the dance. He didn't ask what I'd forgiven him for, his lips parting slightly as he looked at me.

The guilt I found there nearly stole the breath from my lungs. He wouldn't ask me what I'd forgiven him for, not when doing so might force him to reveal what he couldn't.

Instead, we danced in silence, our secrets hanging between us. I knew his secret, but he couldn't know what I planned to do with it.

The weight of that was mine alone to bear.

33

Caldris

I left my mate to her dancing later that evening, stepping to the side and allowing her to shine. And dance, she did, allowing Kahlo to spin her at the center of the room. The Fae around her watched as she smiled, her face lit with the joy she so rarely got to experience. Even Mab stood from her throne as Estrella raised her hands, tiny, shimmering stars rising from her opened palms.

She sent them up toward the ceiling, beaming up at them as they cast the appearance of a night sky down upon the previously haunted throne room. Rheaghan looked at my mate, approaching her side and drawing her away from the God of Beasts so that he could dance with her once more. Kahlo glared at the God of the Sun, his displeasure in having his dance partner stolen by his enemy evident, but Estrella was oblivious to the fight brewing between them. It had been centuries since they'd last tried to kill one another in an all-out brawl.

They were overdue.

Rheaghan slid a hand around the small of Estrella's back, taking her for a turn around the apex of the room as he raised his hand. He extinguished the flames in the cages, winking them out one by one as they made their slow, methodical circle.

The room plunged into darkness, only the stars above to light the dance floor. Mab stepped down from her throne, descending the dais. But my mate held the room captivated, her laughter striking me deep in the place where the thread of our bond connected with my heart.

No one turned to look at the Queen of Air and Darkness as she approached the edge of the dance floor. No one bothered to ask her to dance. I joined her from the side where I'd taken up vigil in watching the love of my life seduce the Gods to her side with nothing but the shine of her inner light.

"They can't take their eyes off her," I said, keeping my voice low.

Mab spun to look at me. Her eyes narrowed into a glare as she huffed and turned back to the room of her followers. Of her minions and those she'd bound to obey her.

But fear didn't equal respect, and Estrella would slowly win the latter by doing nothing other than being herself.

The song increased in volume as Rheaghan tossed his head back and laughed, dancing beneath the stars with my mate. I longed to dance with her again, to feel her body move beneath my hands and let her chase away the shadows of the torment I'd tolerated earlier.

Watching her smile was almost as good.

Estrella wound her body in movements that were sharp when they needed to be, moving to the beat of the drums, and the fluid sway of her hips when the violin struck a chord that she felt within her.

"Men have always been blinded by beauty," Mab said, her voice dismissive.

"I thought she was a dressed up pig?" I asked, thinking of the words Malazan had murmured against my mate when she cut my flesh to ribbons, watching it heal so that she could do it all over again. Mab pursed her lips, pressing the deep red flesh together as she always did when presented with a problem she couldn't solve.

She couldn't kill Estrella and use her, but she couldn't allow her court to be turned against her either.

She smirked, the half-smile lacking the disdain it normally did. "Nobody said there was any accounting for the taste of males."

As if in answer, Kahlo took my mate from Rheaghan and dipped her low. Her head snapped back in tune with the music, her hair forming a dark curtain as it nearly touched the ground. She lifted a single leg to help her balance, her dress parting to reveal more of her beautiful bronze skin.

Kahlo drew her back up to stand before him, the rare ghost of a smile lighting the God's face as he shook his head at Estrella.

Taste, indeed.

I suppressed the surge of jealousy in my stomach, allowing my mate to do what was needed to open everyone's eyes to how monotonous and boring life had become without any light in it.

Under the hand of Mab, we'd forgotten to *live*.

Estrella remembered.

"They don't want to fuck her," I said, leaning my head toward my stepmother. She glared up at me, dark eyes glinting with the harshness of onyx. We both knew I would never allow Estrella to dance with males if that was their aim for the evening. "They just want to be near her. To let her shine her light on them for a little while."

One of Mab's captive children stepped into the fray, holding out a hand for Estrella. She took it, letting him move her into the motions of a dance as she grinned. He hesitated for a moment, his smile shy before he returned it and shook his head.

He was one who often warmed Mab's bed; perhaps her favored nighttime companion for centuries, aside from Octavian and Malachi. He drew Estrella into the dance, touching her only where necessary but staring down at her face as if he couldn't help himself.

Mab swallowed, shifting on her feet and looking far more offended than I'd ever seen her. I wondered for a moment about that little girl who was hidden somewhere beneath the evil that had consumed her. The one Rheaghan swore still lived, held captive in her own body.

"Then what is it?"

"She is everything you will never be," I said, keeping all harshness out of my words. I didn't want them to be an insult, only the truth. "She is life itself."

Fallon stepped up to Estrella's side, and she abandoned her male companion in favor of dancing with the sister the Fates had granted her. They might not have been blood sisters, but something in me rejoiced in seeing them smile at one another.

Estrella grasped Fallon's hands in hers and they spun through the throne room—sharing a single, joyful moment between them. They should have had lifetimes together, their bond something that had been threaded through destiny itself.

Both girls looked toward the ceiling as Estrella closed her eyes, raising their tightly clutched hands to form two swirling balls of light. They rose toward the ceiling, growing in size until they nestled amid the stars. A smaller direct echo of the two moons shining outside the walls of Tar Mesa.

The Prophecy of the Twin Moons.

The moon on the back of the girl's hands seemed to glow in response, the mark given to them by the Lunar Witches pulsing light throughout the room as they danced.

No one dared to interrupt.

Estrella shattered the moment when she spun, finding Nila standing against the walls with an *acalica*. The female was one of the most nightmarish of the humanoid species among the Llaidhe, reduced to making rounds throughout the throne room with Faerie wine to offer. Estrella danced her way over to her handmaiden, taking the serving tray from the *acalica* with a grin. She handed it to the Sidhe standing nearest to the female, looked right into the wide, protruding eyes of the Llaidhe creature, and took her by the hand.

The female looked down at her in shock, and if she'd had eyelids, she would have blinked. She had no lips, her skin a pale, leathery white as her long, bony fingers wrapped around Estrella's hand and wrist gently. Her nails were long enough to cut to the bone, but she held my mate in her grasp as if she was the most precious thing she'd ever touched. Her skin peeled back to reveal razor-sharp teeth that formed some semblance of a smile as Estrella walked backward slowly, guiding the *acalica* into the dance.

The room went silent but for the sound of the music as Estrella moved her body, guiding the Llaidhe to join her in her dance. Fallon came up at her side, taking the *acalica's* other hand as the room watched in stunned, horrified silence.

Nila and Imelda joined them from the sidelines, the *acalica's* ears and pointed fly-like wings fluttering as she learned the steps to the dance she'd never been allowed to partake in. The other Llaidhe in the room watched in rapt fixation, their faces lit with the first hints of hope.

Hope for a new world. The one Estrella would create if they only helped her. If they took their power back.

Kahlo stepped into the fray, the God of Beasts not fearing the *acalica* in the slightest as he took her free hand from Estrella and began to dance with her. Estrella smiled, spinning in her dance and staring Mab in the eye for a brief moment as she shifted her attention to Soren.

She took him to the outskirts of the room, placing the hand of a *maa alused* into his. The female smiled shyly, staring at the God of Twilight and turning that shocked stare to Estrella as she flitted off, already turning her attention to Rheaghan.

Soren didn't hesitate to draw the half-bald, dark-eyed creature into the center of the dance, showing patience as he taught her the moves for the song.

I smiled, crossing my arms over my chest as I watched my mate work to undermine the very structures that had kept Alfheimr functioning for centuries. Her smile was knowing every time she glanced toward me, and while she acted out of desire to see the Llaidhe treated equally, she wasn't unaware of what she was doing.

With a dance, she painted herself as a savior—offering freedom from centuries of systemic oppression.

She made them love her, and as such, took the first step in building her army.

34

Estrella

The music stopped.

Caldris froze where he'd joined me—along with the others dancing around us—turning his gaze forward slowly. Malachi led a group of human mates toward the front of the throne room. A smirk graced his face as the attention of every Fae went to the men and women they led forward.

I turned my shocked stare to Caldris, watching as he squeezed his eyes closed in horror. "Estrella—"

I strode forward, only stopping when he wrapped his arms around my waist and held me back.

"Let go!" I hissed, my eyes landing upon some of the very same people who'd been cruel to me on our journey back to Alfheimr.

Their time in Tar Mesa hadn't been kind—the clothing they wore was nothing but rags as they wrapped their arms around themselves and allowed themselves to be shuffled toward where Mab waited for them.

Caldris pulled me back more firmly, a strong forearm wrapping across my chest as I lifted my feet and tried to shift him off balance. But my mate was too familiar with every strategy I used when fighting, leaving me gasping for breath.

Rheaghan came up at my side as Soren stepped in front of me, blocking my view of what happened at the front.

"You are not responsible for her actions," Rheaghan said, his voice low. The disappointment that was there hinted at his eternity of suffering—of blaming himself for the monster his sister had become.

"She's doing this because of me," I said, my voice dropping low as the fight slipped out of my body. I'd challenged her status quo too openly, and she *couldn't* punish me publicly—not without strengthening my bond with the Llaidhe.

"She's doing this because it makes her feel powerful to hold mates over our heads. She's using you as a scapegoat because she wants to break you, and she knows that you will carry the weight of her crimes if she tells you to. No one here blames you," Caldris said, using his free hand to tuck my hair behind my ear as I settled in his grip.

"Do these belong to anyone here?" Mab asked, looking around the room as she reached the top of her dais. *These.* Her words demeaned the mates, turning them into things instead of people—living and breathing.

She lowered herself into her throne, looking down upon the revelry and the human mates waiting to be claimed. Only three Fae stepped forward, two males and a female waiting to take what was theirs. The Fae Marks upon their skin swirled in tune with the ones on their matching human mates, but the humans didn't cower in the face of what they'd once feared.

There was no light in their eyes as they shied away from Malachi and another of the guards who took up his place at the side.

"Return the other two," Mab said, waving a hand.

The other guard guided the two who were unclaimed toward the throne room doors as one of the male Fae stepped forward.

"Please, my Queen," he begged, cutting off when Mab turned her glare to him.

"I am feeling generous tonight. One of you will be allowed to leave here with your mate and complete your bond with my blessing, under the condition that you swear your allegiance to me," she said, looking down upon the three who had gathered in front of her. I couldn't see enough of them to decide if I knew them, if I'd spoken to them.

It was probably better that way.

The Fae waited for Mab's decision, waited to know how much longer they would have to wait to leave with their mates if they weren't chosen that evening. I suspected there were countless others in the throne room who had yet to even see the mate waiting for them, trapped in an endless game of Mab's will.

Mab clicked her tongue as she studied them intently. "The blue," she said, waving a dismissive hand.

One of the males hurried forward, grabbing the woman who had the same markings as he by the hands and pulling her out of the fray. They blended back in with the crowd, coming closer to us as he ran frantic hands over her face—her arms—searching for injuries.

At the front of the throne room, a woman screamed.

My eyes flashed toward it just in time to watch as Malachi swung his sword. The male's head fell from his shoulders, dropping to the floor and rolling to the Fae female's feet. She howled again, the shrill sound of her voice splitting the air in two.

The agony in it was too familiar. The same as that day the Veil fell.

I turned, burying my face into Caldris's chest. I couldn't bear to watch as the male pleaded for his mate's life, but I forced myself to watch, anyway.

To remember.

The remaining woman turned terrified eyes toward the same male she'd probably feared before coming to Alfheimr. The desperation in them stole my breath away, time seeming to slow as her lips parted to speak.

Malachi's blade cut through her neck in one swift swing. Her body hit the ground as silence reigned.

Her Fae mate didn't scream. He didn't cry as he picked up her severed head and approached her body. There was nothing left in him as he knelt by her side, hanging his face forward and grasping her corpse. He pulled it to his chest, holding the mate he'd never been allowed to touch in life.

It was with his face turned toward Mab that he raised the iron dagger from his side, looking for all purposes like he might attack the Queen of Air and Darkness herself. She raised a brow, unimpressed with the male who would be her murderer.

Caldris guided us forward, moving to the side so that we could see more fully. Rheaghan and Soren followed with us— until I watched from the sidelines as the male turned his blade toward himself.

"*No*," I gasped, only Caldris's arm across my chest keeping me still as the male pushed the blade forward.

And stabbed himself through the heart.

35

Estrella

The walk down the halls was overshadowed by the deaths in the throne room.

Caldris had pulled my stunned body away from the carnage as the Llaidhe dealt with the three bodies. The female Fae who was left without a mate had needed to be dragged away from his remains as she wept and screamed. I didn't want to think of what would happen to her now. How many years would she have to wait before he reincarnated if that hadn't been his final life?

"Where are we going?" I asked, hating that she'd taken a rare moment of happiness and ruined it. I didn't know if I'd ever be able to dance again, not knowing what she'd begun when I'd been too preoccupied to notice.

"The Cove," Caldris answered, his hand at my waist guiding me forward. Gods and Fae alike shuffled forward along with us, paired off into couples that didn't bode well for the evening's events. "You have to snap out of it for this, my star."

I nodded, glancing toward the crystal waters of the Cove as it came into view. That same voice whispered in my head, the shimmer drawing me forward as I clutched Caldris's hand tighter in mine. I didn't let on how drawn to the water I was, forcing myself away as we followed the group toward the path through the trees.

The burning embers from the holly tree rained ash down upon the forest, but it somehow never caught flame.

I immediately wondered about the creatures that called the Cove home, finding their sanctuary within the woods that no longer seemed safe. Where would they go if they couldn't stay here?

The walk through the forest was blissfully short, bringing us to the clearing as the group of thirteen Gods that had been selected spread out. They lingered beneath the canopy of the burning tree, turning to the Fae they'd brought with them.

Mab took up her place with Malachi at her side. "We will all participate in the ritual," she said, her gaze sliding around the tree to look at each of us. She and Malachi stepped forward, and they each pressed a palm to the tree trunk.

We took up our place closest to Rheaghan and his partner on one side, with Kahlo and his on the other. Twyla was as far from Caldris as possible, lingering near Mab even though she hated her.

I swallowed, not wanting to think about what the ritual entailed if family members were spreading themselves out.

Caldris took my hand in his, curling his front against my back as we approached the tree. He waited until the others had all laid their hands upon the trunk to press our joined hands into the bark.

A rush of warmth flooded my back as golden embers left the tree, fluttering down to us. Caldris's hand glowed golden where it covered mine, the light spreading up through his arm as I turned to look at him over my shoulder. His Fae Marks pulsed with golden light where they peeked out from his tunic, and his eyes were lost to gold as his hair warmed beneath the magic surging through him.

"What the fuck?" I asked, flinching back from the expression that didn't seem like his. His head tilted to the side, and he looked more like a God in those moments than ever before. "Caelum."

I lifted my hand off the tree, jumping in shock when a branch slithered around my wrist and pulled me back. It wrapped around me, grabbing my other hand with another branch and keeping my hands trapped against the bark.

"It won't hurt you. Don't fight it," Caldris said, his voice still his own as he ran his nose up the back of my neck. Those golden hands swept the hair off my neck as he breathed me in, and something within me settled for the briefest of moments.

It ended the next, when tree roots pushed through the dirt beneath my feet, wrapping around my ankles and spreading my legs slightly, pulling my stance away from the tree so that I had to arch my back. Around us, the others had stepped away from the tree. I couldn't see Mab or Twyla, only Rheaghan and Kahlo as they drew their partners back to the grass covered part of the forest clearing and lingered just on the outskirts of where I could see. They didn't hesitate to strip clothing off as I turned my shocked stare back to the tree.

Caldris chuckled, his voice low in my ear. "Good girl. I don't want you looking at them," he said.

I kept my eyes forward, my legs trembling beneath me. I hated the idea of being chained, of being trapped and unable to free myself. No matter how I pulled at the restraints, the tree held me steady. The branches holding my wrists vibrated as if the tree itself was *laughing*.

I heard the sound of fabric shifting as Caldris took off his tunic, felt his body move as he stripped off his boots and pants. The next time he pressed against me, he was nude and hard against the curve of my ass as he leaned over me.

"I'm going to fuck you now," he said, his voice both his and not. I had no doubt my mate was in there somewhere, but he was trapped beneath the undercurrent of magic within him.

"*Here?*" I gasped, wincing when someone laughed—the sound deep and rough, as if the person didn't laugh often.

Kahlo.

"Yes, my star. *Here.*"

He grasped the laces at the back of my dress, untying the neat bow Nila had done earlier that evening. He fed the ribbon through the holes slowly, forcing my dress to hang off my body as he made his way toward my waist. It finally fell to the ground, surrounding the feet I couldn't move.

My mate trailed clawed fingers up my spine. The touch sent a ripple through me as he reached the base of my neck. He buried his hand in my hair, grasping it and using it to wrench my head back toward him. My spine bowed, arching for him as my breathing turned ragged.

"Tell me to stop, and it all ends here," he said, leaning forward to press his lips to the curve of my shoulder. His teeth trailed over the skin there; the slightest threat of pain amid the shiver that shot straight to my core.

I laughed uncomfortably, my eyes dropping back to where the tree still held me captive. "The tree disagrees with you. I don't know what I'm agreeing to. Why aren't the others—"

"Every Tithe, the tree chooses one God to channel the magic of the ritual," Caldris explained, that deep voice patient and understanding even as he ground his cock into my ass like he couldn't help himself. "The tree chose me, and as my partner, you're to be the conduit."

"The conduit?" I asked, gasping when his hand freed my hair, sliding around to the front of my neck. He grasped me there, his palm pressing firmly into my jugular as his nails pressed into the side of my throat.

"The tree feeds on sex to help it rise from the ashes after the Tithe. The others' desire will feed into me because of the magic it's given me for the night. Desire that I will use to fuck you until morning. The tree will feed from you—your pleasure," he said, his voice trailing into a growl as his hand lowered, sliding between the valley of my breasts. He moved it toward the apex of my thighs, stopping at the lowest part of my belly and pausing there, lingering, waiting for my answer.

His fingers made small, teasing circles against my skin, making that creature within me rise to the surface as if he'd toyed with her. I felt his chuckle against my spine, felt the smile on his face. The self-satisfied grin of a male who'd triumphed over his prey; he took pleasure in the fact that my monster was his to command—at least in this.

He'd already dominated the most monstrous part of me, and she'd let him.

A growl came from my lips, strange and animalistic as heat slithered through my body in response. The faintest hint of starlight and scales moved on my skin, like the ghost of a memory of what those things were. I immediately thought of the skeletal face I'd seen on Caldris when he claimed me, shock striking me in the chest as my fingernails elongated into claws.

"There you are," he murmured as my hips writhed, seeking out the pleasure he'd offered.

The undeniable urge to claim him, to let him take what he wanted, was so, so much stronger when she threatened to tear through my skin.

"Give me the words, *min asteren.*"

"Gods," someone muttered, and I was too far gone to recognize the voice—to wonder if it was about me and what Caldris had revealed or if it had more to do with their own partner.

I growled again, trying to slide my body along that tormenting hand. Just a little farther, and he'd put it exactly where I needed it. I looked to my side, to the others who were mostly lost in the pleasure of their partners, but never fully took their attention off the glowing golden male behind me.

We'd had sex with an audience before, fucked while people watched, but something about this moment felt more important. It felt like finally ridding myself of my human sensibilities and embracing the less restricted nature of the Fae.

"Would you shut up and fuck me already?" I growled, looking at Caldris over my shoulder.

My mate laughed, but finally slid that hand lower on my body. His fingers trailed through me, brushing against my clit so softly that my hips jolted forward.

"Oh no, my star. I have all night to fuck you."

His free hand wrapped around my front, grasping my breast in his hand and pinching the nipple as he worked the flesh. His other moved between my thighs, sliding first one finger inside of me and working it slowly.

Too slowly

"By the end of the night, you'll be so full of cum that it drips down your thighs," he said, and the creature inside of me purred. "I'm going to make a fucking mess of you. So before you get my cock, you're going to come on my fingers, and then you're going to ride my tongue."

I whimpered as he added a second finger to my pussy, pumping them more quickly and kneading the flesh of my breast in perfect harmony. I tossed my head back, laying it upon his chest as he held me pinned at those two points of contact.

Over and over, those fingers pumped within me, slow and patient—as if he had all the time in the world and wasn't holding my orgasm over me. Controlling it perfectly as he played my body like a harp.

I growled his name, pulling the restraints of the tree against my wrists. "Caldris."

"I think I like you just like this," he said, repositioning the heel of his palm so that it pressed against my clit. The branches at my wrist pulsed with golden light that they seemed to draw from my body, taking my pleasure as it approached my orgasm. "All tied up and desperate for me, willing to let me do *anything* to you."

"Please," I begged, my voice half a sob as he and that tree surrounded me in desire.

The *need* of everyone fed into him, flooding the thread between us. The others wanted to fuck their partners, teasing and torturing them as Caldris did to me, but there was nothing in our bond but desire for *me*.

His attention was solely focused on the places he touched me, on the need filling me as he ground his palm against my clit and fucked me with his fingers. I writhed on his hand, taking what I needed from the delicious friction he offered.

The tree fed as I clawed my orgasm into its bark, shredding pieces from the trunk and whimpering. My mate's hand left my body, but it did nothing to stop the desire from building within me even as I came. It did nothing to appease the wanton part of me, my voice a strangled gasp as he slapped his palm down on my ass.

"It's going to be a long night, Little One," Caldris said, chuckling as he lowered himself to his knees behind me. I turned to look at him over my shoulder, flattening my back so that I could see his face.

I could see him lay a hand upon each of my ass cheeks, lifting and spreading me so that he could see the wet flesh between my legs. I flushed, thinking of just how on display the position had put me to the couples behind us.

"Caldris," I said, shifting my weight from one leg to the other. I couldn't move, couldn't do anything to hide myself as he blew a warm breath against me.

"Let them see the paradise I get to sink inside at night. Never again will they question why I would destroy worlds for you," he said, leaning forward to lick a single line through me.

Everything in me tightened, my entire being centering around that one touch. His eyes sparked with golden embers as he pulled back, his body the flawless canvas of a God and the ghost of a skull on half his face.

"Let them see what they'll never have for themselves, because you're *mine*," he growled, burying his face in my flesh. This was no teasing lick or slow torment, only the devouring of a male who would live with his face between my legs if I allowed it.

"Fuck," I groaned, dropping my head forward.

The God of the Dead ate me like he was starved, working his tongue inside of me and circling my entrance when he pulled back, shifting his attention to my clit and doing it all over and over again so fast that it became a haze.

I became a mess of want and need, and all traces of the woman who would have shied away from such things disappeared.

My hips moved in time with him, riding his tongue as he worked it over me. Through me. Inside of me.

And when I came, it was with his face so tightly pressed to my pussy that I couldn't tell where he finished and I began.

The tree fed, the branches shimmering as it took from me. The edge of my need never went away, making me whimper as my body begged for more—even as I sagged in the tree's grip.

I hated that fucking tree for taking what was mine—for taking the pleasure I was owed and needed. The branches rumbled around my wrist as if it could hear my thoughts, and I growled my warning at it. A single branch came toward me, brushing a leaf against my cheek in a tender gesture that made me look at it with newfound fear.

"It likes you," my mate murmured, standing behind me.

His cock spread through my pussy, gliding along the wet, soaked flesh from my orgasms and stimulating my oversensitive clit all over again.

"How could it not when you're feeding it so well with your greedy little cunt?" Caldris drove inside me to prove his point, sliding through me with ease after all the preparations of his fingers and his tongue.

With how much I needed to be fucked.

My back arched immediately, allowing him to wrap both his hands around the front of my throat and hold me still as he used me in slow, hard thrusts that I felt in every corner of my body. I stretched up onto my toes with each battering of him within me—the tree keeping me from getting away from the torment.

My voice was a garbled groan beneath the press of his hands. The words slurred together, becoming a disaster of pleasure that never seemed to end.

"Fuck. Fuck. Fuck," I gasped with every drive inside of me, and I lost track as one orgasm bled into another.

Caldris drew me back, shifting a hand to my hair and wrenching me toward him. Forcing my back to bow. He touched his tongue and teeth to that spot he'd bloodied on my neck, my shoulder. Everything in me went lax, submitting to him more fully as he moved me how he wanted, fucked me how he wanted. Worrying the flesh with his teeth, squeezing until I bruised beneath him, he roared out his first release and filled me with it.

The tree drank from him through me, and my mate never bothered to pull out—never bothered to stop moving within me before he moved on from his orgasm. He kept fucking me, his cock somehow as hard as solid steel within me.

I became nothing but flesh and need, everything that was *me* fading into nothingness. Only after Caldris came a second time did he pull out of me, and my body immediately mourned the loss of him—clenching around nothing. My eyes rolled back in my head as I raised my ass, seeking more, wanting more, even as my body threatened to collapse.

He appeared at my side, his cock hard and glistening as the branches gave me more slack and allowed my head to lower. Bending me in half at the waist, putting me in line with his cock as Caldris stroked hair back from my face gently. I felt eyes on the part of me he'd used, wetness from both of our releases slipping down my thighs as someone watched.

"You made a mess," Caldris said, gathering my hair into his fist and turning my head how he wanted it. The head of his cock rubbed over the seam of my lips, enticing me to open for him. "Lick me clean."

I opened, letting him drive forward into my mouth. The taste of him—of me—coated my tongue as he hit the back of my throat and made me gag. Two fingers pinched my nose, brutal and unyielding as he took my ability to breathe and pushed forward slowly.

"Swallow."

The order came with unforgiving golden eyes bearing down on me, the male I loved lost to the sex magic of the tree. He would take and take and take until there was nothing left of me. I swallowed around him as he pushed forward, sliding into the narrow expanse of my throat. He tossed his head back, groaning loudly as he pumped within my throat.

I needed air. Needed to breathe.

My fingers curled into the tree, clawing with that need as Caldris used my throat. He looked down at me, smirking cruelly, as he pulled back into my mouth and released my nose. Air flooded my lungs finally, as he made shallow thrusts, rubbing himself over my tongue.

He allowed me a few moments of breath before he worked himself back into my throat, depriving me of air all over again as he sought his own release. Each repetition of the pattern awakened something primal within me, the creature beneath the surface growling as she demanded her own pleasure.

I lost track of how many times he took my air, of how many times he made shallow thrusts over my tongue. My hips writhed, waiting for him to fill me in the place that throbbed with need. He stared down at me as if he knew exactly how badly I needed it, pulling out of my throat as he groaned.

He came, filling my mouth and covering my tongue. The tree fed from him through me, drinking down his pleasure as he pulled free.

"Show me. I want to see my cum on your pretty tongue."

I opened, sticking out my tongue so that he could see the reward he'd spilled in my mouth. He stroked a thumb over the outer corner of my mouth, gathering what slipped free and pressing it into my mouth. I closed around him, sucking that clean too as he smiled down at me.

He turned that smile toward the tree, staring at it as if he was speaking to it. The branches holding me captive moved, lengthening and repositioning. The roots around my ankles released, sinking back into the ground as the limbs holding my wrists twisted my body and pulled my back against the trunk. They lifted, leaves sprouting from the branches to cushion me as they pulled my feet off the ground.

Caldris stepped in front of me, his face in line with mine as he touched his mouth to mine gently. His calm, steady hands grasped me by the inner thighs, spreading them apart as he lifted me before him. Branches stretched down, sliding around my thighs where he held me and pinning my legs to the tree so that he could stare down my body from neck to pussy.

His eyes held mine as he stepped forward into the cradle of my thighs, guiding himself into my drenched pussy.

I tossed my head back, slamming it into the tree trunk as my mate chuckled with something dark lurking beneath the surface of his skin.

And he fucked me all over again.

36

Caldris

Estrella leaned to the side, shifting her weight as she sat upon the stone in the arena. Discomfort flashed over her face as her eyes drifted shut, her exhaustion evident in every movement of her body.

My satisfaction knew no bounds, knowing that I'd been the cause of it. That I'd fucked her immortal body until she had nothing left to give. Until her whimpers of need had turned to sobs, begging me for it to end. For the tree to stop taking her pleasure, to allow her the feeling of fulfillment that could only come after the tree had devoured everything I'd given her.

From sex came life anew, the tree preparing itself to be reborn from the ashes of what remained the following day when it burned to the ground.

She'd been limp, pliant in the tree's hold as it pinned her there suspended for me to fuck over and over again. The magic riding my body had rendered me unable to stop, seeking out my own pleasure that never quite seemed to satisfy that deep hunger within me.

Only when the tree had finally had enough, when the others had collapsed to the ground and found their sleep while Estrella and I rode out the last waves of desire, did the tree let us crash into the orgasm we kept for ourselves.

Its way of thanking us for giving so much.

I watched her as Eryx lunged for me, tossing a handful of sleep dust toward my face. The God of Sleep was doing everything he could to win against me as we fought in the arena. Around us, the clatter of swords resounded through the space, unending from the moment the sun had risen through the Eastern Pillars that Estrella and I had crafted in ice.

I bent back, narrowly avoiding the powder that would make my movements sluggish. I wouldn't allow the magically induced haze to threaten my place at my mate's side for the rest of eternity.

"We both know you aren't going to win this battle," I said, yawning even though he'd missed my face.

While Estrella's sleepiness satisfied that primal, male urge within me to see her exhausted from my cock every day, my own was an inconvenience.

Mab had been cruel to have the arena fights the day after the Cove, when thirteen of the Gods were so tired they wanted to sleep for a year. The Fae partners they'd chosen still slumbered in that Cove, unable to be awoken.

"I'm not going to go quietly into Tartarus," he grunted, swinging his sword toward my neck.

I parried, meeting it with my blade and sending it skittering to the side as it was flung from his grip. I lashed out with a foot, kicking him backward until he landed on the sand with a thump. Staring up at me as I stepped over him, he shook his head in a plea. He only needed to best one of us.

It wouldn't be me.

I slid my sword into his gut, watching as his blood bubbled to the surface and flowed over his armor. Pulling back, I walked to the sidelines to wait for the next paired-off Gods to finish their current battle.

At the very least, I would survive. I wasn't the weakest and wouldn't be the sacrifice to pay for the centuries of missing

Tithes—even if guilt settled over me as I watched Eryx get to his feet. His wound healed over slowly with the absence of iron weapons in the arena.

Still, he clutched his bleeding stomach and made his way to the other side. I would continue to fight the next victor, proving myself as the strongest of the Gods if I was the last one standing. I didn't need them all to know of the strength within me or the ways I could fight. I didn't need to show off, usually preferring to stick to the shadows I called home and not draw attention to myself.

But with Estrella's watchful gaze upon me, that male part of me needed to prove to her that she'd been mated to the strongest of us. No matter what Mab believed about Estrella as far as her heritage went—whether she truly believed her to be one of the missing Primordials—she hadn't allowed my mate to take part in the fights.

Part of me regretted that, having very much looked forward to watching her make quick work of the lower Gods and Goddesses who would have a superiority complex against her until she proved herself as *more*.

The other part of me was grateful she wouldn't have to out herself just yet. While they knew of her magic and resourcefulness, most didn't know of her skill with a blade.

I'd like to keep it that way for as long as possible.

When the truth of her power came into the light, many would seek to use her to their advantage in the same way Mab wanted. I'd die before I ever allowed her to be put in another cage—especially knowing that this one was entirely my fault.

Tiam stepped away from Ilaria where he'd left her bleeding on the sand, stepping over to me. The King of the Spring

Court met me in the space Eryx and I had vacated, his sword hoisted into his hands and prepared for the fight ahead.

I. Would. Not. Lose.

And when the battles were over, I would lay my sword at my mate's feet and make sure they all knew exactly who I would serve the moment we freed ourselves.

37

Estrella

Nila leaned into my side, helping to support my head when it felt too heavy. I couldn't take my eyes off the four figures who still battled within the arena. On one side, Ilaria, the Goddess of Love, fought with Eryx, who Nila claimed was the God of Sleep. The crowd of Sidhe watching quieted as Eryx blew a puff of yellow dust into her face, her body immediately sagging as she wiped it away. She forced her eyes open, though her sword hung limply at her side.

"Sleep dust," Nila murmured, grasping my hand in hers. Whoever won would survive, while whoever lost…

Would be dead the next day.

Body parts littered the sands where the Gods had cut one another down. Rotting even after they'd regrown the missing limbs. The smell was of them as the first stages of rot set in beneath the blazing sun was… unfortunate.

Surely, they could have been used to feed the gnomes.

I swallowed, leaning my head onto Nila's shoulder. Mab watched from her seat a few places down from where I sat in the front row. Her face twisted into disgust as I leaned on my handmaiden. Mab showed no signs of being as tired as I was from the activities the night before, my body suffering for having been the conduit for all that energy.

"You never told me what happened in that Cove," Nila whispered, and I could hear the amusement in her voice.

It was no secret that I felt every bit of soreness within my body, that I didn't want to sit. She'd witnessed it when Caldris had carried my limp body back to my room, lowering me into the bath she'd quickly prepared. I'd hissed when the hot water scalded every tender part of my body, cursing that kinky fucking tree to Helheim and back.

Even after my bath that morning, I could still feel the evidence of my mate slipping free from my body every so often—as it did when I laughed at Nila's words.

"Let's not talk about it."

Caldris smirked as he and Kahlo circled each other at the opposite end of the arena. The two of them were bloodied, the result of small wounds that had already healed from their previous battles. My mate's eyes came to rest on me as if he could scent himself from across the arena, and his knowing gaze trailed down my body, distracting him from the battle at hand.

There was very little at stake for Caldris in proving himself to be the strongest of the Gods, yet he turned to face the God of Beasts when he snarled.

The other God said something, his face twisting in rage as Caldris laughed at him.

"He can't even pay attention to me, because he's still got his mind between his mate's thighs!" Kahlo yelled to the crowd.

I flushed as knowing eyes darted to me, then lifted my chin, refusing to feel the horror that would have once consumed me. Caldris growled a warning in response, but I let a shame-free smile claim my face as I leaned toward the arena.

"There's no need to be jealous, Kahlo! I'm sure you'll understand one day."

The God of Beasts grinned at me as I leaned back in my seat, ignoring the way Nila chuckled at my side.

"That must have been quite the evening," she said, those fingers squeezing me through my dress as she touched an affectionate hand to my knee.

"Not another word," I said, a smile tugging at my mouth as I turned to look at the woman who had quickly become a friend—a light in the darkness of Tar Mesa. When Mab was dealt with, I had no doubt she would fit right in and find a home with Imelda, Fallon, and I.

A strangled gasp came from the ring as Ilaria dropped to her knees. She grasped her throat, blood pouring from the gash cut across her deep beige skin. It would heal, as the weapon hadn't been iron, but it didn't matter.

She'd lost her final fight.

Eryx huffed out a breath, smiling in relief that quickly faded as he watched tears pool in Ilaria's eyes. He lowered himself to his knees as her skin began to heal itself, pulling her into his arms and holding her as she wept for the life she would no longer have.

Tears gathered in my own eyes as I watched. Caldris and Kahlo stopped fighting, turning to watch Eryx comfort Ilaria. They exchanged a single glance between themselves, their chests heaving with exertion.

Then they dropped their swords upon the sand, their fight over. What had seemed so important only a few moments before hardly mattered any longer.

Not when one of their own prepared to say goodbye.

My mate's eyes met mine, and I read the apology in them. We both knew he'd wanted to win for me, to prove whatever part of him wondered if he was worthy of what he saw as my goodness.

He didn't realize that he proved that far more efficiently by ending the fight than he would have by winning.

38

Estrella

I didn't go to Caldris's rooms that night. I couldn't stomach the thought of spending my evening with him, knowing that somewhere within the palace of Tar Mesa, a Goddess prepared to lose her life. Seven people didn't know they'd be walking to their death the next day.

I closed my eyes after Nila left, the violence simmering in me taking charge. Rheaghan's words the night before washed over me, the reminder of what Mab and Malazan had done to my mate. What he'd *allowed* them to do to him to save me from suffering.

The creature rose within me, dancing over my skin as I summoned the shadows to my bidding. They answered, swirling around me and sending a gust of night air into my face. The shadow realm opened to me as I slowly pried my eyes open, staring into the pathway.

No one could know.

I glanced toward the door, listening for any hint of activity on the other side. Malachi, or whoever had taken over for him, was silent, and I hoped whoever it was hadn't fallen asleep.

I needed my alibi to be awake.

I stepped into the shadows, letting them surround me as I thought of my destination. As I imagined *her*, I let the shadows shift and mold in front of me. I reached the shield around my rooms that prevented shadow walking, touching a single hand to the boundary. It parted to allow me to pass, reshaping itself once I was through.

I followed the path, walking slowly. I'd killed before—Fae and human alike. I knew what it was to have blood on my hands and regret it—to wonder if it could have been avoided. But each and every time I'd acted and brought death upon someone, I'd done it in defense of myself.

This was different. This was cold-blooded murder, and even as I walked alongside the halls of Tar Mesa, I knew this would leave a different kind of mark on my soul.

In a better world, I would have brought Caldris and allowed him to be the one to end his abuser's life. He would have been able to have his own revenge, but Mab could force the truth from him. If he was involved in any way, she would know without a doubt who had committed the crime.

This was my secret to keep.

Rheaghan's warning echoed in my head, a confirmation that I needed to be smart about seeking my vengeance. For the way she'd brushed her hand against Caldris's groin as she forced him to dance with her. For all the little touches I'd pretended not to notice as I danced and smiled, plotting my revenge even as I moved my body to the drums.

For each of those, she would suffer.

It didn't surprise me that Malazan's rooms were right next to Mab's—that the two women would stay so close to one another made sense. Malazan was the closest thing Mab had to a friend, though I didn't doubt that the latter would sacrifice the former if it worked to her advantage.

I strolled past the hallway, walking into her darkened room as she slept. Stepping out of the shadows, I sent them skittering to the corners, waiting until I needed to call upon them once more.

Malazan's life thread swayed in the air as it called to me, the simplest of solutions presenting itself. I could end her before she ever woke, snuff out her life and be back in my room before anyone had the chance to realize I was gone.

But I didn't know what trace that magic might leave, what might come back to me if there was no sign of violence on her body. It needed to look as if it could have been *anybody*.

I touched a gloved hand to the knife I found perched atop her stack of clothing for the next day. The iron blade glinted in the light of the candle Malazan had left burning as I turned it from one side to the other, studying the craftsmanship of the blade. The hilt was carved in silver, an intricate, winding pattern of swirls adorning it. Those continued over the iron blade that was curved and wavy itself. Not a straight line, Malazan's weapon of choice, but almost as if it mimicked the waves of the ocean.

For a brief moment, I wondered if it was the very blade she had used to cut my mate, to torture him as Mab watched. I gritted my teeth, the thought fueling me toward what needed to be done.

I stepped away from the candle, leaving it burning behind me as I focused on that cold well at my center. Darkness spread through the room, smothering the flames burning in the fireplace opposite of her bed. The room plunged into complete and total darkness, the only light shining from that one lone candle atop the table.

Striking out with Caldris's magic, I wrapped his shadows around her mouth and the back of her head, muffling her scream as she awakened. I allowed those shadows to hold her pinned down to her bed for me.

Helpless, as I imagined my mate had been each and every time she violated him.

My face remained darkened as I approached the bed slowly, wondering if she'd raped him in this very bed. If she'd gone to his, if I'd unknowingly let him take me in the bed that had been the location of such suffering for centuries.

Her panicked eyes darted about in the darkness as I passed the end of the bed. She couldn't see the way I could, couldn't comprehend what was happening to her as I allowed that starlight to drift over my skin, forming tiny pinpricks of stars that I sent to linger about my body.

Her eyes widened as she tried to scream, to warn Mab that I'd escaped the prison of my room.

"Shh," I whispered, lowering myself to sit on the side of her bed. Her chest heaved with her frantic breaths as the mattress compressed beneath my weight. "I can't have you ruining my fun before I've even started."

It pained me that she couldn't speak, that she couldn't spew her venom and ease the pain of letting go of that final shred of my humanity. If she reminded me of how vile she was, perhaps it wouldn't be so difficult to embrace the monster I'd never wanted to be.

"We're going to play a game, you and I," I whispered, trailing the tip of the blade along her chest. I cut the fabric of her nightgown away from her breasts, parting it slowly down the middle until she was nude on the bed. "I'm going to ask you a question, and you are either going to nod or shake your head. If you lie, I will take a piece of you. If you tell the truth, I will merely leave a scar."

She shook her head, her eyes pleading as I leaned in until my face filled her vision. Nothing but the rage burning in my eyes existed for her as she held them, her lip trembling in fear.

"We shall see how long you survive when you are the victim and not the abuser," I growled, leaning back finally.

I touched my blade to her hand where Caldris's shadows kept it pinned to the bed. Her pinky twitched beneath the knife as she shook her head slightly.

"Did you rape my mate in this very bed?" I asked, my jaw clenched as I studied her. Her eyes flew wide, her expression panicked as she shook from side to side.

Lie.

I swallowed as I met her stare, both of us wondering if I was capable of this. I pressed the blade down, cutting through bone slowly as the mattress didn't provide me with the resistance needed. Blood spewed from the cut as she wailed beneath the shadows keeping her quiet, and the urge to vomit rose within me.

It was one thing to see my own blood spilled. It was another to be the one to do it to a Fae who couldn't fight back.

I shoved down the gag reflex, grimacing as I forced myself not to reveal the weakness. My hand paused, unable to push the blade deeper as I fought my own nausea. The monster within me awoke, shaking off her sleepy haze as she stood. She raised her head, her fury filling me.

She had no such qualms about bloodying the woman who'd harmed our mate.

My lips twisted into a snarl that was an echo of the sound she emitted in my throat. Pushing the blade further into her flesh, she didn't let me wince when the finger cracked beneath the pressure—the bone cleaving before I finally cut through to the other side.

I lifted her severed pinky into my hand beside the knife, dangling it before her face before I tossed it to the side of the bed. Her screams pushed against the shadows, but they held firm. Restraining her, silencing her.

Just as Mab had done with her victims.

I moved to the second finger on her hand, positioning my knife as I repeated my question. "Did. You. Rape. My. Mate. In. This. Bed?" I asked, my voice quiet and seething as I glared down at her. My jaw clenched with the need to kill her and be done with it, but I forced myself to suffer through the knowledge of what had been done to the male I loved.

It didn't matter that centuries had passed. Wounds like that never healed completely; they never went away. By some gift of the Gods, Caldris had survived what she'd done and become a light in the darkness in spite of it, but that didn't mean the memory of that violation didn't haunt him daily.

She nodded slowly, her tears drying as she met my glare with one of her own. I slashed my blade across her hand, cutting through sinew and tendon so that I could scar her skin. It wouldn't matter by morning. She had to know that.

Beauty didn't matter when you were dead and rotting in the ground.

"Isn't that better?" I asked, laying the tip of my knife to the fleshy part of her stomach. She growled, the sound humming up her throat and getting muffled once it hit her mouth. "Were you the first to violate him?" I asked, hating each and every question.

She shook her head; vehemently, in fact.

Truth.

Her eyes gleamed with it, and that primal part of me knew the response had been honest. I wished I could allow her to speak, to give me the names of all who still breathed. I'd have to get them from Caldris eventually, to remedy the mistake the Fates had made by allowing them to live.

I cut a long line across her stomach for her truth, trying not to look at the way blood seeped along her skin. It slid lower, covering the vile part of her that even I couldn't bring myself to touch.

Torture and murder were one thing, but I couldn't bring myself to violate her the way she'd done to Caldris—even if it would serve her right.

On and on, our game went until her body was a mass of slashes and cuts. Blood poured upon the bed, leaving her half-alive and begging for death. I wanted to vomit when I looked at what I'd done—at who I'd become. But the monster within me purred in delight, satisfied with the gift we would give to our mate.

I forced myself to place my blade at her breast, leaning into her face once again. I wanted the last thing she saw to be my face, an avenging fury as her own knife slid up and into her heart. I did exactly that, watching as she turned her stare down to where the hilt of the knife protruded from her chest.

Her face was shocked, her mouth parted. We never thought about that moment when it all ended until it was too late.

Her breath stopped, a ragged gasp leaving her as the shadows parted from her mouth and allowed me to look down upon the mangled remains of her body. I'd lost count of the cuts I'd made, of the times I'd hurt her for each crime she committed against Caldris.

"You're as much a monster as me," she mumbled, the words barely audible.

"For him, I will be." I held her gaze as her final breath left her, her eyes going glazed as I dropped her knife beside the bed and stood from the edge. The feeling that rushed through me wasn't as victorious as I'd thought it would be.

I stumbled as I got my feet beneath me, horror mounting in me. My creature was content to settle down for a nap, purring with pleasure at what we'd done and leaving me to the surge of emotions that came in the wake of her abandonment. I swallowed them down, biting them back as I called to the shadows that lingered around me.

Stepping into them, I let them take me to the shadow realm. I was half in a daze as I passed the hallway that led to that dining room.

The statue of Sarilda seemed to stare up at me, the gleaming stone of her face haunted. I shifted toward her, making the shadows halt with me as they opened up before me. Stepping into reality, I put my feet on solid ground once again as I stared up at her.

I knew nothing about her aside from what Mab had told me, but I couldn't help but feel the similarities between the way Mab had killed her and the way I'd murdered Malazan. I pinched my lip between my teeth as the first tear fell, wondering if I could ever come back from this.

Burying my head in my hands, I resisted the urge to scream. I would have the love of my mate to see me through eventually, but for now, Caldris could never know it had been me. With our bond silenced—the window closed on my end—he would know nothing of what I'd done.

And Mab wouldn't be able to pry the answers from him.

I pulled my hands away, sucking back deep breaths and reminding myself that Malazan had been a predator. Whether or not she'd hurt me in that moment, she'd tortured me. She'd tortured my mate and violated him—as well as countless others.

I turned toward the statues lining the halls, the Gods and Goddesses who had already lost their lives to Mab's reign.

My shadows crept through the hall, reaching behind each and every one of those statues and busts.

I bit my tongue as I pulled them forward, the sound of stone smashing upon the floor echoing up the hall. They cracked, pieces breaking off and ruining Mab's testament to her conquest.

I destroyed her trophies of war, the heads she kept as reminders of exactly what she was capable of. Voices came from the mouth of the hallway; the sound of the destruction having alerted the guards to my presence.

I stepped into the shadows once more. They took me to the last place I wanted to go that night—to the one place I shouldn't be. It was the only place I could go to change *anything* about the next day.

But it was also the only place that would tell Mab *exactly* who had been responsible.

I sighed when I reached the shadows of the boundary she'd formed, preparing myself for the way they would press against me, shoving me back.

They parted without a fight, recognizing me as one of them as I stepped through, moving toward the pits where the humans had been kept. Where they awaited their death in a matter of days.

I stepped forward, prepared to have to work quickly as I glanced down at the guards who would be the greatest problem with sneaking the humans into the shadows.

I took another step, drawing deep breaths.

And smacked my face into a wall of heat that kicked me back.

Light exploded through the shadows, singing my skin as I flew back through the shadow realm. For a moment, I wondered if the realm would fail, if the shadows would part and reveal me to the guards who walked around the edges of the pit outside of the realm that offered me haven.

They held, embracing me and picking me up from the ground. They cradled my body as they put me back to my feet, lingering affectionately as I shook off my disorientation. At the end of the shadow realm, the inky tendrils of darkness bled into the brightness of the sun.

Night met day. Dark met light. And through the hazy, shimmering boundary, a male stepped forward.

He adjusted the collar of his tunic, rolling his neck as I glanced at the darkness that surrounded him.

And Rheaghan smiled.

39

Estrella

"You," I said, my mouth parting in shock. He'd been the very male who planted the idea of murdering Malazan in my head, the one who *knew* I wouldn't be in my room that night.

"Now don't look at me like that, Princess," the God of the Sun said, his smile fading into a teasing smirk. "You know I cannot allow you to pass."

I shook my head, grimacing, as I took a step forward. Putting myself in his face, I growled as my creature reawakened. She didn't like that he'd knocked us on our ass, not in the shadows.

This realm was *ours.*

"They don't deserve to die," I said, enunciating the words slowly. Carefully. Allowing him to feel that this was not a battle I would relent easily.

"Neither do the thousands of lives you stand to save if you would just stop and *think*," Rheaghan argued. He growled down at me, all traces of the light-hearted male disappearing in his rage. "You're thinking like a human again." His lip curled as if disgusted and disappointed by the behavior, a flash of flames and scales trailing over his face.

"I am a human!" I shrieked, tired of everyone telling me not to be what I'd been for my entire life. That girl would always be a part of me, and it could save seven people.

Rheaghan's face softened. "You are the furthest thing from human I've seen in centuries. And seven lives are nothing in the grand scheme of all we stand to gain from Mab not knowing of your ability to shadow walk. Protecting that secret is worth the sacrifice, especially since she will just replace those people with seven new ones before the Tithe. You cannot stop those deaths from happening."

I looked down to the pits, staring at the humans who were huddled among themselves. Even from here, their fear was palpable, their spirits nearly broken. Tears stung my eyes, my lip trembling as my throat burned.

"I can't just leave them," I said, looking up at the King of the Seelie.

He sighed and smiled sadly, raising a single hand to catch me under the chin. The gesture was too sweet, too understanding as he nodded.

"I know, Princess. That's why I'm here." He pulled his hand back, shoving his free hand into the pockets of his trousers. "Do try not to hate me come morning," he said, his brow furrowing as I stared at him in confusion.

That other hand lashed out, striking me in the chest as blinding heat knocked me backward. It seared through me, burning my flesh as I flew through the shadow realm. The tendrils of darkness fumbled, blown backward by the light of the sun as Rheaghan stole them from me. He scattered them to the wind with the power of the sun, consuming my tunnel as I flew through it.

My head snapped back as I landed on something soft.

Air returned to my lungs as I clawed at my chest, fighting against the burning fabric of my clothing and tearing it with black talons.

My chest burned, the flesh sizzling as I finally laid eyes upon my skin. Rheaghan's handprint was seared into my flesh, marking my chest in the place he'd struck me.

My magic worked to heal it slowly, soothing the burn as I looked at where I'd landed.

The walls of my bedroom surrounded me.

40

Caldris

I walked through the pathway up the center of the throne room after Mab summoned me. Estrella was already present, kneeling at the front of the crowd as Mab lingered on her throne. Her face was unblemished, no trace of the exhaustion from two nights before.

The bond between us was still silent, and my concern settled at seeing her unharmed.

I raised a brow at her in question, that blank, careful face turning up to stare back at me. Her eyes gave me no hint as to why she'd closed the window on our thread, keeping me from feeling whatever she was experiencing internally.

"You called for me?" I asked, dropping to my knee in front of the dais.

Mab rose from her throne, approaching the steps as she nodded to the male at her side. He stepped out of view, ducking behind the column carved with snakes.

"Where were you last night?" she asked, raising a hand.

That pull of her snake upon my heart struck me in the chest, lurching my body forward as she summoned the truth from me.

"I was with Rheaghan," I said, gasping as my hand rose to rub at my chest. She released her grip on my heart, shifting her glare from me to behind me.

I followed her gaze as Rheaghan laid a hand upon my shoulder, looking at his sister. I turned my stare up to him as he nodded to confirm my claim.

"I asked him to assist me with returning the arena to its natural state as you requested, sister. He was working there all night."

"Is this true?" Mab asked me, the threat of that bond forcing me to speak the truth.

It didn't matter much, because Rheaghan hadn't lied. "Yes. I never made it to bed before you summoned me."

"Can anyone else confirm this?" Mab asked, looking at her brother now.

He smiled, shrugging his shoulders as he looked about the room. "Only the entirety of the Summer Court Fae who have joined us for the Tithe. All of us were working tirelessly to meet your demand on such short notice."

Mab grimaced, her face twisting into a full scowl as she waved a hand. Davorin emerged from behind the column, the body of a woman hoisted over his shoulder. He dropped her upon the stone at the top of the dais, her hand falling to reveal a missing pinky. Her flesh had been carved—the crisscross pattern of torture cut into every bit of her skin.

Across her chest, her assailant had carved a word.

Vengeance.

I forced myself not to look at Estrella as the corpse turned toward us, the face far too familiar. Those eyes had stared up at me far too many times as Mab forced my body to move, to react to the touch of the woman I hated more than nearly anyone. They'd looked down at me in triumph when she'd settled herself on my cock...

I clenched my jaw, trying to stop the smile that spread my lips at the sight of her dead, mangled corpse.

I tossed my head back and laughed, disbelief striking me in the gut. I'd thought I'd never be rid of her, rid of her touch or the way she'd force me to watch as she violated another in my stead.

"How dare you?" Mab seethed, her voice dropping into a low command as she squeezed around my heart. "I know you had something to do with this."

I chuckled again. "I know nothing of who might have done this, but they have my eternal gratitude," I said, the words torn from my throat as Mab refused to release her grip on me. The words were true, because my mate had made sure of it.

How she had come to know of my deal with Mab, I didn't know. But there was no doubt in me that she had somehow, and that she'd put an end to what she could.

"You," Mab said, turning her attention to where my mate knelt.

She descended the steps, skirting the body of her friend in her haste to reach my mate. Power rushed through the room as she stopped in front of Estrella, reaching down with clawed fingers to grasp her by the chin and jerk that calm, blank face up to look at her.

"Where were *you* last night?"

"I was in my room. Malachi delivered me there himself after dinner," Estrella said, staring up at Mab. The faintest hint of a coy smile played about her mouth, and Rheaghan's gaze was intent upon her smile.

Watching her toy with his sister.

He squeezed his lips together to suppress his smile, shoving his hands into the pockets of his trousers. *He knew,* I realized, suspicion rising in me. He'd conspired with my mate and made sure there wasn't a single doubt of my innocence.

Malachi shifted, drawing Mab's attention to him where he stood behind Estrella. "She didn't leave her room all night, my Queen. I'm sure of it."

"That's impossible!" Mab shrieked at him, lashing out at him with her power and driving him to his knees. "You must have fallen asleep, you incompetent fool! Tell me the truth!"

"I did not," he said, the words ringing true. With his inability to lie, there wasn't a chance the words were false. "Perhaps your shields—"

"They are intact. She did not shadow walk out of that room, and I sincerely doubt the bitch even knows how," Mab snarled, turning her attention back down to my mate's calm face. Calm, because she knew, for all purposes, walking out of her room was an impossibility.

Estrella excelled at the impossible.

A grin spread across Estrella's mouth at Mab's frustration.

"I know you killed her," the Queen of Air and Darkness said, staring down into the smiling face of my mate.

"I assure you, I had nothing to do with her death, but I can't say I'm sad someone got rid of the cunt," Estrella said, the words loud and clear in the throne room. Everyone heard them, heard what *had* to have been the truth fall free.

Except it wasn't.

The lie tumbled from her lips so easily, even I questioned if it was true. Until the realization settled over me, sending a shock through my chest at the confirmation of what Mab had already suspected.

Estrella wasn't Fae.

"You're lying," Mab hissed, squeezing her nails tighter until blood welled beneath the claws.

"How? The Fae cannot lie," Estrella said, maneuvering Mab right into the trap she had so skillfully set.

Mab either had to admit her suspicions of what Estrella was to the gathered crowd of allies and enemies alike, or she had to relent that Estrella couldn't have done it.

As if they realized it too, whispers broke out through the throne room as they looked at my mate with new questions.

Mab released Estrella, spinning back toward her throne. She ran her hands through her hair as she ascended the dais, stepping over the body of her friend. She twisted to look at Estrella over her shoulder, snarling a quiet "Get out".

Nobody moved.

"I said, GET OUT!" she screamed, leaning forward with the force of the words.

Estrella stood smoothly under the weight of Mab's gaze, her eyes drifting to the side so that she could smirk at Rheaghan and me in turn. She was the first to leave the throne room, Malachi trailing at her heels as she walked through the crowd of gathered Fae with her head held high.

I stared at her back as we followed, moving far too slowly for Mab's liking.

"I am still Queen! Get out of my sight!" she shrieked, her voice becoming more and more unhinged with each repetition.

The silence rang in response, one thought filtering through my mind and in an echo of all who followed my mate:

Not for long.

41

Estrella

Malachi had replaced my collar within the hour. Even without any *logical* explanation for how I'd managed to slip out of my room, Mab wouldn't be taking any chances, it seemed.

Nila spent far more time than normal tending to my face and the circles beneath my eyes. Getting me ready for the final evening before the sacrifices. Even Caldris had been allowed to join us in my room, as if the collar were merely a formality.

We both knew there was nothing I could do to stop the Tithe from happening. I'd tried and failed, thanks to Rheaghan's interference, but even in my anger with him, I knew he'd been right. It would have been foolish to give up my advantage when I wouldn't really save any lives.

As soon as Malachi had left the three of us in the relative privacy of my room, my mate had stepped up to me—his silent stare demanding. We spoke not a word as I shoved the window—opening myself to our bond once again. He leaned in, kissing me tenderly. Both of us knew what I'd done, but we wouldn't speak of it—wouldn't give him anything more than a suspicion to protect that knowledge from Mab.

His gratitude still surged down the thread hours later, rippling over each fiber.

Nila brushed my face with powder and liquid, disguising the hints of exhaustion so that no one could see them. For all anyone knew, I'd had a night of solid rest—not spent it out torturing a rapist.

Caldris lingered in the background, infuriating me with his lack of shirt as he read a book on my bed. The fact that he could just stand up and toss on some clothes before attending a ball that took hours of effort from me seemed grossly unfair. Nila hadn't stopped being flustered by his presence, but I couldn't fault her for it. Not when he was so distracting.

The dress Mab had sent for me to wear hung over the edge of the mirror, the fabric dark and foreboding. Tendrils of black inched their way toward my throat, like shadows that would cling to my skin.

Nila glanced at Caldris over my shoulder, nodding at him in some silent communication that left me uneasy. As she stepped away from me and gave me room to stand, I moved toward the dress I'd been told to wear for the evening.

Nila disappeared into the closet instead of helping me into the heavy garment, emerging with a thin piece of fabric. It was as white as the veil, as transparent as it swayed through the wind. But sewn into the fabric were golden gems, a pattern going through the cloth that was breathtaking as it shimmered.

"I don't understand," I said, glancing toward my mate.

He'd stood from the bed, shrugging his tunic on as he seemed to dress for the evening without a care. The black folds of his tunic held the subtlety of gold stitching, something far less delicate for him to wear.

Nila untied my robe, shrugging it off my shoulders. "We must hurry," she said, tugging the thin fabric over my head. It was like wearing the Veil itself, like wrapping myself in the magic of the Lunar Witches and the God who'd given his life to the creation of the boundary.

One strap of the fabric rested upon my shoulder as she pulled the subtle laces tight at the back, pressing the corset into my body. It was the perfect color match for my bronze skin, as if it had been designed with me in mind. The other sleeve hung off my shoulder, draping delicately to wrap loosely around my elbow.

The fabric shimmered as I moved, a slit in the fabric going up to my waist. There were no undergarments beneath it. Nothing to protect me from prying eyes if I moved less-than gracefully.

"Why am I wearing this?"

"Mab wants you to dress as she wills. She wants to bathe you in shadows to call attention to your similarities. But you are not the Queen of Air and Darkness, Estrella," Nila explained, resting a hand upon each of my biceps as Caldris threw open the door.

He moved quickly, snatching the sword from Malachi before the other man could blink. I bolted toward the door, watching in horror as my mate shoved his forearm against Malachi's throat. The shout he'd been drawing in air for died at the impact, leaving the guard gasping for breath as Caldris stole his air and crushed his windpipe.

Caldris swung that blade down, slicing through the flesh of Malachi's wrist. His hand fell to the floor, flopping uselessly to the stone as Caldris turned the sword in his grip and dragged it across the other male's throat in a smooth arc. Malachi collapsed, his back sliding down the wall as he pressed his hand and the bloody stump into his bleeding throat. The wound, despite the iron blade, wouldn't be fatal.

He bent down, picking up Malachi's severed hand and striding back into my rooms. He pulled the door closed behind him, leaving my guard's body slumped against the wall. That wound could heal in time.

"Turn around, *min asteren*," Caldris murmured, his jaw clenched as I did what he said. I spun as Nila swept my hair to the side, revealing the magical lock at the back of my collar.

He pressed Malachi's severed hand to it. The iron fell away as my body hummed. Dropping to the floor at my feet, the metal lump no longer served any purpose as the creature within me rose from her iron-induced slumber. She rolled her head from one side to the other, growling at the device that had effectively stolen her voice for weeks.

I bent down as golden light pulsed up my arm, illuminating my Fae Mark in a wave that began at my fingers and slithered up to the side of my neck and my chest. I grasped the collar, my hand burning as I carried it to the window and thrust open the panes.

I cocked my arm back, resisting the urge to scream as I threw it as far as I could. It landed out of sight, and I imagined it sliding across the white salt of Tar Mesa. As I turned back to face my mate, he raised his chin to me.

It seemed I wasn't the only one who had been keeping secrets.

His mouth cocked into a smirk, and I glanced toward the door.

"What's the plan?" I asked, meeting that arrogant stare with one of my own.

I rolled my neck from one side to the other, reveling in the feeling of freedom without that damn collar. I felt more animal than human—than Fae—as I waited to hear what my mate and handmaiden had conspired to do.

"We're going to make a statement," Caldris said.

I pursed my lips, glancing toward the door once more. "Is there any particular reason why he's still breathing?" I asked.

Caldris shrugged as if it was inconsequential to him, making his way to the door. He hauled it open, grabbing Malachi by the arm and dragging his body into the privacy of my room. I stared down at the unconscious but alive body of the guard who'd caused so much suffering.

The memory of his blade cutting through the neck of the human mates brought a snarl to my lips.

"This feels like playing the short-term game," I muttered as Caldris knelt at Malachi's side. His attention turned to me, the motion slow and furious as he met my stare.

"You," he said, baring his teeth. "Have been spending far too much time with Rheaghan, my star."

I swallowed, grinning back at the face of his jealousy as he plunged his fist into Malachi's chest. His hand disappeared as breastbone cracked beneath his punch, emerging only when he pulled a heart free.

The God of the Dead rose to his feet, striding toward me slowly. When he reached me, that heart still clutched within his grasp, he knelt before me. Holding up the bloody flesh, he held my stare as he offered me the heart of a male who had caused me so much suffering.

"My Queen," he murmured.

I smiled down at him, reaching out to take Malachi's heart in my hand. "Did my status rise?" I asked, making a bark of laughter rumble from him in response.

"It's only a matter of time, Little One," he said, glancing back toward Malachi's body.

With his heart clasped in my palm, I shifted my attention to him and walked around the kneeling form of my mate. Dead, unseeing eyes stared up at the ceiling, his heart ceasing to beat. I cocked my head to the side as I lowered myself beside him, something malicious washing over me.

All those centuries my mate had served as a slave, all those years commanded against his will. Malachi had been a willing part of that, taking free will from the man I loved.

I touched a finger to his cheek, watching as a tendril of darkness spread across his skin like rot. His eyes flung open suddenly as his gaze met mine, leaving me to stand tall as I stared down at him.

The golden thread of his soul lingered just out of reach, unable to reconnect with his body. But I did not desire their reunion, only for him to watch as his body was used against him. To be helpless as I made it *mine*.

I looked at the specter lingering behind the body, cocking my head to the side as I studied his rage-filled face.

"Your body is mine now, Malachi. You were my enemy in life, but you will fight for me in your death." I wouldn't keep his soul from moving to the Void, leaving where he wandered from here up to him to decide.

But I wouldn't allow anyone to place coins on his eyes or pay his fee to the ferryman either.

He couldn't speak. Couldn't answer as I condemned him to his suffering. Caldris stared at me, unsurprised, though I suspected he couldn't see the specter of the man he'd killed. He knew better than any that some tortures didn't require physical pain.

Some torments came in forced obedience.

Twyla stepped up outside my door, looking both ways before she stepped inside and closed it behind her. She eyed

Malachi's slit throat and the hole in his chest, reaching into the satchel that hung by her side. Her gaze went to her son, who nodded, making her heave a sigh as she pulled something free from the bag.

The crown was studded with diamonds, a gleaming thing with arches that spiked toward the sky. The gems were massive as she held it out in front of her.

"Are you sure about this?" she asked, glancing toward her son.

"Sure about *what*?" I asked, propping a hand onto my hip. I'd grown tired of being kept in the dark, of the way Caldris made plans without me.

"Already, Tar Mesa is filled with whispers of what you did outside the palace. People watched from their windows when you made the sky go black," Nila said, looking at my mate. "Soon enough, the court royals will go home. They'll carry those whispers with them. You stand no chance of defeating her now. Not when she has Caldris bonded to her, but you can give them something to talk about. You can give them a show they will never forget, so that when you rise, they will follow."

I drew in a breath, turning to face where Caldris watched me expectantly. I knew if I was too afraid to move forward, he wouldn't force it. But we'd already killed Malachi. I'd already claimed him as mine. We'd come too far to turn back now.

I picked up the knife from the dining room table, dragging the blade up my wrist until blood dripped onto the floor at my feet. Carefully holding it away from my body so that I wouldn't ruin the splendor of my gown, I chose to trust Nila and Twyla with the information that might have been damning in the wrong hands. Caldris raised my wrist to his mouth, drinking from me as I gathered a single drop of blood onto my pointer finger.

I touched it to Malachi's lips as Caldris let my blood pour over his tongue. The corpse of my enemy shuddered, his eyes drifting closed. They filled with golden light when he opened them, the muscles of his face relaxing into something completely obedient. There was not a trace of the personality that belonged to the soul that had inhabited him in his life.

There was only me.

Caldris drew away a moment later, the white lines of his Fae mark pulsing with gold where it peeked out from the top of his tunic. His blue eyes sparkled with gold, his features tense as he narrowed his gaze on me. Then he reached out to his mother, taking the crown from her hands. Golden light reflected off the diamonds as he raised it to my head, settling it atop my hair as Nila fussed to make sure that he didn't mess up her diligent work.

"This is foolish," Twyla said, her face twisting into a scowl. She leveled her son with a stern glare. "Who do you think she will punish for this insolence? It will be you who suffers the consequences."

"Then so be it," Caldris said. "We cannot raise an army unless they know that there is someone who could stand against Mab. This is the only way."

"But she cannot stand against Mab. Not yet. You act too soon," Twyla protested.

"Better I act too soon for your tastes than I remain complacent after *centuries* of tyranny. She killed your mate. She cost you your husband. She took your *child*. When will you say enough, mother?" Caldris asked, settling his hand around my waist as if he needed the comfort. "I would sooner die than remain a slave any longer."

"And leave Estrella to Mab's will?"

"What Mab fails to understand is that she cannot kill Caldris without killing me. Our lives are bound by a blood vow. When one goes, the other will follow," I said, watching as her eyes filled with revulsion.

"Why would you do such a foolish thing?" she asked, and I recognized the emotion hiding in the horror. The thought of losing her only son was unbearable, and I was a liability at the moment.

"You may be content to live in a world where your mate no longer exists, but I am not. I've no desire to remain here without her," Caldris answered, raising his chin in defiance.

"I'm going to save him," I whispered, the vulnerable words feeling torn from my soul. I didn't know how or when I'd remove Mab's serpent from where it wrapped around his heart.

Only that I would.

"And who will save you?" Twyla asked, shaking her head.

"The same person who always has," I answered, glancing down at the golden marks on my skin as my nerves threatened to tear me in two. "I'm going to save myself."

42

Estrella

The doors to the ballroom were closed, probably sealed shut when we'd been more than fashionably late. Malachi led the way through the halls, approaching them without hesitation. The guards standing outside looked at him in confusion, stepping in to stop him just a moment before he crashed a hand against the heavy doors.

A burst of golden light flashed through the darkened hall at the moment of impact, thrusting the doors open. People who had lingered too close scattered, shrieking as they escaped the corpse that stepped into their midst.

Caldris followed after him, leaving me standing in the hallway and unable to breathe as I thought of what was to come. As I tried to channel the energy to don the mask I needed to wear for the performance I hadn't asked for. Twyla and Nila had made themselves scarce, hopefully finding a way to blend in with the crowd so that no one would know of the role they played.

"Caldris, what is the meaning of this? Put him to rest!" Mab yelled, the command washing over my skin. I could practically feel the answering smirk on my mate's face, the way he would smile back at her with the knowledge that he did not need to follow that order.

He couldn't, after all.

Because Malachi was mine to command.

I let out a breath, loosing the power that lingered beneath my skin. It was like breathing, like letting out the part of me that was begging for release. The flames in the torches on the wall were smothered, dying out beneath the wash of power as I stepped into the darkened ballroom.

Only the light pulsing off my Fae Mark lit the room, making the gems on my dress and the diamonds of my crown pulse with warmth.

Light in the darkness.

Hope.

I raised a hand, drawing in a slow breath as I allowed the flames to return to each of the torches. One by one, starting with the one closest to me, they returned as I walked through the center of the ballroom floor. Caldris stepped to the side, moving out of my path as I approached the Queen of Air and Darkness.

Shadows and Starlight.

"I'm afraid he can't do that," I said, my voice humming. It was quiet, a subtle echo in the undertones of my words. "I am the one who raised Malachi from the dead, and as such, I will be the one to put him to rest."

"Then do it," Mab ordered, gritting her teeth as she studied the spectacle I'd made of myself.

I raised my chin, smirking slightly as I bared the corner of my teeth. Caldris moved to stand behind me, a silent sentry, and placed his hand atop my bare shoulder. I felt the moment my Fae mark sparked to life with the contact, that mix of golden glow and inky darkness illuminating my skin.

"No," I said, my smile deepening alongside Mab's scowl.

Her brow furrowed as her nostrils flared, her anger pulsing off her as she raised a hand. I couldn't fight her when Caldris's knees buckled slightly, and I felt him resist the urge to touch his heart.

The idea had been to make a spectacle. To give the courts something to whisper about. But I grew tired of whispers and secrets in the dark.

I wanted what was real.

I grasped the shadows pulsing off her hands, pulling on the threads attached to them as she fought to hold tight to the magic held within her grasp. I gripped those threads as I crossed them, watching her eyes widen as the bare glimmer of gold wrapped around her wrist.

"Someone taught me a lesson a long time ago, and I don't think anyone has ever done you the courtesy," I said, taking a single step forward as I pulled the threads taut.

Mab's face twisted as the threads cut through her flesh.

They slashed through flesh and bone—pulling and sawing—until her hand dropped upon the gray stone of the ballroom floor. She stared at it in shock for a moment, blood pulsing off her severed wrist to puddle on the floor beside it.

"You should not play games with that which you cannot control, and you definitely should not toy with the Fates," I said softly, ignoring the frenzied whispers of all who lingered in the throne room.

Mab stared at her wrist in horror, waiting for her hand to grow back. I hadn't cut her with iron after all, so it should be something she could heal. Her face paled, her mouth dropping open into a silent scream. For all purposes, she should have been shrieking. Her pain should have been evident throughout the room.

One of her more loyal followers approached her side, raising her skirt and tearing off a piece of fabric from it. She wrapped it around Mab's wrist, and I was gratified in the knowledge that it would normally have been Malazan who tended to her.

"Summon the witch," the woman snapped, turning to one of Mab's other minions. The other woman fled the ballroom, going in search of whatever witch she could find.

Mab paled as she looked around, realizing the implications of me harming her permanently. I hadn't known it was possible, hadn't known the threads could inflict permanent injury in the same way as iron, but something about it felt *right*.

As soon as she'd tended to Mab, the woman stepped forward, summoning Mab's guards to surround us.

"Kill them all," she snapped, ignoring Mab's protest behind her. Mab and I both knew I was worth far more alive than dead if she could find an efficient way to control me.

I raised a hand, grasping the woman's thread of life between my fingers and plucking it like a harp. She jolted forward the moment she felt me pull on it, raising a hand to signal the men back. They paused, hesitating as they studied me.

"What do you want?" she asked, her voice dropping into the quiet of a whisper.

I grinned as her cheeks flushed with humiliation. "I should think it was obvious. I want all of you to suffer for your part in your people's suffering."

***

My body was on fire—burning from within.

But I remained silent as two witches stepped into the ballroom, making their way to Mab without hesitation. Neither of them was Imelda, and I craned my head to find the witch. She stepped in front of me, appearing from the crowd as if summoned. She dragged me from the center of the chaos, taking me to the edges of the ballroom. I couldn't believe that we'd not been dragged to the dungeon following my outburst.

We'd stoked the flames of rebellion, but I didn't know if it would be enough. If Mab's lack of reaction would somehow hinder our cause.

Imelda's fitted forest green dress clung to her shoulders, showing off a line of cleavage that I couldn't help but wish Holt had been around to see. It was fitted through her like a glove, hugging the flawless curves that defined her body.

She touched a hand to my cheek, flinching back the moment her skin touched mine.

Caldris stepped closer, concern filling his face at whatever lingered in Imelda's gaze when she turned her attention to him.

"She's burning," Imelda whispered, glancing around the ballroom.

Most of the partygoers were distracted, too fixated on the spectacle of Mab shouting at the witches who fought to stem the bleeding.

"What do you mean, she's burning?" my mate asked, touching his hand to my skin. He didn't flinch back, didn't seem bothered by the heat filling my veins like slow poison.

It stemmed from my hands, spreading up through my forearms and reaching my body in a languid fluid. The threads of fate clung to *everything*, surrounding me like a temptation. The beast within me wanted to pull on them, to see what I could change about the world around me with a flick of my fingers.

"There are too many," I murmured, staring into Imelda's mismatched eyes.

"She's channeling too much, too fast. Magic has a price, and she is spiraling. If she keeps using like this, there will be nothing left. Her magic needs to be nurtured. It needs to be trained and fed and taught to obey her," Imelda explained, rummaging through the small pack she'd kept at her side. "Right now, it is wild. It's untamed. If she can't find a way to leash it, it will consume her. She'll become nothing more than a vessel for it, and there's no telling what it will do."

"Help her stop it," Caldris said.

I could hear the panic in his voice even as my sight glazed over. Bright white flooded my vision, blinding me to his plight as his chest pressed into my back, shielding me from view. The spectacle we'd created was at risk, but I suspected there were far greater things to worry about.

"Estrella, look at me. Look at me, sweetheart," Imelda said, the gentle tone in her voice setting what remained of my nerves on fire.

Worry slipped through my fingers. Only the spark of golden threads surrounded me. I couldn't find Imelda, couldn't focus on her face when she was lost to me.

The man from my dreams emerged from the light, stepping through the threads. His golden eyes sparkled with worry as he leaned in front of me. Imelda's voice still pleaded with me in the background, as if she couldn't see the beautiful man who'd stepped out of the light. Shadows clung to him, protecting him from the brightness as he leaned over me.

I couldn't detach from reality, couldn't silence the worried voice of my mate trying to pull me out of the haze that had claimed me. I saw myself standing between Caldris and Imelda, the latter chanting with her eyes closed as she tried to draw me back to myself.

In the same breath, I saw myself kneeling at the feet of the man with the golden eyes. There was something familiar about the curve of his mouth, about the bow of his lips, even as they pressed tightly with worry.

He reached out gently, grasping me by the chin and tilting my head back so that he could meet my stare.

"You've taken too much," he said. There was sympathy in his voice, something soft hidden in the words. As if he understood the pain of burning from the inside, knew the fire that lit my blood and made me want to die.

"Make it stop," I begged, shaking my head from side to side. I would have cried, but my body was lit aflame so thoroughly that the tears would have dried the moment they touched my skin.

That pulsing golden light seemed to glow brighter, sparkling off my skin as I whimpered.

"Give it to me," the man said, holding out his other hand. I hesitated, meeting his gaze as I held onto the power that threatened to consume me. I couldn't give it away, not knowing that it could be used to commit true horrors.

"I can't," I said, shaking my head. I didn't know who the man was or how he appeared to me so often.

"You can," he said, waving subtly. The threads hanging through the air swayed as if he'd stroked them, responding to his motion with a casualness that could only be natural. "You have taken something from me. Something that does not belong to you. All you need to do is give it back, Estrella."

"How do I know it's really yours?" I asked, lurching forward as the burning within me touched my heart. Caldris groaned beside me, the sound of his voice breaking through the haze.

"Like calls to like," the man said, lowering to his knees in front of me. He stared at me across the small space between us, sliding the sharp point of one of his nails across his palm as he held it out to me.

The blood that flowed from his wound wasn't red, but the thick, viscous molten gold. It slid across his skin slowly, painting him with the color as he moved his hand and it trickled down to his wrist.

"Who are you?" I asked, staring at the blood in fixation.

The subtle hints of gold in mine were nothing compared to the vibrance of his.

He touched his thumb to the spot under my eye where tears would have fallen, the coolness of his blood coating my skin.

"I am your father, Estrella," he said, his voice staying gentle as I swayed forward involuntarily. "You've been so brave, but I need you to fight for just a while longer."

He took my hand in his, slicing my palm open with the same nail. My blood slid across my skin.

"At least tell me your name," I said, feeling the power slip from me. He pressed our hands together, taking what was his back as I withered. That loss of power drained me, leaving me feeling weak in comparison.

"The day for you to know who I am will come soon enough," he said, pushing to his feet as the haze began to fade. "It was nice to have a few moments where you do not hate me first."

"Wait—" I protested, pushing to my feet as the haze slammed down upon me.

He vanished into the ballroom, the white light gone as I stared back and forth between Imelda and Caldris. Imelda nodded to my mate, signaling that the burning had passed as she touched a tentative hand to my face.

My mate sighed in relief, pressing his mouth against my forehead. He didn't waste another moment, turning and guiding me toward the doors to the ballroom. We left, escaping the mix of chaos and revelry around us.

Humans danced at the center of the ballroom where Mab had once stood, their feet slipping in the blood upon the stone. Their movements were sluggish, as if they'd danced for hours but couldn't stop.

I stumbled as Caldris led me out the doors.

The humans wouldn't survive until morning—would dance until they died.

43

Estrella

Caldris grasped my hand as soon as we emerged from the throne room, using the distraction of Mab's severed flesh to our advantage.

"We have to go. Now," he said, his voice urgent.

"I won't leave you here," I said, knowing exactly how much he would suffer at Mab's hands if I fled in the night after the display I'd just shown. We'd played our hand too soon, come on too strong with the magic I barely had control over. Even now, having cut Mab's hand from her flesh, it still strove to take her head, to watch that crown clatter to the floor and stride over to claim it for myself.

The vengeance, the monster rising within me, terrified me—even with the surge of power muted by my father.

My father.

"We aren't leaving," Caldris said, taking us out of view of the doors.

He waved a hand—summoning the shadows he called home. The walkway appeared before us, plunging us into darkness as he pulled on the hand he held tightly within his. It was a tether, drawing me into the shadow realm I'd walked through on my own more times than I could count. The portrait of what existed in the real world was foggy, hidden behind mist and shadows as we ran through the realm he created.

We emerged out the other side suddenly, stepping onto solid stone as a familiar hallway drew me in. Two guards waited at the entrance to the underground passage, blocking it from us as they stepped forward, unsheathing their swords as they went.

Caldris swept his shadows out, darkness bleeding from him as they fell to the floor. I felt the moment their hearts stopped beating mid-drop, felt the second they drew their final breath. We strode passed without hesitating, our steps already beyond them by the time they hit the stone with a loud *thump* that made me wince.

I knew this path. Knew the hallway before me as it led to a single doorway. The arch of it was unassuming as Caldris pressed his palm to it. His power lashed out, striking at the magically sealed door with lashes that left gouges in the wood.

Shadows curled around the surface as his eyes bled to black, wrapping around the frame—smothering it. He pulled his hand back slowly, shoving it forward to slap his palm down on the wood in a single, battering hit. Power erupted through the hall as the door finally flung open, clattering off the stone beyond it.

He pulled me forward, stepping into the darkness. There were no flames in the torches to light the way—not when we weren't supposed to be in this hall. The floor turned to rough stone, the steps haphazard as we moved along.

Caldris knew the way, could see in the darkness. I channeled that part of me, drawing it toward me so that I could see enough, *just* enough to follow him without tripping on the crude steps. The light of the moon shone in from overhead in the opening ahead, bleeding into the tunnel as we approached.

The flames of the burning holly tree cast a warm glow about the forest, reflecting off the Cove as we stepped out into the clearing.

Come home.

The voice I'd shut out called, probing along my skin. It felt for any weakness, any ability to manipulate me into those waters.

I squeezed my eyes closed, forcing myself not to focus on it. To focus on the mate at my side, the danger that awaited us once Mab realized we'd escaped while she demanded the healers tend to her missing hand.

I raised my chin, tearing my eyes off the Cove's waters to look at my mate. He met my stare, a deep breath releasing from his lungs as he glanced back the way we'd come. With no sign that we'd been followed, he turned toward me and took my other hand in his. He raised that grip to press my hand to his cheek as his head tilted to the side, his eyes glimmering with something wild.

"Now what?" I asked, swallowing as I considered the possibilities.

I knew what the logical option was—knew why he'd likely snuck us down while everyone was distracted in the chaos. I'd agreed to it once, told him I would accept the bond between us.

But that had been when it had been some distant concept for our future, not when it stared me in the face.

An eternity together—bound as two halves of one soul.

I swallowed.

"Now you run, *min asteren*," my mate said, the dark creature beneath his skin showing itself. His head tilted to the side—something predatory emerging. It seemed so much more than Fae, so much more than the half-feral male I'd fallen in love with. "And when I catch you, you're mine."

I didn't know what waited when he caught me, what else might be required from us to complete the bond. But time was limited, with the chances of discovery growing with every minute that passed.

"What if I don't want to run?" I asked, cocking my head to the side. If I could just accept him, not require him to take me forcefully—

"This is the Court of Shadows, my star. The magic here demands I prove myself worthy of claiming you for eternity," he said, releasing my hands and taking a step back. "Here, we are predator and prey."

He'd barely gotten the final word out before I turned, sprinting into the tree line. I kicked my shoes off as I went, ignoring the tear of brambles and roots in the bottom of my feet. They healed as quickly as they hurt, even with my power more depleted than it had been. Wherever that male with the golden eyes—my father—had siphoned my power, it no longer surged in my veins.

Caldris laughed in the clearing behind me, the sound unnatural. It lacked all the joy of a true laugh, as the instinct to claim his mate overrode his senses. I knew when he caught me, this would be no gentle claiming. He wouldn't gently lay me down upon the sand and make love to me but tackle me to the forest floor and mount me as soon as he'd flipped up my dress.

I winced when I thought of the delicate, beaded fabric being torn, branches already catching on it to steal the gems from me. They fell to the forest floor like a glittering trail, giving my mate a way to track me.

Even knowing what waited for me, I couldn't bring myself to fear Caldris. It wasn't terror that made my heart pound in my chest.

It was excitement.

Gods be damned, I couldn't wait for the moment he caught me. Couldn't wait to be united with him—even if I was terrified of what that meant. Of the implications for our future.

Would I still be me? Would he still be him?

Or would we simply be *us*?

I heard the moment Caldris followed after me, his footsteps thundering through the forest. The pace was too fast, his legs so much longer than mine, eating up the distance between us.

I looked over my shoulder, trying to decide how much time I had as I rounded a tree and swerved in the other direction.

And ran straight into the male in front of me.

44

Caldris

I ran.

I sprinted over the log that blocked my entrance into the tree line. I'd given Estrella the head-start the magic of the Cove demanded, given her the chance to escape me long enough to be deemed worthy of having her as my mate.

As soon as that magic pull released me, I laughed, darting after her and following the trail of her scent. Her excitement washed over me, striking me in the chest as I ran and sending a growl rumbling up my throat.

Something in the forest laughed, the faintest chuckle on the wind that circulated through those trees. The Cove delighted in this moment, in the opportunity it too had been deprived of for centuries under Mab's control.

I bared my teeth as I hunted for my mate, then caught a glimpse of a gem glittering on the ground. She'd unintentionally left me a trail of breadcrumbs, and in other circumstances, I knew she might have stripped off her dress to keep me from finding her.

But time was of the essence, so even though she ran…

She didn't try to hide where she went, running palms slick with her own scent all over the trees she passed. Amusement rippled down the thread, consuming me as if I could see her smiling face as she ran.

The bond was stronger here, as if that thread knew we were *so* close to completion.

Her amusement fled suddenly, the bond between us going silent for a single moment that made me falter and pause my steps as I looked around the forest.

The scream that tore through the air made everything inside me freeze.

Never. Never had I heard that sound come from Estrella's mouth. Never in all the pain she'd experienced had such sheer, utter *terror* been ripped from her body.

"ESTRELLA!" I shouted.

I forced my legs to move past my blinding fear. I didn't know where mine ended and hers began, only knowing that darkness curled at the edges of my vision. The shadows came closer, driving me forward as if they reached beneath my feet and gave me the speed I needed to reach her.

Estrella screamed again. The sound cut off sharply, her voice muffled as she grunted. I roared my rage, putting everything I had into that warning call.

The rumble that replied shook the ground, making me stumble to the side. Horror flooded my veins.

I *knew* that sound. Would know it anywhere—no matter how many centuries separated me from my father's life and death.

Mab might have killed my father in his sleep, but she'd only been able to do so because he'd been weakened. Because his magic had been stolen.

By the creature that now had my mate.

No.

I jumped over a fallen log, racing toward that burning tree at the apex of the forest.

Estrella hung limp from the creature's grip, held aloft by a single clawed hand wrapped around the front of her throat. It forced her head back, hanging at an unnatural angle because of the sheer size of his hand. It was bigger than her neck, two fingers splayed across her collarbone—smoke billowing off her where he touched her skin and dress.

Her feet dangled above the ground—her legs too short to touch as the enormous monster lifted her to his mouth. Four tusks pointed out from his mouth, parallel to the ground and in line with what might have been lips if it hadn't been for the horrific, razor-sharp teeth that he bared at my mate.

"Stop," I ordered, taking a step toward it. I moved slowly—cautiously, trying to distract the thing from Estrella's limp form.

How much had he taken from her to leave her unconscious? How much had he fed off my mate?

I swallowed down my panic, taking another step forward. Golden eyes snapped to me—another growl.

"You don't want her," I said, willing the shadows to gather around me. Showing him the magic I had, whereas Estrella...

I didn't dare think it.

His body faded into the glimmer of shadows, his being becoming more and more ethereal with every breath of power he inhaled. Only the faintest tint of shadows remained at the top of his head—wafting off his back.

He dropped Estrella, those long, clawed fingers uncurling from her neck. She dropped to the ground—forgotten—her broken body striking the roots beneath her. She crumpled upon herself as the daemon stepped away from her.

She did not move.

I took a step back, raising two hands placatingly as I willed the creature to put distance between himself and the love of my life.

I had not waited centuries to have her—only for her to be torn away from me so soon.

I unsheathed the sole dagger I'd been permitted to carry at Tar Mesa, watching as the creature's eyes dropped to the iron blade. I couldn't use my magic against it, not when feeding it would only make it stronger.

He struck—the center of that massive palm colliding with my chest. Something cracked within my body, propelling me backward. A tree broke my fall, the rough bark digging into my spine as the trunk snapped in half.

"Pathetic little Faerie is nothing without his magic," the daemon said in that eternal, rough voice.

The creature was both nothing and everything, a void of all magic and life—consuming everything it touched. Plants died beneath his feet as he stepped toward me, a ripple of rot spreading through the forest.

I pushed to get to my feet, white hot pain filling my chest. Whatever he'd broken hadn't been clean. Agony consumed me as I moved. Still, I pushed until I got my feet beneath me, curling over myself as I glared up at the creature.

Time. I needed to buy more time.

Estrella stirred behind the creature as I swung my dagger, distracting him as he chuckled and pulled his arm away. She rose, her legs collapsing beneath her as she cradled her arm to her chest and looked disoriented. That arm was bent at an unnatural angle, broken and bleeding from where the bone protruded from her skin.

I slashed again, silently willing her to run. Sending the command down our thread.

The daemon stole my blade, swiping it out of my hand and tossing it to the side before the back of his hand collided with my face.

Bones crushed; the crunching sound far too loud in my ears as my vision swam. I collapsed to the ground, spitting blood on the leaves.

It was too red for this place, too jarring against all the green.

The creature spun to look over his shoulder at the same time I did, far too late, as Estrella raced forward with a grimace. She grabbed my knife in one hand, a branch of the holly tree clutched in her other. She slid through the creature's legs—stabbing my iron dagger into the back of one knee.

Time slowed as I watched her pull that blade free, twisting it in her hand and stabbing into his other kneecap as she came out the other side. Her ruined arm clutched that holly tree, shoving it against my chest to hand it to me as she brought the iron dagger down upon the top of the creature's foot.

He howled in pain finally, blood pouring from his wounds as I shoved to my feet. One end of the holly branch was still on fire, the eternal flame burning as I thrust it up into the underside of the creature's chin.

He roared, wrapping his taloned hands around mine. Shredding the skin of my arms through my armor and crushing my bones into dust. My grip loosened, refusing to let go altogether, but the strength was gone.

I couldn't drive the branch farther into his skull, not with my flesh and bones in tatters. Estrella swept her blade across his stomach, disemboweling him. His innards fell to the forest floor in a wet splash. Estrella moved to the creature's back when he still didn't let go of the branch.

He couldn't, not when he'd be dead the moment the burning holly found his brain. The daemon howled as she thrust her dagger into his back, using it to pull herself up onto his shoulders. She abandoned the blade there, wrapping both her good and injured hands around the front of the creature's forehead. She pulled, her scream of pain sounding through the clearing as she tipped his head back.

He fought her, releasing the branch with one hand to reach behind him. The scent of her blood washed over me as he swept those claws across her face, leaving her cheek in shreds. I shoved higher, pushing that branch through tissue and bone just as Estrella kicked out with one of her legs, colliding with the creature's arm that still clutched the branch.

She pulled back, stomping that foot down on it again as the creature clawed at her.

Blood.

There was too much blood.

"Estrella!" I warned as she kicked again. The daemon's hand left the branch. I thrust it up into his skull as soon as his resistance left, piercing his brain.

He vanished into shadows with a pop, his yell sounding through the clearing as he returned to Helheim, where he belonged. The branch continued upward with the momentum of my shove, narrowly missing Estrella's face as she flung her body backward.

The flame singed her cheek, illuminating the damage she'd suffered in order for us to kill the creature that would have claimed both our lives.

Estrella crumpled to the ground, blood pouring from her wounds as I dropped the branch and fell to her side. Her face was a ruined map of skin and flesh, her cheek hanging off in strips.

He'd shredded her arms, the back of her neck, her shoulders. The deep gashes pumped blood onto the leaves below us as I drew her into my arms.

"Need to complete the bond," she gasped, looking into the forest.

We both knew our time had run out, that any chance we'd had of completion had been lost to the daemon stalking through land meant to be sacred. I had no doubt who had unleashed the beast upon the Cove—who had allowed the monster to keep me from claiming my mate.

"You're hurt," I said, leaning my body over hers. Protecting her from the other monster who stepped into the Cove. I felt Mab's wrath the moment she emerged into the clearing.

Estrella's flesh started to heal over itself—slowly, too slowly—but it was enough. That magic that existed within her was still there, the creature who had stolen the rest of it dead and gone.

"Where is my pet?" Mab asked, stepping into the clearing. She eyed the damage done to my mate and me with a glare, searching for the daemon that no longer existed.

Estrella's gaze merely dropped to Mab's hand, or rather, her *missing* hand. A bandage had been wrapped around her wrist, the hand still missing.

If it hadn't grown back by now…

Estrella smiled, her face sleepy as that eerie golden light pulsed through the ribbons of her cheek, reconnecting the tissue. "Dead," she muttered, forcing herself to sit in my grip.

She leaned back into my chest, the ache spreading from that point where my bones had cracked.

I didn't care. I'd suffer through it endlessly just to hold her while we faced our punishment.

"I wondered how long it would take you to try. I must say, I'm so very disappointed in you, Estrella," Mab said, her lips peeling back to show her teeth in a moment of all-consuming rage. "There is a ruthlessness in you that reminds me of myself. If only you could sever your mate from your soul, you just might become something great."

Estrella coughed, blood trickling from her lip. She raised a single, shredded hand to wipe it away, wiping it on her dress — or what remained of it.

"You mean I might go mad like you? I will *never* choose that fate."

Mab grimaced, holding out her hand for the guard at her side. Davorin placed a knife within her open palm, wincing back when Mab drew a line upon her bad forearm.

Blood dripped down onto the earth, her lips moving silently in an incantation. Tendrils of smoke rose from the ground where her blood set it on fire, lifting and shifting, blowing in the breeze to form a creature.

The daemon that emerged from the smoke was a different one than Estrella and I had only just banished, but his eyes gleamed as if he knew us all the same. Estrella shuddered in my grasp, leaning back into me as her fear reached a new height.

Mab couldn't mean to take Estrella's magic, not if she wanted to use her for her own purposes.

"Take the girl to her room and keep her there. Only harm her if she fights you." Mab said, her dark eyes glittering like onyx. "I need her whole for tomorrow."

45

Estrella

After a sleepless night spent staring at the daemon who refused to leave my room, I was forced to dress under his watchful eye. Nila had been beaten, her face bloodied and each wrist bound in iron so that she could not heal herself from her injuries for the part she'd played in the antics the day before.

"I'm sorry," I murmured to her softly, hanging my head forward.

She didn't so much as look back at the daemon who occupied himself by rifling through the food they'd sent up for my breakfast, to the extent that I knew I would not be eating that day. His mangled claws had touched everything, shoving it into his jowl-like mouth as if it was all that kept him from devouring the power he felt rebuilding within me slowly.

Too slowly.

I felt the press of it beneath my skin, barely there and just a whisper. Between my father having taken the excess and the magic the daemon had stolen before I realized what he'd done, I felt almost as useless as if iron was on my own wrists.

"It was worth it," Nila whispered, leaning forward to grasp a hair clip resting atop the bone vanity. "To see the way they looked at you. They finally saw you, Princess. They saw everything that you could be in the war with Mab. I'll never regret that. Even if they send me to The Mother's embrace for it."

"Don't speak like that," I said, scolding her as I met her eyes in the mirror. I refused to think of what Mab would do to any who helped me organize a rebellion against her.

Her curiosity with me only went so far. The moment I'd become a real threat, *that* was the moment she would dispose of me.

"Time to go," the daemon grunted, dropping what remained of the barley bread loaf he'd been gnawing on.

"But she isn't ready yet," Nila protested, hurrying to clip the top layers of my hair back from my face. The rest hung down the back of my black dress that seemed to melt into shadows. The gauzy fabric was more solid in vital parts, covering my breasts and intimate areas, and then fading to transparency on my stomach and thighs.

Nila had painted golden symbols on my skin beneath it, echoing the golden swirls of my Fae mark. A golden line trailed over the center of my stomach, starlight twinkling to the sides. Upon the thigh that peeked out from the dress were bands that wrapped around my leg, similar marks placed strategically on my ankle.

"All the Gods will wear similar markings," she'd explained, distinguishing them from the rest of the Fae in attendance. I supposed Mab intended to treat me like one of the Gods now that she'd determined I was a Primordial, even if she did have to be mistaken in that knowledge.

"Don't care," the daemon grunted, grasping me around the bicep and pulling me from my chair. He shoved me forward, making me stumble over the slippers I wore upon my feet.

I'd forgone the heels Mab selected, a small protest if I was to be walking upon the sands of the Cove. I could hardly function in the heeled shoes she chose on solid ground, let alone if the ground shifted beneath me as I walked.

Nila hurried to follow at my side, brushing rouge upon my lips as we walked through the halls. It didn't take nearly long enough to reach the entrance to the Cove where the door was still blown open. Three guards lurked there, guarding it as if we weren't meant to enter.

Everyone was expected to be present for the sacrifice — even me.

I didn't relish the thought of all those deaths, but something in me had become desensitized to it. With how close Caldris and I had been to death the night before, with how many people I'd watch Mab and her like slaughter over the course of these weeks I'd spent in the Court of Shadows, somehow it stopped hurting just a little.

I *hated* it.

We emerged into the Cove, walking toward the sands where the rest had already gathered. Mab stood beside Caldris. His hands were bound in iron. She'd not bound me — not with the daemon to keep me company through the night. There was no need, not when he would eat whatever magic I released.

I walked to Caldris's side, ignoring Mab's watchful eye as I stopped beside him. He was less dressed than I was used to seeing him, shirtless, as he knelt upon the sand. He wore his typical black trousers, but his chest had been painted in black and white symbols that were similar to the style of mine.

I glanced down the line of the Gods, finding all the males shirtless and the females wearing dresses similar to mine. Even Mab had dressed accordingly, her black gown an exact replica of my own with the same markings on her skin.

"Begin," Mab said sharply, staring forward into the Cove.

In the distance, the light of the burning tree dimmed as it reached the end. The flames began to extinguish, and I knew that the last leaf would fall only when all lives ended.

A group of guards shuffled the humans into the Cove. Their fear-filled features and screams echoed through the cavern. I couldn't take it but refused to look away.

I refused to dishonor their memory by not bearing witness to what was done to them. Skye turned, looking through the crowd of Fae as if she might find a friendly face. Her eyes landed on Caldris first, recognizing him. Her mouth dropped open in shock, as if she might say his name. She noticed the shackles on his wrists, turning her gaze to me.

I felt the moment she recognized me, that she realized I was no longer human. Her brow furrowed in confusion, twisting into rage the longer she stared at me while they forced her to walk forward.

"You fucking Fae bitch!" she screamed. The words tore through me.

"A friend of yours, I take it," someone said beside me.

I turned, glaring into Rheaghan's face as he grinned. It didn't reach his eyes in the same way, as if, even after centuries of these sacrifices, they still affected him.

I ignored him, turning away as the humans walked into the Cove. The water was still as they strode to waist deep. The guards hurried out of the water as quickly as possible, leaving them standing there.

They stared at us in horror as Mab raised a single hand. Shadows bled from her, spreading across the surface of the water. The humans panicked. They split up, hurrying toward the shore in their desperation to get away.

Skye reached the edge, colliding face-first with an invisible barrier. She struck it with a fist, like beating on glass, and her eyes met mine. There was a plea in them, a question I couldn't answer. I couldn't tell her why this was necessary—couldn't give her the assurance that I would help.

Not with the daemon lurking and my mate so vulnerable in irons.

I frowned at her, refusing to let the burn of tears reach my eyes. The shadows approached, coming close to their targets, and the humans seemed to realize the inevitability of what would happen.

They stopped fighting, stopped moving. But Skye held my gaze as the shadow touched her hand. It crawled up her arm, slithering over her shoulder like a serpent. It wrapped around her neck, squeezing and then twisting to the side so sharply that I heard the crack through the barrier between us.

Her body fell, sliding down to the surface of the water as the shadows did the same to the other humans.

I couldn't take my eyes off them, couldn't pry my gaze away from the needless death—

A wet, rasping gasp came from my left. Caldris moved at my side, shifting forward a step as I spun to look at him suddenly.

His eyes were on mine, blinking in rapid succession. He turned his attention down, leading my gaze as he raised his shackled hands.

Silence roared in my head as my eyes caught on the iron blade protruding from his chest.

From his heart.

46

Estrella

Someone screamed.

Mab pulled back the blade, leaving a surge of blood to pulse from the front of the wound. My mate fell to his knees, blood trickling between his lips as those blazing blue eyes came back to mine.

That person was still screaming. The sound echoed off the walls of the cavern as I dropped to my knees at his side, pressing my hands to his wound as he toppled to the side. I caught him, pulling him into my lap. Tears splashed down on his face, and it was only when he reached up with a shaking hand to wipe them away that I realized the screaming wasn't coming from someone else.

It was me.

"There's been a change of plans," Mab said, her voice calm and cool as if she hadn't just killed my mate. As if she hadn't driven a knife through his heart, leaving him to bleed out in my arms as I held him close. She wiped her knife on the fabric of her dress, staining it with his blood.

"I love you," he said, and I felt death come for me.

Mab didn't know that I would follow him, that our oath meant both of us died. But I wasn't ready to step into the Void yet, wasn't willing to let her win.

"Caldris will be the Godly sacrifice. Consider yourself fortunate, Ilaria," Mab said, and the words rang in my head.

I didn't care. I didn't care that Mab would know the secret of my blood. I didn't care about anything but him as his eyes started to glaze, his lips turning pale and lifeless.

My claws extended into talons that I dragged over my wrist. One sharp slice across my skin, and the scent of my blood coated the air.

"Please don't leave me," I begged, crying as I pressed that wrist to Caldris's mouth.

His eyes closed, and I felt our bond fray. I felt the life leaving him, his soul readying for the afterlife. But my blood didn't pool in his mouth, and it was bleeding enough that it went *somewhere*.

"If you are not strong enough to free yourself from this bond that cripples you, then I will do it for you, Little Mouse," Mab said, a sneer on her face as I turned my eyes up to her.

I tilted my head to the side as my blood poured into my mate's mouth, the promise of retribution lighting my gaze with gold.

Mab took a step back, motioning toward the daemon as if he would step in and consume the magic I prepared to use against her.

Mab's men grasped Caldris by the legs, trying to drag his limp form from my grip. I held tight, continuing to bleed on his face, his mouth, anywhere I could get that blood. It was a fool's chance, my only option to keep him with me as I clung to the remnants of our mate bond—holding that hint of life that still remained within him.

That golden thread swayed, feeling more and more fragile with every moment that passed.

Until it didn't.

Until the golden thread reknit itself, surging brighter than ever.

Caldris's eyes flung open, the blue lost to the golden light of Fate. Mab gasped, and the daemon swung his sword.

I didn't realize until it was too late that it came for *my* head, shielding Caldris with my body as I laid myself over him. The blade was a mere breath from my skin. I felt the wind in the motion as I drew in a shuddering breath.

Knowing it would be my last.

Caldris reached up, his arm moving faster than lightning arcing through the sky.

He caught the blade in his bare hand. Stopped it with an explosion of golden light that tore through the cavern.

The daemon was flung back as Caldris curled me beneath him, covering me with his body. He got to his feet as the daemon hit the ground, scattering into dust on impact. The guards charged him as I scrambled to stand, staring at him in shock.

He reached out a hand, his shadows no longer dark but glowing as he sent the tendrils sweeping toward those who advanced. They wrapped around the guards' throats, squeezing as the royals of the other courts stepped back from the fray.

I turned, my stare landing upon Mab as she raised a single hand. Her face tipped to the side as I met her glare, watching as those eyes trailed down to the blood dripping from my wrist. The wound had already healed over, but the faintest golden shimmer accompanied my blood as the light from Caldris's tendrils played off it.

She squeezed her hand when my mate rounded on her, heading for the bigger threat in the cavern. He grimaced but continued on, pushing through her control on him even as his chest stopped heaving with breath.

I tried to send him what remained of my magic, but there was nothing there to give. The daemon and my father had stolen most of it, taken it from me for one reason or another. To protect me or to hurt me—all that mattered in those moments was the way Caldris dropped to his knees.

His eyes flashed back and forth between the gold from my blood and his bright blue, and my own heart stalled in my chest as Mab squeezed.

"Stop!" I begged, squeezing my eyes closed. I couldn't lose him—not when those few moments without him had been unbearable. "Name your price."

"My star," Caldris wheezed, stretching up with a hand to try to convince me not to do it. Not to give her the one thing we both knew she wanted. Mab grinned, clearly pleased with the turn of events.

She tossed her head back and laughed. The sound filled the cavern. She hadn't anticipated my saving him—hadn't considered it a possibility.

"We both know there is only one thing I want from you, Little Mouse," she said, stepping closer slowly. She stopped when she was in front of me, pressing the tip of the blade into the skin above my heart.

"Estrella, NO!" Caldris called.

"Don't do it," a male pleaded.

Mab turned her gaze swiftly as her brother stepped up beside us. Rheaghan raised his hands placatingly, trying to convince her that he was no threat, despite his words. "It cannot be undone. I don't think you understand what an eternity of servitude will mean."

"I consent. As long as he lives," I said, the words torn from the depths of me.

Caldris's horror pulsed along our thread, striking me deep in the chest. Mab wasted no time gliding the edge of her blade along my skin. It tore through the tissue, cutting through the muscle and sinew to create a gash that leaked blood upon my dress.

She raised her other arm—a small snake twining itself around her wrist. He hissed at me, showing iron-tipped teeth just before he pressed his face to that hole in my skin.

I held her gaze as he slithered inside. As he shoved through my ribcage, maneuvering through my body until he found my heart. I felt the moment he reached it, winding his way around the beating flesh.

Everything within me tightened—became unfamiliar. Mab's will pressed down on me, a heavy weight upon my soul. She took a step back.

"What have you done?" Rheaghan asked, running a hand through his hair.

I turned to look at him in slow motion, my every thought delayed as my skin worked to heal itself. As my body tried to grasp the invader, to find a way to get it *out* before it was too late.

The tip of Mab's iron blade lashed out so fast, I blinked in a daze, waiting for my life to end.

Thinking she'd changed her mind.

A thin line of red appeared on Rheaghan's throat. His mouth dropped open as he sputtered. He pressed both hands to that line, that unnaturally straight line that marred his fair skin.

Blood poured free. Slid over his hands in a thick, viscous ooze.

He dropped to his knees at my side. Mab drove her blade into his heart, effectively silencing him. I took a step toward him, readying myself to give him blood. Mab abandoned her blade and squeezed her hand, my feet halting beneath me as her will pressed down on me. I couldn't move, couldn't get to Rheaghan as he bled out. Only when I stopped moving did Mab grasp the hilt once more, yanking the iron free from her brother's heart. Blood sputtered from the wound, pouring down his chest.

It wasn't his sister he looked to in those final moments— not his murderer.

But me.

He dropped onto the sand face first, bleeding out upon the white silt. There was no movement in his chest. Not a breath in his body.

Because the King of Summer was dead.

47

Caldris

Shoving to my feet when Rheaghan dropped, I dashed to my mate's side. Her hand was pressed to her heart, to the wound that had sealed and trapped Mab's snake within. She was just as much a prisoner as I now, unable to defy any of Mab's commands.

My regret knew no bounds. My guilt for being the reason she no longer had any hope of a life of her own.

The daemon grabbed Rheaghan's body, hauling him into the Cove as Mab stared passively at her brother. She didn't appear to care that she'd murdered her only remaining family, that he'd loved her enough to not be able to rise against her all this time.

She only cared for his insolence, that he'd dared to speak against her so publicly.

"You're mine now," Mab said, snapping out a hand to catch Estrella by the chin.

Estrella screamed in pain, undoubtedly trying to deny the words that had wrapped themselves around the center of her soul. Mab's talons cut into Estrella's skin, the sides of her jaw bleeding as she held her.

I opened my mouth, the words to beg for Estrella's freedom dying before I could even speak them. Estrella's hand reached out to grasp mine, her fingers intertwining as she sought out that single trace of comfort.

I still remembered those first moments of being bound. The battle of wills that had happened within me. I'd only been a child, barely been old enough to understand, but even I'd known the darkness settling upon me wasn't right.

"I have need of something that is locked within Tartarus," Mab said, clicking her tongue as she turned to look at the shimmering Cove. It looked innocent—the perfect disguise for the horrors that slept within.

"No," I rasped.

I'd seen what remained of those who returned. Seen the absolute terror that consumed them. Most never set foot on solid ground again, never emerging from the entrance to Tartarus—but the ones who did...

They were never the same. Most almost begged for death.

Mab continued on as Estrella clenched her teeth together, grinding them as she looked at the Cove. She'd seemed drawn to it that first day, and even now, there was the strangest sense of longing in our bond.

Strangled by Mab's hold on both of us, but there, no less.

"Bring me a snake from the crown of Medusa," Mab ordered, nodding toward that shimmering pool.

Estrella moved to obey, her legs shifting even as she grimaced. Mab gestured to one of the guards behind her, and the male unclasped the scabbard from his waist. Stepping up, he ignored my growl as he settled it about Estrella's waist. The sword was far too large for her small grip.

She shifted to stare down at it, realization dawning for what kind of task this would be. It wouldn't be any simple trip to the market, not with an iron blade at her side. Imelda hurried through the crowd, though Fallon remained back ever-so-slightly. The male at her side, her betrothed, blanched as he looked at all the blood up close.

Rheaghan had been his king, and without an heir...

Etan was the new King of the Summer Court, at least until one of the other surviving Gods stepped up to take Rheaghan's place. Mab had strategically placed her daughter to become queen, as if she'd known that Rheaghan's time approached. His body floated in the water as Imelda pressed a small pouch into Estrella's hands.

I had no doubt it was filled with herbs. With medicines, and maybe a few plants that Estrella could use to her advantage in battle—if she'd had any of the knowledge Imelda did.

But she didn't—couldn't. Not when she hadn't had Imelda's centuries of training.

Not when she didn't have that kind of magic.

Estrella took a step toward the Cove, her eyes connecting with mine as she gripped my hand more tightly. I stepped alongside her.

I'd go with her. Anywhere.

Even to Tartarus.

One of Mab's men grabbed me around the back of the neck, hauling me off my feet and tossing me back to the sand behind him. Estrella spun, her eyes landing on me where I lay upon the sand. The fear there, the terror that lingered in her green gaze, would haunt me for the rest of my life. She wasn't afraid of the prison itself, only of what might be done to me while she was gone.

Of coming back to me dead.

"You have thirteen days to complete your task. If you do not complete this order in time, or to my satisfaction, Caldris will die. You will not be here to save him, and I will shred his heart until there is nothing left for you to repair. You will not get close enough to give your mate your blood a second time," Mab commanded, waving a hand.

A burst of shadows spread out from her, catching Estrella around the ankles and urging her forward. I hauled myself to my feet, falling back when Mab squeezed her hand and willed me still.

Estrella's feet touched the water.

She sloshed through the surface as she stepped into the carnage of the eight bodies, then moved to the deepest part of the Cove. I knew the moment the ground faded out beneath her, when the water grew too deep.

Her arms moved frantically as she attempted to swim, her life in Mistfell always keeping her from the waters surrounding her village. She sank below the surface, sputtering as she struggled and managed to get her head above water.

Fear pulsed down the bond, along with the strangest sort of song. It radiated through me as Estrella turned to face me.

The water rippled.

Something came from the depths.

Tendrils spread through the water like ink, like tentacles. In the crystal-clear water of the Cove, I watched Estrella's terror widen her eyes in shock as those tendrils wrapped around her ankle.

As they stretched up and grasped the bodies of the sacrifices.

"Caelum!" Estrella called, her mouth filling with water as she was pulled under.

And then my mate was gone.

Glossary of Terms

Alfheimr: The Fae realm.

Calfalls: The Ruined City that was once a tribute to the God of the Dead before he destroyed it in the war between the Fae and humans.

Cwn annwn: The three white wolves associated with the God of the Dead and the Wild Hunt

Folkvangr: A meadow in the afterlife ruled over by The Mother

Helheim: The part of the afterlife where the souls of the damned go.

High Priest/Priestess: The top Priest and Priestess who profess to commune with The Father and The Mother and pass along their messages.

Ineburn City: The capital of the human realm, a gleaming city of gold.

Llaidhe: Opposite of the Sidhe. The Fae who are conventionally afforded less rights for their non-humanoid appearance.

Mistfell: The village at the edge of the Veil, where it is closest to Alfheimr. Serves as the access point between realms when the Veil does not block passage.

Mist Guard: A separate army with the sole purpose of protecting the Veil from harm and fighting the Fae should it ever fall.

New Gods: The Father and The Mother. Worshiped by humans after they discovered the truth that the Old Gods were truly Fae. The Father and The Mother make the choice of whether a soul goes to Valhalla, Folkvangr, or Helheim after the true death at the end of the thirteen-life cycle.

Nothrek: The human realm.

Old Gods: The Old Gods are the most powerful of the Fae race known as the Sidhe. Most commonly, these are the offspring of the Primordials.

The Pillars: The forest at the center of the Shadow Court

Priest/Priestess: The men and women who lead the Temple in service of the New Gods and their wishes (The Father and The Mother).

Primordials: The first beings in all of creation. They do not have a human form by nature, though they can choose to take one for various reasons) and are simply the personification of what they represent.

Resistance, The: A secret society living in the tunnels of the Hollow Mountains (as well as elsewhere in Nothrek) that resist the rules of the kingdom and live their lives as they please. They also resist the Fae and offer protection to the Fae Marked and other refugees from fleeing the Royal or Mist Guard.

Royal Guard: The army that works on behalf of the King of Nothrek, ensuring that the Kingdom remains peaceful and compliant with his wishes.

Sidhe: The human-like Fae who are *not* of the first generations and are less powerful than the Old Gods. Their magic exists, but is far more limited than their older counterparts.

Tar Mesa: The capital of the Court of Shadows

Tartarus: The Faerie prison intended for the most powerful of creatures.

Valhalla: The great hall of the afterlife presided over by The Father.

Veil: The magical boundary that separates the human realm of Nothrek from the Fae realm of Alfheimr.

Viniculum: The physical symbol of the Fae Marked. Swirling ink in the color of the Fae's home court extending from the hand to the shoulder/chest.

Void: The space between life and the afterlife where the soul goes to wait—either for reincarnation or to be selected for their permanent resting place.

Wild Hunt: The group of ghost-like Fae from the Shadow Court that are tasked with tracking down the Fae Marked to return them to their mates in Alfheimr, as well as hunting any who may be deemed enemies to the Fae.

Witches: Immortal beings with powers relating to the elements and celestial bodies; i.e. the Shadow Witches, Lunar Witches, Natural Witches, Water Witches, etc.

Hierarchy of the Gods & Fae

Primordials

Khaos: The Primordial of the Void that existed before all creation.

Ilta: The Primordial of the Night

Edrus: The Primordial of Darkness

Zain: Primordial of the Sky

Diell: Primordial of the Day

Ubel: Primordial responsible for the prison of Tartarus

Bryn: Primordial of Nature

Oshun: Primordial of the Sea

Gerwyn: Primordial of Love

Aerwyna: Primordial of the Sea Creatures

Tempest: Primordial of Storms

Peri: Primordial of the Mountains

Sauda: Primordial of Poisons

Anke: Primordial of Compulsion

Marat: Primordial of Light

Eylam: Primordial of Time

The Fates: Primordial of Destiny

Ahimoth: Primordial of Impending Doom

Old Gods of Note:

Aderyn: Goddess of the Harvest & Queen of the Autumn Court.

Aesira: Goddess of the Hunt

Alastor: King of the Winter Court and husband to Twyla before his death.

Basilius: God of the Sea

Caldris: God of the Dead.

Eryx: God of Sleep

Ilaria: Goddess of Love

Jonab: God of Changing Seasons. Killed during the First Fae War.

Kahlo: God of Beasts & King of the Autumn Court.

Levana: Goddess of Witchcraft & Magic

Mab: Queen of the Shadow Court. Known mainly as the Queen of Air and Darkness. Sister to Rheaghan (King of the Summer Court).

Rheaghan: God of the Sun & King of the Summer Court. Rightful King of the Seelie.

Sarilda: Goddess of War

Sephtis: God of the Underworld & King of the Shadow Court.

Shena: Goddess of Plant Life & Queen of the Spring Court.

Soren: God of Twilight

Tiam: God of Youth & King of the Spring Court.

Twyla: Goddess of the Moon & Queen of the Winter Court. Rightful Queen of the Unseelie.

The Wild Hunt

Sidhe

WANT MORE?

If you enjoyed this
and would like to
find out about similar
books we publish,
we'd love you to
join our online Sci-Fi,
Fantasy and Horror
community, Hodderscape.

Visit hodderscape.co.uk for
exclusive content from our authors, news, competitions
and general musings, and feel free to comment, contribute
or just keep an eye on what we are up to.

See you there!

H**O**DDERSCAPE

NEVER AFRAID TO BE OUT OF THIS WORLD